"A moving and powerful tale that should delight all fans of Spock and the planet Vulcan. I've always wanted to see the story of Spock's early years on his home planet and here it is at long last. Reading *VULCAN'S FORGE* is the only *logical* thing to do!"

—A. C. Crispin, author of *Sarek* and *Yesterday's Son*

"*Truly fascinating!* The 'silent years' of the young Spock . . . his family life on Vulcan . . . coupled with a difficult and dangerous mission in the present, where old friends and older enemies reassert themselves."

—Diane Duane, author of *Spock's World*

"*I love this book!* These women *know* Spock. They know Sarek. They understand the relationship between the two and how Amanda felt about both of them. They understand Vulcan, that desert world, and its harshness and beauty. I'm putting *VULCAN'S FORGE* right next to *Spock's World* and *Sarek* on my Star Trek hardcover shelf."

—Mary Taylor, Science Fiction and Fantasy Media Forum, CompuServe

STAR TREK®

VULCAN'S FORGE

JOSEPHA SHERMAN & SUSAN SHWARTZ

POCKET BOOKS
New York   London   Toronto   Sydney   Tokyo   Singapore

POCKET BOOKS, a division of Simon & Schuster Inc.
1230 Avenue of the Americas, New York, NY 10020

This book is published by Pocket Books, a division of
Simon & Schuster Inc., under exclusive license from
Paramount Pictures.

ISBN: 0-671-00927-3

First Pocket Books paperback printing March 1998

10 9 8 7 6 5 4 3 2 1

To the young women of Bellatrix,
past, present, and future,
Mount Holyoke College's science fiction society

and

To the memory of
Mark Lenard

VULCAN'S FORGE

ONE

Captain David Rabin of Starfleet stood leaning wearily against one wall of the Federation outpost, snatching this rare bit of free time to look out over the stark, clean beauty of the desert and at least try to relax. He was a not-quite-youngish man of Earth Israeli descent, olive-skinned and sturdy, his hair and beard a curly brown, but right now he felt twice his age and as though he'd spent all his life wandering in the wilderness.

Whoever named this planet Obsidian, Rabin thought, *really caught the feel of the place.*

Sharp gray peaks like a row of fangs rimmed the horizon, and plains of black volcanic glass gleamed beneath the savage sun. This was very much a hard-edged world, beautiful if you had an eye for such things, reminding Rabin of Vulcan or the desert preserves in Earth's Negev, where he'd grown up.

1

Now there's a good comparison, the Negev, with all its history of wars and fanatics!

When Rabin had been assigned to planetary duty here on Obsidian, he'd been told, "This is a perfect spot for you, Captain Rabin. Why, with your background, your desert experience, your knowledge of hydrostatics, you'll have no trouble at all."

Of course not. Help the people. Introduce them to a better life without, of course, damaging the Prime Directive. Oh, and keep an eye out for Romulan intrusions while you're at it, yes? This world does lie right on the edge of the Romulan Empire. Of course, we can't spare you any extra personnel since this is only a small outpost, a scientific outpost at that, but that won't be a problem, will it?

Rabin grinned wryly, then shrugged. You didn't rise to the rank of captain without knowing something about bureaucracy. And things could, as the old story went, always be worse. At least Obsidian's air was breathable, its gravity almost Earth-standard: no special gear required. Nothing but the wisdom of Solomon and the patience of Job.

Obsidian's people, not surprisingly, were as hard-edged as their world. Humanoid, with sharp features, dusky-olive skin, and lean, angular bodies (what you could see of them under those flowing robes), they were very much like his own Israeli ancestors: tough, stubborn, and indomitable.

All of which they needed to be. As his superiors had so delicately reminded him, Obsidian did lie perilously close to the Romulan Empire. Worse, it had a very active sun producing ever more frequent solar flares. Not a healthy combination. The folks here in the bustling (and as far as probes from space had shown, the only) city, Kalara, shielded themselves from the flares as best they could. But they were a low-tech people, deliberately so, kept that way by a network of conservative customs That Just Were Not

Broken. And veils, hooded robes, and even thick mud brick walls might be proper and picturesque, but they simply weren't enough protection. Rabin winced at the thought of the resulting abnormally high rates of cancer and lethal mutations.

No wonder everyone seems so bitter. So fatalistic. Yes, and has so much rage buried just below the surface. Amazing that they even contacted the Federation!

More amazing that they had been able to, if not actually break, at least bend their customs enough to go the next step and accept provisional Federation status. But then, Rabin thought, you'd have to be pretty stupid, customs or no, not to want the kinder, more benevolent life the Federation promised, particularly for your children. The child mortality rate here, poor kids, was frightening.

And yet, what has the Federation done for them so far? We've managed to treat a few children, but most of the parents don't trust us. And why should they? We've told them that their sun's growing increasingly unstable. Well, they knew that! We promised them a better harvest, then gave them just the one good season followed by a blighted crop of what was supposed *to be perfectly desert-adapted quadrotriticale—didn't* that *make the Federation look stupid!*

The crop failure *could* have been due to faulty genetic coding hitting in the second generation. Some of the technicians had dubiously proposed that excuse, since there weren't any major signs of insect damage or recognizable disease. But excuses didn't help anyone.

Yes, and then there had been the failed hydroponics facility—the sand that had fouled the machinery and destroyed the entire operation *could* have somehow filtered in past the controls. Unlikely, but maybe someone had failed to make sure a seal was airtight.

Oh, and then there had been the supply dump that had

mysteriously been attacked by desert beetles, *hikiri* as large as a man's hand and with pincers that could take off a finger—well now, the locals had claimed that *they* never had trouble with *hikiri* beetles: it must have been poor Federation planning.

Right. And all those misfortunes coming so closely one on the other were strictly coincidental. Romulan interference? They could hardly be unaware of the Federation presence. But there had been not the slightest trace of activity on the Romulans' part; they seemed content to merely watch and wait.

Besides, you don't need outsiders to help you stir up a good case of paranoia. There are more than enough suspects right here on Obsidian.

The saboteur wasn't Leshon or any of his city folk, nor did they know who the criminal was; the aristocratic mayor had sworn to that by one of his people's convoluted and quite unbreakable oaths, a glint of satisfaction in his eyes at seeing the mighty Federation discomfited. But who knew how many other lives were out there in the desert? And this was, after all, a major trading center, with caravans in and out of the city every day.

And I just don't have the personnel to one, watch for Romulans, two, guard the outpost, three, watch every supply dump plus the fields and hydroponics facility, and four, scan everyone who goes in and out of the city!

A Federation science ship was supposed to be en route to Obsidian, its goal to study the deterioration of the planet's ozone layer; maybe when it got here he could beg or steal some extra personnel from the captain.

And maybe *siniki,* Obsidian's answer to pigs, could fly.

Rabin could hear the city's noise even through the thick walls: business as usual in there, everyone studiously ignoring the Federation presence just outside. He snorted, listening to the normal babble of voices, the grunts and bleats of animals and a snatch of flutesong; the air was hot and dusty as always, but he caught a tantalizing whiff of something spicy being barbecued. Another plus: Humans could eat most Obsidian meals. He'd walked through the marketplace several politic times, smiling and nodding, listening to music, watching street performers, sampling the food.

And just barely managing to not get lost. Kalara was a sprawling maze of low, flat-roofed mud brick buildings, each one covered with intricate clan patterns in reds and blues. After much negotiation, the Federation outpost, built up against one of the city's outer walls, had been designed to look very much like a Kalaran building, even to being faced with the same mud brick. David, thinking that the Federation needed some clan patterns too if they were to keep up status, had over the weeks added various human symbols, including the Hebrew signs *Shalom* and *L'chaim*, Peace and To Life. The locals, when he'd told them the translations, had very much appreciated that! It was one of the few times he had actually gained face since coming to this world.

"Captain Dafit Rabeen."

Rabin turned, biting back a sigh and forcing an amiable smile onto his face. Just what the day needed: politics. "Sern Leshon." Fortunately remembering local custom, he dipped his head three times in courtesy.

The lean, red-robed figure returned the three shallow bows, while his ritual entourage (three men, three women, never more or less), in their dull brown robes, bent nearly in half. Leshon waved them away casually, not deigning to look over his shoulder, his sharp, narrow face unreadable. "Ah, again you study the desert!" He spoke Federation standard rather well, though with a guttural accent. "What, Captain, if asking may be permitted, find you so fascinating in the desert?"

"It's clean." But Leshon could hardly be expected to recognize a quote from the old Earth movie *Lawrence of Arabia*, so David added, "My own ancestors came from such a place."

"As did mine." There was no mistaking the irony in Leshon's voice. "But we left it as quickly as possible."

Point to your side. "Yet you have to admit it's beautiful."

"Beauty? Heat and dust and emptiness." Leshon gave a sharp tongue-click of disapproval. "We are *not* wild nomads to appreciate such miseries. Yes," he added with a sideways flash of cool eyes, "I am aware that you have attempted to contact them."

"Without success."

Again Rabin heard that disapproving tongue-click. "They are nothing. Little more than animals unworthy of your time."

Federation Directive Whatever-It-Is: Don't try to argue the natives out of their prejudices. "It wasn't 'wild nomads' who let beetles into our supply dump, Sern Leshon."

"What's this? Do you accuse my people—"

"Of nothing, Sern Leshon."

Except, Rabin thought dryly, a slight touch of hypocrisy. Leshon and the good folks of Kalara might not be behind any acts of sabotage or know who was, but that didn't mean Leshon wasn't enjoying the proceedings. He could hardly have wanted his authority undermined by a Federation presence and, David knew, still held a grudge against the city council for overruling him.

"Sern Leshon, I don't blame you or your people for being wary of strangers who aren't even from your—" Rabin broke off sharply as Junior Lieutenant Shara Albright hurried forward. Young and earnest, with not a blonde hair out of place, she stopped short, clearly aching to speak but determinedly obeying protocol. *Why oh why,* David thought, *did they send me someone who not only isn't biologically suited to this climate but who doesn't have a scrap of humor as well?* At least her passion for spit and polish meant that she followed orders about keeping her head covered and protecting her too fair skin. "Go ahead, Lieutenant, say something before you burst."

Her blink told him she didn't approve of his levity, but of course a junior lieutenant didn't scold a captain. "Sir!" she began, almost explosively, cautiously in Earth English so Leshon couldn't understand. "There's another of them. The hermit types, I mean."

Rabin groaned. "The usual zealot, I suppose? All right, let's see what this one has to say."

This one, clad in the usual worn-out robe, was firmly in the mold of hermit: the fanatic and determinedly unkempt sort. He was an older man, filthy, painfully thin and with the eyes of someone who enjoyed watching heretics burn. Standing carefully upwind, Rabin gave him the courtesy of a triple dip of the head, very well aware that Leshon was watching.

"Demon!" the old man said severely in return.

"Ah, no. I'm sorry to disappoint you, but I and my people are definitely mortal flesh and blood."

"Demon, I say! Can you deny you were not born of this world? Can you deny you come from the Outer Dark?"

A crowd of locals had begun to gather, a little too coincidentally, and the hair at the back of David's neck began to prickle. Judging from the growing tension in the air, this was a mob in the making, and if he didn't defuse things quickly—

"I come," Rabin said very gently, "from the Federation, that is, the United Federation of Planets, a peaceful association of equals. And I—we, all of us, we come—we come in peace."

"You come to destroy us!"

No reasoning with a fanatic. "Why?"

That stopped the hermit short. But he recovered all too quickly. "You dare to mock me! You, your Federation with its plot, its secret plot to destroy us!"

"No. We—"

"Yes! You plot to destroy our water tunnels and enslave us all!"

Obsidian, like many other desert worlds, depended on its ancient network of water tunnels; even the fiercest of wild nomads would die before damaging one. The crowd gasped in outrage, and David cut in hastily, "How? You, all of you, you've seen what we've brought: food, medical supplies—if we were the monsters this" *benighted old idiot* "this elder claims, wouldn't we have brought weapons instead? Yes," he added wryly, "and if we were such monsters, would we have ever been the victims of acts of sabotage?" That translated as "well-spoiling," and roused wary murmurs of agreement from the crowd.

"Poison!" the old man shouted. "You have poisoned the water!"

"Really? Then go, bring me some of that 'poisoned' water. Bring some for yourself, too! *Now!* Ready? *L'chaim!*"

The hermit clearly didn't want to be part of the friendly ritual of sharing water, but just as clearly didn't dare refuse and risk accusal. Rabin glanced down at the earthenware cup. It looked like water, tasted like water. He drank with a flourish and made a mental note to have himself checked out later, just in case.

Lowering the now-empty cup, Rabin smiled, looked around at the crowd, seeing doubt then embarrassment replacing anger. "Quite pleasant. Nice and cool. And not a drop of poison, either. It's very easy to hate, isn't it? When your crops fail, your children sicken, it's very easy to believe that *he's a demon, she's a witch* just because he or she isn't exactly like you. Believe me, I know. I come from a land very much like yours." *Save for the sun; Earth never had a sun like this, thank the good Lord.* "But we settled our differences and made the desert bloom, and so can you. You can see an end to shortened lives, see your happy, healthy children play—but only if you let us help you."

"As slaves," the old man muttered, but the fire had gone out of him.

"As friends," Rabin corrected firmly. "And we—"

Shouts broke into the rest of his words. Rabin smelled acrid smoke and swore under his breath. Now what?

"Fire!" someone yelled—in Federation standard. Spitting out an oath, Rabin ran.

Sure enough, another precious supply dump had been sabotaged. *Of course,* Rabin thought. *The hermit's ravings made a perfect distraction, especially understaffed as we are.* Yes, and more shouts were telling him that another dump had been caught just about to burst into flame. *Someone* had known enough to bypass the controls and get in there, but—

No Romulans on Obsidian, assuming Federation instruments were doing their job. No double agents among his crew, assuming *he* was doing his job. No locals with sufficient knowledge of technology; that was a given. Rabin looked wildly out at the desert.

Just who is out there? Who—or what?

"It does not seem that Obsidian likes you," Leshon purred, and Rabin whirled to him.

"You'd like us to just go away, wouldn't you? Return things to the way they were. But they aren't going back that way! They aren't going to get better, either, not with your sun turned enemy. We aren't trying to cut into your power, Sern Leshon, surely you see that? I *like* these people, Sern

9

Leshon. I don't want to see any more of them suffer. I don't want to see any more children die!"

"Nor do I," Leshon returned flatly. "But I—"

"Captain!" That was Albright, her eyes wide with alarm. "There are reports of sabotage coming in from Supply Dumps Four and Five."

"Those, too?" Rabin groaned.

No hope for it. He was understaffed and overpressured, and now, with the harsh desert summer almost here with its promise of death for the unprepared, one more loss would mean the end of the mission.

All those poor, sick kids!

They couldn't wait for that Federation science vessel to make its scheduled visit. No choice, Rabin thought reluctantly, but to call for emergency Federation assistance. He ducked into the outpost's command center, absently returning greetings from the personnel, amazingly reassured after the low-tech, dusty, maddening world outside to be suddenly surrounded again by all the gleaming, ultramodern equipment and clean, cool, if somewhat antiseptic, air.

"Ensign Liverakos."

The young man, slender, dark, and competent, glanced up from his console. "Sir."

"I want an encrypted message sent right away to that science ship, the . . ." Blast, what was its name?

Ensign Liverakos had already turned back to his console, his long-fingered, graceful hands flying over the controls. "The *Intrepid II*, sir."

"Ah, of course. Named after that first *Intrepid* lost in action years back. And the captain is . . . ?"

"One moment, sir . . . here it is. Captain Spock, sir, homeworld Vulcan."

Rabin stared. "You're joking."

"Uh, no, sir. It is Captain Spock, formerly—"

"Of the *U.S.S. Enterprise*. Yes, Ensign, I know. Believe me, I know." Rabin felt himself all at once grinning like a kid. Like the kids he and Spock had both been. "Don't worry, Ensign. The strain hasn't gotten to me. It's just that suddenly there's hope. For the first time since all this trouble began, there is hope."

TWO

Intrepid II, Deep Space
Year 2296

The science vessel *Intrepid II* moved silently through space. Spock, once science officer on a very different vessel, now captain of this new ship, sat as still as a Vulcan statue in the command chair, very well aware of every passing moment.

There, now: It was the exact instant when he was scheduled to go off watch. One must be precise at the beginning of a mission, especially with a new crew, if they were to settle into the right routine. Getting to his feet, he told the helmsman, "You have the bridge, Mr. Duchamps."

Lieutenant Duchamps had the round, cheerful type of face that seemed always about to break into a smile. But he replied with rigid formality, "I relieve you, sir," far too stiffly for a normal human response.

Not unusual, Spock mused. For the first few weeks of any mission over the past three decades of his service in Starfleet, crew members who had never served with Spock or

12

other Vulcans tended to be just as rigidly uncomfortable in his presence.

Company manners, Leonard McCoy called it. Spock suspected the stiff-necked, wary behavior was more a matter of those bizarre tales no one *quite* believed about Vulcans: that their complete self-control meant they had no emotions.

Fact: the newcomers—no, that was not precisely accurate—the portion of the crew with whom Spock had never served were still on their best behavior with him. With, for that matter, the former *Enterprise* crew members who had transferred with Spock onto the *Intrepid II* on what humans called a "shakedown" cruise.

Odd phrase. I can observe nothing even approximating shakiness in the performance of any of the systems functioning on board. Indeed, more and more of them are becoming fully operational by the hour.

A flash of memory brought Montgomery Scott's message to him: "Och, be good to her, lad." Scotty's accent had been set for maximum density, his voice pleading as if Spock might actually neglect his duties. "She's only a wee lassie. Let her have some life, not like the other one, that poor lost first *Intrepid.*"

Trust Scotty to see familiar relationships in the inanimate. The situations, Spock thought, were not at all similar, nor were the vessels. The *Intrepid II,* designed for exploration and research, was a modified *Oberth*-class ship, a smaller, lighter craft than the *Enterprise* but still carrying enough weapons to hold her own in ship-to-ship action. She was, indeed, a far cry from Scotty's "wee lassie."

On the day I truly understand Scotty's anthropomorphisms, Spock thought with the smallest hint of wry humor, *I will also truly understand every gene of my own halfhumanity.*

But the crew were hardly machines. Dr. McCoy had been

making psychological generalizations about mourning, periods of adjustments, and stress since the *Intrepid II* had left its docking bay. It had, after all, been just over one Earth standard year since the loss of Captain Kirk, and while a Vulcan might be able to portion away grief, one year was hardly sufficient time for humans to adapt.

Doors too new to have acquired scratches from use whispered quietly, efficiently shut behind Spock *(satisfactory)*, and the turbolift began to take him down to quarters without the smallest hesitation. *(Satisfactory, again.)*

He expected nothing less. Lieutenant Commander Atherton's work and reports were consistently superb. According to the crew rumor that Spock's keen hearing had overheard, Atherton diverted any human passions he might have into his engines—"and he hasn't even got the excuse of being Vulcan!"

Spock permitted himself the slightest upward tilt of an eyebrow at that. Atherton did have his odd habits. Of Earth British descent, he spoke with a crisp if archaic English accent. While it admittedly conveyed information clearly and concisely, it did seem to bother some of the crew.

Why? Because it is an archaic accent?

No. There must be more. Uhura, here on the *Intrepid II* with Spock and a full commander in her own right, had once told him regretfully that she missed Scotty's familiar warm burr. That the burr had been just as carefully cultivated as Atherton's crisp accent was a matter neither Spock nor Uhura had mentioned.

Humans, Spock thought, did harbor a tendency for what they called "nostalgia." But it was illogical to regret or yearn for the past. The sooner the new crew members recovered from their "company manners" and integrated into the whole, the sooner the ship would run at peak efficiency. Morale would then be higher: a desirable goal and a stimulus to even greater success.

Sarek, Spock realized with a start. *"A stimulus to greater success"—that is one of my father's favorite phrases. Fascinating that I should use it now.*

And not quite welcome.

As for the others, those who had transferred from the original *Enterprise,* those who still mourned . . . Spock hesitated, admitting to himself with total honesty that Captain Kirk would have known what to do to comfort the mourners and reassure crew members still awed by the *Enterprise* veterans. But Jim was gone.

That Spock himself might feel more comfortable with a perfectly integrated crew was not a variable in the equation. *The calculus of captaincy,* he mused, deriving an austere satisfaction from the phrase.

But austerity could become sterility. Perhaps after he meditated, he would balance the cold equation with music. In his quarters was the lytherette that had been Ambassador Sarek's gift to him.

Spock straightened ever so slightly. Ridiculous after so many years to still react this . . . irrationally. Yet it seemed that these days he and his father could not even agree on music: Sarek considered Spock's transcriptions of Earth compositions frivolous. Surely the act of transcribing music from one instrument to another, with all the care necessary to maintain the composer's intent, was a legitimate exercise in logic.

Still, there was undeniable emotion in all human music. Was a shakedown cruise with a crew half in awe, half in mourning, a time for even a suggestion of frivolity?

That was too emotional a question in itself. Spock brushed his fingers across the control panel, overriding the elevator's programmed speed, testing. It would be interesting to see how the mechanism functioned when the elevator stopped.

The stop was smooth. *Quite satisfactory.* A panel flashed

green, signaling acceptable life-support levels in the corridor beyond—another refinement introduced by Chief Engineer Atherton. Spock stepped out into a corridor partially dimmed to hint at ship's "night," striding past a few crew members also going off-watch. Starfleet Medical had long ago decreed, quite reasonably, that every ship must have a period of "night" to reflect transspecies biological imperatives. Spock knew that his own metabolism, even after so long away from his native world, was still driven by the brilliant, hot days and deep nights of Vulcan. He might need considerably less sleep than a human, but he nonetheless required the rhythm of day and night.

Alone in the corridor now, Spock let his hand rest on a bulkhead, testing once more. The ship's vibrations were both so subtle and so all-pervasive that only a Vulcan—or perhaps an engineer who bonded with his ship almost as a symbiote—could perceive them. Machinery, Spock had been given to understand, had a "feel," though he could sense no more than how expertly the chief engineer managed the deadly raving of matter-antimatter flow into the great engines, how meticulously he had calibrated the ship's life-support. For a chief engineering officer to operate at peak efficiency, however, he must manage his staff as expertly as his engines.

That, Spock reminded himself, was equally true for starship captains. The integration of the crew might have been a simpler task if more of the *Enterprise* officers remained. Sulu had long since left to take command of the *Excelsior*. Chekov had joined him as first officer, and Scotty had retired to the Norphin Colony. Of the bridge crew, only McCoy and Uhura remained of his comrades on . . . Spock's eyes narrowed fractionally, but he mastered his expression almost immediately . . . *Jim Kirk's bridge.*

Is this human "nostalgia"? Illogical.

A light suddenly flashed on his belt. Lieutenant Richards, the new science officer, had presented Spock almost hesitantly with this, his latest refinement on paging technology: It kept the entire crew from hearing their captain being hailed. Messages awaited Spock in his quarters, one carrying the red light indicating urgency.

Quickly entering his quarters, Spock just as quickly turned down the light until it was a more comfortable reddish glow, turned up climate control—adjusted to a frugal Earth-normal in his absence—to something approaching Vulcan-normal, then sat before his personal viewscreen and signaled for communications.

Interesting, he thought, scrolling through the encrypted data, translating it as he read. *No, fascinating.*

Spock's long fingers flew over the keypad, quickly calling up a visual. A stocky, sturdy figure appeared. A bearded face with wry dark eyes seemed to stare at him, and Spock felt the smallest thrill of recognition. The years had changed the human, of course, but Spock mentally removed the beard and visualized the face as far younger: Yes. David Rabin—now, it would seem, Captain David Rabin. Spock played the audio, unscrambled:

"Spock, or at least I hope it's you: Yes, it's your old desert pal, assigned to planetary duty on Obsidian. What am I doing here? Making the desert bloom, my pointy-eared friend. Or at least trying."

Quickly, all humor gone from his voice, Rabin cataloged the list of problems, ending with, "I like these people, Spock. They deserve better. We really need your help, my friend. Rabin out."

"Obsidian," Spock repeated thoughtfully, staring at the now-empty screen for an instant. His fingers flew over the keypad once more, bringing up first the planet's position—on the edge of the Romulan/Federation Neutral Zone—then an executive summary of planetological, biological, and anthropological data, and finally his old friend's official biography.

Excellent fitness reports, of course; Rabin was not the sort to be idle. A good many successful desert excursions on a good many worlds: his friend had become as much a nomad as Rabin's ancestors.

He has also cross-trained in hydrostatics, I see. Only logical, under the circumstances.

Successful missions, yes, although comments about Captain Rabin's "initiative" had been duly entered. Such comments, Spock knew, were ironic: there had been several such in James Kirk's records. And none at all in his.

What was Rabin doing on an outpost this small?

I'm making the desert bloom, my pointy-eared friend.

One corner of Spock's mouth quirked up in what would have been wild mirth for a human. Rapidly processing the data, he saw that Medical had red-flagged Obsidian; glancing at its star's spectrographic assay, he saw the cause. Loki could be called a main-sequence G-type star, but its recent level of solar flares and sunspot activity made the worlds orbiting it less than healthy places to live, complicated by the fact that Obsidian had almost no ozone layer.

High infant mortality, high death rate of adults as well, mostly due to melanomas, carcinomas . . . Spock downloaded the medical data, preempting his science officer's task for the sake of efficiency; after all these years, he knew far better than Lieutenant Richards what Dr. McCoy would need, and the science officer would never reproach him.

A new flash of light: an upgraded message from Rabin.

"We've got trouble, Spock. The grain supplies are contaminated. The level of raiding against the cities by the wild nomads has stepped up. *Someone is poisoning the wells!*"

Both of Spock's eyebrows shot up. "They're poisoning the

wells!" was Rabin's personal metaphor, meaning damage. Prejudice. Danger. A long finger stabbed at a control button, opening a direct line to Lieutenant Duchamps.

"Captain?"

When will he stop sounding astonished? And when will the title stop sounding incongruous to me?

Illogical.

"Lieutenant, divert course to Obsidian, with all deliberate speed. I should suggest maximum scan and yellow alert as we parallel the Neutral Zone."

"Aye-aye, sir." Curiosity tinged Duchamps' voice, but "aye-aye" was the only acceptable answer.

Meditation was out of the question. One did not need to be a Vulcan to know that diverting course was likely to bring questions, if not outright debate. Spock took down his lytherette from where it hung near his copy of Chagall's *Expulsion* and began to tune it. Perhaps he could at least—

Of course, the first interruption struck right then. "Yes, Mr. Atherton?"

"Captain, I have just calibrated my engines and was counting on testing them at lower speeds when your order came." Atherton's clipped British accent almost trembled with protective outrage, just barely skirting insubordination. "I would hate to put undue pressure on the dilithium crystal mounts just because this David Rabin you mentioned has overreacted."

Me bairns, me puir wee bairns.

That echo of Scotty's frequent wails kept Spock from giving the human a precise, perfectly logical dressing-down. Instead, he took a deep breath, knowing how many people had no doubt patched into ship's communication or would have this message relayed to them, and said only, "The rest of the ship is in such exemplary order, Mr. Atherton, that I think you might countenance the speed." He kept his voice coolly patient, more for the memory of Scotty's concern than Atherton's present worries. "I knew Captain Rabin when we were boys together on Vulcan. I have traveled with him. He would not send out a distress call without great need."

The viewscreen showed how thoroughly Atherton's pale face reddened. "Aye-aye, sir," the chief engineer said crisply, and Spock's screen went blank. It was illogical, Spock told himself, to be grateful to a formula that had been old even in the days when *Jane's Fighting Ships* meant naval vessels, not faster-than-light craft.

There were no further messages of import. Spock returned to tuning the ancient lytherette, his fingers caressing pegs and the luminous varnish of its sound box, then glanced at the chronometer and made a private estimate before striking the opening notes of a slow, meditative piece by that most logical of human composers, Johann Sebastian Bach.

Quite within the time frame Spock had projected, the doors to his quarters parted, his privacy coding overridden as only a privileged character might do.

The privileged character glowered at him from the doorway. "Spock," McCoy blurted, "you never told me you had a human buddy on Vulcan when you were a kid!"

Ah yes, the news must have spread through the *Intrepid* at better than warp factor ten. Gossip always could outpace even a starship. Rather than replying immediately, Spock allowed himself the luxury of a few more notes of Bach's "Air on the G String," then lifted his fingers from the instrument and let the vibrations dissipate.

"Since you have already intruded, Doctor, please sit down."

McCoy ambled into the red-lit cabin, mimed ostentatious discomfort at the heat, and sank into the chair opposite Spock, setting a square crystal bottle down on the desk with a thump that made the cobalt blue liquid inside slosh from side to side. It boiled up, threatening to overflow, and McCoy glared at it.

"If you were a drinking man, Spock, I'd say you could use a drink. Where do you keep your beer glasses?"

"I see no logic to the ingestion of ethanol," Spock retorted. "Especially not before what might be a ship's action."

A quick foray by McCoy to one of Spock's meticulously neat shelves produced, if not beer glasses, a substitute the human considered at least adequate: a pair of translucent stone goblets. He poured the frothing ale.

"Now, if this were Saurian brandy or Tennessee bourbon, I wouldn't waste it on you. But Romulan ale . . . if your Romulan cousins can drink it, you certainly can."

"Romulans do many things no sane Vulcan would do," Spock observed, studying the liquid. The ale was the exact color of antique computer screens.

"Sane Vulcan?" There went McCoy's eyebrow, raised in his usual jesting mockery. "Isn't that somewhat of a redundancy?"

"Believe me, Doctor," Spock admitted reluctantly, "I have known of cases . . ."

No. McCoy had often harassed Jim Kirk with these nocturnal visits. *Ship's doctor's responsible for the captain's health,* he'd insisted. "'You're a bartender, not a doctor,'" Spock quoted Kirk without warning, almost making McCoy choke on his drink.

The doctor raised his glass in appreciation. "Absent friends." The old toast was the most military thing about him.

Spock knew he must comply or risk a serious breach of custom. "Absent friends," he responded and took a meager sip of the burning ale.

"I miss him too, Spock."

A flash of memory: the sharp stab of grief, logical but no less painful, the memorial ceremony, with humans allowed to show that grief while he, he must keep his face forever properly impassive . . . Spock glanced up from his glass. "What would you have me say, Doctor? One cannot change the past."

His cool tone, Spock thought, would surely provoke McCoy into a rant. But if the usual diatribe about Spock's coldness brought the doctor any ease of heart, he was welcome to it.

But McCoy said nothing, and there was a suspicious warmth in his eyes that Spock recognized as human sympathy. "It grows late," Spock said. "This is not your watch. Should you not be sleeping?"

"What about you? I've checked computer access, Spock. You haven't slept for—"

"Ten days, fifteen hours, and thirty-five minutes—"

"Stop!" McCoy flung up his free hand. "You haven't slept since we left Tarin Four."

"Really, Doctor." Spock raised an eyebrow to the position his crew called (not to his face, though they never did realize the efficiency of Vulcan hearing) "eyebrow on stun." "I must protest your cross-training as a computer hacker. I had no idea you were so accomplished."

McCoy flushed awkwardly. "Access time is tied to medical records," he admitted. "In case of obsessions, compulsions, people spending all their off-hours plugged in. *Including,*" he reverted to his unwelcome subject with a vengeance, "this ship's captain. I remember the last time you played sleepless wonder."

"We returned home safely then, did we not?"

McCoy glared. "You're worried about this friend of yours."

"David Rabin is a very distinguished officer. He was a capable individual even before he entered Starfleet. Did I ever tell you," Spock continued, calculatedly offering diversionary tactics, "of when I met him . . . and his mother, who was at that time a Starfleet captain as well?"

He could all but feel McCoy restraining himself from chasing after the story. "Nevertheless," the doctor continued resolutely, "you're worried about him. Why, Spock?"

"Because Captain Rabin is worried, and I trust him. Obsidian is of strategic importance because of its location on the border of the Neutral Zone."

He called up the star map and turned the screen to allow McCoy to see it.

"That star's got the jitters," McCoy grumbled. "Naming it Loki was bad cess. Do you have any idea of the incidence of lethal mutations on that planet?" he asked, almost accusingly. "Carcinomas? Melanomas? Place makes metastasis an occupational hazard."

Wordlessly, Spock handed the physician the data he had downloaded. McCoy practically grabbed the printout from him. "A bribe, Spock?"

"Data are never a bribe, Doctor. Let us call it a briefing."

"Didn't have time to get this from Richards, though. Micromanaging, eh Spock? Science officer wouldn't thank you for stepping in. Oh well, every man—all right, every Vulcan—yields to temptation every now and then."

"I judged that I could approximate your requirements more closely than Science Officer Richards. Please, examine the data."

"This is another reason Rabin's worried, isn't it?" McCoy asked, looking up after a time, his voice compassionate. "Obsidian's a low-tech world. Only reason it tolerates a Federation outpost at all is for the medical technology. And maybe the water engineering and agronomy."

Spock highlighted a graph on-screen. "In the generation since that outpost has been operational, the average age of the townspeople of Obsidian—we have no way of calculating population trends for the nomads—has risen two years. That is a significant change. Another generation or so . . ."

"So it's not just tactics. It isn't even loss of face if the Romulans—"

"No evidence of Romulan interference has been reported."

"I don't believe in the tooth fairy, Spock!"

Spock sipped his ale rather than pander to the doctor's improbabilities about dentition and the supernatural. "It would be a loss if the Federation were compelled to abandon the outpost."

"It's the *waste* that's scaring your friend, isn't it, Spock? The loss of life. The children who will never have a chance *at* life, much less health. The people who will never be without misery." McCoy's voice thinned in pain.

Spock turned away, remembering Rabin's mobile face, smeared with grit from Vulcan's deep desert, a trail of dried blood at one corner of his mouth, tears making clean streaks in the mess: "I cry because I'm relieved. I'm *proud* to care so much."

McCoy poured himself more ale. "Spock, you're a phony. Don't tell me your heart doesn't bleed for these people."

Spock glanced at him, face a cool mask. "In diagnosis, if nothing else, you are the logical peer of a Vulcan. However, if you seek to elicit a reaction for which I am not equipped, you are in error."

"Tell it to the stars." McCoy drained his glass, then set it down with a bang. Spock lowered his own drink more gently. His aim, rather to his bemusement, was not as unerring as it should have been.

"Function's deteriorating, Spock!" McCoy pounced. "Are

you going to sleep? I'll make a bargain with you. You sleep *now,* and you can sleep here, not in sickbay. Though how you can sleep in this heat . . ."

"One does not bargain with duty," Spock pointed out. "And you had best acclimatize yourself to 'this heat' if you are to accompany me to Obsidian's surface."

"Try and *keep* me away," said McCoy, a hunter on the trail of his most hated quarry: suffering.

"Doctor, I would never interfere in the performance of your duty."

McCoy tentatively raised a hand, then let it fall back to his side.

You almost forgot, did you not? Had I been Jim, you would have patted me on the shoulder.

But one did not casually touch Vulcans. "It's okay, Spock," McCoy continued as though that awkward little moment had never occurred, "I won't tell anyone that your heart's in the right place. Assuming that the right place is where normal people have their livers."

He rose. "Get some rest, Captain. We've got more work than any two men, or Vulcans, can handle facing us on Obsidian. Someone, I forget who, once said that 'the desert is a forge on which to try the' . . . hell, I forget. Soul, probably."

A shock of memory surprised Spock. Forge, indeed. Long ago, he and Rabin had been hammered out on another such forge. "You have convinced me, Doctor. However, without belaboring the point, may I remind you that I am better able than you to tolerate extremes of heat—or of sleep deprivation?"

"I'd like to see what your subconscious comes up with when you're *really* sleep-deprived," McCoy grumbled. Spock sat waiting. McCoy usually delivered his true message just when he seemed about to leave.

"Spock, forget I'm your doctor for a minute. Pretend I'm your friend. I'm telling you, as a friend: Dammit, get some sleep."

He slouched out, muttering to himself, "Hypertamoxifen, recombinant interferon, genetic splicing . . ."

It would be profoundly tempting to anticipate McCoy's research. But McCoy's points about micromanaging and usurping his officers' functions had made sense, and Spock had given him what amounted to an implied promise that he would comply.

Replacing the lytherette on its wall mount, Spock darkened the cabin and stretched out on his bed. If the bridge needed him, he was a signal away. He hoped—emotion though that was—that they would.

And then, drifting at last into sleep, hoped that at least for a short while they would not.

THREE

**Vulcan, Sarek's Estate
Day 3, Fourth Week of Tasmeen,
Year 2247**

The view from his father's estate was tranquil in Vulcan's early morning, the air still cool and sweet with the scent of desert vegetation, the vast red sweep of desert and mountains still blue with shadow. Spock, already nearly his father's height at seven Vulcan standard years—seventeen Terran years—though not yet grown out of a boy's gangliness, stood on the wide stone terrace trying to empty his mind of all but the tranquility before him . . . trying but not quite succeeding.

This was illogical. He had survived his *kahs-wan* trial, proved himself a true Vulcan despite his mixed heritage. There should be no reason for doubt.

And yet the question remained. Surely it was not illogical to wonder about himself? Spock had studied genetics as part of his schooling; he was quite well aware of his own hybrid complexity. But a reasoning being was more than a mere assemblage of genes.

What, then, am I?

His father would probably say that introspection was an interesting mental discipline only as long as it did not devolve into unseemly self-absorption. His mother would probably smile that cryptically amused human smile of hers and murmur in Earth English something about "teenage angst."

Neither view was particularly helpful.

So. The question should be, perhaps, less "What am I" than "What am I to be?" Spock was sure that he lacked the temperament to become a teacher as his mother had been, and while the thought of pure scientific research was intriguing, it did not seem right for him as a career, either. To be an ambassador like his father . . . again, intriguing—but that was Sarek's path, not his. A fact, Spock thought, that Sarek could not or would not see.

No. Calmness. Anger is a dangerous emotion.

A flash of color caught the young Vulcan's attention: a *lara,* a desert bird dazzlingly blue against the red sands, soared up into the brightening sky, racing upward on a thermal. Spock's gaze followed it up, up, climbing as though fleeing the known, the safe—

Ridiculous fancy. Illogical.

And yet, were it not illogical to do so, he might almost envy the bird its freedom. The thought of seeing strange new places—

"Spock."

He just barely managed to properly compose his face, to turn without unseemly haste. "Father. Is it time?"

Sarek, an impressive figure in his somber red ambassadorial finery, nodded. "Come, my son."

Private—and indeed often public—meetings were traditionally held in the early morning, one of the coolest parts of the desert day. Sered, Spock knew, had once been a class-mate of his father's at the Vulcan Science Academy, though the two had never been close. Now Sered was Sarek's political antagonist, one who advocated Vulcan's withdrawal from the Federation.

Withdrawal, Spock thought with the certainty of his nearly seventeen years, *is hardly a wise or a logical position.*

But of course it was not his place to speak up. It was his place merely to watch and witness as Sered came to their home to debate with Sarek.

Why? Sarek does not legally or morally require a witness. Does my father think me his ambassadorial apprentice? I am not, I will not be, that.

As they reentered their home, Sarek commented, as though aware of his son's thoughts, "Sered always was a brilliant student, brilliant and philosophical. Quite charming. Deliberately so. Do not let him charm you, my son."

"No."

Sarek raised a wry brow but said nothing more. Spock stood politely to one side as Sered was ushered into his father's quiet, simply furnished study—a table, chairs, several cases holding books and scrolls and one elegant wall hanging in muted brown and sepia tones by the famous scholar-artist T'Resik. The young Vulcan, still keeping out of the way as was proper, listened to the two political rivals greet each other with just the proper amount of cool civility.

They are saying a good deal in only a few words, yet at the same time never really saying anything. Spock marveled at that bizarre juggling-with-words skill, then reminded himself that of course they were masters at such. That was part of how the game of diplomacy was played.

It is not my game. Despite what my father may believe.

But one could learn from any experience, and Spock determined to learn what he could from this, all the while trying to study Sered without being noticed.

Sered was worthy of study. He was a striking figure, taller than Sarek, lean almost to the point of thinness, with the clean, sharp features of a noble from Vulcan's distant past. He was dressed almost too austerely in a simple brown robe of archaic cut that emphasized the link with the past.

Arrogance, Spock thought in disapproval, then chided himself: Illogical to judge merely on physical appearance.

"Colleague Sered, this is my son, Spock. Spock, this is the scholar Sered."

Spock started at hearing his name suddenly spoken. He bowed politely, then straightened to find himself caught by Sered's intense stare, a stare that seemed to sum up all he was and would ever be—and which found him lacking.

"He does look truly of our people," Sered said after a moment. "I see nothing of humanity in his appearance."

Sarek's almost imperceptible crook of a hand sent Spock back to his corner, struggling to keep his face impassive. What Sered had said had most definitely been intended as an insult. Why? The only logical reasons could be to force Sarek from his calm—or to display deliberate prejudice.

Sarek never stirred. "There is no shame in my son's parentage," he said, totally without expression. "Nor is there shame in that of my lady wife."

"A fine and sadly rare thing," Sered retorted. "To see so strong a bond, I mean. Even if perhaps it is—this is not meant as an insult, Sarek, but as simple fact—even if it is misplaced."

"How so?"

"Ah, Sarek, you know exactly what I mean. We have had similar discussions in the past."

"And came to no satisfactory conclusions."

"I grant that. But you cannot deny the truth: Ours is a long and proud heritage worthy of protection."

"And I grant that. Your point, Sered?"

"My point is that some of that precious heritage has already been lost."

"Because of our alliance with the other Federation worlds."

"In part, yes. And yes, of course we have debated this before. You cannot deny that diffusion and assimilation are both perils when one deals with outsiders."

"We have, indeed, debated this before."

"Of course. And I will not waste our time in going over old ground. More important for our people than outside influences is that we not let ouselves forget Surak's teachings." Sered gave the smallest hiss of disapproval, barely audible. "Too much has already been lost through misinterpretations and false doctrine. Yes, and almost worse than this warping of logic has been the sundering of our kind."

"Those who abandoned Vulcan, you mean." In Sarek's voice was the faintest warning hint of *we have been here before as well.*

"Exactly. Think of it, Sarek. Consider it well. Our own cousins are lost to us—unless we turn back from the treacherous path we walk."

Sarek's slight lift of an eyebrow spoke volumes of skepticism. "To do what? Rejoin a people who have chosen the path of violence?"

"Ah, my colleague, consider this: Our ways have become stale, rigid, far from the healthy whole proposed by Surak. Can you deny this?"

"Yes."

"You spend so much time in your ambassadorial duties—no shame in that, but you do not see, you do not know what happens outside the many embassies. Ours is, indeed, a stagnant culture. While who can say what our cousins have become?" Sered paused, the faintest hint of a charming smile barely touching his lips. "Can you honestly claim you are not curious? Come, Sarek, tell me: Do you not wish to see what glories our sundered cousins might have accomplished?"

"Of course," Sarek retorted dryly, "but not if it involves surrendering all that we are and may become."

Sered stepped back from the confrontation, turning to study the intricate wall hanging. "T'Resik's work, is it not?"

"Indeed."

"A most logically woven piece. See how the twist of fiber here leads the eye to follow it along till it joins this thread and becomes one with it. Stronger than before." He turned smoothly back to Sarek. "And that is exactly what I propose. We cannot survive as we are. Ultimately, there must be a merging of the sundered cultures, the two halves made whole. We must use the fierce, healthy—yes, the *emotional* strain to rejuvenate Vulcan's tired bloodlines." Sered's glance flicked to Spock, flicked away. "In a new joining, a new, better order, those of . . . lesser blood—" Again his glance flicked delicately to Spock, then away. "—those of lesser blood might be deemed less than worthy."

"'Lesser blood,'" Sarek said to the air. "There, I believe, is an illogical thought if ever there was such a thing. Blood is but a substance, in itself neither superior nor inferior. Odd that it, whether from one species or two commingled, should so often be used as an excuse for bias—even, it would seem, in these enlightened times. But of course," he added directly to Sered, "you would never stoop to employing such illogic. The fault must then be mine for misunderstanding you. If you wish to leave, Sered, after such a lack of communication, there is no loss of dignity in that."

Sered, face a stony mask, dipped his head almost curtly to Sarek, ignored Spock completely, and left with precise, cold dignity.

"That," Sarek said after Sered was gone, "is, alas, a sadly warped and dangerous being."

"But . . ." Spock began tentatively. "He does seem to make some interesting points, Father."

Sarek turned to him, revealing nothing at all of his thoughts. "And what points might those be, my son?"

Spock hesitated, trying to focus, to put his thoughts into clear, concise order. "I must postulate that, since emotion and mystery are a part of the Vulcan soul—as T'Pau so eloquently put it—is it not illogical not to study such issues?"

"Ah, my son waxes philosophical."

"I merely meant—"

"Spock, I did warn you. Sered can be totally charming to even one fully grown. And you are still far from that."

Was his father trying to goad him? No, that would hardly be logical. A test, then, for him to prove his own logical thinking to Sarek. "I am not yet adult, Father. I admit that. But surely even a child may see the value of certain matters."

"There can be no value in any matters that include a return to the practice of violence. My son, I do not mean to belittle your thinking. But you must admit that I have had many more years of study—many more years of life and its experiences."

"Yes, of course, but—"

"You are letting control slip, Spock."

And you—you patronize me, my father. But Spock wisely kept silent, willing himself to emotionless calm. After a moment, Sarek nodded approval. "Yes, the words of Sered sound intriguing. Who would not wish to learn more about our sundered cousins? But as a mature adult, Spock, I truly am more aware of the warning lessons of history. Yes, those ancient days must sound fascinating to one as young as yourself, full of what your mother would call 'romance.' I remember when I was your age and felt the same. But there is nothing romantic about war, nothing fascinating about mindless bloodshed. As I grew, I learned that not all paths are safe to walk."

The lecture was rapidly becoming more than a young Vulcan's self-control could endure. Before he could disgrace himself by blurting out something such as *But I'm not you,* Spock dipped his head courteously to his father and said instead, "You have given me much to ponder. If I may . . . ?"

Sarek nodded, the ever so slight upward crook of his mouth hinting at his amusement.

At me. At my youth. At my thinking in other ways than his and—no. Emotion. Control it.

Spock gladly fled to the sanctuary of his mother's wet-planet conservatory. There he stood alone amid unfamiliarly damp air and strange, lush-leaved plants, seeing little of them, willing himself back to proper Vulcan reserve.

"Spock!" said a startled voice. "I thought you were with your father."

Spock turned to see Amanda, looking every bit a true Vulcan lady in her simple, elegant grey robes for all her undeniably human features. "I was," he told her. "Till now."

Amanda moved closer, comprehension lighting her eyes. "Oh. I see. He doesn't mean to lecture you, Spock, truly he doesn't. He—I—we are concerned about you. I'll even use an emotional term if you'll excuse me the lapse of good taste: We're worried about you."

"Why? Because I am not truly Vulcan?"

"Because," Amanda countered gently, "you haven't yet puzzled out who and what you are." She held up a hand before he could speak. "And that, believe it or not, has nothing to do with mixed heritages. Spock, *everyone* goes through the 'Who am I?' stage. It's part of growing up, no matter what the sentient species, particularly when the being involved is also going through what my people used to call, with dread, 'the teenage years!' And—you aren't hearing a word of this, are you?"

"Mother, forgive me. I have heard too many lectures this day."

"Teenagers," she muttered, but there was a wry smile on her face. "They're all the same. Come to think of it, *everyone's* the same."

"I fail to see—"

"Oh, I don't mean in surface things like appearance"—one finger lightly touched an Earthly orchid, very foreign in appearance to any Vulcan bloom—"or culture. But you know that I've been studying the various Federation races. And the more I study, the more I realize that there are greater similarities than differences among us. I'm finding certain constants in all the sentient races."

Spock frowned slightly, as much in confusion as denial. "I will grant that all peoples have concepts of what they consider moral or immoral. But more than that—I would not criticize your logic, Mother—"

"Why, thank you, dear," dryly.

"—but how can your statement be true?"

Amanda paused to delicately pinch off a wilted leaf. "Have you never heard that ancient children's tale of the hero transformed into a hideous beast, a guise from which he's rescued by the heroine?"

"Yes, of course. That is 'Sikan and T'Risa,' though no one tells such a tale to children nowadays."

"A pity."

She clearly meant it. Spock blinked. "Surely you do not claim to find truth in such a . . . a foolishly emotional story."

"Oh, I do. To you that tale is 'Sikan and T'risa.' To me that's 'Beauty and the Beast,' and to Andorians it becomes 'The Prince Trapped in Monster Form.' Spock, archetypes, certain set figures and concepts, are built into all of us. Even Vulcans, with all their self-control, have them."

"I do not see—"

"The Eater of Souls," she challenged, and laughed when Spock could not quite suppress a tiny flinch. "You see?"

The Eater of Souls was an ancient Vulcan myth, a demonic being that had once been said to manifest in sandstorms during the summer solstice—a being that could devour Vulcan essences, even down to the *katra*.

Spock shook his head in disapproval. "This proves nothing. The Eater of Souls is a foolish relic far removed from the cold equations of science."

"Properly logically stated. And yet, like it or not, you reacted."

"I . . ."

"Spock, even Vulcans can't—and shouldn't!—deny their basic mythic roots. Those are a part of every sentient being. And I know that Vulcans don't want to throw away their honored heritage."

Spock opened his mouth, shut it, finding absolutely nothing to say. The day had begun with confusion, and his father and mother were only adding to that. By now he was no longer sure where he stood. And anything he said, Spock knew, was going to be disgracefully emotional.

Rather than breaching good manners, Spock bowed and withdrew without a word. The doors of the conservatory sealed shut behind him.

FOUR

Obsidian, Deep Desert
Day 3, Seventh Week, Month of the Raging *Durak*,
Year 2296

He spurned even the faintest shadow of the sheltering rock cliff and strode out into the deep desert, his arms outstretched as if to welcome the light of a star that both gave life and took it, agonizingly, away. The world's sun flashed into his eyes, and the veil, in instinctive reflex, descended over his eyes, and he permitted it to remain—for that instant.

He lifted his hand further, baring his head to the light. The star was at zenith. It was too bright a gold and more poisonous than the star under which he had been born and that he would never see again unless the Faithful and his sundered brothers helped him wrest its control from weaklings and traitors.

He was too old for the blood fever. Still, his blood was fire. His eyes were fire. He stripped the veils from them and gazed directly into the sunlight.

The Faithful who had followed him from their rock fastnesses now assembled behind him. They moved softly, lest his meditations be disturbed and he be angered.

They feared him more than they feared their own deadly sun!

The light burned. His eyes were fire, and that was good.

The Faithful ventured forward. He heard the whisper of worn cloth and knew that one or two, perhaps more, had followed his example and dared uncover there in the pitiless light.

Would you skulk your puny lives away underneath a rock because you fear your star and its gifts of life and death? he had demanded only the night before. *Pale you are, and call it safety.*

As a Terran maggot was safe, whether it crawled or walked abroad on two legs and made futile attempts to make the desert bloom. Deserts were not supposed to bloom; they were a forge on which the strong must be tested if the race were to thrive and conquer.

At that, the nomads' carefully swathed pallor was at least a survival positive, unlike the arrogance with which the city-dwellers squandered their substance on Federation drugs and exposed themselves to the sunlight for no better reason than to display their wealth and that they could. The Faithful despised those of the cities. If their hatred were as strong as their faith, they would serve him well.

He heard one of the Faithful tumble to the ground: that dawn, the man's breath had come too fast, and he had raised a hand to his chest as if a spear had transfixed it.

Behind him, the others groaned at this proof of weakness, unworthiness.

"Drag that back to shelter," he commanded. "He will not stand here upon the sands with us again."

Or anyplace else. The man had stopped breathing.

"When shall *we* be worthy?" Eldest of the Faithful, Arakan-ikaran dared speak to him, dared even to question.

"When you are ready!" he snapped.

They whispered briefly among themselves, saving their strength for endurance and to contemplate the garden that he had promised to set in the middle of the deepest waste, filled with sweet water, abundant food, and strong children. In that paradise, no one's skin fissured or blossomed with evil, deadly colors. No one collapsed and died. But there was a world to win before paradise could be regained.

He allowed the translucent veil to shield his eyes once more. There was endurance and there was stupidity. And there was meditation, as well. His keen hearing heard the whisper of every grain of sand that shifted or the faint flicker of air that brushed against the lesions that had begun to open even on his skin. If he strained his hearing in the dry air, he could fancy he heard ionization itself as energy built up for the next set of solar flares, prominences leaping past the star's corona, attempting to embrace this world. Blurred by the veil, dune and rock promontory acquired a halo as if rainbows turned malignant and extended past the spectrum visible to the Faithful into fascinating patterns of ultraviolet and infrared.

His eyes were fire. His blood was fire.

And his brothers were calling.

To meet him here at the appointed place, far away from the concealment of rock or the reassurance of shielded equipment, when solar flares were imminent was a risk worthy of his warrior forebears. Energy pooled, static crackling as a sudden, turbulent shimmering erupted on the desert plain. For an instant, the brothers who were more outsiders than true kindred seemed to float above the sand and gravel, sheathed in light, crowned with fierce colors. They flickered out, then returned, stronger than before.

"They come! Without a ship, they come!" the Faithful whispered. "Crowned in glory, they walk, so tall and so unscarred."

To these primitives, he thought with sharp contempt, the Romulans with their lean height, their arrogant bearing, ready for thought or warfare combined, would look like messengers from that paradise he had prophesied for them. Now their dreams *must* come true.

And his along with them.

It was not illogical to dream: it was merely illogical to pour one's blood out upon the sand.

Far better that it be Federation blood.

The Romulans—even here, he would not willingly speak the name they had for themselves or call them brothers before lesser creatures—saluted him, to which he replied with a stately inclination of his head.

"Even these messengers from the heavens honor him. Our Prophet. Ours," whispered one of the Faithful.

It was more to the point, he thought as the Romulans, heavily armed, clasped his arm in the warrior's greeting, to say not that he was *their* prophet, but that they were his sacrifices.

Or anything else he needed.

If you can bear to hear an insult and not blindly kill to avenge the slight, the young centurion had once heard a senator say, *you can bear to salute a traitor.* Even here, it was not safe even to think the name of the senator: one never knew who among these savages just might bear telepathic abilities.

And it was not, after all, as if the tall figure casting a long shadow over the sand were a traitor to the senator his own commander served, much less to the Praetor himself. He was simply a traitor to his own race. The young centurion thought that he could very well endure another world's treachery, especially if the traitor declared himself open to alliance against the Federation. They would use him. And when they had won, they would turn and conquer the traitor's world as well, giving him his dream of a reunited breed—only not in the way he had hoped.

After all, alliances, especially covert ones, could always be disavowed.

The Romulan touched the amulet at his throat. He was a warrior born and had learned more than a warrior's skills. Still, the amulet helped him face the traitor and his band of mad primitives with suitable composure.

If it were not for this planet's location and the embarrassment that expulsion from it would cause the Federation, he would not have remained here for longer than it took to request removal.

The young centurion nodded respect to the one who faced the sun with naked eyes and bared head—no one had ever said that *Romulans* could not or did not lie, especially not to beings they held in contempt. Then he turned toward the rocks as if studying them. Gradually, he let himself drift toward the nearest escarpment. The rest of his landing party spread out, attempting to distract the natives that their contact called the Faithful.

His boots crunched on the sharp black rock that littered the ground. Sound carried a long way in the desert. If the cursed Federation risked an agent out this far (and they had one mad enough and almost brave enough that it would be no disgrace for a Romulan to fight him), he would hear, just as he would hear if their catspaw and madman moved toward him.

Protected by the striated rock, momentarily somewhat cooler, he snapped open his communicator. Shielded though it was against the miserable static on this irradiated world, static crackled from it. He muttered and adjusted the gain. Perhaps the interference—and the exceedingly narrow communications band that any Romulan signals officer knew to monitor—would prevent any Federation meddlers from eavesdropping, as was their contemptible habit.

A faint beep came from the communicator, and he whispered words, implanted by drug therapy, that he had not even known he had learned and that he would later forget.

There was a pause during which the young Romulan listened to the electrons dance between here and the Warbird he wished to his ancestors he had never left. Then:

"Well?"

Only that one word. Avrak, sister's son to Senator Pardek—he who proclaimed so eloquently the reasons (if you could call them such) that he desired more knowledge of the Federation—rarely spoke more than needful. It was far safer that way. The senator stood in place of a father to Avrak, who was in turn the centurion's own patron. If he were to make a career, win a share of his family's estate, even select a suitable consort, he could do nothing without Pardek's consent. As a military client, the young officer rose and fell, lived or died, with Avrak.

"Sir!" He could be as sparing of speech as Avrak.

"How is our traitor?" That Avrak asked at all was high praise.

"This malfunctioning star hasn't cooked his brains. Not quite yet. Even if he does think he's in charge."

"Excellent. Keep it that way."

The communicator went dead.

Had that been a chuckle he had heard?

Despite the heat of the deep desert and the restraint bred into him, the Romulan shuddered.

FIVE

**Intrepid II and Obsidian
Day 4, Fifth Week, Month of the Raging Durak,
Year 2296**

Lieutenant Duchamps, staring at the sight of Obsidian growing ever larger in the viewscreen, pursed his lips in a silent whistle. "Would you look at that?"

Spock, who had been studying the viewscreen as well, glanced quickly at the helmsman. "Lieutenant?"

Duchamps, predictably, went back into too-formal mode at this sudden attention. "The surface of Obsidian, sir. I was thinking how well named it is, sir. All those sheets of that black volcanic glass glittering in the sun. Sir."

"That black volcanic glass is, indeed, what constitutes the substance known as obsidian," Spock observed, though only someone extremely familiar with Vulcans could have read any dry humor into his matter-of-fact voice. *Jim, for instance.* Getting to his feet, Spock added to Uhura, "I am leaving for the transporter room, Commander. You have the conn."

"Yes, sir."

He waited to see her seated in the command chair, knowing how important this new role was to her, then acknowledged Uhura's right to be there with the smallest of nods. She solemnly nodded back, aware that he had just offered her silent congratulations. But Uhura being Uhura, she added in quick mischief, "Now, don't forget to write!"

After so many years among humans, Spock knew perfectly well that this was meant as a good-natured, tongue-in-cheek farewell, but he obligingly retorted, "I see no reason why I should utilize so inappropriate a means of communication," and was secretly gratified to see Uhura's grin.

He was less gratified at the gasps of shock from the rest of the bridge crew. Did they not see the witticism as such? Or were they shocked that Uhura could dare be so familiar? Spock firmly blocked a twinge of very illogical nostalgia; illogical, he told himself, because the past was exactly that.

McCoy was waiting for him, for once silent on the subject of "having my molecules scattered all over Creation." With the doctor were several members of Security and a few specialists such as the friendly, sensible Lieutenant Clayton, an agronomist, and the efficient young Lieutenant Diver, a geologist so new to Starfleet that her insignia still looked like they'd just come out of the box. Various other engineering and medical personnel would be following later. The heaviest of the doctor's supplies had already been beamed down with other equipment, but he stubbornly clung to the medical satchel—his "little black bag," as McCoy so anachronistically called it—slung over his shoulder.

"I decided to go," he told Spock unnecessarily. "That outrageously high rate of skin cancer and lethal mutations makes it a fascinating place."

That seemingly pure-science air, Spock mused, fooled no

one. No doctor worthy of the title could turn away from so many hurting people.

"Besides," McCoy added acerbically, "someone's got to make sure you all wear your sunhats."

"Indeed. Energize," Spock commanded, and . . .

. . . was elsewhere, from the unpleasantly cool, relatively dim ship—cool and dim to Vulcan senses, at any rate—to the dazzlingly bright light and welcoming heat of Obsidian. The veils instantly slid down over Spock's eyes, then up again as his desert-born vision adapted, while the humans hastily adjusted their sun visors. He glanced about at this new world, seeing a flat, gravelly surface, tan brown-gray stretching to the horizon of jagged, clearly volcanic peaks. A hot wind teased grit and sand into miniature spirals, and the sun glinted off shards of the black volcanic glass that had given this world its Federation name.

"Picturesque," someone commented wryly, but Spock ignored that. Humans, he knew, used sarcasm to cover uneasiness. Or perhaps it was discomfort; perhaps they felt the higher level of ionization in the air as he did, prickling at their skin.

No matter. One accepted what could not be changed. They had, at David Rabin's request, beamed down to these coordinates a distance away from the city: "The locals are uneasy enough as it is without a sudden 'invasion' in their midst."

Logical. And there was the Federation detail he had been told to expect, at its head a sturdy, familiar figure: David Rabin. He stepped forward, clad in a standard Federation hot-weather outfit save for his decidedly non-standard-issue headgear of some loose, flowing material caught by a circle of corded rope. Sensible, Spock thought, to adapt what was clearly an effective local solution to the problem of sunstroke.

"Rabin of Arabia," McCoy muttered, but Spock let that pass. Captain Rabin, grinning widely, was offering him the split-fingered Vulcan Greeting of the Raised Hand and saying, "Live long and prosper."

There could be no response but one. Spock returned the salute and replied simply, "Shalom."

This time McCoy had nothing to say.

It was only a short drive to the outpost. "Solar-powered vehicles, of course," Rabin noted. "No shortage of solar power on this world! The locals don't really mind our getting around like this as long as we don't bring any vehicles into Kalara or frighten the *chuchaki*—those cameloid critters over there."

Spock forbore to criticize the taxonomy.

Kalara, he mused, looked very much the standard desert city to be found on many low-tech—and some high-tech—worlds. Mud brick really was the most practical organic building material, and thick walls and high windows provided quite efficient passive air cooling. Kalara was, of course, an oasis town; he didn't need to see the oasis to extrapolate that conclusion. No desert city came into being without a steady, reliable source of water and, therefore, a steady, reliable source of food. Spock noted the tips of some feathery green branches peeking over the high walls and nodded. Good planning for both economic and safety reasons to have some of that reliable water source be within the walls. Add to that the vast underground network of irrigation canals and wells, and these people were clearly doing a clever job of exploiting their meager resources.

Or would be, were it not for that treacherous sun.

And, judging from what Rabin had already warned, for that all too common problem in times of crisis: fanaticism.

It is illogical for any one person or persons to claim to know

46

a One True Path to enlightenment. And I must, he added honestly, *include my own distant ancestors in that thought.*

And, he reluctantly added, some Vulcans not so far removed in time.

"What's *that?*" McCoy exclaimed suddenly. "Hebrew graffiti?"

"Deuteronomy," Rabin replied succinctly, adding, "We're home, everybody."

They left the vehicles and entered the Federation outpost, and in the process made a jarring jump from timelessness to gleaming modernity. Spock paused only an instant at the shock of what to him was a wall of unwelcome coolness; around him, the humans were all breathing sighs of relief. McCoy put down his shoulder pack with a grunt. "Hot as Vulcan out there."

"Just about," Rabin agreed cheerfully, pulling off his native headgear. "And if you think this is bad, wait till Obsidian's summer. This sun, good old unstable Loki, will kill you quite efficiently.

"Please, everyone, relax for a bit. Drink something even if you don't feel thirsty. It's ridiculously easy to dehydrate here, especially when none of you are desert-acclimated. Or rather," he added before Spock could comment, "when even the desert-born among you haven't been *in* any deserts for a while. While you're resting, I'll fill you in on what's been happening here."

Quickly and efficiently, Rabin set out the various problems, the failed hydroponics program, the beetles, the mysterious fires and spoiled supply dumps. When he was finished, Spock noted, "One, two, or even three incidents might be considered no more than unpleasant coincidence. But taken as a whole, this series of incidents can logically only add up to deliberate sabotage."

"Which is what I was thinking," Rabin agreed. " 'One's accident, two's coincidence, three's enemy action,' or however the quote goes. The trouble is: Who *is* the enemy? Or rather, which one?"

Spock raised an eyebrow ever so slightly. "These are, if the records are indeed correct, a desert people with a relatively low level of technology."

"They are that. And before you ask, no, there's absolutely no trace of Romulan or any other offworld involvement."

"Then we need ask: Who of this world would have sufficient organization and initiative to work such an elaborate scheme of destruction?"

The human sighed. "Who, indeed? We've got a good many local dissidents; we both know how many nonconformists a desert can breed. But none of the local brand of agitators could ever band together long enough to mount a definite threat: they hate each other as much or maybe even more than they hate us."

"And in the desert?"

"Ah, Spock, old buddy, just how much manpower do you think I have? Much as I'd love to up and search all that vastness . . ."

"It would mean leaving the outpost unguarded. I understand."

"Besides," Rabin added thoughtfully, "I can't believe that any of the desert people, even the 'wild nomads,' as the folks in Kalara call the deep-desert tribes, would do anything to destroy precious resources, even those from offworld. They might destroy *us,* but not food or water."

"Logic," Spock retorted, "requires that someone is working this harm. Whether you find the subject pleasant or not, *someone* is 'poisoning the wells.'"

"Excuse me, sir," Lieutenant Clayton said, "but wouldn't it be relatively simple for the *Intrepid* to do a scan of the entire planet?"

"It could—"

"But that," Rabin cut in, "wouldn't work. The trouble is

that those 'wild nomads' are a pain in the—well, they're a nuisance to find by scanning, because they tend to hide out against solar flares. And where they hide is in hollows shielded by rock that's difficult or downright impossible for scanners to penetrate. We have no idea how many nomads are out there, nor do the city folk. Oh, and if that wasn't enough," he added wryly, "the high level of ionization in the atmosphere, thank you very much, Loki, provides a high amount of static to signal."

Spock moved to the banks of equipment set up to measure ionization, quickly scanning the data. "The levels do fluctuate within the percentages of possibility. A successful scan is unlikely but not improbable during the lower ranges of the scale. We will attempt one. I have a science officer who will regard this as a personal challenge." *As do I.* A Vulcan could, after all, assemble the data far more swiftly than a human who—no. McCoy had quite wisely warned him against "micromanaging." He was not what he had been, Spock reminded himself severely. And only an emotional being longed for what had been and was no more.

Commander Uhura had to admit that sitting in a captain's chair felt . . . just fine. Being called "Commander" was fine, too, for that matter. *You could have gone after your own ship,* she chided herself. *Had enough of "Hailing frequencies open," didn't you? Had just about sufficient seniority. Yet you turned down the chance, foolish you.*

Maybe not so foolish. When it came right down to it, Uhura knew that the command chair was figuratively a bit uncomfortable. Restricting. She never had settled down in any traditional fashion: no husband, no children, no regrets. A Federation captaincy left very little time for anything else *but* restriction. If she hadn't married a man, she was not, Uhura thought dryly, ready to be married to a ship.

Was Spock? That was a question she'd asked herself often enough in the last three years—a question Uhura rather suspected even he, for all his Vulcan logic, couldn't answer. Vulcans never fidgeted, but there were times when Captain Spock looked as if he found the command chair an uncomfortable fit. And if he couldn't decide—

"Commander," Lieutenant Duchamps said suddenly. "A message is coming in from Captain Spock."

Just in time to keep me from getting sentimental. "I'll take it here."

"Commander Uhura." No mistaking Spock's precise voice. "I would appreciate the crew performing a planetary scan."

"Yes, sir. Looking for . . . ?"

"Life, Commander. Preferably intelligent. Science Officer Richards will want to coordinate with Medical for the requisite parameters and brain-wave complexities."

He said no more. But the sudden silence spoke volumes. *Fascinating,* Uhura thought. *Wonder what's going on. And trust Spock not to say anything melodramatic like, "I can say nothing further for reasons of security." But it's "reasons of security," all right.* She contented herself with, "We'll start that scan right away, Captain."

"Thank you, Commander. Spock out."

They would have to shift position, Uhura thought. Lieutenant Commander Atherton had been counting on maintaining a geosynchronous orbit. He was *not* going to like this. Or rather, to be charitable, he was going to *act* as though he didn't like this.

Sure enough, when Uhura advised the engineer of the forthcoming scan, she was treated to a series of precise, peevish, but strangely happy complaints about "It may put an undue strain on my test configurations," and "It will take some time to straighten things out without upsetting previous calibrations," not to mention, "It will completely derange my training schedule."

Scotty, Uhura thought, bemused. *The accent may be different—ohh, yes!—but underneath that prickly façade, he really is just like Scotty. If a captain is married to the ship,* she added wryly, *then a good engineer is that ship's lover.*

Well, well. They might have a new ship, they might have a crew half veterans still in mourning, half newcomers wary of the veterans, but maybe they were going to be able to mesh into an efficient unit after all.

Though I doubt I'll ever get used to that British Colonial accent!

"Commander?" It was Ensign Chang, a small, wiry young man, one of the newer crew members and still somewhat tentative about what and where he was. "I . . . uh . . . think I just . . . uh . . . spotted something. Something odd."

"Odd."

"Yes, Commander. While we were unscrambling ground communications, there was the weirdest blip on the screen." His voice became more sure as he continued. "It emerged from the Neutral Zone, just for a second, then vanished. I recorded it, though."

"Good man!" Uhura quickly moved to his side. "Play it back."

"And . . . there! Did you see it?"

"I did, indeed," Uhura said grimly. "Open a hailing frequency, narrow beam, Captain Spock only." Even in this urgent moment, she couldn't help but enjoy ordering someone else to do that. "And scramble it."

"Hailing frequency open, Commander. Scramble activated."

Uhura leaned over the control panel. "Captain Spock: Urgent. We have just uncovered signs of a Romulan Warbird. It's cloaked, but they lowered that cloaking just now

51

for a few moments. And that suggests to me that someone just beamed down to Obsidian."

Spock replied almost instantly, "Excellent logic, Commander."

Uhura stiffened in a moment's pleased surprise. That was high praise from a Vulcan! "Why, thank you, sir," she said, and returned to the command chair, trying very hard not to grin. The chair felt a little less restricting now.

McCoy, there in the Federation outpost on Obsidian, overheard Spock's transmission to Uhura. "Why, Spock," the doctor drawled, "I didn't know you had it in you."

Spock glanced at him, catching just a hint of an edge to the jesting words, almost as though McCoy were feeling left out. It would hardly be rational for the doctor to be envying David Rabin his prior friendship with Spock. More probably, McCoy was longing for the old *Enterprise* camaraderie. It would not, Spock thought, be wise to say that. Instead, he merely raised an eyebrow and pointed out, "Common courtesy is never amiss. Nor is it illogical to commend someone for being logical. Particularly," he added, voice totally without expression, "when that someone is human."

McCoy nearly choked on a laugh. Spock, satisfied that the issue had been defused, turned to David Rabin. "I think we must speak together. In private."

"Just what I was thinking. We can talk in the closet they call my office."

The space was, indeed, barely more than a closet, but the blank walls and smooth, unornamented furnishings left no place for spy devices. Spock, nevertheless, ran a quick check. Yes. Secure. Which brought him to his first point. "Security on Obsidian has almost certainly been breached. There are too many examples of a supposedly low-tech people knowing too much about activities here: this can only point to inside involvement."

Rabin sighed. "I thought as much, though I haven't been able to prove a damned thing."

"We cannot rely on information from the *Intrepid* alone."

"Right. No matter how good the equipment on your ship is, it's not going to be able to pinpoint what's going on in that wilderness outside. It can give us some idea of where to look, but . . ." He paused, looking at Spock, the two of them in perfect understanding, then shrugged and added, with the tone of someone saying the obvious, "Someone has to get out there and search."

"Indeed. But since we do not know the extent of infiltration, the locals, even those seemingly friendly or helpful, cannot be trusted. Logically, it must be Federation personnel, and they alone, who investigate in the desert."

"And equally logically," Rabin added, "it's going to have to be those with the most desert survival experience." He stopped with a wry grin, considering what he'd just said. "Guess what, Spock?"

"There is no 'guess' to this. We are the most logical choices."

"You've got it. It's been a long time, my friend, but it looks like we're a team again."

SIX

**Vulcan, Mount Seleya
Day 6, Seventh Week of Tasmeen,
Year 2247**

Dawn hovered over Mount Seleya. A huge *shavokh* glided
down on a thermal from the peak, balanced on a wingtip,
then soared out toward the desert. Spock heard its hunting
call.

*Where it stoops, one may find ground water or a soak not
too deeply buried,* Spock recalled from his survival training.
He had no need of such information now. Nevertheless, his
gaze followed the creature's effortless flight.

The stairs that swept upward to the narrow bridge still lay
in shadow. Faint mist rose about the mountain, perhaps
from the snow that capped it, alone of Vulcan's peaks, or
perhaps from the lava that bubbled sullenly a thousand
meters below. Soon, 40 Eridani A would rise, and the ritual
honoring Spock and his agemates would begin.

It was illogical, Spock told himself, for him to assume that
all eyes were upon him as he followed his parents. Instead,

he concentrated on his parents' progress. Sustained only by the light touch of Sarek's fingers upon hers, veiled against the coming sunrise, Amanda crossed the narrow span as if she had not conquered her fear of the unrailed bridge only after long meditation.

Few of the many participants from the outworld scientific, diplomatic, and military enclaves on Vulcan could equal her grace. Some had actually arranged to be flown to the amphitheater just to allow them to bypass the bridge that had served as a final defense for the warband that had ruled here in ancient days. Others of the guests crossed unsteadily or too quickly for dignity.

Vertigo might be a reasonable assumption, Spock thought, for beings acclimating themselves to Vulcan's thin air or the altitude of the bridge.

"The air is the air," one of his agemates remarked in the tone of one quoting his elders. "I have heard these *humans* take drugs to help them breathe."

All of the boys eyed the representatives from the Federation as if they were xenobiological specimens in a laboratory. Especially, they surveyed the officials' sons and daughters, who might, one day, be people with whom they would study and work.

"They look sickly," the same boy spoke. His name, Spock recalled, was Stonn. Not only was he a distant kinsman to Sered, he was one of the youths who also eyed Spock as if he expected Spock's human blood to make him fall wheezing to his knees, preferably just when he was supposed to lead his agemates up to the platform where T'Lar and T'Pau would present them with the hereditary—and now symbolic—weapons of their Great Houses. By slipping out early into the desert to undergo his *kahs-wan* ordeal before the others, Spock had made himself forever Eldest among the boys of his year. It was not logical that some, like Stonn, would not forgive him for his presumption, or his survival; but it was so.

A woman's voice provided a welcome interruption. "Let's assume your tricorder is broken or missing—*David, don't lean over like that or you'll give me a heart attack!* Your tricorder's crashed, and you have to calculate how long it'll take you to hit the lava down there and turn into shish kebab. Say it's a thousand-meter drop."

One thousand point five nine, Spock corrected automatically, but in silence.

"Remember, you'll have to account for less air resistance; the air's thinner. Get *back,* no, you're not stretching out flat on the bridge, and you can't see the lava from here! I gave you an assignment, David!"

From the corner of his eye, Spock could see a woman in the glittering uniform of a Starfleet captain tug a boy who resembled her back from the edge of the bridge. Allowing for variations in species and body type, the human youth seemed close to his own age—perhaps a little old for such brusque treatment, although he seemed amused rather than annoyed. He had courage, if not judgment, Spock decided. If it were not that emotion was impermissible at any time and completely unacceptable this morning so close to the Shrine, Spock might have envied the boy his excited grin and that eager gaze darting from Mount Seleya's peak to the bridge and the desert.

He might also, were emotion not unacceptable, have envied the way the Starfleet officer, clearly his mother, did not rebuke her son with a politeness that would be worse than any human rage, but instead distracted him with mathematics.

Almost absently, Spock solved the simple equation, then estimated how long it would take the Terran boy to produce a reasonably correct solution. The answer came within the parameters he had set: a sign of quick intelligence in the human.

"That's better," said the Starfleet captain. "Believe me, David, if you don't settle down, I've got more snap quizzes where that one came from. I know you're excited about seeing Vulcan—"

"Aren't you?" the boy countered. "I mean, look at that *desert!* It makes Sinai National Preserve look like a sandbox!"

Fascinating. Even Spock's mother did not speak of the deserts that occupied much of her adopted world with such admiration.

"David, I swear, someone spiked your tri-ox with adrenaline."

The tri-ox compound did, Spock mused, sometimes have such an effect on some already excitable humans. But he was too intrigued by this show of blatant emotion to comment.

"Calm down!" the woman was ordering. "Before we return to Earth, I may be able to arrange a field trip. But not if you create an interstellar incident."

That sparked a wry grin from the boy but no repentance, and his mother sighed and continued, "Once you actually start at the Academy, you'll learn how important diplomacy is for a Starfleet officer—even one who plans to be an explorer."

"Yes, ma'am." The boy subsided, tugging at his close-fitting formal tunic, so much less suitable for Vulcan's heat than Spock's loose, dark robe with its embossed metallic heir's sigils.

Lecturing offspring seemed to be a constant among all sentient beings, Spock observed.

Then he had to force himself not to start. Not fifty meters away stood Sered, in a more formal version of the austere brown robe he had worn for his visit to Sarek's house. The robe bore the bronze symbols that denoted Head of House, but he had chosen the most archaic forms of the complex glyphs. Intriguing.

"We shall pause here, my wife," murmured Sarek to Amanda. He added, "Captain Rabin." The ambassador had not raised his impeccably modulated voice, but the captain turned and came to . . . *military attention,* Spock knew from his studies, although he had never actually seen the posture before.

"Ambassador Sarek."

"Do you find your stay on Vulcan instructive?"

The Starfleet officer's face was impassive. "My highest function is to strengthen the figurative bridge—like the literal one we just crossed—between your world and mine. My assignment honors me."

Remarkable. Her son had achieved stillness, if not her military bearing.

"You do your service justice, Captain. My wife, may I present Starfleet Captain Nechama Rabin, from the planet of your birth? Captain, this is the Lady Amanda, my wife."

Amanda, who had courteously raised her light veil, somehow managed to seem taller and more stately than the woman who snipped roses in a wet-planet conservatory and admitted to worrying about the son whom she lectured. "Shalom, Captain," she said, hand raised in the Vulcan greeting.

"Live long and prosper, Lady Amanda." The two human women studied each other for an instant, then smiled.

"Peace and prosperity," said Lady Amanda. "Could we have better greetings between compatriots on such a fine morning?"

"Let us hope," Sarek took up her words, "that such greetings extend as well to . . . friends."

With a raised eyebrow, he acknowledged the captain's son. Sered, Spock noted, stood all this while as if paralyzed by *le-matya* venom, watching. *My father delivers an object lesson,* Spock realized.

"May I present my son, David?" asked the captain. "He enters Starfleet Academy next year."

"Another generation of service?" Sarek said. "Highly commendable."

Spock knew that Sarek, like most Vulcans, held the military in low esteem. Did diplomacy require the speaking of lies? No, Sarek had said that "service" was laudable; he had said nothing of its type. And his approval drove home his "lesson" to Sered: Sarek favored both today's ceremony and the invitation of Federation representatives.

The boy stepped forward fearlessly (*Of course,* Spock thought), looking up into Sarek's keen eyes, then raised his hand in the proper salute. "I am honored, sir." His Old High Vulcan formal greeting was hesitant, but correctly phrased; he had even mastered the glottal stop. "I also thank you for the opportunity to witness this ceremony."

Sarek managed without the slightest change in expression or posture to register his approval. "It has its parallels in the customs of your own people, does it not?"

His father was being positively expansive to this stranger! *Jealousy,* Spock reminded himself, *is an emotion. A perilous one. Why should he not be polite to a visitor?*

Spock wasn't the only one who had noticed. He saw Sered's expression alter in a way that would have been imperceptible to a human, but to a Vulcan looked as blatant as a grimace of revulsion. *Contempt is an emotion as well,* Spock thought. Then the tall, austere Vulcan vanished into the crowd.

"Yes, sir," David was continuing. "Boys undergo a ritual that confirms them as adults. But not just boys. What about . . ."

Captain Rabin's hand came down firmly upon her son's shoulder, cutting off what Spock was certain would have been a most revealing question. "My son has completed advanced desert survival training, Ambassador Sarek. All morning, he has told me how magnificent he finds the view. He is hoping for an opportunity to visit the Forge."

It seemed that humans knew the art of using words as a diversion as well.

Sarek dipped his head a polite fraction. "A most feasible ambition, David. Captain Rabin, with your permission, I shall have one of my aides arrange an excursion."

No mention was made of including Spock. Again he warned himself against emotion. Against jealousy. And almost succeeded.

David visibly *glowed.* He glanced over at Spock, who kept his face impassive.

"We have presumed upon your time, sir," said Captain Rabin. "I know you must be eager to see . . . your son?" She raised an eyebrow inquiringly at the ambassador. ". . . welcomed into the ranks of adult Vulcan males."

"Spock," Sarek introduced him briefly. Spock bowed in silence.

Was Captain Rabin disconcerted by the brusqueness? "Lady Amanda, my congratulations," she said carefully.

"We are very proud of Spock," Amanda replied, just as carefully.

With a noncommittal smile, the captain withdrew, towing a reluctant David as though he were a much younger child. He, giving up the struggle for dignity, left trailing questions. "Do you think they'd let him go with me? I'd love to talk with a Vulcan my age. Who else would come? You know, everyone's talking about Vulcan boys. What about *girls?*"

Lady Amanda's shoulders shook almost imperceptibly. Captain Rabin stopped in her tracks. "I tell you what, David. Ask that question, which probably breaks every privacy code the Vulcans have—and they've got *plenty*—create your interplanetary scandal, and you can forget seeing the Forge. In fact, it would be a wonder if we weren't kicked off Vulcan."

"But what *about* girls?" he whispered, clearly forgetting about keen Vulcan hearing. "It's not as though they were secondary citizens. I mean, what about T'Pau? She's important enough, isn't she? Yes, and what about T'Lar of—of Gol?"

The captain's expression changed to what Spock's mother called her "give me strength" face, used when her patience was severely tried. "Will you please stop thinking about Vulcan girls? They probably all have dates for Saturday night anyway."

David flushed. "Mother, please. You know I wasn't talking about that. And you mean you approve—"

"Look, son," said Nechama Rabin. "As you just lectured me, T'Lar of Gol and T'Pau will be honoring these boys. Is it logical to assume that they, as women, would slight girls— who one day may grow up to be Elders themselves?"

"But we don't know—"

"And aren't likely to. Before you ask, I am *not* about to try to find out. And neither are you. Now, *quiet* or you go back to Base. This is not, incidentally, your mother speaking. This is the captain. Understood, mister?"

"Aye-aye," said the boy. Spock suspected he would behave appropriately now—until his next attack of "why." But surely there was nothing improper about an inquiring mind! It would be interesting to speak with this Terran who shared a trait with him that—

But Sarek would probably not allow his son to risk exposure to human emotionalism by learning more about this boy or any of the others.

A deferential three paces behind his parents and two to the side of Sarek, Spock strode past a series of deeply incised pits—the result of laser cannon fire two millennia back— and up to the entrance of the amphitheater. Two masked guards bearing ceremonial *lirpa* presented arms before his father, then saluted Spock for the first time as an adult. For all his attempts at total control, he felt a little shiver race through him as he returned the salutes as an adult for the first time. The clublike weights that formed the *lirpa* bases shone, a luster of dark metal. The dawn light flashed red on the blades that the guards carried over their shoulders. At the guards' hips, they wore stone-hilted daggers, but no energy weapons—*phasers*—such as a Starfleet officer might wear on duty. Of course, no such weapons might be brought here.

Lady Amanda removed her fingers from her husband's and smiled faintly. "I shall join the other ladies of our House now, my husband, while you bring our son before the Elders. Spock, I shall be watching for you. And I am indeed *very* proud."

As, her gaze told him, *is your father.*

She glided away, a grace note among the taller Vulcans.

Spock fell into step with his father, head high, as if his blood bore no human admixture. *As it was in the beginning* . . . Silently, he reviewed the beginning of the Chant of Generations as he glided down the stairs.

Long ago, some cataclysm or some unspeakable weapon had peeled half the face of the mountain away, leaving only a ridge above the crater that had been shaped into a natural amphitheater. Beneath this roof was a platform from which two pillars reared up. Centered between the pillars stood an altar of dark stone on which rested the greatest treasures of each Great House on Vulcan: ceremonial swords, of which Spock and his agemates would receive replicas.

We are trained to abhor violence. Yet we are taught combat and, to honor us, we are awarded archaic weapons. This is not logical.

None of the other boys accompanying their fathers seemed to have such reservations. The Federation guests simply watched, the adults clearly impressed, the youngsters honestly openmouthed. Sered, Spock thought, would no doubt think that awe was a highly appropriate reaction.

Behind the pillars glistened a pool, ruddy with 40 Eridani A's dawn. To either side of the pillars, dark-robed students of the disciplines of Gol stepped forward to shake frameworks of bells. Another, whose robes bore the sigil of a third-degree adept, swung a great mallet at a hexagonal gong so ancient that its precious iron central boss had turned deep red. Again, the bells rang, dying into a whisper and a rustle.

Everyone in the amphitheater rose. T'Lar, adept and First Student, walked onto the platform. Then, two guards, their *lirpa* set aside for the purpose, entered with a curtained carrying chair. From it, robed in black, but with all the crimsons of the dawn in her brocaded overrobe, stepped T'Pau. She leaned on an intricately carved stick.

Spock's father stepped forward as if to help her.

"Thee is kind, Sarek," said the Elder of their House, "but thee is premature. When I can no longer preside unassisted over this rite, it will be time to release my *katra.*"

Sarek bowed. "I ask pardon for my presumption."

"Courtesy," T'Pau held up a thin, imperious hand, "is never presumptuous." Her long eyes moved over the people in the amphitheater as if delivering some lesson of her own—but to whom? Carefully, she approached the altar and bowed to T'Lar. "Eldest of All, I beg leave to assist thee."

"You honor me," replied T'Lar.

"I live to serve," said T'Pau, an observation that would have left Spock gasping had he not been getting sufficient oxygen.

Both women bowed, this time to the youths who stood waiting their presentation.

Again, the adept struck the gong.

T'Lar raised both arms, the white and silver of her sleeves

63

falling like great wings. *"As it was in the beginning, so shall it always be. These sons of our House have shown their worthiness . . ."*

"I protest!" came a shout from the amphitheater.

Even the Vulcans murmured what would have been astonishment in any other people as Sered, his heavy robes swinging about him, strode down the center aisle to stand before the altar.

"I protest," he declared, "the profanation of these rites. I protest the way they have been stripped of their meaning, contaminated as one might pollute a well in the desert. I protest the way our deepest mysteries have been revealed to *outsiders.*"

T'Pau's eyebrows rose at that last word, which was in the seldom-used invective mode.

"Has thee finished?" asked T'Lar. Adept of *Kolinahr*, she would remain serene if Mount Seleya split along its many fissures and this entire amphitheater crumbled into the pit below.

"No!" Sered cried, his voice sharp as the cry of a *shavokh*. "Above all, I protest the inclusion of an outsider in our rites—yes, as leader of the men to be honored today—when other and worthier men, our exiled cousins, go unhonored and unrecognized."

Sarek drew deep, measured breaths. *He prepares for combat,* Spock realized, and was astonished to feel his own body tensing, alert, aware as he had only been during his *kahs-wan,* when he had faced a full-grown *le-matya* in the deep desert and knew, logically, he could not survive such an encounter. *Fight or flight,* his mother had once called it. That too was a constant across species. *But not here. There must not be combat here.*

"Thee speaks of those who exiled themselves, Sered." Not the slightest trace of emotion tinged T'Pau's voice. "Return lies in their power, not in ours."

"So it does!" Sered shouted. "And so they do!"

He tore off his austere robe. Gasps of astonishment and hisses of outrage sounded as he stood forth in the garb of a Captain of the Hosts from the ancient days. Sunlight picked out the metal of his harness in violent red and exploded into rainbow fire where it touched the gem forming the grip of the ancient energy weapon Sered held—a weapon he had brought, against all law, into Mount Seleya's amphitheater.

"Welcome our lost kindred!" he commanded and gestured as if leading a charge.

A rainbow shimmer rose about the stage. *Transporter effect,* Spock thought even as it died, leaving behind six tall figures in black and silver. At first glance they were as much like Sered as brothers in their mother's womb. But where Sered wore his rage like a cloak of ceremony, these seemed accustomed to emotion and casual violence.

For an instant no one moved, the Vulcans too stunned by this glaring breach of custom, the Federation guests not sure what they were permitted to do. Then, as the intruders raised their weapons, the amphitheater erupted into shouts and motion. From all sides, the guards advanced, holding their *lirpa* at a deadly angle. But *lirpa* were futile against laser rifles.

As the ceremonial guard was cut down, Sarek whispered quick, urgent words to other Vulcans. They nodded. Spock sensed power summoned and joined:

"Now!" whispered the ambassador.

In a phalanx, the Vulcans rushed the dais. They swept across it, bearing T'Pau and T'Lar with them. They, at least, were safe. Only one remained behind. Green blood puddled from his ruined skull, seeping into the dark stone where no blood had flowed for countless generations.

"You dare rise up against me?" Sered shrilled. "One sacrifice is not enough to show the lesser worlds!" He waved his weapon at the boys, at the gorgeously dressed Federation guests. "Take them! We shall make these folk of lesser spirit *crawl.*"

Spock darted forward, not sure what he could do, knowing only that it was not logical to wait meekly for death. And these intruders were not mindless *le-matyas!* They were kindred, of Vulcan stock; surely they could be reasoned with—

As Sered could not. Spock faltered at the sight of the drawn features, the too-bright eyes staring beyond this chaos to a vision only Sered could see. Few Vulcans ever went insane, but here was true madness. Surely his followers, though, clearly Vulcan's long-lost cousins, would not ally themselves with such insanity!

Desperately calm, Spock raised his hand in formal greeting. Surak had been slain trying to bring peace: if Spock fell thus, at least his father would have final proof that he was worthy to be the ambassador's son.

They suddenly seemed to be in a tense little circle of calm. One of the "cousins" pointed at him, while a second nodded, then gestured out into the chaos around them. The language had greatly changed in the sundered years, but Spock understood:

"This one."

"Him."

It may work. They may listen to me. They—

"Get back, son!" a Starfleet officer shouted, racing forward, phaser in outstretched hand, straight at Sered. "Drop that weapon!"

Sered threw back his head. He actually laughed. Then, firing at point-blank range, reflexes swifter than human, he shot the man. The human flared up into flame so fierce that the heat scorched Spock's face and the veils slipped across his eyes, blurring his sight. He blinked, blinked again to clear it, and saw the conflagration that had been a man flash out of existence.

Dead. He's dead. A moment ago alive, and now— Spock stared at Sered across the small space that had held a man, his mind refusing to process what he'd just seen. "Half-blood," muttered Sered. "Weakling shoot of Surak's house. But you will serve—"

"Got him!" came a shout. David Rabin hurled himself into Sered, bringing them both down. The weapon flew from Sered's hand, and Captain Rabin and Sered both scrambled for it. The woman touched it, Sered knocked her hand aside—

And the weapon slid right to Spock. He snatched it up, heart racing faster than a proper Vulcan should permit, and pointed it at Sered.

"Can you kill a brother Vulcan?" Sered hissed, unafraid, from where he lay. "Can you?"

Could he? For an endless moment, Spock froze, seeing Sered's fearless stare, feeling the weapon in his hand. Dimly he was aware of the struggle all around him as the invaders grabbed hostages, but all he could think was that all he need do was one tiny move, only the smallest tightening of a finger—

Can you kill a brother Vulcan?

He'd hesitated too long. What felt like half of Mount Seleya fell on him. Spock thought he heard his father saying, *Exaggeration. Remember your control.*

Then the fierce dawn went black.

SEVEN

Obsidian, Deep Desert
Day 1, First Week, Month of the Shining *Chara*,
Year 2296

He stood in noble, straight-backed isolation in the desert's cleansing forge, the sun blazing all about him, fire to burn impurities from him, from those who followed him—fire to destroy those who would not yield. And fire, just incidentally, to highlight him impressively, like one of those hero-deities out of these primitives' childish mythologies. Behind him, his keen ears warned, some folk had gathered. A handful of his Faithful, not quite daring to intrude on his meditations.

I do not meditate. I wait for my plotting to blaze into flame. But these weak things need not know my plans.

"What?" he called over his shoulder without deigning to turn, and heard the small rustlings of amazement, of *how did he know we were here?*

Fools. They had not yet realized just how keen were his senses. "You disturb me. Why?"

"The spy . . ." That was Arakan-ikaran's voice. "There has been a report from the Outsider base."

That was, of course, the Federation outpost. "Has the spy left his post?" It was the softest of purrs. "I did not give him permission for that."

"Oh, no, no," Arakan-ikaran assured him hastily. "He remains faithful to our cause. To you! He sent word, though, to Rharik, who sent it to Kheral, who—"

"I am pleased to see that the network remains intact. What is the information?"

"A small force of the Outsiders has set out into the desert, headed by the Outsider Fool and . . . another."

That hesitation was hardly accidental. "Which?"

A nervous pause. "One like you, Master."

It took every atom of his will not to start. He could not have been betrayed. It could not be part of a Federation trap; they could not know what, who, he was. But there were traitors among his kind, that he knew quite well. Traitors who would willingly turn from the True Path to fawn on those Outsiders. Traitors, too, or at least treacherous ones, among the Sundered.

"Master . . . ?" Arakan-ikaran asked warily. "*Is* this of your holy kind? Another you have summoned to guide us?"

Oh, you weak idiot. "No." He turned, slowly and dramatically, well aware of how splendidly the sun's fires haloed him. "Think, you who call yourselves my Faithful. Think! Who would bear my seeming yet be of the Outsiders?"

They picked up the bait without hesitation. "The Fiery One!" The whispers flew through the gathering. "The Fiery One has come!" "The Outsiders have sent us the Fiery One!"

Predictable. They had come to the proper conclusion, all without his needing to say a single untruth. The Fiery One in their primitive belief was the Tempter, the Evil Force that was not the purifying fire but the foul and all-destroying blaze.

Good. Very good. "This is not the Fiery One," he said before unseemly yet useful frenzy could become hysteria, his voice cutting easily through the noise. "This is not the Fiery One but his agent."

"But—but what shall we do?"

"Nothing." His face a perfect, elegant mask of tranquility, he told them, "Leave that one to me. I shall be a clear white flame to protect you. But you must serve me."

"We do!" they cried in orgiastic worship. "We always will! You are our lord and we are the Faithful! Let us serve!"

He suppressed a sigh. Once again, they used their absurd, so useful faith to incite themselves to a frenzy such as a Vulcan might only experience in the depths of *plak-tow*. "Yes," he said. "In time. Now you must tell me what else our spy had to say."

"It is of the Outsiders, Master. Their route into the desert is too sure. It seems to say, 'We know where the Faithful are hiding.' Can this be so? Is the Fiery One's slave guiding them to—"

"Be calm. They know only what I allow. They know only where we have been. The desert is vast, and I will provide shelter for my children." He glanced at Arikan-ikaran. "There is yet more. What?"

"With the Outsiders, it is said, rides one they call the—the—" Arikan-ikaran stumbled over the unfamiliar, alien words. "The 'chief medical officer.' Is this one not a sha-man? A person of some importance among them?"

"It is." But even as he said this, he wondered, *Chief medical officer? From which ship? Is the Federation calling in new vessels?*

Arikan-ikaran took his hesitation for encouragement. "Is this not a useful thing? Would he not make a valuable hostage?"

Ahh. Now and again, one of these primitive creatures did show a spark of logic. "Yes. Indeed yes. You are wise." Watching Arikan-ikaran's proud face fairly glow from the praise, he continued, "But you have missed the major point. This one, this 'chief medical officer,' might prove even more than a mere hostage." Turning back to study the sun, the pure, cleansing fire, he added over his shoulder, "He should make a most valuable lure as well."

"You *bet* I'm going with you," McCoy exploded. "That's a desert out there!"

Spock glanced blandly at David Rabin. "Dr. McCoy does have a tendency to state the obvious."

McCoy snorted. "You know perfectly well what I mean, Spock. That's a wilderness, full of accidents just waiting to happen, and—"

"And we need an adaptable medical officer to accompany us. Quite logical."

"I—oh. Well, we certainly can't head out there in standard Federation uniforms, so I guess you, Captain Rabin, have gear for us."

He exited with just a touch of haste. Rabin glanced at Spock again, then grinned. "Not fair. Humans don't expect humor from Vulcans."

"I? I merely stated the obvious."

"Right. Of course. Come, my humor-impaired friend, let's get going."

The desert robe, Spock thought, felt comfortably familiar, very similar in weight and weave to those from Vulcan. There were, after all, only so many logical ways to design desert garb, he concluded, and pulled the robe's hood up over his head: Good. Deep enough to provide more than adequate shade.

Ahead stood the rest of the party, five humans, four of

them with the darker complexions that indicated genes of desert stock. The fifth was Lieutenant Diver, looking very small and delicate amid all the flowing robes; her specialty was igneous geology, which made her a logical part of the group. Six humans, Spock thought, including McCoy, plus himself. The shuttlecraft would be almost full but not overburdened. There would be sufficient room for a prisoner, should such a need arise.

McCoy, medical gear slung over his shoulder, was looking about at the rest of the party, shaking his head. "When I said we weren't going to wear standard uniforms, I never expected *this.*" His sweep of a hand took in all the loose, flowing desert gear.

Captain Rabin, resplendent in a white desert robe and flowing headscarf that made only the vaguest nods to regulations, frowned slightly. "Maybe it's not Federation textbook." It was said as much for the clearly disapproving Junior Lieutenant Albright, who was *not* going along and who, perspiring in full Federation uniform, still looked the very image of the proper Federation officer, as for McCoy. "But it's damned practical."

"Huh. Probably. But," McCoy added, tongue firmly in cheek, "I'm a doctor, not Lawrence of Arabia."

Rabin, not missing a beat, gave him an elaborate salaam. Several of the others stifled laughs, and one, a handsome, olive-skinned young man, murmured, "Most elegantly done, sir."

"Why, thank you, Ensign Prince."

Spock raised an eyebrow at the subtle emphasis on "prince." "That is not merely a name, I think. Do you refer to an ancient title?"

The ensign grinned, perfect teeth gleaming, and glanced quickly at David Rabin as though this was an old joke between them. "Yes, Captain Spock, he does. I am Prince Faisal ibn Saud ibn Turki and so on and so on of the ancient

Saudi line—for what that's worth. This, by Father's calcula-
tion, makes me seventy-ninth in line for the throne."

"While he's waiting for the crown," Rabin added dryly,
"he'll be the pilot of our shuttlecraft. Not as fast or elegant
as the cruisers he'd prefer, but . . ." His shrug was eloquent.
This, apparently, was also a long-standing joke. Interesting,
to see a captain and crew so at ease with each other. A
human thing, though, Spock admitted; it required the sharing of common emotions.

He turned his attention to the shuttlecraft, not quite
frowning. The craft seemed in good working order, but it
was decidedly antiquated. "Its lines seem very similar to the
Galileo model."

Rabin nodded. "That's exactly what it is, modified somewhat for the desert climate."

"Damnation!" McCoy exploded. "The Federation never
throws anything away, does it?"

"'Waste not, want not,' that's the outpost way," Rabin
retorted dryly. "It would be nice if we had something better
suited to low atmospheric flight, but you take what you've
got." He squinted up at the cloudless, blindingly bright sky.
"Our meteorologists have assured us that there are no
nearby storms."

"There are none," Spock agreed, weather-sensitive as
were all the desert-born.

"Yes, but unfortunately Obsidian's weather is too unpredictable for any serious long-range forecasting. On that
interesting note, gentlefolk, let's go."

There was, Spock thought, no truly logical way to arrange
seating. He took the seat directly behind Ensign Prince,
Captain Rabin beside him, and, with Rabin's agreement, let
Lieutenant Diver, as geologist, have the forward seat beside
their pilot, since she would need to have the clearest view of
the terrain.

The ancient shuttlecraft groaned, shuddered, then, metal

complaining, lifted itself off the ground, occasional vibrations still shaking it. Ensign Prince fought with the controls, swearing under his breath in what was decidedly not regal Arabic and was certainly not meant to be overheard (though two of the crew, a man and woman evidently familiar with the language, stifled snickers), then gave a recalcitrant panel a hard kick.

The shuttlecraft's flight leveled out.

"Works every time," the ensign said over his shoulder.

"Glad to hear it," McCoy drawled from where he sat behind Spock. "I'd hate to have to walk back."

"No danger of that," Rabin countered. "If the *serenti* didn't get you, the *qatarak* would."

"Trying to scare me? Captain Rabin, I've seen some things out there," in space, said the sweep of McCoy's arm, "that would give your desert beasties nightmares. Treated some of them, too," he added thoughtfully.

Spock's frown was barely more than the faintest twitch. Was this continuing jesting between the two humans turning into true rivalry? Such things happened all too frequently aboard the *Intrepid II,* but on the ship he had usually let the crewmen work out their own solutions; humans, he had learned, did not often appreciate Vulcan interference, no matter how logical. Yet aboard the *Intrepid II,* there had been time enough and room enough for settling quarrels. Here there were no such luxuries.

But before he could work out a logical progression of arguments to settle matters between the two men, Lieutenant Diver, who had been looking intently out of the forward window, said, "Sir, there are clear traces of ancient watercourses down there. They probably can't be seen from the ground."

Spock looked down at the vast expanse of gray-tan-brown and found the traces to which the lieutenant referred: the faintest darker lines, as though he were glancing down at some faded drawing—were that not too fanciful a concept. The network of underground irrigation tunnels could be seen from the air as well as unnaturally straight disturbances in the soil—but these ancient watercourses led away from that network. Even, Spock mused, as the faint data trail the *Intrepid* had been able to send had led away. "Indeed. Continue with your thought, Lieutenant."

"Whoever's doing the sabotage has to have a safe base of operations, as well as a source of water. If they're not using the local wells—"

"They're not," Rabin cut in. "The locals do *not* let strangers use their water."

"Well, then, their base has to be a distance away. Quite a distance. I'd guess that there's still water up in those mountains to the northwest, and that if we follow the watercourses, dried-up though they are, back along their route, we'll come to that water."

"And hopefully the base," Rabin added. "Scanners picking up anything, Ensign Kavousi?"

Rustam Kavousi, a burly young man originally from New Persia, was one of the two who'd understood Ensign Prince's muttered curses. Now he clearly was just barely stifling some of his own. "I keep getting readings, Captain Rabin, but the blasted things fade out before I can confirm them. Static."

Rabin glanced at Spock. "So much for high tech. What do you suggest?"

"That we follow Lieutenant Diver's advice and what clues we have and investigate the mountains."

"Seems the most likely choice to me. Ensign Prince, change our course to . . ." He leaned forward to study the instrument panel. "Assuming that compass is still functioning, to bearing forty-nine point five."

"Bearing forty-nine point five it is, sir. Though if I may, sir: We're not going to reach those mountains today."

"Understood," Spock and Rabin said almost as one: they

were both well aware of how deceptive distance could be in a desert, even from the air.

"We can put down there, twelve degrees off starboard," Rabin said after some study of instruments and landscape. "That's a Turani oasis. Nobody home right now," he added, peering down, "but they've got relatives in Kalara who are friendly toward the Federation. They won't begrudge us a little water."

Ensign Prince landed the shuttlecraft with remarkable smoothness considering the rock-strewn, hard-packed desert floor. "I don't dare be rough," he replied to his captain's wry congratulations, "not with a ship this old."

It took only a short while to set up camp. "We won't use any wood," Rabin said, glancing up at the lacy trees framing the tiny pool. "It's scarce enough as it is."

"And," Spock added, "I do not doubt that the Turani, like most desert people, have severe penalties for any who harm a tree."

"Exactly. Sorry, everyone, no hot-dog roast tonight." That archaism got a chuckle from his crew, but McCoy stared at Rabin as though not quite approving of his levity.

"Is something wrong, Doctor?" Rabin asked, a touch too casually.

McCoy shrugged. "Each to his own methods."

"Indeed." Rabin continued to his crew, "Artificial light and heating only. We'll use the portable generator."

Spock watched keenly to catch any further not-quite-animosity between Rabin and the doctor before it could grow into true hostility, but there was none. This was not precisely satisfying, since one never knew when humans might not decide to call an issue settled.

David has never been a somber or overly logical type, but he is certainly experienced enough to avoid foolishness. And McCoy is . . . as McCoy is.

The brief, gaudy desert sunset quickly faded into a

moonless night bright with stars. Spock exchanged brief comments with Uhura as the *Intrepid* passed overhead, a bright, swiftly moving dot of unblinking golden light amid the seemingly unmoving stars. Soon the ship would be out of range on the far side of the planet, but there was time to assure each other that there was nothing to report.

Snapping his communicator shut, Spock moved apart from the others, standing alone in the darkness, robe wrapped tightly about himself against the growing chill. The humans would probably think him meditating and therefore not disturb him, but Spock knew that he was simply finding enjoyment in the night: the sweet, dry scent of cooling desert, the whisper of wind, the soft singing of sand against rock, the chirping of insects that existed even here—

Someone else was here. Not by the slightest tightening of muscles did Spock reveal that he knew they were being watched. He moved forward as calmly as though aimlessly strolling. There was only the one spy. . . .

He pounced. The spy was a scrawny desert nomad with no spare flesh to him but with muscles like wire. But Spock's Vulcan strength was the greater, and he dragged his struggling, frantic catch back to the others, who sprang to their feet, grabbing for phasers. "There is no need for alarm," Spock assured them. "He was alone."

But the spy had squirmed about to stare up at him, and pure horror contorted the nomad's face. "The Fiery One . . ."

"I fail to understand—"

"Please, please do not do it. Do not burn my soul."

Spock straightened, all at once comprehending. This was not the first time some low-tech (and even the occasional not low-tech) being had mistaken him for a figure of evil. *Though I fail to see why slanted brows and pointed ears should be considered anything but mere physical features.* "I will not burn your soul," Spock told the nomad, and felt the man sag in relief. "You will not be harmed. But you must answer my questions."

"Y-yes, oh Mighty One. If—if I may."

"First, why were you spying?"

"Th-those were my orders."

"Indeed? From whom?"

A shudder shook his captive. "No . . . I don't . . . I can't . . ."

"We will not harm you," Spock repeated. "But you must tell us who sent you to spy on us."

"No . . ."

"Who sent you to spy on us?"

"The Master," the nomad blurted in terror. "Please, please, I cannot say more!"

In a surge of panicky strength, he tore free, racing off into the night. "Phasers on stun!" Rabin commanded. "Don't let him escape."

Phaser beams cut the darkness. The nomad fell, and they rushed to where he lay. McCoy got there first, kneeling at the side of the crumpled figure.

"Damn. Damn, damn, *damn*. I hate having to say this." The doctor glanced up, eyes shadowed. "He's dead, Spock."

"That's impossible," Rabin cut in. "The phasers were—"

"It wasn't the phasers." McCoy got slowly to his feet. "The poor terrified idiot took some type of fast-acting poison. Did a really efficient job on himself."

"You can't . . . do something?"

"Not in this life."

Lieutenant Diver wrapped her arms about herself, shivering. "W-we can't just leave him there."

Spock, well aware by now of the human need for ritual even in the most unlikely cases—such as now, with the death of a perfect stranger and a spy as well—did not argue. Wordlessly, he gathered rocks, wordlessly piled them over the body, aided by the others. "Now there remains the question raised: Who sent him?"

"The Master," Rabin said. "Who or whatever the Master may be."

Ensign Kavousi muttered, "Some religious fanatic, no doubt," and spat. "We do not need an alien Mahdi."

Rabin glanced at Spock. "Looks like we have one. Feel up to the challenge, oh Fiery One?"

Spock frowned ever so slightly. "What do you know of the religious beliefs of these people, Captain Rabin?"

"Not as much as I might. They're pretty closed-mouthed about that. There's your basic Force for Good, and yes, your basic demonic Force for Evil, the Fiery One."

"How is that one usually portrayed?"

"Redheaded, fiery eyes . . ." Rabin's voice trailed into silence as he stared at Spock. "But never anything about pointed ears or black hair or dark eyes!"

"Indeed. Then we have a new question. Since I do not look at all like their image of Evil, how did he know to call me the Fiery One?"

"He . . . couldn't have known, could he? Unless he had been told."

"By this mysterious Master, who would seem to be acquainted with the appearance of Vulcans. Or perhaps with Romulans. Either implies an offworld origin for the Master, or too-great familiarity with the Romulans."

Rabin groaned. "And someone or someones from a Romulan Warbird did just beam down, didn't they? Nothing's ever simple, is it?"

"That, I take it, is a 'rhetorical question.'"

"Spock, in times like this, I can only say . . . nothing at all except good night and try to get some rest."

The morning found the ancient shuttlecraft soaring as best it could, heading closer to the mountains. The flight went without incident or evidence until midday, when Rabin noted, "You're going off-course, Ensign Prince. Heading should be twenty-nine point six West, Forty-three point two North."

"Aye-aye, sir."

"That's twenty-nine point six, Ensign."

"No disrespect, sir, but I'm *trying* to stay on course. There's a tricky wind starting up. Ship doesn't want to—"

The shuttlecraft rocked as though a giant hand had slapped it. Ensign Prince gave up attempting to explain and concentrated totally on holding the course steady.

Spock and Rabin exchanged quick glances. "Weather reading, Mr. Kavousi," the human ordered.

"Doesn't look too good, sir," the ensign replied after a moment. "Sudden shift of wind: hot air swirling up off the desert floor hitting the colder air coming down off those mountains."

He didn't have to explain anything more to the others. All the party knew that this sudden desert shift of winds, very probably with the layer of colder air forced underneath the hot, could only mean one thing: a sandstorm was being born. This was not a sandy desert, but that didn't mean there wasn't enough grit and dirt to form a true menace.

Yes. With eerie swiftness, a wall of dirty brown was rousing off the desert floor, swirling higher, higher. Spock knew that similar storms had been known to reach heights of ten or more kilometers and had to force himself to remain properly, logically calm and not grip the armrests of his seat.

Rabin, of course, couldn't, as captain, show his alarm either. His voice was almost convincingly steady as he said, "Take her higher, Ensign Prince. Upper stratosphere if you can. Get us out of here."

"Right." The ensign was too busy fighting the controls to worry about formality. "Should be a calmer layer up there. Somewhere."

The shuttlecraft lurched, then climbed abruptly—only to be just as abruptly thrust down again, banking sharply, shuddering, engines whining.

"We can't get above the storm," Ensign Prince cried. "The wind's too fierce!"

"Ensign Kavousi," Rabin snapped. "Get us a reading. What's beneath us?"

Kavousi struggled with the sensors, at last admitting, "Can't tell, sir. There's far too much static."

The wind was still rising, engulfing the wildly lurching shuttlecraft in a world of swirling brown. "This old wreck isn't going to hold together much longer!" Ensign Prince warned.

Spock and Rabin glanced at each other, each knowing the other was remembering being caught in another, equally perilous storm from their boyhood. "When positive data are lacking," Spock said, "extrapolation of the last known facts becomes necessary."

"In other words," Rabin retorted, "guess. Take her down, Ensign Prince."

"Yes, sir."

Engines whining with strain, the shuttlecraft descended through brown and brown . . . descended . . .

"We're coming in!" Ensign Prince yelled suddenly.

And then, with bone-jarring force, they were down.

EIGHT

Intrepid II, Obsidian Orbit
Year 2296

"Captain's Log," Uhura began her entry with vast satisfaction. This was one piece of communications equipment she had tested but never thought to use. *"Stardate 9814.3. Commander Uhura, Recording, Intrepid II.*

"Captain Spock has beamed down to Obsidian's surface along with Chief Medical Officer McCoy, and Lieutenants Clayton and Diver. Lieutenant Clayton has already filed a preliminary report and requested additional plant pathology data. We are conducting a full-planet scan for intelligent life while Captain Spock, Captain Rabin, Lieutenant Diver, and several of the outpost's key personnel are overflying an area in which nomads have recently been seen. It has been approximately forty-nine point one eight—"

Is that accurate enough for you, Spock? Uhura thought with a grin.

"—hours since Captain Spock has reported in. This is only

partly due to increased ionization levels. I have placed an emergency transmission reporting the likely presence in-system of a hostile ship, most probably Romulan, to the nearest starbase, but do not expect to receive an answer for several days.

"I have become concerned about Captain Spock; Meteorology reports a growing storm in precisely the sectors for which his flight plan was filed.

"Uhura out."

He had praised her logic in public. *I won't let you down, Spock, and I'll keep the ship safe for you.*

She could almost hear his reply, dry, but with a sly amusement far in the back of those wise, dark eyes: *"Certainly, Commander. I would expect nothing else of you."*

Nothing less, he meant.

"Commander?" Lieutenant Richards turned from the massed screens of the science officer's station. "That dust storm in planetary sectors seven point three four to nine point six eight that I've been monitoring—sensors are showing turbulence up to about ten kilometers into the atmosphere."

The outpost's shuttles might be old, Uhura thought, *but they were built to withstand deceleration through atmosphere. They ought to be able to withstand some dust . . . shouldn't they?*

"Storm's already built up to what would be Force I hurricane strength on Earth," Richards continued. "Now, it's showing signs of turning into a coriolis storm."

Uhura raised an inquiring eyebrow. *I haven't got time for a learning experience, mister.*

Richards missed the significance of that eyebrow. "A coriolis storm," he continued earnestly, "gains strength from the rotation of the planet itself."

That struck home. Given the composition of Obsidian's

deserts, a storm like that could carve the flesh off bones, then reduce the bones to splinters. *Small* splinters. As long as the shuttle maintained altitude, it could ride out the storm. But what if Spock decided to land? Or what if he *had* to?

"Open a hailing frequency, mister," Uhura ordered Lieutenant Duchamps. "Uhura to Captain Spock. Narrow beam. Encrypt."

Her ears, attuned after a career spent with such equipment, detected infinitesimal shifts in tone as Duchamps tried to filter out the storm-borne static and refine his signal. Her fingers itched for the familiar duty station, and she bit back the words, *Out of the way, mister. That's* my *job*, that threatened to leap out at the unsuspecting officer.

It wasn't her job. Not anymore. Now, her job was to sit there while Duchamps sweated with frustration.

As she opened her mouth to acknowledge Richards's efforts, the science officer broke in, "Commander, I'm reading increased sunspot activity and a buildup of energy that could mean a massive solar eruption."

Oh, wonderful. Just what we needed.

Richards bent over his duty station, and what had to be one of the most threatening spectroscopic analyses Uhura had ever seen exploded onto a viewscreen: perturbations deep within the solar core, building up until they erupted out from Loki into deadly prominences and hard radiation.

"How long?"

"Until the flares actually erupt? Loki's treacherous even in its timing. It could be six minutes or six hours from now. Or six weeks. Look at the fluctuations in Loki's corona—" He projected what looked like a halo in convulsions above the star's blacked-out disk. "Here's historical data superimposed on the present scan."

"What about radiation levels?" The Loki of Terran mythology, she knew, lay tied beneath a rock upon which a serpent coiled, dripping poison down upon him. *This* Loki spat its own poison in the form of hard radiation that, even this far out from the star, could put *Intrepid*'s crew at risk.

"Uhura to sickbay."

"Mercier here." Station-born, Medical Officer Frances Mercier understood better than any groundsider who had spent his or her childhood sheltered by atmosphere the damage an ion storm could inflict, or the nasty things hard radiation did when it passed through material such as the hull of a starship. "I gather Loki's acting up again."

Uhura grinned to herself. McCoy must be teaching Mercier every trick in his little black satchel, including the telepathy and clairvoyance every medical officer seemed to have and that all of them lied about.

"I've started issuing new radiation badges," the medical officer continued. "I'm sending someone up to the bridge with yours, Captain—I mean Commander."

Captain. Now that was a hint if ever there was one.

"I'm going to move the ship so we're shielded by the planet itself," Uhura warned. "Better make sure you put away all the glassware, Doctor. When the storm hits, you could get some breakage."

"Aye-aye," Mercier said, and ended her transmission.

"Helm!" Uhura called. "Prepare to come about. Move us into Obsidian's shadow. I want planetary mass between us and Loki."

"God help them," murmured an ensign, one of the newcomers who was most shy of the former *Enterprise* crew.

"God help *all* of them down there," Uhura corrected. "Don't forget we've also got an outpost on Obsidian and several million people with provisional Federation status. We're already having . . . Any luck getting through there?"

A headshake. Damn.

". . . trouble reaching the captain. He'll know the storm's building up and expect us to take appropriate action to protect the . . . uh . . . the *Intrepid* and its crew."

She had almost said *Enterprise.* Better watch it.

The needs of the many outweigh the needs of the few, Spock often said. *Or the one.*

He'd lived his belief. Once, he'd actually died for it when, in a desperate attempt to restore warp power to the *Enterprise* as it hid from Khan Noonien Singh in the Mutara Nebula, he had exposed himself to hard radiation. Once was far too often. *I've lost Captain Kirk. If anything happens to Spock or McCoy . . .*

The ship banked, its turn more perceptible in the smaller *Intrepid* than it would have been in the *Constitution*-class *Enterprise.* Had the original ship survived, Uhura realized with a little shock, it would be obsolete now.

A scream of static leapt from the science officer's workstation. Loki's disk in the viewscreen darkened as Richards augmented filters rather than burn out the screen. The corona rippled and acquired a ghostly afterimage.

"Better strap down," he said. "When that first shock wave hits . . ."

Uhura fastened the restraints over her thighs, glad that no one was going to try to ride this one out. "If any of the crew feel like going out for a breath of fresh air right about now, tell them to forget it," she said. Captain Kirk had always known when to joke.

The bridge crew laughed shakily, but at least they laughed.

"Got an ETA for the radiation front now," Richards offered. "Eight minutes thirty-five seconds . . ."

"Thank you, Lieutenant. Status report, Mr. Duchamps: any sign of that Warbird?"

"Negative, Commander. Negative." She could almost hear Duchamps' skeptical *In this mess?*

"Keep looking, mister. The cloaking device might distort

the ion flux just enough so that we can spot it. Look for anomalies." Right. Loki was practically *all* anomalies. Besides, it was too easy to retreat into a technician's role now that she had the center seat. "Keep an eye on any 'dead' space. Wherever there's Romulans, there's usually something dead."

That drew another laugh. *Gallows humor,* thought Uhura. *If there* is *a gallows, though, it's not going to be ours.*

Groans. Stirrings. Then: "Anything broken?" Dr. McCoy asked.

Spock observed a reddish lump on the doctor's forehead and scrutinized him more closely: McCoy's pupils were not dilated, and he gave no more evidence of disorientation than "a man who'd been thrown out of the sky and dumped on his sore backside," as the doctor had managed to complain almost as they'd hit.

David Rabin disentangled himself from the collision gear. "Just Ensign Prince's pride, I'd say. Trying to stick Brother Abdullah with being seventy-ninth in line for the throne, mister?"

"It's a dirty job," the ensign retorted, "but someone's got to do it. Sir, you know what they say about landings. A good landing is any one you can walk away from."

"Let's see what we've got left to walk away from."

Lieutenant Diver, hair fallen over one eye, was struggling to pull free of restraints and a warped chair, all the while calling up cartography from a flickering screen. "I—"

But her voice broke off in a startled yelp as the shuttle suddenly lurched and slid what Spock's kinesthetic sense told him was 3.2 meters—downward. A series of impacts boomed and vibrated on the shuttle's hull: rocks, Spock assumed, torn loose from a hillside above them. Were they merely on the side of a steep slope—or did the slope end in a cliff?

The entire craft seemed to swerve sideways, then slid again before it stopped sharply—1.59 meters later, Spock knew—its nose tilted awkwardly downward. Wind buffeted the shuttle, sending a shrilling storm of grit lashing at the vessel's hull.

"I would suggest," Spock raised his voice over the storm, "that no one move more than he or she must. This slippage leads me to conclude . . ."

Rabin held up a hand. "Spock, let me suggest that first we all shift our weight toward the far end of the shuttle as a counterbalance. *Then,* no one moves."

"Ensign Prince," Spock asked, "were you able to see our landing site at all?"

"In this mess, sir?" the ensign asked. "Got some quick glimpses of mountains or at least steep hills. Some cliffs. Then we were caught in the storm but good and even the instruments weren't registering much."

"Lieutenant Diver?" Spock raised an eyebrow.

Hastily brushing back her hair, she began again, "Cartography calls this the Rupathan Range . . . not sure about the accuracy, not with that rock composition . . . highly friable . . . hey!"

The ship lurched again under a fresh roar of wind and a new cascade of rocks. The shuttle was ruggedly built, but nothing was *that* rugged. They were already clearly on a precarious angle. If the wind was of sufficient force . . .

"Ensign Prince," Rabin ordered, "see if you can lift us off. Now!" he added as the shuttle slipped a little further.

The ensign's fingers flew over the controls as he muttered under his breath. "Landing gear's damaged. No . . ." he added, looking at his screens. "Landing gear's *gone.* Let me see . . ."

More keyboard tappings brought up a rockscape half shrouded by veils of blowing grit and larger debris. He leaned forward as though in disbelief, then spat something guttural.

"Surely not camels *and* goats, Ensign?" Rabin asked. "Let alone diseased ones?"

"Sir, that last slide brought us up against a large rock— the last thing between us and what looks like a drop of approximately one hundred meters. If we're dislodged by a big enough rock or if the cliff's edge crumbles . . ."

"Oh great," McCoy said. "A man goes over a cliff and grabs a root, and then the root starts to pull free . . ."

Rabin sighed. "So much for staying with the ship."

"But we can't sit out that storm in the open! Isn't a lot of the blowing grit volcanic glass? We wouldn't last a minute."

"Doctor," Spock began, "if we fall a hundred meters . . ."

"Spock, now's no time for a lesson in physics."

Spock ignored that. "What can we expect of this region, Captain Rabin? Are there caves?"

"Yes! There are caves all through here, like on the Forge. Lieutenant Diver, try to locate one with a sonic scan. Meanwhile," Rabin added, leaning over a console, "let's see if we can reach the base . . . bah, no. Nothing."

Spock thumbed open his own communicator and was not surprised when static, then silence greeted him. "I shall assume that the *Intrepid* has shifted orbit to place the planet between it and Loki. The communicator's power is insufficient to pierce this storm, much less planetary mass. When the storm subsides . . ."

"Dammit, Spock," McCoy snapped, "we may be confetti before this thing subsides, especially if—"

"I'm getting something," Lieutenant Diver said abruptly. "A cave . . . maybe fifty meters away."

"Yes!" Rabin exclaimed. Moving very gingerly, he pulled open the cabinets holding survival gear: rations, water containers, lights, heavy visors to protect their eyes. "Spock, what are the odds of our making it to that cave?"

"Before this shuttle falls from the cliff?" Spock asked. "Or are you asking what the odds are of our making it to that cave without rocks hitting individual crew members or of the cave being uninhabited by something inimical to life?"

Rabin sighed. "How many years have you served with him?" he murmured to McCoy. "And he's still alive?"

"I must have been crazy," McCoy admitted. "He kind of grew on me."

Rabin eyed him quizzically, then shrugged. "Judgment call, Spock. Which do you think is safer? Riding it out in the shuttle or making a run for it?"

"If we leave the ship, can we survive, however briefly, in this type of storm?"

Rabin nodded. "If we cover every bit of skin and nothing hits us, yes. In the deep desert, people dig into the ground itself and survive, and they don't have any fancy gear."

"Never fancied myself a cave man," McCoy muttered.

Nevertheless, he gathered his gear about him, then nearly fell against Rabin as the ship lurched again.

"No time to worry about it!" Rabin snapped. "We've got to get out of here."

"Port's stuck!" Ensign Prince shouted. "I can't get it to open." He hurled himself at the port's manual controls. "Damnation! Whatever tore off the landing gear jammed the controls, too."

Cautiously, feeling the shuttle shifting subtly under his feet, Spock moved to the pilot's side, trying . . . no. The door was jammed beyond even Vulcan strength.

"Stand aside, Ensign."

Spock drew his phaser, using it as delicately as a surgeon's tool to burn the damaged controls away. He paused, drawing a series of deep, rhythmic breaths, summoning the Disciplines learned on the Plains of Gol, however imperfectly, that would briefly give him greater strength.

"Come on, Spock," McCoy urged him. "You don't have time to analyze the situation."

There was no distraction. McCoy's words were nothing. As if detached from his body, Spock watched himself force the port open just wide enough for his fingertips to fit between the door itself and the shuttle's bulkheads, and shoved. There was no pain. There was no effort. There was only need.

The wind shrieked, driving sharp-edged grit through the narrow gap into the shuttle.

"Get those visors on *now!*" McCoy ordered. "Spock, you get those fossil eyelids of yours down, y'hear?"

Spock, hardly hearing him, took another deep, steadying breath, then braced his fingers against the metal. The port began to slide open, painfully slowly. He almost lost his grip when the shuttle lurched again, sliding free, stopping with a jolt. Rabin launched himself from the opposite bulkhead, adding his strength and, fortunately, helping to counterbalance the shuttle. Ensign Kavousi joined them, grunting with effort. The port slid open a tantalizing bit more. At least slender Lieutenant Diver would be able to squeeze through, but the rest of them . . .

"Again," Spock heard himself gasp. His control must be slipping. He sounded almost weary.

This time, their combined strength moved the port open almost wide enough—

The shuttle jolted, jolted again.

"That rock's breaking up!" Lieutenant Diver's voice was a little too agitated for a reporting officer's.

"On the count of three, Spock," Rabin panted. "One, two, *three!*"

The port flew open. Obsidian's winds gusted in their

faces, and rock dust swirled into the shuttle's cabin. For an instant, Spock could see the promised cave refuge, tantalizingly close.

"Buddy system!" shouted Rabin over the gale. "I want one of my people to link up with *Intrepid's* crew. If they don't make it, you don't. Now, move, move, move!"

He practically hurled Ensign Prince and Lieutenant Diver out of the shuttle.

"Mr. Kavousi, take the doctor . . ."

"I can make it out under my own steam," McCoy grumbled, hastening to avoid Kavousi's hand at the small of his back. He clutched his tricorder possessively, covering it with a fold of his desert survival gear.

The ship slid again. Spock heard shouts of alarm from outside and knew the shuttle was very close to falling.

"Not long now, Spock," Rabin gasped. "Move!"

"Do not be heroic. Go! I will follow you."

"Not a chance. This is my planet. Now, *git!*"

He sounded like the doctor, Spock thought, and sprang clear of the shuttle. But he twisted in mid-jump, snatching at Rabin, hand closing on the human's arm as the shuttle, now wildly unbalanced, lurched away. Rabin jumped blindly, Spock pulled, and the two of them went sprawling.

"Too close," Rabin gasped from where he lay. "Thanks."

Spock raised his head just in time to see the shuttle upend and vanish over the cliff. The wind howled so loudly he could not even hear the impact of its landing.

They sat huddled in the cave, Spock and Rabin's crew together, winded and too weary to speak, humans overwhelmed, Spock thought, by the calm more of shock than military training.

"Everyone here?" Rabin asked. "Come on, folks, rouse: roll call."

As the crew called off name after name, Spock straightened sharply, missing one familiar face. "McCoy," he cut in over their voices. "Where is Dr. McCoy?"

"Don't see him—"

"Not here—"

"Wasn't he with you?" Rabin asked Ensign Kavousi.

"All the way!" the burly ensign protested. "I pushed him halfway up the hill! You could hear his complaints over the storm."

"Yes, but did anyone see the doctor actually make it into the cave?"

"I did," said Lieutenant Diver. "He was grumbling something about heavy-handed Farsi-types—sorry, Ensign. Then he started all over again about . . . I'm not sure, something about him not having the sense to come in out of the rain. It didn't make too much sense to me, but by then I was too busy scouting out the cave." Her eyes widened. "Captain Spock, you don't suppose . . . ?"

"I do not make vague suppositions, Lieutenant. What are you trying to say?"

"W-what if he went back out there?"

Cutting the sudden tense silence, Spock told her, "It is illogical to assume that he merely . . . wandered off. The doctor, while erratic, is rarely illogical."

"You saw that bump on the head he took," Rabin said. "Might have confused him."

"Or maybe he dropped some of his medical equipment in the struggle and went back for it," Lieutenant Diver added. "That would explain that 'come in out of the rain' comment. Captain, he really could be wandering about outside!" Her eyes were wide with the *Captain, do something* look that people had always directed at James Kirk.

"Lieutenant," Spock retorted dryly, "if Dr. McCoy were 'wandering about outside,' he would long ago have ceased to wander."

Humans did not find blunt logic reassuring. Lieutenant

93

Diver stiffened as though she'd been slapped. "You're just going to *leave* him?"

"If it is written . . ." Ensign Prince began warily.

"I do not believe that the doctor is dead," Spock said. "But I will not risk lives in a search for him until the storm subsides. I suggest, Lieutenant, that you join the others in seeing how this cave can be made habitable."

"Aye-aye, sir," she said, and left him, her shoulders expressing her dejection and disappointment more than the words she was too well trained to utter.

"What you said about McCoy," Rabin murmured in Spock's ear. "Is that logic or do you really know something the rest of us don't?"

"I would know," Spock said without explanation, "if McCoy were dead."

He remembered the brilliant welter of passion and compassion that had been McCoy's mind from the time his *katra* had resided in it until the *fal-tor-pan* replaced his essence within a physical shell. Impossible that such a spirit would be extinguished and Spock not sense it. He reached for what tenuous link might remain between him and the doctor. . . .

No, Spock realized abruptly, McCoy was most certainly not dead. Instead, in true McCoy fashion, he was . . . furious.

"He lives," Spock added shortly, awarding Rabin one level glance, knowing his friend would respect Vulcan codes of privacy.

Rabin raised an eyebrow, clearly wanting more data than he was getting, then gave up and turned to the others. "All right, folks. I don't have to tell anyone not to go for a stroll out there." That roused some feeble laughter from the others. "But remember the spy Captain Spock caught? I don't want anyone to go *anywhere* alone. For *any* reason whatsoever."

"I wasn't planning on going anywhere, sir," Ensign Prince said and, without further preamble, stretched out on the rocky floor, head cushioned on an arm. Spock understood: an odd, uncomfortable way for the man to sleep, but a simple, highly logical method of judging the force of the storm and the likelihood of further rockfalls through vibrations in the rock itself.

"The wind's shifted, sirs," the ensign told both captains suddenly. "Hopefully, it means that the storm's going to stop. Sooner rather than later, that is."

He fell silent once more, eyes closing.

"Ensign Prince has the right idea," Rabin said. "All of you, get some rest. We'll discuss our options later."

Cautiously, the crew members found places to sit or lie, making themselves as comfortable as was possible.

"What do you think, Spock?" Rabin asked softly.

"I think that our limited supplies cannot provide sufficient nourishment, water in particular, for all. In fact, the odds of survival for the entire party for more than four days drop to—"

"Ah, never mind. I get the picture. What if we split up?"

"The removal of even two members of the party will greatly raise the survival odds of those remaining from four days to a full Federation-standard week."

"Two, eh? I can see where this is leading."

"And so, logically," Spock continued with a slight nod, "those of us most experienced in desert survival must hunt for water and possible aid, while the others must remain here to call your base and await pickup."

"The 'most experienced of us' being you and me."

"So it would seem."

"Ah, what about Dr. McCoy?"

"We will search as soon as the storm ceases, of course. But I . . . doubt that we will find him." Again he challenged Rabin with a level glance to ask more; again, Rabin merely raised a brow and said nothing. Spock continued, "The next experienced would, I would assume, be Ensign Prince."

"He would. Our Saudi Prince spends his holidays on Earth, wandering with the Bedouins of the Rub al-Khali, the Empty Quarter."

"Good. Then, regardless of rank, he must take charge of those who stay behind."

"That leaves us to do the roving. Partners again, eh, Spock?"

"Indeed. But first we must provide a means of communications for those staying." Spock reached for a communicator, opened it, and began, heedless of fingers that only now he realized had been abraded in the struggle, to dismantle it. "If we combine all communicators and possibly a tricorder, if there is still one undamaged, there should be sufficient power for at least a brief distress call."

"If you say so. Haven't pulled an all-nighter since Starfleet Academy."

Spock raised a brow. "Not you. You are human. Go to sleep, my friend."

"But—"

"Sleep."

Rabin grinned. "Yes, Mother," he said, and went to find himself a space. Spock felt the corner of his mouth crook up ever so slightly. It was illogical, perhaps, but strangely heartening to know that even now, David Rabin was as irrepressible as ever.

He could already hear minute changes in the wind's howling, as if a master conductor signaled his orchestra for a softer tone. The storm would die before morning.

And McCoy?

Survive, Spock told him silently. *Wherever you are, do what you must, but—survive.*

NINE

**Vulcan, Location Unknown
Day 6, Seventh Week of Tasmeen,
Year 2247**

Spock woke in slow, dizzy stages, not at all sure where he was. There seemed to be a hollowness under him, a lack of solid ground. . . . His head ached, his vision refused to focus, and his stomach was protesting that the world did not seem to be as firm as was proper. *There is no pain.* He began the discipline as best he could. *It is only an illusion* . . . Gradually he began to remember . . . there had been the ceremony gone so terribly wrong . . . Sered . . . the Starfleet officer destroyed in a blink of time . . .

Yes, and then someone had clearly struck him with sufficient force to stun him. Fortunate that his mixed heritage had given him a Vulcan rather than human skull; if it had been the latter, he suspected that he would be suffering a severe concussion.

Instead, he just felt ill enough to almost wish it were,

illogical or not, otherwise. It was, a corner of his mind noted, not as though his father were present to observe and instruct. He need not worry about being a true Vulcan, acting in accordance with his full potential.

But the pain was gradually fading to an ache, and Spock managed to summon enough self-control to block it totally. The world finally came into focus around him: a significantly restricted world. He was in . . . in a shuttlecraft of some sort, yes, and strapped into a seat. Sered's doing?

Yes, Sered, indeed. That was he, straight-backed and proud, sitting beside the "cousin" piloting this craft. The other occupants . . . Spock glanced warily from side to side and bit back a groan. Not only had Sered escaped, he had managed to take his hostages with him.

And I am clearly one of those hostages.

Were they not his responsibility? After all, he was Eldest of his year.

"Are you all right?" an earnest voice whispered. "No, no, don't look at me. They haven't noticed we're awake yet. It's me, David Rabin."

Yes. Spock recognized that much.

"Are you all right?" David persisted.

"If you mean, am I injured," Spock whispered back, "not as badly as I might—"

He broke off as the shuttlecraft lurched roughly to one side then the other, which did not make his aching head feel any better. Eyes shut, Spock once again willed the pain back under control. A subtle glance out a window—once he could see clearly again—revealed nothing but a swirling curtain of brown—

A storm! A sandstorm! And Sered was deliberately ordering the craft right into the midst of its ferocity. Why would even a madman risk—

"We can't go on," the pilot was protesting. "I can't hold us steady!"

"Continue," Sered commanded coldly. "They will be unable to track us. Their sensors will be confused by the storm's static, and all communications will be destroyed."

"What good does that do us if we crash?"

"Do you question me? I tell you, my calculations indicate that this craft's tolerances exceed even the full force of the storm. Continue! We shall succeed. We shall hide from the fools far beyond the Forge!"

The pilot glanced at Sered in alarm. "Are you jesting? There's nothing out there but wilderness! Unstable, volcanic wilderness at that. It looks like—bah, perhaps my ancestors had more sense than I ever believed when they packed up and left—"

"It is the Forge of our people," Sered cut in. "'And in the wilderness shall we find shelter.'"

That, Spock thought with a touch of disapproval, was surely a misquote from one of Surak's lectures.

Sered continued, "In that wilderness is a cavernous region, a vast underground realm naturally shielded from all detection and known as . . ." He paused, clearly for dramatic effect. "The Womb of Fire."

The Womb of Fire! Spock echoed in silent shock. He knew very little about the region save for the fact that it was said to be truely seismically unstable, highly volcanic, and perilous to the point of—

Of insanity. His control wavered. Sered might as well have invoked the Eater of Souls. *Racial memory,* his mother had called it. Illogical to think of such things now—or was it?

But Sered had not finished. Ranting outright by now, he told the grim-faced pilot, "You should understand. Vulcan has lost the true meaning of Surak's teachings. You would know that, you must, you of the sundered kindred."

"If you say so."

"Fool! Vulcan *has* lost the true message! We have gone too far into logical aridity and in the process become weak. The only course of salvation is a return to the earliest forms of our rituals. And that," he concluded, face gone cold and empty of all emotion, "we shall find in the Womb of Fire. There shall we be annealed, there shall we be reborn in a stronger, purer guise."

But even as he finished, a crackling, static-filled message came over the shuttlecraft's instruments, and terror was clear even in the broken words: "Bearing twenty-four point nine . . . west . . . twenty-four point . . . storm . . . sand . . . engines failing . . . going down . . . we—"

The transmission stopped with terrifying suddenness. "Oh God." David's voice was a horrified murmur. "Oh God. They've crashed." No longer even trying to pretend he was unconscious, he stared at Spock, wild-eyed. "My—my mother might have been on it."

"We do not know that." Spock said it as gently as he could. "We do not even know if she was taken hostage."

Sered was transmitting to other craft, "Follow us. Do not deviate from our path."

"You see?" Spock told David. "There are other vehicles. Even if your mother was captured, she may be safe on one of those."

"Enough talking," a guard said brusquely, and both boys wisely fell silent.

There were no further crashes. The storm at last died away, but by that point, the shuttlecraft had already entered the rugged, mountainous region considered unlivable even by the hardiest of Vulcans. All about them, jagged volcanic peaks, sharp-edged as so many dark knives, thrust up stark against the sky, and ancient or sometimes alarmingly recent lava flows covered the landscape in twisted black ropes.

"There," Sered commanded. "Land there."

It was the smallest trace of level ground. The shuttlecraft landed with a jolt, listing slightly to one side. "Best I could do," the pilot muttered, "considering."

Sered ignored him. At the Vulcan's imperious gesture, Spock, David, and the other young hostages were ushered out. David looked around their fierce surroundings then shrugged. "Not a great place for a picnic, is it?"

Brave, Spock thought. *Foolhardy, perhaps, but decidedly brave.*

The warriors were forcing the hostages into a cavernous opening. "We must not allow this," Spock whispered to the human.

"Right. Go in there, don't come out."

But what could they do? Helpless against laser rifles, they obediently entered the cavern. Rough walls, Spock noted, with a good deal of rock fracture. Unstable, indeed. And:

"Unstable," David agreed softly. "But what can we— *are!*"

The ground shook, shook again, stilled. Spock steadied David, who had fallen against him, coughing, then pointed as inconspicuously as he could. "One more tremor," he whispered, "and that wall will be breached."

David nodded almost imperceptibly, understanding. Only one more tremor . . .

"C'mon, earthquake," he whispered, and Spock only just managed to keep his face properly stoic. The human was incorrigible.

Better that than hysterics.

The tremor came. Hidden by a torrent of falling rocks and a cloud of dust, Spock and David scrambled their frantic way through the newly opened rift in the wall and kept going out into the open and the maze of volcanic peaks, ducking behind boulders, dodging between clefts in the rocks, sure that laser rifles were going to fire, sure that they were going to be maimed or killed or—

No. Now that the ground had settled, Spock could see that the quake had caused enough damage to confuse even Sered. He dared to stop to catch his breath.

"By the time they realize we are missing," he told David, "assuming that they do realize it, we will be far from here."

"I . . . can't . . . " David gasped, white-faced. "I . . . I can't . . . breathe."

Of course, Spock realized after a startled moment. David was human, not Vulcan; the volcanic region of the Forge lay at a relatively high elevation, high enough that a human undergoing exertion would need help to breathe the thinner atmosphere. If they were ever to reach civilization, David was going to need tri-ox compound, yes, and desert gear better than the bedraggled finery he still wore. At least, Spock thought, sternly quelling his growing alarm, the boy seemed to be in excellent physical condition for one of his age and species. That would help for a time.

"Rest," Spock said. "Breathe as deeply, as rhythmically, as you can." His voice wasn't quite as properly steady as he would wish. "Then we shall find you some tri-ox compound."

David tensed. They both knew, without a word needing to be exchanged, that the only place for such a find would be the wrecked shuttlecraft. That David's mother might be one of its victims was something neither boy wanted to mention.

But where had the craft crashed? Searching his memory for clues, Spock knew that it would have to be fairly close; they had landed not too long after the crash. Ah yes, and the pilot of the doomed craft had mentioned a bearing . . . yes, 24.9 West. It would be impossible to pinpoint the exact location without instruments, but there was still a chance. Spock told David, "I believe I know approximately where we may locate the crash."

David, for all that he was still clearly suffering from the lack of oxygen, struggled to his feet with a melodramatic bow. "Lead on, my friend, lead on."

Spock forbore to add the obvious: that they must reach the site before *le-matya*s and other predators did.

The storm had left few traces behind, and the sun blazed in Vulcan's clear, bright desert sky. The two boys set out across a barren waste of gray flint and red rock and ancient black lava flows, moving carefully over the treacherous footing.

"Be wary," Spock said. "Now that the sun is warming the desert floor again, poisonous reptiles will be sunning themselves on the rocks."

"Just like Earth's deserts. Almost stepped on a sunbathing snake once. In the Negev. Don't know which of us was more scared."

The curtness made sense. David was clearly keeping his words to a minimum, saving breath. Used to desert terrain though he was, without that tri-ox compound he needed to rest more and more frequently, his face reddening, one hand pressed to his ribs. During one of the stops, he glanced about at the rugged wilderness and shook his head. "Can't imagine anyone living here."

"Other than the desert flora and fauna? No."

"Why not? Couldn't you guys put up force shields? Or maybe even domes?" At Spock's puzzled nod, David continued, "Then how come you have this blasted wasteland?"

"It is a part of the natural order," Spock retorted. "We prefer to keep some portions of our planet primal. It makes us careful."

"Careful. Right."

They set out once more, over terrain that grew more and more savage. Spires of twisted black volcanic rock rose on all sides, and the ground was so littered with sharp bits of flint that Spock and David needed to choose each step with care. It would be all too easy to cut a foot or break an ankle here.

"And such an injury," Spock warned, "would most surely prove fatal."

"If the air doesn't kill me first," David said tersely.

His breathing was growing more and more labored, and even his brave, cocky spirit was clearly failing. *We must reach the wreck soon*, Spock thought, *or he will not survive.* He surprised himself by adding, *I would not wish such a brave, bold intelligence to be lost.*

But then they came out of a maze of lava spikes and found themselves faced with a sharp, steep, rocky slope like the side of a small mountain. Spock scouted from left to right and back again, then returned to David's side with a sigh.

"There is no way around. We can only go up. But," Spock added, studying the slope above them, "I believe that we have all but found the crashed shuttlecraft. See, there and there, where the rocks have been scraped and burned. The craft must have come in over them. It must lie on the far side of the slope."

David made one gallant attempt to climb, then groaned, collapsing to a rock, head down. "Can't . . ."

Spock watched the human uneasily for a moment, not sure what to do, then decided, "Wait here. I shall go ahead. I will not be long."

"No. Wait." David struggled to his feet, face drawn. "You must not—"

"I must. If the shuttlecraft's . . . just ahead . . . I want to be there, too."

Brave but foolhardy, Spock repeated to himself. But one could not help but admire the human's determination. With Spock's help, David struggled up the slope, gasping painfully for breath, staggering, falling, yet stubbornly refusing to give up. Those were not coughs, Spock realized. At least not all of them. Some were sobs.

But at last they crested the slope.

"There it is," David said grimly. "Down there. There's the shuttlecraft."

What had once been a sleek, modern craft was now nothing but a broken, twisted mass of metal and composite.

No one, Spock thought, could have survived. Surely, David knew it, too. But all the human said was "Come on."

He staggered down the far side of the slope, falling more than walking, then collapsed at the bottom. Before Spock could help him, David struggled back to his feet, trying to run. But Spock, stronger than the exhausted human, caught his arm, forcing him to a more cautious pace.

"It will serve no logical purpose for you to kill yourself."

David said nothing. Doubtless, by this point speech was impossible. But he continued to plow doggedly forward until they both stood at the shuttlecraft's crumpled side.

It is illogical to be afraid, Spock scolded himself. He must not think of what lay within as once-living beings but merely as objects. He must ignore whatever he saw and concentrate only on finding the tri-ox compound and some protective gear for David.

But it took all his training in self-discipline to stay calmly analytical at the sight of the broken bodies flung like so many dolls within the shuttlecraft, limbs skewed at impossible angles, head twisted on broken necks. The reek of darkening red and green blood threatened his control and brought David, retching dryly, to his knees.

But the human refused to surrender. Rising white-faced and shaking, David searched body after body. All at once he raced from the wreck, collapsing into a gasping, sobbing heap. Had he found his mother's body? Spock ached to run after him, but forced himself to continue to hunt. He even managed not to hiss in fury when he found the communications gear shattered and the one whole laser rifle useless.

Wait, though. Matters could have been far worse. Here was a good supply of the tri-ox compound, and there, spilling out of a ruptured storage compartment, was protective gear that might fit. He dragged it out of the craft, then hurried to David's side, only to stand in awkward uncertainty. Was this mourning, or merely exhaustion?

"Captain Rabin . . . ?" he asked hesitantly.

"She wasn't there!" David sobbed. "My mother wasn't there!"

"But that is good news!" Spock said in confusion. "She is surely still alive."

"Y-yes!"

Now truly bewildered, Spock asked, "Why, then, do you weep?"

"Oh God, Spock, don't you understand?" David wiped his eyes with a shaky hand, struggling to catch his breath. "I couldn't help it; I mean, I feel sorry for those poor people in there, but—but you *don't* understand, do you?"

"I . . . fear not." An unwanted image of Lady Amanda, broken and still in death like the bodies within the shuttle, thrust itself into his consciousness, and he just as brusquely thrust it away. *Control, Spock,* he told himself, echoing his father. *Where is your control?* "Doubtless, anoxia is adding to your fears." At least so he assumed. "Wait."

At David's nod, Spock carefully injected him with the tri-ox compound. David took a wary breath, then another, relief plain on his face.

"Better. Much better. Thought I wasn't going to make it." He wiped his eyes again, and Spock frowned.

"It is illogical to weep if one is not mourning."

"I guess it's a human thing, Spock, a—a sign of human caring, and a . . . well, a release of stress. Humans don't consider it a weakness, either," he added almost defiantly. "In fact, I'm proud that I'm able to care so very much. You . . . still don't get it, do you? Ah well, never mind, never mind."

He was almost babbling with physical and emotional relief, so near to hysteria that it grated on Spock's Vulcan nerves.

"It would be illogical for me to worry about a human

emotion," Spock pointed out, and was surprised to hear David laugh and agree, "I guess it would."

Illogical, indeed. But a very human thing. A fascinating new thing to ponder.

David wormed his way into the protective gear. "Not exactly the height of fashion, is it?" he asked, waving a too-long sleeve. "Boy, I'm glad none of the girls, human or Vulcan, can see me!"

Spock blinked. "Why should survival equipment need to be fashionable? And why should such a thing matter to anyone, girl or boy?"

"A joke," David said gently. "It was a joke." He shook his head. "We have a long way to go, don't we?"

"Toward understanding each other? Yes, I believe we do. But we also quite literally have a long way to go to reach civilization."

David stiffened. "We . . . ah . . . can make it, can't we?"

Spock hesitated. "I survived my *kahs-wan* trial," he said at last, "the ordeal that pits a Vulcan boy alone against the desert."

"But you didn't have to worry about having a human with you," David finished dryly, then shrugged. "Desert training in the Negev wasn't exactly a picnic, either. But I survived that." His sweep of a hand took in the vast expanse of wilderness before them. "Shall we?"

"Indeed."

Together, they set out into the desert.

TEN

Obsidian, Deep Desert
Day Unknown, First Week, Month of the Shining *Chara*, Year 2296

Dr. Leonard McCoy was having a rotten day. Or night. Or whatever you wanted to call time on this benighted ball of black glass circling a star with the spectroscopic analysis of a serial killer. One moment, Captain Rabin's ten-ton Farsi security chief was manhandling him out of the shuttle teetering on a damn precipice and frog-marching him into a cave. His face still ached from being pelted by grit and black glass, which was bad; he hadn't been able to tend the others, which was worse; and not five minutes later, the fact that three men even stronger than Ensign Kavousi had jumped him meant that he was now a weapon in someone's hands. And that was worst of all.

He had fought, of course, but it had been three against one. His captors had taken communicator, phaser, tricorder, and medical kit from him. Someone, veiled against Obsidian's disastrous environment, had stomped his

108

tricorder into uselessness—*except as a lure for Spock and the others.*

Then they had stashed him in one of the caves that seemed to honeycomb this range until the storm subsided. They'd stored him without food, water, or a clue about what was going on until, in the last howlings and lashings of the warning storm, he had been hauled outside, blindfolded, and spirited off in some rough, whining vehicle for far too long to wherever the hell they were now. Another damn cave.

At least, this time, they'd left him a tiny light, a primitive little candle flame, so he could see his prison. It wasn't encouraging. The rock faces weren't rough stone, they were obsidian (lava tubes? he wondered, and hoped that the volcano that had created them was at least dormant), and the volcanic stuff had been polished so he could see himself—*sorry-looking imitation of an officer and a gentleman, son?*—but not break off a chunk to use as a weapon.

Footsteps padded toward his cell. *Can't say I think much of the hotel staff,* McCoy groused, working himself up into a fine rage. If he could find a use for it to annoy his enemies, so much the better. If not, it relieved his spirits. *Spock,* he thought, *Spock, dammit . . .*

Tall figures swathed in desert robes and protective face veils circled McCoy. Their posture wasn't just military, he realized. It looked Vulcan.

Just when he thought things couldn't get much worse! Vulcans were the last people he could hope to manipulate. He rubbed his hand over his face, where a growing beard and tiny cuts itched abominably.

"Here. Eat."

The wrapped bar that the arrogant figure tossed in front of him bore the blocky glyphs that passed for lettering among Klingons. McCoy couldn't read them, but he knew the

Klingons ate as much meat as they could as often as they could. As opposed to Vulcans, whose code of nonviolence—hah!—made them vegetarians. This unappetizing cube was sure to be mostly protein, possibly animal in origin. And "origin" really didn't bear thinking about.

He got the message with the meal: deliberate insult.

"Like my old grandma back in Tennessee said when she taught Sunday School, 'Thou preparest a table before me in the presence of mine enemies.' If that's what you're doing, son, you're doing a rotten job."

"Eat," McCoy's captor said again, unveiling. The doctor was gratified to see that what he had taken for an accent was, in fact, a split lip. And a dark-green bruise marred one of his captor's pointed ears.

"This . . . stuff is probably incompatible enough with human physiology that I'll get a terminal case of the runs, if not worse," McCoy told his jailer. "I'm hot. I'm tired. I'm dirty. I probably stink from here to high heavens—an offense to your fine sensibilities. And on top of everything else, you feed me stuff you wouldn't throw a stray *sehlat.*"

No response. Maybe their Anglic wasn't good enough to understand his rant, and they'd swiped his tricorder. Rotten as his Vulcan was, he'd try to make them understand in that language.

He rasped his throat dry on it, and the tall figures looked at one another. One of them laughed, sharply and briefly.

Say what? McCoy asked himself. *If you're laughing, mister, not only have you got a lousy sense of humor, but you're no Vulcan.*

He suppressed a groan. If it looked like a Vulcan but laughed, it had to be a Romulan. He didn't need Vulcan logic to tell him that the presence of Romulans on Obsidian, bordering the Neutral Zone, was the worst possible news. If these Romulans felt secure enough to reveal themselves, that meant that unless McCoy was very, very lucky, he could forget about a comfy ride back to the base when they were done with him.

"We are now engaged in a great civil war . . . another one," McCoy muttered. "The perfect ending to a perfect day."

"This . . . weakling is the war criminal Makkhoi?" a Romulan behind him asked the one he was trying to face down. "I heard they called him Bones because of experiments he performed on prisoners' bone marrow. . . ."

Now, just a damn minute! McCoy felt his blood pressure spike up. *The name's McCoy, not Mengele!*

"Quiet!" said their officer. Probably a centurion and young for the rank at that. "Those charges were never proved."

Well, what do you know? Out of the mouths of babes . . .

The centurion spoiled the good impression McCoy was getting of him by his next words. "He may be a notorious meddler and spy, but he was James Kirk's battle companion and as wily as the captain, respect to his shade. He was a great killer, but no torturer. Whatever else this Makkhoi is, he is loyal to his own. I would offer him honorable parole if that traitor did not forbid."

What traitor was that?

Centuries of inherited forlorn hopes had made McCoy good at grabbing any opportunity, however slight.

"You have my name, sir," he said, bowing in his best Southern Cavalier style to the centurion. "May I know yours?"

"Ruanek," the centurion told him. "Centurion of the Empire. Of House Minor Strevon."

McCoy cudgeled his brains for his last Intelligence briefing and came up with only a headache.

"In service to . . . ?" he probed.

111

Centurion Ruanek shook his head. "I was warned you would try to trick me. You have the courtesy of my name. Be content with that."

"Hard to be content where the room service is as bad as this, son," McCoy improvised.

"If you were my father, I would fall on my sword."

Aha! "If you were my son," McCoy retorted, "I would have exposed you at birth. Or I'd lock up all the sharp toys in the house till you learned some sense."

He saw reluctant humor glint in this Ruanek's eyes. *Good. Maybe I can work on him. Time to change tactics.* "Now that we've exchanged fire," McCoy continued, deliberately softening his tone, "how about some information? Like, where are you taking me and what's happened to my friends?"

"You will be told. If you will not eat, come now."

No one pulled a weapon on him, which McCoy supposed was some sort of social promotion, Romulan style. He left the revolting bar of goo sitting on the rock. Fasting in moderation was good for the system. With luck, no helpless creature would find it.

The Romulans prodded McCoy through a maze of tunnels, pushing him past intersecting corridors where he could see people, their backs to him, working feverishly, or caches of stored goods, some covered with the types of dropcloths the Federation routinely used for valuable supplies—*Nice little thieves' ring here, maybe, as a sideline to the sabotage?* From one or two tunnels he caught distinct whiffs of the sorts of chemicals one found in primitive armories.

The ancient rock was honeycombed with these tunnels, which probably allowed the "wild nomads" to communicate during storms. So they weren't truly primitives, despite city-dweller prejudice. McCoy hadn't seen this many tunnels since Janus VI. *I could use a nice friendly Horta or two about now,* he thought. Even if "friendly" was hardly the word to describe what was left when a Horta with a grudge got done with an intruder.

Their path slanted down. McCoy almost lost his footing on a patch of slick obsidian he wasn't expecting. *Great. Let's all go sliding down into wherever . . . wouldn't that reflect credit on the Federation? We come in peace for all mankind—oooops!*

Fortunately for the remnants of his dignity, he didn't have to traverse the rest of the tunnel on his backside. One of the Romulans steadied him roughly. He found himself standing in what looked like a huge natural cave, roughly the size of a shuttlebay on a Federation spacecraft, its walls smoothed and painted with symbols such as McCoy had seen on rocks here and there in his brief visit to this world.

Pictoglyphs . . . graphs . . . whatever the hell they're called. Wonder what they mean.

In some past era, the cave had been equipped with two enormous metal doors that sealed it off from what must surely be the desert. McCoy tried and failed to pick up any residual vibrations from the storm. Clear skies, maybe? He hoped Spock and Rabin wouldn't waste time going after him.

He took a second look at those doors. Damned impressive! Etched with similar glyphs and figures, they were probably as much a work of faith as of protection and technology. Metal-poor as Obsidian was, simply mining and smelting enough metal or trading for it with the city-dwellers must have been the work of generations.

The Romulans came to military attention. *A little slow to salute, aren't we? Is this your traitor?* He raised an eyebrow as Centurion Ruanek brought his fist to his chest in seemingly reluctant deference to . . .

Standing with his back to the Romulans was a tall

mysterious figure in pure white robes. Slowly, the figure turned and acknowledged the saluting Romulans as if his acknowledgment was an honor, even a blessing. He was taller and leaner than the Romulans and veiled to the eyes.

A little overdressed for the vast indoors, aren't you? McCoy wanted to ask. It had to be all this desert melodrama that was getting on his nerves, not the threat to his life or to his crew or to Obsidian's Federation or the planet itself, right? Right. *And maybe pigs can fly.*

With the same sense of ritual that he had shown before, the tall figure unveiled, revealing a cold face with high cheekbones planing up to elegantly angled pointed ears.

I'm dead anyway. Might as well make it good. Rejecting the idea of an exaggerated salaam, which probably wouldn't translate from one culture into another, McCoy groaned melodramatically and set his hands on his hips. "Well, look what we've got here. Another Romulan just crawled out from under a rock."

He heard a faint choking noise from one of his guards.

"Vulcans do not crawl out from under rocks," said the figure in white.

Does Spock know about this? was McCoy's first thought. Just when he thought things had gotten as bad as they could, a renegade Vulcan would have to turn up. He supposed that if he wished this one "live long and prosper," he wouldn't reply with "peace and long life." Not unless renegade Vulcans lied as well as betrayed.

He had had years of practice in riling Vulcans, or one particular Vulcan, and some good luck in fooling Vulcans as eminent as T'Pau herself. He'd give it his best try.

"Vulcans don't attack their allies either. When I last looked, mister, Vulcan was a part of the Federation, and the Romulans weren't. Seems to me that you've got things mixed up, haven't you? What's the logic in that?"

The Vulcan studied him as if he were a Rigelian flatworm.

Worse: he might have had some scientific respect for Rigelian flatworms. Contempt glinted in the absolutely flat, cold eyes. Bones had last seen that fixed intensity on Khan as his madness worsened, but there was more to this gaze than simple madness.

When McCoy had been a boy, he had sneaked off to a revival meeting, one of the last held on Terra, by a man later remanded for treatment for an attempt on the Andorian ambassador's life. "God created *man* in His image. *Man,* not aliens that creep or crawl or have blue skin."

The Vulcan who stood before him had the look of a religious fanatic. McCoy thought of holy wars from centuries and planets past—some now little more than radioactive asteroids orbiting desolate stars—and suppressed a groan of real pain.

The Vulcan barely stirred. "If you are in truth the physician McCoy, as my long-sundered cousins tell me, then he who leads you is Spock, half-breed and outsider, flawed from his boyhood and usurping the place of those worthier than he."

Bad as McCoy's Old High Vulcan was, he recognized the gutturals of invective mode. Linguistics said it was vanishing from the language, but, as far as McCoy was concerned, it couldn't disappear fast enough.

Well, wasn't it a small galaxy? How did this madman know Spock? No, wait a minute. The birth of a half-human baby, particularly one who was the son of Ambassador Sarek, certainly would have made the equivalent of the front pages all over Vulcan. Not unusual at all that this guy should know about Spock. Definitely not unusual that he'd single Spock out as an example of all that was wrong with Vulcan: they'd gone through the same deadly nonsense back on Earth with such nasty terms as "miscegenation" and "half-breeds."

Yeah, but we outgrew it. Vulcans are formidable enough.

115

Vulcan religious fanatics, with their logic and their physical strength perverted—God, that doesn't bear thinking about.

"All right, maybe you think Spock's nothing more than a half-breed," McCoy accused. "But you're a fine one to talk, turning your back on your own people and double-dealing with Romulans."

"They are our brothers," the Vulcan said. "You others are creatures of a lesser breed."

"And what do you call the people around here?" McCoy gestured in the direction of the cave warren and the feverish workers within. "Cannon fodder?"

The Vulcan might not have understood the archaic term, but he certainly understood the point. "The Faithful will receive their reward in the fullness of time. And so will you. Come, there is a task you must perform for me."

He held out McCoy's communicator. Hell, he practically dangled it in front of McCoy's nose.

"The storm has ended for now. You will communicate with your captain"—disdain slimed the military title— "Spock. You will be well paid for your words."

"Go fish." If this madman pushed him, the next thing McCoy said wasn't going to be a tenth as polite and would probably break every privacy taboo on the planet.

"There are no fish on Obsidian. Just fools and puppets and my long-lost cousins. If you seek to force me into ancient brutality, learn that my will is stronger than that of any lesser being."

"How nice for you."

Not the faintest flicker of emotion crossed the cold, insane face. "We shall consolidate power here, eliminating the man your Federation has set up as puppet-master among slaves. He is a fool, but capable of causing damage just as a backward child playing with fire can burn down a house."

"So, you insult my captain, threaten a brother officer, then expect me to sing for my supper?" McCoy asked. "That's hardly logical, let alone coin enough to buy me."

Behind McCoy, the centurion stirred.

"I believe I have your price, *Doctor,*" the Vulcan told him. If he'd poured any more acid sarcasm on the word, it would probably have disintegrated. "Let me demonstrate."

His gesture of "after you, sir" was not convincing. The gemmed blaster he pulled was. McCoy went. It beat being dragged. Or burnt and dragged.

He was guided back into the maze of caves, taking a sharp turn away from where McCoy had first been brought. The passage wound on for what McCoy guessed was a couple of hundred meters, then opened into another chamber.

McCoy looked up at its ceiling. Impressive. When this range heaved itself up from the planet's core, gas bubbles must have formed in the rock, which hardened about them, forming huge natural caves. Or else this was one hell of a lava tube.

"These are my Faithful," the Vulcan told McCoy. "And I am their Master. Observe."

A few artificial lights set in the cave's roof glowed faintly. But more light came from outside: the so-called Faithful had opened a smaller, unornamented version of the massive metal doors. Three nomads entered the cave, dragging a fourth. None wore headcloths or protective robes; in fact, they were ridiculously exposed for this climate, let alone for sunlight as tricky as Loki's.

"That man's collapsed," McCoy said.

"A stunning demonstration of the obvious," the Master replied. "Your deductive skills overwhelm me."

"Heat prostration . . . no . . ." He watched while the sick man's friends set his emaciated form down—laid him out, rather—against the rock wall. McCoy drew in his breath sharply at the sight of the multicolored blotches marring the nomad's flesh, large, raised, unevenly shaped. Some bled sluggishly.

"God. Man's dying of metastatic melanoma if he's not dead already."

More nomads entered. McCoy looked about in growing horror, seeing similar, if smaller tumors on many. One or two sat quietly, their eyes blank—burnt out by the sun. A thin woman coughed rackingly: silicosis or the equivalent, from all the dust. Many more bore signs of malnutrition or mistreatment in addition to the cancers that rose on their skin, birthmarks from Loki's treachery.

"It's bad enough to make them go out there unprotected," McCoy exploded. "But you're working them to death and starving them, too! Dammit, man—"

"I am Vulcan, not 'man,'" the Master interrupted coolly. "I make them do nothing: they have chosen to serve me of their own free will. As will you, *physician*. Serve me, and I will give you your price: permission to go among my Faithful and help them. I will also give you *this*."

He snapped his fingers. One of the Faithful ran up, inflamed eyes wide. This loyal follower was scarcely more than a child. McCoy's diagnostic instincts came alive: squamous carcinoma, a bloated belly, and what looked like trachoma or something else that would probably leave him blind within the year, if he didn't die first of sunstroke or overwork. Hungrily, McCoy eyed what the child presented to his master as if it were a sacred relic—McCoy's satchel of medical supplies.

Let me help. It was one of the greatest phrases in the language, and had won the off-Earth writer who had made it the theme of his masterwork a Nobel Prize. McCoy's Starfleet oath restrained him, but an older oath by far overrode it. *I swear by Apollo the Physician, and Aesculapius, and Hygeia and Panacaea His daughters, and by all the other*

Gods and Goddesses, and the One above Them Whose Name we do not know . . .

"Give me that!" He lunged forward at his medical kit. A protoplaser used as a weapon could create a nasty burn. That, too, violated his oath, but maybe he could buy enough time to help *someone.*

"Earn it," the Master told McCoy. Then, appallingly, he smiled.

McCoy's eyes watered. *It's the damn sunlight,* he told himself. And knew he was lying.

Spock, where are you? Get me out of this hell! Let me get them all out of it! Spock!

But of course there was no answer other than the groans of the dying.

ELEVEN

**Vulcan, Deep Desert
Day 4, Eighth Week of Tasmeen,
Year 2247**

Spock's faster metabolism woke him with a shock: He was hungry. For a moment, he lay staring up at the barely light sky of early morning, startled to find himself out in the desert when he had been dreaming of home and bed.

Desert, yes. A neat twist extricated him from the grit into which both boys had dug for warmth the night before. Exhausted from the brutal heat of Vulcan's Forge, David still slept deeply, curled in on himself like a child.

"David, it is time."

Two days into their trip across the Forge, and they had already fallen into a routine. If they rose now, they could travel until the sun hammered the Forge and David's footsteps as well as his ready flow of speech faltered. Even a Vulcan needed to seek shadow by midday, sleeping or meditating through the worst of Vulcan's heat. Then, as the sun waned, they would rise and hike on until the darkness and the predators—any predator surviving on the Forge was a highly efficient one—grew too dangerous.

The fact that the headgear of their salvaged protective suits contained a visor allowing David to see in the dark as efficiently as a Vulcan had let them come farther than Spock's most optimistic estimate. That estimate, he realized, had been predicated on bigoted observations from the likes of Stonn.

Illogical. I should have drawn my data from closer to home. After all, Mother has proven herself able to adapt to this world.

Could she, he wondered, have survived *kahs-wan?* Speculation was fruitless. So was idling in the coolness of the waking desert to watch the dawn, beautiful though it promised to be.

"David," Spock repeated more loudly, "it is time."

The human stirred. "Another scenic day in hell," David muttered. He coughed, then shook himself free of the grit and stretched. "I don't suppose you'd let me call school and say I'm sick."

"Are you ill?" If so, their chances of survival plunged.

"It was a joke, Spock. I'm fine, honest. Grubs for breakfast again today? The ones in the Negev tasted better. And I got to grill them."

"Half a ration bar for you," Spock said. Perhaps he should allot the survival rations entirely to David rather than letting the human risk eating off the land.

"Hogging all the good stuff, are you?" David's grin turned into a yawn.

"Hogging?"

The human groaned. "I was kidding. And they say Vulcans have no sense of humor."

He could, Spock thought, chart the passage of the day by the type and quantity of his companion's observations. But the idea of David ill, David delirious and dying, David buried in the desert with flat rocks heaped over a lonely part of Vulcan that would henceforward be human territory— Spock drew a deep breath, summoned his control, and decided he preferred the ready babble of speech even this early in the morning.

Together, they reached for their water bottles.

"L'chaim!" David toasted. "In Hebrew that means 'to life.'"

"Highly appropriate," Spock nodded. He drank, scanning the desert, then, as David munched the tasteless rations, face wrinkled in disgust, began a morning hunt. A flat rock flipped over produced several grubs, which he passed over to David, who neatly nipped off their heads with a fingernail, then resolutely ate them.

"Better than ration bars. What isn't?"

Meanwhile, Spock stripped several stalks from a hardy *khara* bush to reach its moisture-laden core, carefully leaving most of the plant to regenerate, then nibbled the soft, slightly salty pulp. This, too, was better than ration bars!

"Are you ready, David?"

"Just a minute." The human boy searched in his makeshift pack for a spray hypo and one of the precious vials of tri-ox. He injected himself, breathed deeply, then paused, looking at the empty vial.

"Spock," he said slowly, "I've been thinking this over. And the tri-ox won't let me ignore this. I've got tri-ox to help me. But what about the others, back there with that religious fanatic? True, they're not as active as I'm being, and that should buy them a little more time. But still . . . even if we do manage to walk out of the deep desert, maybe reach one of those science outposts on the Perimeter, there's no way we're going to make it before people—maybe all the hostages—start to die."

"I . . . have considered that."

"Right, and what odds do you give on that madman getting them proper medical care?"

"Approximately—" Spock began.

"I know you're some sort of math genius!" David interrupted. "It was one thing to raid the—the shuttle as long as we thought we could find communication gear. But it all got fried by the crash. So, where are the closest communicators?"

"Either at the research stations—"

"Or back at Sered's hideout. Spock, I think we ought to turn back."

Spock fought down a wince. He had been thinking the same thing. But logic insisted that he point out, "Two youths against armed Romulans and an adult Vulcan male, David. The odds against—"

"I'm not saying we go in like the cavalry, lasers blasting. We haven't got any, at any rate. But, Spock, if we got out, we can sneak back in."

"If Sered finds us, he will put us under heavy guard."

"Wanna bet? He despises us. I'm a human, and you—you heard what he called you. To him, we're kids, Spock. We can't do anything. Even if he found us, he'd just say we were so scared we came back. If we picked our moment, we could steal a communicator—"

"Logically, he would have them watched," Spock said. "Our safest plan—"

"Are the hostages safe?" David countered. "Listen, my mother's Starfleet, and that means she'll do everything in her power to help people. Maybe we can run interference for her and the other adults—if we get there in time. If they haven't all collapsed from oxygen deprivation or the heat. Now calculate your math," he challenged fiercely. "What's the odds on either of these plans working out?"

Spock paused, mind turned inward, calculating strengths, weaknesses. "Odds are approximately equal," he admitted after a moment. "And equally bad. David, is this an example of what humans call 'a dirty job, but someone has to do it'?"

"Spock, my friend, this is about as rotten an example as we'll ever find. So, we're agreed? Back the way we came?"

"No," said Spock. He knelt and smoothed a patch of sand. "Let us say that here is Sered's cave, here is the shuttle, and here is our relative position." He drew lines joining each position. "We actually gain time not by retracing our footsteps, but by charting our course along the hypotenuse of this triangle."

"You think you can find Sered's hideout again? What if there's a lava pool or something lying across our path?"

"There are no open lava pools on the Forge," Spock told him patiently. "And even if we must detour around obstacles, we are hardly likely to go astray. Surely you remember that there are some notable rock formations near the hideout."

"None of which we can see from here. What do we do till we can?"

"We navigate by the stars."

"Right! Clear desert nights, no light pollution, and all that. I should have remembered that." David packed up his scanty gear. "Okay, Spock, this devil's advocate is all out of objections. Ready when you are."

Devil's advocate? Spock made a mental note to ask his mother for a definition of David's latest exotic terminology.

They started back the way they had come, up some hills crumpled up from Vulcan's crust, and out onto the slick, wrinkled black surface of an ancient lava flow. Here and there, earthquakes had shattered the surface, allowing scrawny plants with vicious-looking thorns to gain root-holds.

"Walk warily," Spock warned. "The lava looks thick, but there may be gas bubbles hiding just beneath the surface. If you break through the crust, you risk a broken or badly lacerated ankle."

David was actually silent as they picked their way across the glossy, treacherous plain.

"Watch out for the plants as well," Spock continued.

"Boots ought to be all right," David grunted. He raised his protective visor and studied the horizon, squinting against the brightness.

"It is not your boots that concern me," Spock replied. "It is the plant life. Merely brushing against some of these shrubs will dislodge toxic spines."

"Meat-eaters?" David asked, eyeing them. "Fascinating—no, that's your line, isn't it? What about these lichen-looking things?"

Spock followed David's gaze. "Those? They are, indeed, true lichen. You cannot get a rash from touching them, but if ingested, they are a powerful hallucinogen, even for Vulcans."

"And what do Vulcans hallucinate? Talking theorems?" David laughed for the first time that morning.

Spock blinked. Was this odd placing of laughter a human defense against stress? Curious, he said, "I fail to see how humans can display such illogical levity in a crisis."

David lowered his visor with the finality of a Terran knight going into battle. "One more time: It's a dirty job, but someone's got to do it."

He strode boldly forward, Spock at his side.

Amazing. I know that I am keeping David going—but I think that David is keeping me going, too!

He had never sensed in another such a fierce desire not just to survive but to keep observing as well, even when false logic might dictate giving up. It was highly commendable in a Vulcan. In a human, it was . . . highly commendable as well.

"Hey, snake!" David yelped suddenly, twisting aside. His

feet slipped out from under him and he went down with a thud and another yell, this time adding what Spock suspected were highly improper expressions in the invective mode of several human languages.

"David! Are you badly hurt?"

"Nothing's broken but that damn bush I landed on. You weren't kidding about those thorns. Look at this! They shredded my sleeve. Ow, and me."

Both boys stared down in dismay at the long black thorn embedded in his forearm.

"At least I'm right-handed," David observed weakly.

"No! Don't try to pull it out. Such thorns are barbed."

"Great," David said. "Just great. I'll be the only one-handed first-year student in the Academy." He reached for his knife, but Spock forestalled him.

"We have been using our knives to pry up rocks and slash vegetation. Not only would they be difficult to sterilize properly, by now, neither has a fine enough point or edge for this type of work."

"Yeah, right, kids don't get the good stuff, do they? It's a shame none of those lasers in the shuttle were functional, huh, Spock? Otherwise we could use one of them on low power to vaporize the thorn."

"And possibly your arm as well. Neither of us are trained in laser surgery." Spock rummaged through the medical supplies they had taken from the shuttle . . . yes. He took out a small, thin scalpel and a tiny vial of a sterilizing solution.

David grimaced. "You sure you can use that? Too bad you can't just use an obsidian blade, all the shards lying around here."

"I could not achieve a sharp enough point."

"Right, right, and the stuff's brittle as glass—it *is* glass. Volcanic glass. They used to use obsidian for trephining, Aztecs or someone, performed brain surgery with it four thousand years ago. No, wait, it was the Egyptians who did the surgeries. The Aztecs used obsidian to cut out people's hearts. And I'm babbling, right?"

"You are on the edge of shock." While he spoke, Spock carefully cleaned the scalpel. Trying to keep the human from sliding further into shock, he asked, "Were these Egyptians of Terra noted surgeons?"

"For their time, they were. And the Aztecs were pretty clever, too. Bloodthirsty lot, though. Thought their gods would die if they weren't fed human blood. Heh, hope Sered isn't *that* far gone!"

Spock froze. "I trust not."

David, struggling one-handed, managed to tear a strip of cloth from his tunic. "Bandage. Reasonably clean. You think we need to worry about infection out here in the desert?"

"The desert is clean," Spock assured him. "But that thorn has to come out. Even the slightest piece left in your arm could create a highly unpleasant condition."

David grimaced. "Good thing I've had my shots." Then he grit his teeth and gestured for Spock to proceed. Spock clamped his hand down upon David's wrist with Vulcan strength, immobilizing it and, he hoped, numbing it as well. He made a careful incision. David flinched, then held still with quite commendable control. The small wound bled more than Spock had expected, not dangerously so, but the red of it staining his fingers and the scent of it, clear to his keen Vulcan senses, were almost shocking. He shut his eyes for a moment, trying to thrust memories of the ruined bodies in the downed shuttle from his thoughts.

A shadow crossed David's arm and both boys glanced up. High overhead, a *shavokh* circled, drawn by the sight of a prone body. The human glared up at the bird. "You can just wait till hell freezes over."

"At least," Spock tried to distract David as he worked, "it fills its ecological niche by seeking carrion . . ."

"Thanks a lot, Spock—hey, any deeper and you'll need a search warrant!"

". . . rather than souls. On Vulcan, we have a tale of the Eater of Souls . . . a night creature which stalks and destroys the spiritual essence of its sapient prey. My mother says that belief in such a creature is common to all sentient beings. Have you ever encountered such stories?"

David continued to glare up at the circling *shavokh*. "I can't believe we're having—*ouch!*—this conversation right now. Aren't you finished yet?"

"One more spine . . . there. I believe we did include an antiseptic with the other medical supplies . . . ah."

He sprayed the antiseptic over the wound, then bandaged it. David sagged back against the rock in relief, his eyes closed, arm cradled against his body and face greenish beneath its tan.

"Do you wish to rest?" Spock asked.

"How long until midday?"

"Approximately one point five three of your hours."

David forced himself to his feet. "Stop this early? We don't dare. You're the one with the built-in range finder, Spock. Lead on."

"This is, I believe, an example of what humans call 'macho behavior.' And it is not logical. David, one point five three of your hours is hardly a long time, and you will do neither us nor the hostages much good if you collapse."

"I'm not going to . . ." David sat down suddenly. "Well, I guess we *can* spare one point five three hours," he said with a shaky grin, and closed his eyes.

David, relatively recovered after the heat of the day, had not objected when Spock had pushed their pace, but by the time they stopped for the night, the human youth dropped to the ground. He was spent and breathing hard, but he still managed to exclaim over the beauty of the sunset. The light bathed the desert floor like a flood of molten bronze. Even the ancient lava flows seemed to ripple, liquid once again.

"My son, you indulge in metaphorical thinking." Spock could almost hear Sarek saying that, and he retorted silently, *If you saw the Womb of Fire at sunset, you too would use metaphor. My description is exceedingly logical.*

Since the human boy was still favoring his left arm, Spock took on himself the task of digging shallow sleeping trenches in the loose ground for the night.

"Don't you think it's still too early to stop, Spock?" David asked, looking wistfully at the sky. "You did say we'd have to steer by the stars. We could get in a couple of hours of travel before the hunters came out."

"I observed that you have been somewhat unsteady on your feet for the past three point two kilometers. We will both be more effective after a meal and a night's rest."

However effective the two of them could be against armed Romulans and Sered. . . .

David had set out provisions: two ration bars, one dried-out root. Now, he sat twisting straps of some supple fiber about his good hand. "You know, Spock, you wouldn't believe how much I hate being taken care of. You really wouldn't believe it. Back home, I'm considered pretty competent. Had to be, or I wouldn't have gotten into Starfleet Academy." He reached down for a small chunk of lava, then whispered, "Freeze!"

Another metaphor? Fascinating. Spock's sensitive ears picked out the sound of some small creature, perhaps a *hayalit* too far from its burrow. David's eyes were very bright. Fever? No, that was the alertness of a hunter.

The *hayalit* stopped for an instant against a rock, its carapace taking on the rock's color. David quickly slipped the lava chunk into his makeshift sling, whirled it over his head, then sent the chunk flying. The *hayalit* had time for one desperate leap, then crumpled.

"I will retrieve it." Somehow that came out in a casual voice. Spock, determinedly hiding his reaction, needed the brief walk to give him time to compose himself. Were all Terrans such efficient predators? Only that morning, he had shed David Rabin's blood, felt the other youth flinch under an improvised obsidian blade, mortally vulnerable. Now, the victim had turned into a hunter.

"You said we needed a decent meal," David called after him. "I've had my immunizations, remember, or those grubs you fed me would have killed me already. I need the protein. And, if you'll excuse my saying it, you do too."

"I can obtain sufficient protein from the desert legumes. I have no need or desire to eat meat. But you are human."

"Heh. You sound almost like Sered." David skinned, cleaned, and disjointed the creature with rapid efficiency. "I . . . don't suppose there's anything around here that will burn?"

The thought of David devouring his kill raw was more unpleasant than the risk of their fire being seen. Spock reluctantly gathered bits of dead vegetation, which David set alight with a spark from his firestarter. At least, Spock told himself, the *hayalit* was low enough on the scale of evolutionary being to barely qualify as animal.

"Tastes just like chicken," the human observed between bites, clearly intending it as a jest.

Looking for a safe subject, Spock said, "You build a commendable sling."

David grinned. "It kind of comes with the name. King David was a hero of my people. As a boy, he had to face a giant, Goliath. Everyone expected the kid to be pulverized, but David wouldn't listen to the odds. He slew the giant with nothing more than a stone from his slingshot. I guess he's a good role model about right now, don't you, Spock?"

"Indeed."

The small fire quickly burned out. The two boys raked the ashes aside, lying side by side on the warmed ground, looking up into the vast dome of the night sky. By unspoken consent, they said nothing of the trials ahead.

"If you seek Captain Rabin's ship," Spock observed, "its disk is so small that parallax is insufficient for observation. However, you can observe one hundred and sixty-eight first-magnitude stars and—"

"As my mother would say, at ease! We're not in class right now."

Silence fell. Spock let himself slowly relax, muscle by muscle, and was almost asleep when David asked suddenly, "Do you ever think of . . . well . . . girls?"

Spock frowned in confusion. "In what context?"

"Well, as girls. Different from us, but . . . attractive. As, uh, mates. One of these days. When we're grown, of course."

Spock felt one eyebrow shoot up. David could not know how gravely his question violated Vulcan codes of privacy. "For me, the topic is academic. I am already bonded."

"You're *married?*" David's voice shot up an octave. "But you're just a kid!"

"It is our custom. I was bonded to T'Pring when we were both seven."

"T'Pring . . . wasn't she at the ceremony? Tall, slim, wearing silver? Very alert?"

"Yes," Spock said, bemused that David should have seen and remembered her.

"Hey, she's really something! Really . . . beautiful." From the hesitation in David's usual flow of talk, Spock inferred that the Terran had meant to add something, then decided against it. "But, Spock, the two of you didn't even talk to each other."

"Talk about what? She will meet me at the appointed time. There will be time enough for speech thereafter." He could feel his face heating. *Control,* he told himself. It was a perfectly normal psychological and physiological process. And he had years before he must confront it.

"I thought you people were advanced," David protested. "Look at your parents . . . I mean . . ."

Yes, and look at me. Half-caste, so that the first madman to disgrace Vulcan in hundreds of years can denounce me before the Adepts of Gol.

No. Control. "My father's parents left him unbonded," Spock replied. "My father and mother chose otherwise for me."

David snorted. "I'd say they did." He fell silent for a long time. "Spock," he asked, "are you scared?"

Spock, too, paused. "The unknown," he conceded, "is always disturbing." Then, because David seemed to expect more, he added, "So is the thought of facing something overwhelming."

"Overwhelming" was the word for it. For two boys to go up against Romulans and an adult Vulcan in full training went beyond illogical all the way to what a human might well call "preposterous."

But then, a human might, like his friend David's namesake, try to beat the odds. Try and succeed. David had taught him a word from David's people's history: *"chutzpah."* Yes. The *chutzpah* of that was almost reassuring.

"David," Spock began tentatively. "May I ask you a personal question?"

"Go right ahead."

"Why did you choose Starfleet Academy? I see no logic in enthusiasm for a military career."

"It's not military, not entirely. It's . . . well, at the Academy, you can study anything you want, ask any question you need to ask—in fact, you're supposed to. You get to go anywhere in the galaxy and maybe even somewhere no one has ever, ever gone—can you imagine anything more exciting than discovering a new intelligent race? And while you're traveling and studying, you sometimes get to help people, too."

Spock bit back a totally human sigh. Starfleet sounded like precisely the sort of institution to hold the answers to his inner questions. "But the weapons," he insisted. "Your ships are armed."

"My mother says that only a fool goes into a situation with lasers firing. Our people—not the Federation, but the people of the very small nation I call home on Terra—have been scientists and artists and teachers—"

"And warriors."

"Yes, sometimes warriors too, when we had to be . . . for more than six thousand years. We are very old, almost as old as Vulcan civilization, perhaps. There were times when, like Vulcans, we turned away from the path of the warrior. But when we left ourselves unprotected, evil men tried to wipe us out so that we said 'never again.' My mother says that 'never again' is optimistic. But she also says that 'not this time' as a motto is something you can build your life around. They won't kill the weak. Not this time. They won't destroy the city. Not this time. They won't launch a sneak attack on a weaker civilization. Not this time. Not while Starfleet's there.

"Not while *I'm* there," David added, and he was clearly speaking a vow. "Not here, either."

"It seems," Spock had to force the words past his lips, and his hands had turned very cold, "extremely logical."

"It is for me," said David. "I know it is. I only hope I can measure up. Maybe, if I get through this all right, if we get back . . . Spock . . ." He drew breath for what Spock knew was going to be an explosion of enthusiastic tactlessness. "Why don't you apply to Starfleet too? There'd be no question of you getting in; they've been hoping to get some Vulcans, and it sounds like—"

"My parents have other plans for me," Spock told him in exactly the same tone that Sarek used in reprimanding him. The Bonding. *Kahs-wan*. The Science Academy. A distinguished, peaceful career for the next two hundred years. His path was set.

"That's such a waste." David sighed, but the sigh turned into a yawn.

"If we are to be strong enough to face the desert tomorrow," Spock said, "we had both better sleep."

"Right," muttered David. "G'night, Spock."

Spock could hear the human's breathing slow and deepen as he slid into sleep. It was a long time, however, before his meditations could bring him to a point where he could even think of rest. He pictured Sered's proud, elegant, countenance. Thought of his treachery. David and his mother were right, Spock decided. Not this time. Not. This. Time.

David claimed that the Academy set him a standard he must strive to match. Spock must now try to match a human's dedication. Perhaps he and David could discuss the entire issue at some later time.

Assuming, of course, that they survived.

TWELVE

Obsidian, Deep Desert
Day 2, First Week, Month of the Shining *Chara*,
Year 2296

The crew of the ill-fated shuttle woke to silence and clear skies. Rabin and Spock moved to the cave entrance, flanked by the others, everyone eager to see exactly where they were.

Someone swore, very softly. Someone else whistled in shock. Their cave sanctuary looked out on a perilously narrow strip of flat ledge, scored and blackened where the shuttlecraft had made its crash landing and almost deadly slide.

"One meter of error," Ensign Kavousi murmured, "that's all it would have taken. One meter of error in landing and we'd be dead."

Captain Rabin shook his head in wonder. "Ensign Prince, I think I speak for all of us when I tell you that was one hell of a piloting job you did."

The ensign shrugged, olive skin flushing slightly. "Ah well, it was written that we not crash, but thank you, sir."

Spock stepped carefully to the edge of the cliff, wary of crumbling soil, studying the formation. Yes . . . it would be a difficult climb down without mountaineering gear, but it could be done. Indeed, if his suspicions were correct, it had already been done. . . .

He prowled the narrow rim of the ledge, hunting, a wary Rabin in his wake.

"You don't suppose . . ." Rabin began tentatively.

"You speak of McCoy?"

"If he was out here, walking blind . . . I mean . . ."

"He is not dead."

"Then where *is* he? Not too many places for a man to be hiding."

Spock acknowledged that with the slightest of nods, then stopped sharply, going to one knee. There at the very lip of the cliff, boldly placed so that it could not possibly be missed, lay a tricorder bearing the insignia of Starfleet Medical Corps. And it was shattered beyond repair.

"The storm must have smashed it," Rabin said in the tone of someone who didn't quite believe what he was saying.

"Hardly. If you will observe the damage closely, you will see that it has been quite deliberately done by a suddenly applied force."

"Like the force from someone's boot."

"Precisely. Someone also made quite certain that we should find the tricorder and, presumably, assume that the doctor had fallen to his death. That, I assure you, is not the case."

Spock straightened, looking out across the desert. A vast, rocky plain stretched out before him, glinting here and there with fresh-strewn shards of black glass over a layer of tan soil and pale sand. But he did note some hints of green; there was, therefore, at least some water. The far horizon was rimmed by a dark, jagged ridge of mountains, clearly igneous and possibly still seismically active. They seemed no more than a few days' walking away, but Spock knew from experience with the deceptive light of other deserts that they were much farther away than they appeared.

And in all that vastness, he saw not the smallest sign of habitation. "Either Dr. McCoy's captors are truly skilled in covering this terrain, or they had a small, swift craft. Either way, the doctor is surely a captive."

That, he added to himself, *would explain why he is so very furious. But where is he? And who has captured him?*

The "why" was simple enough: a Federation medical officer would make a valuable hostage, indeed. Someone obviously knew about Starfleet, presumably the same someone who knew enough to convince a native spy that a Vulcan was the Fiery One. "Do you recognize this region?" Spock asked Rabin.

"I'm not sure." Rabin studied the desert, hand shading his eyes. "That's due west . . . then that must be the Taragishar Range. At least I *think* it is; never saw it from this angle before. If we bear north-northwest, we should be only . . ." His voice faltered. "Only unbelievably far from the Federation base. With a hell of a lot of uncharted desert in between."

"There is no need for alarm. You are as much an experienced desert inhabitant as I."

"Spock, it's been a good many years since our last outing. Maybe time doesn't mean as much to you Vulcans, but it sure does to humans."

Spock waited.

"True," Rabin continued, as Spock had expected, "I haven't tied myself down to a desk job, and I try to keep myself fit, but still . . . all that . . ."

Spock only raised an eyebrow. Rabin hesitated, then gave Spock a lopsided grin. "You read me all too well, don't you? What can I say? The boy's still part of the man, and the boy's still got the taste—logical or not—for adventure. At least I don't need tri-ox here. Ah, what are you looking at down—oh."

The shuttle was an alarmingly small mass of shiny metal there at the base of the cliff. Rabin winced and turned away, to find himself being watched by the crew. "Ensign Kavousi, Captain Spock worked long and hard on that transmitter. Stop gawking and see if you can raise our base or the *Intrepid*. Ensign Prince, go help him."

"Aye-aye. I still wish you'd let me go with you and Captain Spock, though, sir."

"Ensign Prince, we've gone over this already. Three or four times already, for that matter. One last time: Only you have the experience these people need. You have the responsibility for insuring their well-being." Rabin set a hand on the young man's shoulder, adding too softly for the others to hear, "I need you here, Faisal."

Ensign Prince blinked and clasped a hand to his belt, only to brush his phaser and frown as though surprised. Rabin grinned.

"You were expecting a Meccan dagger, weren't you? Wrong desert."

"Shalom, Captain." The ensign touched heart, lips, and brow.

"Aleikum salaam," Captain Rabin replied, returning the salute. "Go with God."

Spock nodded at Lieutenant Diver and Rabin's crew, who all looked somewhat—he sought for a word and settled on "forlorn." "I have every confidence in you," he told them, "and in those at the base. When we return to that base, we will speak again. I am certain your experiences will be highly instructive."

Now, why did that make them smile?

"Well," Rabin said with clearly forced cheer, "the day's

not getting any younger. Think we can get down that cliff safely, Spock?"

"Others did."

"Then—let's trek, Spock."

With a reluctance that surprised him, Spock turned his back on the sheltering cave. Overhead, Loki glared, an angry eye in a quiescent sky. Spock frowned ever so slightly, sensing the first new perturbations in the air. Was there to be another storm? Worse, was he sensing the first air pressure changes signaling a solar flare? If so, it might well occur while he and Rabin were out on the open desert, forcing him to find shelter for Rabin and himself, just as he had on Vulcan.

Until then, however, Rabin knew this world better than did he, and so Rabin would lead.

The struggle down the steep, nearly sheer slope of the cliff took a good part of the morning and brought Spock and Rabin unnervingly near—unnervingly for the human, at least—the wrecked shuttlecraft.

Rabin whistled soundlessly. "Looks even worse up close. That isn't going anywhere, ever. Nothing worth salvaging, either."

"Indeed not."

Rabin glanced at Spock. "You're remembering, too, aren't you? That other wrecked craft, back on Vulcan?"

"Yes." *And another, earlier, wreck of a* Galileo *craft.* "But there is nothing in that memory or this wreck that can help us, and we surely have a considerable journey ahead."

"So don't waste time in reminiscing," Rabin finished dryly. "Got it." He looked about, getting his bearings. "We really couldn't have picked a less convenient place for a crash if we'd planned it. *Nothing* nearby, not even an oasis town."

"The land cannot be totally lifeless if the nomads cross it. And I did see signs of vegetation, indicating moisture."

"Then: Onward."

Spock paused, glancing about the open wilderness with a desert-dweller's instinctive caution. Rabin stopped with him, warily silent.

They had been walking with a steady, ground-eating, energy-saving stride, taking advantage of the morning's relative coolness, and by now they could no longer see the cave in which the rest of their party sheltered. All about them stretched the rocky plain with its glittering black coating of bits of obsidian over the tan, hard-packed soil. The wind whispered harmlessly, stirring the hot, dry, dusty air, tugging at Spock's hood.

There. His keen Vulcan hearing had caught the clear, steady chirping of some desert fowl. Where there was wildlife, there was water. The wind shifted slightly, and Spock sniffed the air, analyzing.

"Water," he said after a moment. "This way."

It was a bare seepage from between two rocks, but it was clean. No desert-dweller passed up the chance for moisture, particularly when it meant precious supplies could be conserved, so Spock and Rabin took advantage of the chance to drink, then sat back, resting for a moment.

"I admit," Rabin began, "I was a little leery about taking only the two small canteens with us."

"Had I not seen vegetation, I never would have proposed bringing so small an amount," Spock agreed. "But the crew needed the water more than did we."

"Right. 'The needs of the many,' and all that. And I'd forgotten how you really can smell out water if you know what you're hunting. That funny not-quite-wet rock smell. Almost like hot metal."

"Exactly."

"Ha, look at this," Rabin said, studying the relatively lush plants growing along the line of seepage. *"Liak* root." He pulled one free with some effort, then brushed the soil away from the tuberous roots. "See?" Breaking off a piece, he crunched it happily. "You usually find these near water," the man said around his mouthful. "Nice flavor, crunchy texture, and it's got vitamins human and presumably Vulcan metabolisms can use."

Spock, curious, sampled a piece. "Yes," he said, swallowing. "Quite palatable. Will it store well?"

"Easily. For days, maybe even a week."

"Excellent. Then let us supplement our rations with fresh food while we may."

They added several of the *liak* roots to their packs, leaving the majority of the plants behind to replenish themselves, then set out again. The walking so far had not been particularly difficult, Spock mused, hearing gravel crunch under his feet. Aside from such local variations in the sparse, thorny vegetation as the *liak,* this seemed little different from many another desert plain he had crossed in his life; there were, after all, only so many ways for similar ecological systems to be formed.

Of course, as with all deserts, there were perils. Obsidian could be treacherously fragile and slick underfoot. And one needed to keep a keen eye for such predators as whatever cold-blooded species might need to warm themselves on sun-heated surfaces.

"You still aren't a meat-eater, I take it?" Rabin asked suddenly.

"That has not changed."

"A pity. Some tasty wild critters about, such as . . ." He pounced swift as a predator himself, and came up with a good-sized lizardlike something, wriggling frantically in his grip as Rabin held it firmly just behind the head. *"Bok-tarik.* That's what the good folks of Kalara call them, anyhow. But if you aren't going to join me . . ." He put the *boktarik* down again with careful gentleness, watching it scuttle away. " 'Sorry, sir, but we can't kill a whole *bok-tarik* for just one steak.' "

"That," Spock commented, "is a jest, originally from Earth, originally told about a man desiring to eat elephant and being rebuffed by the chef. It is older, my friend, than both of our ages added together."

"Aha! He *has* learned something of human ways!"

"It would be illogical, to say nothing of highly improbable, of me not to have done just that. And you," Spock added without the slightest trace of expression, "have not lost your gift for, I believe the proper word for it is, 'wisecracking.' "

That forced a genuine laugh out of Rabin. "God, Spock, it *has* been a long time. I never meant to drop out of sight like that."

"Lives often diverge, whether one wills it or not."

"And isn't *that* the truth! I've heard bits and pieces about your career, of course; hard to avoid hearing about the first *Enterprise* and its heroic mission. Missions. *Enterprises—* ah, you know what I mean."

"Yes. The sun is rapidly approaching its zenith."

"I've noticed. And smart desert critters should rest in whatever shade they can find."

There was none. This, Spock knew, was hardly a problem. He and Rabin sat, if not totally comfortably, at least tolerably well, under the makeshift canopies that flowing desert robes could create. For a long while they said nothing, sharing a canteen between them, both too desert-wise to move more than was absolutely necessary or take more than a mouth-wetting swallow at a time, or to stint themselves on water, either. Spock watched to be sure that the human, more water-dependent than he, took the larger share.

Then Rabin stirred slightly. "So, what *have* you been doing? Besides rising through Starfleet ranks, that is?"

Spock hesitated. *I have lost my captain . . . and my friend.* But all he said was "Experienced much. Learned what I could."

Rabin snorted. "Such as how to field unwanted questions. Don't worry; I've had some experience in that myself."

Time passed and the desert grew utterly still with heat, too warm for even the human's innate cockiness. He napped sitting up, and Spock used the desert quiet to slip into meditation. It would be far too simple to let worry intrude, about the crew, back in their rock shelter, about himself and Rabin and the desert about them. But worry was emotion, emotion was insignificant . . . logic was the cornerstone, logic and control . . .

He roused suddenly, feeling refreshed. The sun had slid almost to the horizon, and a cooler breeze was already sweeping over the desert as he got to his feet, brushing off his robes. With a companionable nod to Rabin, who was doing the same, Spock set out again, the human keeping pace but moving a bit stiffly.

"Don't worry about me," he told Spock, who was watching him warily. "Nothing wrong. I just haven't been doing as much long-range hiking as I should."

Spock glanced at the sky, the horizon. "We should be able to go on for a bit longer before nightfall."

"I can do it, if that's what's bothering you."

"I am not bothered. Merely speculative. I trust you are not being what is generally termed, I believe, 'macho.'"

Rabin, mouth full of something he had just snatched from a thorny plant, nearly spit it out, choking on laughter. Chewing frantically, he said, "No. I'm not being 'macho,' honest." He bent over one of the thorny desert plants, then plucked a second object and straightened. "Here, try this. *Challik* fruit, nice and ripe. Watch it! Knock the spines off first."

"I am well acquainted with the typical characteristics of desert succulents." Spock neatly broke the spines off against a convenient rock, then sampled the *challik*. Agreeable, if a touch too sweet for his tastes. "Odd how few intelligent beings realize that a desert is rarely totally barren. There is generally food to be found."

"If one isn't too fussy," Rabin added. "And has an eye that truly sees. What always amazes me is how few intelligent beings realize how beautiful it all is!"

Spock paused, considering the starkness about him. A younger Spock would have agreed stiffly that there was an esthetic correctness to the arrangement of plain and mesa and mountains. Now he could say simply, "Yes. I, too, find it beautiful." Which was, after all, just as logically truthful.

They camped for the night on a level stretch of land slightly higher than the surrounding area; both of them knew the danger of flash floods. The desert floor was far too parched to absorb water quickly, which meant that any rain in the high mountains would come surging down dry gullies or even slight depressions with quick, deadly force.

"Not much in the way of tinder," Rabin commented. He shivered suddenly, drawing his robes about him as the desert rapidly cooled after sunset.

"No matter." Spock had already found three good-sized rocks, checking them for fractures or other dangerous weaknesses. Piling the rocks together, he heated them to a steady, baking warmth with a quick, efficient phaser blast. "They will stay hot, I would estimate, for perhaps five point nine Obsidian hours."

"Long enough. Won't betray our presence with any nasty firelight or smoke, either." Rabin held a *liak* root over one, then sampled the roasted result. "Not bad. Could use some pepper, though. This is how the nomad women cook; a good cooking stone—one that's not going to explode on you from trapped air—is passed down, mother to daughter."

"A similar ritual was performed by women in Vulcan's nomad past."

"Clever, those women." Rabin paused, eyeing Spock slyly. "Speaking of which, my pointed-eared friend, what *have* you been doing in all those years? Married your T'Pring and—"

"No."

The flatness of it made Rabin stare. "No? I thought there . . . ah . . . wasn't a choice about it."

"There was. T'Pring chose otherwise." Memory, still surprisingly sharp after so long, told him: *I chose not to be the consort of a legend.* "As," Spock said in deliberate understatement, "did I."

"Ah."

Spock raised a brow. "Now, if I am not mistaken, you are about to perform that human ritual of 'I told you so.'"

"I wouldn't! But . . ." Rabin grinned. "I did tell you so, didn't I?" The grin faded. "Not that I've done so well on the home front. I . . . was married for a time, 'a nice Jewish girl' and all that. But . . ." He shrugged. "It turned out that I'd wed a wife who didn't like deserts."

"That hardly seems like a logical choice."

Rabin snorted. "Believe me, Spock, logic had nothing to do with it!" He shrugged again. "No kids, no complications, no hard feelings. It happens. My mother, of course, still wants grandchildren, but she's hardly going to nag me across the galaxy! Besides," he added with the return of his grin, "she has her own life. She retired from Starfleet some time ago, went into politics back on Earth and is now both happily remarried and a member of the Israeli government, the Knesset."

Rabin paused as though he'd been slapped. "Hell, Spock, I forgot," he said awkwardly. "The Lady Amanda. I heard about . . . please do accept my condolences." In shaky Old High Vulcan, he added, "I grieve with thee."

"There is no need for embarrassment. One cannot alter what has already passed. But," he added, voice carefully controlled, "thank you. Now I do believe we should rest. I will take the first watch."

Rabin settled himself on the ground, wrapped in his bedroll. Silence fell for a time. Then:

"Spock . . ."

"Yes?"

"Can't help wondering. The crew . . . think they'll make it?"

"If you wish me to 'guess,' you are mistaken, my friend. And as for a rational reply, the chances of the makeshift transmitter working with sufficient strength and sufficient length of time to let the Federation base find the crew are, given fair weather and no solar flares, approximately twenty-four point five to—"

"Not statistics again."

"I cannot predict what the crew will do. But I can remind you of this fact: they are well trained and intelligent, both your party and mine. They will not make foolish mistakes."

"And what about us? Think we'll make it?"

Spock started to reply, then stopped, realizing that there had been the faintest tinge of humor to Rabin's voice; the human was hiding his worries as humans tended to do by pretending he was only joking. Rabin was also deliberately evoking their long-ago struggle for survival.

"Only," Spock said as though he hadn't seen through the subterfuge, "if we achieve sufficient rest."

There was a sound suspiciously like a chuckle from Rabin. "Good night, Spock." It was a parody of a little boy's voice.

"Good night," Spock said and, secure in darkness too thick for human vision, permitted himself the smallest upward crook of his mouth.

Rabin stretched, yawning. "God, what I wouldn't give for a good old-fashioned genuine Earth-grown-bean cup of coffee! It's been far too long since I've slept on the ground, Spock. Getting too old for this."

Spock raised an eyebrow. "I would not believe that to be the truth if you were twice your age."

"Saying I'm still a child at heart?" The human stretched again, wincing. "Wish I could get the rest of the body to agree! Ah well, at least nothing bothered us in the night. I . . . only hope the crew had as peaceful a rest."

"It is illogical to worry about what cannot be affected."

"Easy for you to say! You don't have to answer to Starfleet for the loss of a shuttlecraft."

"Judging from the age of that craft," Spock said in a carefully neutral voice, "I do not believe the bill would be substantial."

"Never underestimate the power of bureaucracy. Well, my friend," Rabin added with a wryly melodramatic bow, "the desert waits."

They walked on into the morning, and on again, the only sounds the soft stirring of wind, the crunch of grit under-foot, and the occasional distant call of what Spock assumed from the incautious shrillness was a hunting bird. The day quickly grew warm, then hot. Not unpleasantly so, Spock thought, at least not for a Vulcan, though Rabin did not seem unduly uncomfortable, either. The terrain remained relatively level, and it was not at all difficult to fall into the mindlessness of step after step after . . .

"Remember the last time we did this?" Rabin said sud-denly. "Having to be heroes when we both were nothing but scared kids—oh, don't look at me like that, Spock. You and

I both know that underneath that Mr. Cool Logic face you were wearing, you were every bit as scared as me and—look at those Indians on the horizon!"

At first, the reference escaped Spock completely. Then a memory with Jim Kirk's voice whispered, *"John Ford Westerns, movies,"* as he saw the line of desert nomads sitting their *chuchaki* on the ridge above them.

"Wild nomads," Rabin murmured. "Look at those *chuchaki*. Lean as greyhounds and pure white, every one of them. Desert breed. Deep desert, these guys."

"I do not believe it would be wise for us to move."

"I'm not moving."

The nomads sat absolutely still, keeping even their *chuchaki* from fidgeting, making a dramatic point. Then the line rode smoothly down the ridge as one to block the way, still without a sound other than the jingling of harness and a grunt from a *chuchaki*.

At first glance, the nomads seemed identical as clones, shrouded in the same deeply hooded flowing robes, tan as the desert floor. But Spock noted subtle changes in the weaving of each robe and less subtle lines of color, red or blue: ritual markings, no doubt, that indicated different clans or rankings.

One thing the nomads all had in common: They were blatantly not happy at finding strangers in their territory. In a movement so smooth that it could only have been rehearsed, the nomads, as one, drew and aimed archaic—but, Spock didn't doubt, still quite deadly—projectile rifles at Rabin and him.

"What the hell's going on?" Rabin whispered. "Why are they calling us the Faithful?"

Spock's translator was picking up the same cryptic words. He also saw fingers beginning to tighten on triggers. Taking a logical chance out of desperation, he raised his hand in the split-fingered Vulcan greeting and said, "Live long and prosper."

This calm, ritual greeting was clearly not what the nomads had been expecting. For the first time Spock saw them stir uneasily, glancing at each other. He followed up on their hesitation by telling them, still in his best calm, logical voice, "We are not of the Faithful—but we do wish to speak of them." He added softly to Rabin, suddenly inspired, "Push back the hood of your cloak. Let them see you."

Rabin warily pushed back the hood. As Spock had hoped, the nomads reacted to his clearly non-native features; this was plainly not one of the mysterious Faithful. More, they were actually *pleased*.

"The Kindly Fool!"

"The Kindly Fool has finally gained the wisdom to find us!"

Rabin raised an eyebrow at that "Kindly Fool" epithet, but Spock cut in before he could say anything, "Yes. This is the good man who seeks to save your children and make the desert bloom."

That started a storm of murmurings among the nomads. At last the one who seemed to be their leader, his robe marked with red *and* blue zigzag weavings, said, "Come."

They were escorted—surrounded, rather—by the mounted nomads, towering over them, to a rocky outcropping. "There," said the nomad's leader. "In there."

Rabin groaned. "Another cave."

"More than that," Spock murmured, entering. "Note the size of the cavern, its height and depth. Yes," he added, "and notice that the nomads have painted pictographs all over the walls. This is a true refuge, not merely a chance convenience, presumably one in which the nomads take shelter during a solar flare."

"I just hope it isn't going to be turned into a prison."

"I do not think that will be the case. Look."

One of the nomads was approaching, the hood of his robe pulled back to reveal dark eyes in a lean, sharp-edged face lacking any surplus flesh—the face, Spock thought, of a true desert-dweller. This uncovering was, he suspected, a sign of respect, as was the earthen cup of precious water he bore.

"The Water Ritual," Rabin muttered. "Never saw it outside of street theater in Kalara. You're right; we *are* being honored."

The nomad made a great ceremony out of offering the cup. With a sideways glance at Rabin, who was gesturing subtly, *go on, take it,* Spock bowed to the nomad, accepted the cup, sipped, then passed it on to Rabin. He, too, sipped, then passed it back to the nomad, who drank in turn. The cup made its rounds three times, then the nomad bowed and left. Rabin whistled under his breath.

"You're in the wrong business, my friend," he murmured to Spock.

"What do you mean?"

"Took me a while to place those tribal weavings. But these are the Benak Haran—they almost always do that 'shoot first, ask questions later' routine! Nice job of diplomacy you did."

Does he take me for my father?

Illogical to feel even quickly suppressed anger at the comparison. "I did what was needed," Spock said flatly.

Time enough to ponder such issues when he and Rabin and all the crew—yes, and Dr. McCoy as well—were safe.

Whenever that might be.

THIRTEEN

**Vulcan, Deep Desert
Day 6, Eighth Week of Tasmeen,
Year 2247**

Spock and David stopped to get their bearings, both boys staring at the far horizon, where a jagged mass of blackened rock hunched up from the reddish desert floor.

"No easy way to get around that," David said.

"No need to get around it. We must, instead, get over it."

"That . . . wasn't a joke, is it?"

"A play on words, I believe you call it? No. I only mean that we must climb over it, quite literally."

"Oh, now you've *got* to be joking!"

"The ascent is not as difficult as it seems. Others have climbed the ridge, and indeed the al-Stakna Mountains beyond, without mountaineering gear." That those others had been scientists trained in mountaineering was a fact he saw no reason to mention to David. "And once we have crossed it, we will be on the edge of the Womb of Fire."

151

"Now, that really makes me feel cheerful." David shaded his eyes with a hand. "I know distances in the desert are deceiving, but it looks like we could reach that thing in about an hour or so of quick hiking. How far away do you think it really is?"

"If my calculations are correct . . ." Spock began.

"If they're not correct, I'm dead and so are the rest of the hostages. I'm assuming that if I stick my head into the hypotenuse of this navigational triangle of yours, we won't both hang."

Spock flicked the human a sharp glance, letting him know what he thought of people who punned on mathematics. David's grin made his lips crack. "Once we cross the ridge," the human continued, giving them a perfunctory swipe with his tongue, "will we be able to see where Sered's got the hostages?"

"We should." Spock studied the rugged landscape, trying to pick out the easiest route: impossible at this range, even for sharp Vulcan vision. "As to your first question, barring unforeseen storms or other hazards, we should reach the ridge in time to rest overnight and start our ascent at first light."

"You think there's water up there?" David asked. "Not that I'm worried or anything, but we're pretty low on liquid supplies."

Spock glanced up. A *shavokh* circled high overhead, but it was clearly watching something other than the boys, and hunting other than dead prey. "The *shavokh* senses water," Spock said, then looked directly at David. "So will every other creature in the range."

"All of which are likely to be fanged, taloned, or toxic. Warning taken."

They started forward, heads down against a sudden sand-laden gust. Ahead, a shower of phantom rain quickly formed, tantalized them for a few moments, then just as swiftly disappeared. David stopped, blinking.

"Spock, what does a Vulcan mirage look like?"

"First I must know what mirages look like on your world."

"Oh . . . pools of water, swaying palm trees, happy camels, that sort of thing. Even buildings, sometimes. On Vulcan, a mirage wouldn't look like a dried-up streambed, would it?"

"Not unless you assume that the planet has turned malicious. Vulcan already possesses significant hazards without such fanciful concepts. And that," he added, following David's glance, "is hardly a mirage."

"Water?"

"Possibly just below the surface. Come, we shall see."

It was a long, shallow channel, faintly darker than the surrounding land, its smoothness broken by a rumble of rocks that had clearly been swept down from higher ground. It was even remotely possible, Spock thought, that this seemingly dried-up watercourse was part of the aquifer that supplied Sered's fortress. He cautiously studied the sky, then gestured to David to fan out some distance to the left.

"We may find water below the surface, but we must be wary."

"Gotcha. Whatever the odds are against a cloudburst anywhere in the vicinity—ha, or even miles away—I don't want to be anywhere near a water channel in a flash flood."

There was mud below the dried surface, and yet more mud below that, and after a time of fruitless digging, both boys gave up.

"Not worth it," David gasped.

"The energy expended in digging would far exceed the energy replaced by whatever water we reached," Spock agreed.

"But there's got to be water somewhere nearby if there's mud under this."

"The *shavokh* would not be hunting if there was not. Come, David, we shall follow its lead."

"And," David said, glaring up at the bird and rubbing his thorn-wounded arm reminiscently, "hope it's not going to be hunting us."

The land grew steadily rougher as the boys hiked toward the ridge, forcing them to pick their way among larger and larger chunks of basalt. By the time Vulcan's fierce sun had slipped behind the horizon, they had reached the sharp slope that was the true base of the ridge.

"You were right about how long it would take," David said, plopping down on a convenient rock, then added a wry, "Not going to say 'I told you so'?"

Spock glanced at him in genuine surprise. "Why? I did tell you so."

"Agh. Save me from literal-minded Vulcans."

"That, I take it, is a rhetorical remark." Recognizing one of the thorny plants clinging to the rough ground, Spock carefully broke off two stalks. "This contains sufficient moisture to keep us at least relatively comfortable."

"Food." David ironically held up one of the nearly inedible ration bars in one hand. "Moisture." He held up the stalk in the other. "And a nice, firm bed. Servants, wake me when it's morning."

"Before morning," Spock corrected. "We cannot waste the precious hours before the day's heat."

"Before," David agreed with a groan, and went flat.

By the time the sun had risen, the boys had been climbing for several hours.

"You're right," David panted. "Don't need special gear. Climbed worse at home. Climbing into a whole new set of hazards, though," he added, stopping to catch his breath. "Who'd have guessed there'd be so many blasted *crystals* in the rocks?"

"It is an unusual formation," Spock agreed.

"Why do I not feel privileged? And yes, that was another rhetorical question."

As the sun continued to rise, its rays beat down on boulders and rock spurs with ever-increasing force, the flare of sunlight on the crystals dazzling the boys despite David's protective visor and the veils of Spock's eyes. The narrow trail they were following blazed as though filled with melted stone, and they climbed slowly, afraid of pitfalls they might not see in time.

"If our path were easy," Spock said, trying to reassure the human and himself both, "predators native to this range would find it so as well."

"Gee, now that's comforting."

This low in the foothills, the temperature was not appreciably cooler. Nevertheless, the smallest increase in humidity brought Spock's head up; he could almost feel the skin of his face, taut against his planet's dryness, relax in proximity to . . .

He sniffed deliberately. The powdery, alkaline scent of a recent rockfall, but something else . . . He sniffed again. Yes! Unmistakably water! There was also the spoor of some animal, acrid enough to be a carnivore, vaguely familiar, but possible threats were overpowered by his survival instincts clamoring at him that *here was water, here was life, he must hurry!*

No. Haste was fatal in the desert, particularly when something had its lair nearby. David had scented it, too, reaching for the sling at his belt and checking his sidepouch for suitable ammunition.

Let David hunt. Fresh meat will keep him healthy.

As for himself, Spock thought, where there was water,

there would surely be edible plants. That would extend how long they could survive out here—

Until David runs out of tri-ox compound. If that happens, what then?

Spock had already worked it out. To save David's life, he would have to be turned over to Sered, even if that put Spock's own chances at risk. He would have to be careful that David, jumping to one of his intuitive conclusions, did not anticipate this line of reasoning.

"Spock," David called softly, "there's something around here. I've spotted tufts of something that looks like fur, camouflaged against the rocks."

"Be careful."

"I will. But I don't see anything around."

Neither do I. A predator prefers not to be seen. Until it springs.

David was already scrambling up over a heap of rocks, and Spock hurried after. Yes, there was the pool, tiny, a deep indigo amid the black rocks, and infinitely welcome to his sight. Beyond the water lay a jumble of immense basalt boulders. Some long-ago earthquake must have sent them tumbling down to end up slanting against each other, forming a wilderness of caves.

How very curious: Although birds circled overhead, no animals came to drink.

"Something's wrong," David whispered. "Think the water's bad?"

Spock shook his head, pointing at animal tracks in the mud at the water's edge; creatures clearly used this pool regularly. "Our presence could be frightening them away."

"Or it could be some nasty predator lurking about."

"Exactly," Spock said softly. "I will stand guard while you fill the water bottles."

The human warily knelt at the water's edge. "Hey," he

whispered, "here's another tuft of that fur. Not too pretty: orange with greenish tinges."

Spock stiffened as memory belatedly processed and returned data, all at once knowing exactly what he had smelled, what had left that fur.

"Le-matya," he murmured.

"Heh?"

"It is a felinoid predator, a deadly mountain hunter. I did not think we had reached its range."

David shrugged. "Predators don't read the guidebooks. Now what?"

But Spock held up a warning hand, listening. He heard a faint mewling coming from the shadow of a rocky overhang. That was hardly the scream of a *le-matya.* Was something injured? Warily, he stalked forward, David following to guard his back.

So. Here were more tufts of fur, orange with green markings, teased by the wind. The mewling grew louder as the boys approached. Moving with exaggerated care, Spock peered into the darkness. Inside was a nest of dried plants and more fur. And within it squirmed six tiny *le-matya*s.

Full memory flashed to life:

A scream of feral rage, a scrabble in the rock dust, and the le-matya *all but cornering him until I-Chaya rose up, growling, the* sehlat*'s shabby coat fluffing upward in a feeble threat display as he showed his broken fangs. I-Chaya hurled himself between the* le-matya *and the child Spock, clearly demanding that his Vulcan "cub" take himself off and hide. Spock heard I-Chaya's yelp of agony as the* le-matya *swiped at him with those poisoned claws, knew his* sehlat *had just given him life at I-Chaya's own expense—*

These babies, so young that the poison sacs at the base of jaws and claws had not had time to fill, would grow into predators such as had killed I-Chaya. His hand clenching around a rock, Spock bent over the nest.

But then he hesitated. Warily, hardly understanding the urge, he reached out to touch one small creature, hearing it hiss in childish defiance. Why, *le-matya* fur was soft, softer than he would have imagined! How tiny the babies were—and how foolishly, marvelously brave, all but helpless yet trying to defend themselves, raising plump little paws that were only a fraction of the size they would one day be. The needle-thin talons that tipped them were more of a promise than a menace. One baby opened its mouth and yowled, showing what would one day be formidable fangs but were now little more than milk teeth. How could he—

"Spock, *look out!*"

With a shriek, the outraged adult *le-matya* lunged toward its nest—her nest—to protect her young. Spock flung himself away from the nest, falling, rolling, scrambling into the cover of a projecting rock, staring at the sheer size of the predator. The ones around Shikahr were big, but this was a creature of the Womb of Fire, perhaps even a successful mutation. He swung up onto the rock, fighting for the advantage of height.

But the creature had clearly caught his scent—and the smell of fear. Once again, Spock was seven years old and paralyzed at the approach of a deadly enemy. Once again, his control slipped as the *le-matya* screamed, exposing discolored fangs that were lethal enough of themselves but that carried a deadly nerve poison.

David! The thought stabbed through his paralysis. *If he moves, the* le-matya *will turn on him!*

Spock's hand fell to a sharp rock. He was no longer a child; he had most of the strength that an adult Vulcan male was supposed to have, and if he hit the *le-matya* just right, he would crush its skull.

But if he killed the creature, what happened to the kits? Ridiculous, illogical, maybe even fatal to hesitate, and yet—

"Move it, Spock!"

Spock had an instant's confused thought that David's shouts put him at risk. Then a rock bounced off the *le-matya*'s head. The creature howled and whirled, just in time for another to hit it on a sensitive ear, drawing green blood. A third rock struck near its eye. The *le-matya* screamed with rage and charged. But David was nowhere in sight.

Oh, clever! Spock thought, and threw a stone at the *le-matya*. The creature whirled, shrieking, and David launched a fusillade of tiny stones from his sling, peppering the *le-matya*'s tawny hide. As the predator spun and spun again, trying to find this enemy that could attack from all sides, Spock saw David gesture frantically, *Let's get out of here!*

Indeed!

He leaped from rock to rock, jumping down as David came running up, water bottles sloshing at his side. The two boys ran together until Spock brought them to a stop, listening.

"We are safe. She will have returned to her nest by now."

"Are you all right?" David was grabbing at him, wildly looking for wounds. "Did that thing claw you? And what in hell *was* it?"

The contact was not unpleasant, but it was a breach of control. As tactfully as he might, Spock freed himself. "That," he said, "was a *le-matya.*"

"The top predator? Well, it looks like about the top of the food chain to me, and I bet it thinks so too. Still," the human added, "to be fair, if I had a litter to protect, I guess I'd be furious, too."

"All *le-matya*s are like that," Spock corrected. "Perpetually raging. Alone of Vulcan's predators, they kill more than they need."

David's eyes widened. "Then why didn't you kill it? Or the kits? Those cute little critters are only going to grow up into monsters like that thing."

"It is wrong to kill an entire litter of even these babies.

And killing their mother would bring about their deaths as well."

"Well, yes, but . . . well . . ."

"Besides, this is her land, not ours; and she was merely defending her young."

"Well," David said again, "at least we got the water. Let's put some distance between us and Mrs. *Le-matya*."

He appointed himself—and his sling—as rear guard. Moving as quickly as they dared while keeping a watch for more *le-matya*s, they clambered up to the crest of the ridge. Spock pointed, not sure if he was satisfied with his navigational skills or—most illogical to feel this—alarmed at their accuracy.

"That," he said, "is the Womb of Fire."

Before them lay a twisted wilderness of black rock and gray cinder. Steam swirled up from fumaroles and pools of superheated water or boiling mud. Crusts of yellow sulfur and patches of blazingly green lichen were the only color in all that vast, tormented landscape, and the air shimmered with heat.

"Oh my God," David said with genuine reverence. "And we're going to cross *that?*"

"It can be done."

"You don't sound too sure about that."

"It can be done," Spock repeated. "We must merely be careful where we step."

"And breathe. Hey, no problem!"

"That, I assume, is sarcasm?"

"It most certainly is." David sank to his haunches with a sigh. "But we're on the right track, right? We're almost at Sered's hideout."

"We are."

"God. Never thought I'd be glad to see anything that looks like a burned-out hell," David said, then straightened, looking out over the waste. "Or maybe not burned-out at that. Still smoking down there somewhere. I just hope whatever's brewing doesn't boil up at us."

"It is illogical to worry about what cannot be helped."

"That's me, good old illogical human that I am." David produced a water bottle and held it out to Spock. "How long since you've had a drink?"

"Twenty-four point eight three six of your hours," Spock replied. He took the bottle and drank, then added, "You must surely know by now that it is a mistake to ask a Vulcan a 'rhetorical question.'"

"As long as you're alive to answer," David said. He looked out at the Womb of Fire. "That thing looks like it really is going to give birth."

"There," Spock said, suddenly realizing where he was and pointing. "We do not need to cross the entire Womb of Fire after all, merely one corner. That is what we seek, at the right edge of the Womb of Fire."

"That mountain? No . . . not a mountain. Bet it's what's left of a caldera all fallen in on itself."

"It is. And Sered's fortress lies within it. I recognize the rock formations."

David shuddered. "They're all in there. My mother, the students in the compound, half the diplomatic community resident on Vulcan. I . . . just hope they're all still alive."

A human, Spock suspected, would have put his hand on David's shoulder, trying to reassure him by touch. He raised a hand, let it fall. For a Vulcan, touch provided no reassurance; and the simple need for contact was a breach of control.

David opened his pouch, looking inside. "I've got three tri-ox shots left," he told Spock. "Maybe I should space them further apart?"

"On the contrary," Spock said, "I would suggest that you

inject yourself all the more regularly because of the sulfur fumes we will encounter as we proceed. Anoxia leads to bad judgment."

"Do *they* have tri-ox?" David demanded. "Do you think that Sered even cares if their hearts or lungs give out?"

"They have us," Spock said. "Such as we are. And such plans as we can contrive."

David settled himself more comfortably, clearly battling with himself for calmness. "We need a communicator. Once we get one, we can signal my mother's ship, Shikahr, oh, anything . . ."

"Including search teams. The authorities have surely been conducting overflights."

"Oh, right. With all this desert to be searched, I don't think we can count on the cavalry to come riding to the rescue."

Spock looked at him blankly. Cavalry? Was that not an archaic form of—ah. Another of David's movie references. One he had made before, equally illogically. "Perhaps not," Spock agreed. "But one of them might be able to provide reinforcements."

"First, we need that communicator. But . . . Spock, who were those people with Sered? Not Vulcans, and yet . . . I heard Sered speak of 'sundered cousins.' "

Spock met David's eyes unflinchingly. He owed the human his life, but privacy guarded the story of the "sundered cousins," one of the most tragic chapters of the calamitous time just before Surak's teachings and the saving transformation of Vulcan society.

David was the first to glance away. "I get it. 'I could tell you, but then I'd have to kill you.' "

Spock stared at him in startled horror. "I would never—"

"No, no, it was just an idiom! You meant it's classified stuff, right? Well, then we can assume a news blackout on material going out of this system. Time enough to worry about that when we get back." He whistled softly. "What a mess security's going to be!"

"As you say, time enough to worry when we are back."

"Still," David mused, "it's obvious those guys are Vulcanoid, so we know that what affects Vulcans affects them. I wish they didn't have all the Vulcan strengths."

Spock shook his head. "They may not," he said softly. "I have not heard that they preserved all of our ancient arts. This much I may tell you: Of the kindred who left Vulcan, not one came from Mount Seleya. Not one was an Adept of Gol."

"And wouldn't Psyops love that information! Never mind, never mind. Spock, we've survived on a wing and a prayer this long—yeah, another movie quote—so here's my plan. We get down there as quickly and safely as we can, and we seize any opportunity we get, just like we did when we escaped. We're bound to find time to set up a rockfall or something, or signal someone."

"You make it sound very simple."

"Well, yes, but remember that we'll have help. I know that the Starfleet folks will be doing everything they can to escape."

"And if they are too ill for that?"

"Oh. Well. We'll just have to . . . well . . ."

"Create a distraction?"

"Yes!"

"One strong enough to confuse an entire troop of armed and well-trained warriors?"

"We'll think of something," David said with a bold sweep of an arm. "After all, it's up to us."

Granted, Spock thought, his experience with humans was limited. But from what he had seen so far, it seemed that when humans made such sweeping statements, they usually did "think of something." Yes, and David was living proof of human resourcefulness—and the sheer will to survive. It might be only logical to trust both one more time.

In any event, Spock thought, looking out on the deadly waste before them, there was hardly a choice. Human wit and Vulcan logic were just about all that they had.

Will it be enough?

As David would say, he answered himself, *it will. It has to be.*

FOURTEEN

**Obsidian, Deep Desert
Day 3, First Week, Month of the Shining *Chara*,
Year 2296**

The good thing about a nightmare, McCoy thought, was that you got to wake up from it. Unfortunately, he was already wide awake and wished he weren't, so he could pinch himself, then go back to sleep.

Someone in the cave hurt. Someone was crying hopelessly, helplessly, and McCoy couldn't find him. Her. Whatever. He couldn't find his communicator either. Dammit, this "Master" and his pet fanatics had smashed his tricorder. They'd stolen his medical bag, and that traitor of a Vulcan—a paranoid schizophrenic, assuming McCoy could even apply that diagnosis to Vulcans—had offered it back to him as a bribe.

All he had to do was sell out his friends. Little thing like that, and he'd be allowed to treat the sick and dying here in what looked and smelled like one of those filthy hospital wards back in the Dark Ages on Earth before they learned about sanitation or anything else. Maybe if he threw his soul into the bargain, this pointy-eared false prophet would give him back his communicator, too.

What keeps you from trying, boy? he asked himself.

Simple. It was one thing to, well, bend the Prime Directive a bit. Hell, he and Jim had sprained it pretty severely a few times in the past! But if he betrayed folks now, he could very well be leading them right into a deadly trap. Even, Romulans and all that, a war.

His guts roiled. Ha, look, here came something edible at last, brought by a contemptuous-looking Romulan who all but hurled it at McCoy.

Lousy waiter, my friend. No tip for you.

The rations consisted of a watersack and some withered roots and the like, but at least it was food.

Yes, but there were others who needed it even more than he did. McCoy wisely took a good drink of the water—he wouldn't do anyone any good if he collapsed from dehydration—and munched on one of the roots—ditto for collapsing from starvation—then got to his feet.

"Here." With hand gestures, he urged the sick folks nearest him to take the rest of the rations, sharing the food and water out as far as he could.

A shadow loomed over him. McCoy, who'd been kneeling beside a moaning woman, trying to get her to drink, turned to find one of the Romulans standing over him: that young centurion, Ruanek, face carefully impassive, body language not quite threatening him.

Aside from his politics, he looks like a fairly decent fellow. And I already know he has a sense of humor. Too bad he has a madman as a commanding officer.

For a time, McCoy tried to ignore the centurion. But Ruanek was standing so close that at last the doctor turned and snapped, "Go right ahead and try."

The Master, madman or no, had to have taken him

prisoner for a reason, which meant, logically enough, that he would want to keep the captive in relatively undamaged condition. The centurion hesitated a moment, then shrugged and turned away: if McCoy wanted to starve himself, the gesture clearly said, it was his own stupidity.

Water dripped down the black rock somewhere in the distance. The sound was driving McCoy almost as crazy as his helplessness to aid these people. Clouds of dust rose from one corner: some idiot smoothing away at the cave wall. Some of it already shone, reflecting the cave's interior, doubling the number of sick and dying. That was hardly an improvement. At least, air was circulating somehow, which meant there was probably a way out, if he could only find it. As a Starfleet officer, he had an obligation to keep trying to escape. But as a physician, his obligation lay here. And without a communicator, he might as well just walk into the desert till it swallowed him, and he wasn't about to do that.

One of the fools hammering away at the rock broke off a huge chunk that crashed down. The slick black stone shattered. So did McCoy's temper.

"You all stop that right now, y'hear!" he shouted. "Some of these people already have pneumonia. Do you want to make it worse?" Might even be a new disease. Desert silicosis, he could call it when he wrote it up—assuming he ever got out of here.

One of the natives looked up at him, shrugged, then struggled up. The man wasn't just emaciated, McCoy realized. That was cachexia, as if he'd been wasting away for months. It was a wonder the poor man could stand, much less begin to undress—not that he had much on as it was. He peeled off all but a single undergarment and started toward what looked like an exit; leastways, that's what it had to be if armed men—Romulans—stood guarding it. McCoy could pick out each bone and individual tumor on the dying man's dark-tanned body. The metastases going on inside were probably beyond even a Starfleet medical center's facilities to treat.

When he almost toppled over at the third step, someone who merely looked like he was at death's hallway, not death's door, rose, too, and went over to him. Wedging what looked like the walking skeleton's left shoulder blade under his arm, he kept him going. The Romulan stood aside, one hand moving in a warding-off gesture.

For a blessed moment, McCoy could smell the clean, hot fragrance of the desert. He even welcomed his brief glimpse of Loki's light, poisonous as it was.

"Where's he going?" McCoy demanded. The only answer he got was a shrug. The nomads understood as much of his language as he did of theirs: none at all. He pointed and got another shrug. That wasn't a lack of understanding, McCoy realized. That was resignation. No one in the cave expected to see those two again, at least not in this life. What their Master told them about the next was another subject entirely. McCoy looked down at the pile of rags the man had left behind. Why, he'd even left his worn-out desert boots. Why'd he gone and done that?

The answer made him shiver. The dying man—and his companion—had up and gone out into the desert the way an old Eskimo used to go out onto an ice floe rather than squander his people's few precious resources on a useless mouth.

"Stop!" McCoy shouted and ran after the two men.

He decided almost immediately that he didn't *like* looking down into the business end of a laser rifle. Not. One. Bit.

He glared at the people carving away in the corner and shouted again. The pounding, grinding, and polishing stopped. After a while, it started up once more. If anything, the rock dust grew worse. Three or four people doubled over in paroxysms of coughing. One spat up blood. McCoy dodged his usual Romulan to try what sips of his own small water supply, shifts in position, a gentle voice—even speaking an unfamiliar language—might do to relieve the pain.

"It's contagious," he told the Romulan. "No cure. Especially not without my medical bag."

The Romulan grinned at him and walked away. He might know there wasn't even a myth that humans couldn't lie, but it seemed as if he didn't care.

Spock, McCoy called out silently. *Spock, where are you?* All those months he'd hosted Spock's *katra* had grown the bond between them. Even if he felt as dizzy as he had before the lexorin he'd taken to relieve the psychic burden had kicked in, he fought toward contact. He'd know, he reassured himself, if Spock were dead or dying. Dammit, if only he knew more, maybe he could use what remained of the link that had united them to contact Spock, and the hell with the damn communicator anyhow!

Stop cussing and calm down, he told himself. *You'll only wear yourself out.* In what felt like happier centuries ago, Spock would have steepled his hands and meditated while Jim paced and McCoy fumed. Then Jim would either have slugged or seduced someone and they'd get to break out and go back home.

God, how he wished he could! This time, McCoy didn't have the option. Or his captain. Or his favorite Vulcan.

Spock, you damn well better be all right.

Spock hadn't been himself long before Jim's death. He'd taken Lady Amanda's passing hard, harder than it looked on the surface, and McCoy knew he'd quarreled in that deadly silent, courteous Vulcan way with his father once again. Amanda had been the glue that held those two together.

McCoy had to admit that one reason he'd re-upped was to accompany Spock on the shakedown cruise on *Intrepid II.* With Jim . . . gone, Spock had no reason—logical or otherwise—to continue to refuse independent command; nevertheless, McCoy knew that the Vulcan fretted, in some deep recess of that incredibly brilliant, convoluted mind, about his ability to lead.

So, instead of a nice shakedown cruise, what would have to go and happen to Spock? A psychotic Vulcan and a planet at risk. Right on the edge of the Neutral Zone. If Spock failed, he not only lost the planet, he jeopardized the fragile entente between the Federation and Vulcan: not that the madman wasn't doing a perfectly wonderful job of that!

Spock needs me with him. All he's got is that Captain Rabin. Captain? He's a standup comic, not a captain!

In his mind's eye, he could see Spock raise an eyebrow at that. *Why, Doctor, I did not know you were a theater critic.*

He wasn't, of course. He was a doctor. And too good a psychiatrist not to know what else he was: angry. Oh, not at Rabin directly, and yet . . .

Dammit, there was just too much time to *think*. To analyze. McCoy admitted reluctantly that somehow, deep inside, he was feeling, stupidly, irrationally angry, that Spock was somehow betraying Jim's memory by reviving a friendship with another human friend.

Now isn't that a poison-mean nonsense? Just because Spock doesn't weep all over the place doesn't mean he can't feel grief. And just because he's glad to see someone from his childhood, it doesn't mean he's forgotten Jim.

McCoy sank down onto the floor beside one of his patients—ha! now that was a rotten joke—and sank his head in his hands.

Physician, heal thyself.

Hell of it was that he kind of liked Rabin's irreverent cheerfulness. Yes, and the man made one fine officer, too, wisecracking joker or no.

Ah well, McCoy thought wryly, at least he knew one thing. He'd finally found where Spock had learned how to reply, deadpan, to human jokes. Rabin must have been quite a friend, or Spock wouldn't have been so pleased—oh, the fellow could put on his best Vulcan face, but McCoy knew when he was happy—to see him. And he wouldn't have been so willing to accept other humans as friends.

It's not like any of us have much else, McCoy thought. He himself had joined Starfleet after his divorce as a way of stopping the hurt. *And what did gallivanting around the galaxy get me? Just more people to hurt about!* Jim had lost most of his family. Spock was estranged from his father, while Rabin, for all his talk of a mother, a home back on Earth, was as much a rolling stone as the rest of them.

And then Jim Kirk just had to leave them and go on all by himself. Leading the way, not that death was a place McCoy wanted to head out for any time soon. He dashed his hand over his eyes and dared anyone to notice.

"Communicator's got to be around here somewhere," he growled, taking his frustration out on the air. "Where'd it go?"

A tug on his sleeve made him whirl around so fast that the woman who'd tried to attract his attention gasped and backed away. Her hands went to her mouth, and McCoy saw the blotches that disfigured them.

"It's all right." He made his voice gentle and extended his open hands, trying to reassure her. "I won't hurt you."

She glanced over at the Romulan, who had been reinforced by one of his companions. Both of them stood turned away from McCoy; both seemed heartily bored.

She gestured at McCoy, then pointed at a small pallet against the wall.

"Is that your child?" he asked, still in that gentle, patient voice, pointing from the pallet to the woman and back again. "Yours?"

She nodded—that being one gesture his folks and hers seemed to have in common—then bowed three times. McCoy imitated the gesture, much to her shock. She must not be used to much respect. Giving a little gasp of relief, she led him to the child, so wrapped up even here against Loki's deadly sun that McCoy couldn't tell from looking whether it was a boy or a girl. Whatever: the child was feverish.

"Water," McCoy ordered. When the mother blinked at him, he pantomimed drinking. She scurried off. *Dammit, these people are parched, and it looks like I get to have all the water I want!* Well, the Romulans had never signed the New Geneva Conventions, and the Master certainly hadn't given McCoy a clue that he respected anything beside his own delusions.

The woman returned with a water bottle. McCoy looked about for a bowl or even a deep dish. Pulling the swathings off the child—a boy, after all—he used them to sponge the child and took the opportunity to examine him. Not a single blemish on him—at least not yet.

He held out his hand for the woman's, marred as it was by large moles, uneven in shape, of colors strange even among aliens. One had cracked and was bleeding. She let him bind it.

"Ought to get you to the outpost med center," he muttered. "I wish there were more I could do. You've still got a chance, but . . ."

She pulled her hand back. He pointed at it, then at her child's body, and shook his head: no blemishes. A wide smile spread over her drawn face.

There must be something else I can do! McCoy thought, continuing to inspect the child. His eyes were almost covered by black crawling things that McCoy cleaned tenderly away.

"Look," he said. "See these? Bad! Watch me wash them away." The woman nodded. "Next time they come back, you do it." She nodded again. McCoy hoped she'd gotten the message.

He looked down. Sure enough, there was the cause of the trouble—a swollen foot. McCoy held it up, despite the child's feeble kicks. The boy had stepped on something that had broken off and gotten the foot infected, for certain.

And me without my kit, McCoy thought, longing for his laser scalpels and antibiotics. Scalpels. That reminded him. Here he was on a planet called Obsidian: why, the place was *made* of scalpels! He picked up a rock shard, one of the thousands that lay underfoot, and tapped it against the wall until he achieved a sharp edge.

An unpleasant few moments later, the bit of thorn causing the trouble had been removed, the child's foot was purged of the blood and matter that had collected in it, and McCoy was tying off as clean a bandage as the child's mother had managed to scrounge for him. Tears poured down her face.

So. Hadn't done all that badly after all, had he? Here was one child who wouldn't die. At least, not this time. Not today.

McCoy let himself grin at the woman: another gesture his and her races had in common. He realized that his stomach had stopped aching for the first time since he'd been brought here.

He poured more water over his hands (that was precaution, not waste) and dried them on a rag—not one of the ones belonging to the man he'd seen walk into the sun, he hoped! The woman seized his hand, kissed it with her cracked lips, and then tugged as if beckoning him to follow her.

Because she had no reason to wish him ill—*Other than that no good deed goes unpunished, of course!* McCoy thought dryly—he followed. Maybe she knew of other people he could help, even with the crude tools he could improvise. Maybe he could get her to show him some of the local herbs; there had to be herbs somewhere on this benighted planet, and from there . . .

She darted over to the rock wall, then glanced fearfully at the Romulans. They were so used to fear they didn't even notice. *She's small, sick, no threat to them,* McCoy realized. *So she's a nonperson.*

Long practice had taught McCoy not to make any such dumb mistakes. Or assumptions of any kind, as the woman returned, something hidden in her hands. She smiled at him again, a mother about to present a child with what it wanted most, and showed him what she held—his communicator.

"Where'd you find this?" he demanded. She shook her head, her eyes fearful. *Better not push too far,* he warned himself. But it was difficult to stay calm. He gave her the triple bow that meant respect. He would have given her the world if he'd had title to it. His communicator! Why, he was halfway home already!

Concealing the precious gift, he retreated to a distant corner of the cave. He even reassured the Romulans from a distance by eating, genuinely hungry and thirsty for the first time in days. Then, he curled up, his back to his guards, against a nice, cozy boulder as if he were sleepy.

The Romulans nodded at each other and knelt, occupied by something on the bare rock of the cave's floor. *Probably shooting craps,* McCoy thought. He knew damn well they weren't playing fizzbin.

When he was certain they were totally distracted, he pulled out the communicator.

"McCoy to *Intrepid,*" he whispered into it. "McCoy to *Intrepid.* Come in, Uhura. Come in!"

Only the frying-bacon sound of heavy static replied. Hastily, McCoy turned down the volume. That had to be a sound the Romulans would recognize. He'd been stupid. Uhura had probably shifted course for safety to put the planet between the ship and Loki. He could try to raise the ship until his communicator's duotronic circuits rusted and not hear a peep. Besides, he realized from the intensity of the static that the ionization was still too strong for *Intrepid* to beam anyone up or down without scattering his atoms all over the star system.

So much for the ship.

McCoy shut his eyes, reaching within as he'd learned how in the days he carried Spock's *katra* in his own consciousness. *Spock, are you there?*

He could gain only what he had before: Spock wasn't dead.

Sighing, McCoy again risked activating his communicator. "Spock . . . McCoy to Spock . . . are you there, Spock?"

More static, but alarmingly faint this time.

No, oh no. The power can't be fading. The circuits can't be scrambled or—or whatever else it is could go wrong with these things. McCoy quickly shut it off, glared at it helplessly, wishing he'd had more than basic training in communicator maintenance. But no, why would a doctor need a more intensive course? *Besides, it's not as though I could get spare parts around here.*

Defiantly, McCoy activated the communitor again, trying to ignore the alarmingly faint crackling. No use conserving power. for all he knew, energy would keep draining even if the communicator *wasn't* on. He'd try again, and keep trying. And if the power died, well, at least he'd go down fighting!

FIFTEEN

David, a half-unwrapped ration bar in one hand, glanced uneasily around the Womb of Fire. Spock and he had taken temporary sanctuary in one of the few spots that did not seem actively dangerous, although that meant that they were still surrounded by waves of heat and pools of bubbling water.

"Are you sure this place isn't radioactive?" he asked yet again. "It really does look like someone nuked it—maybe not long enough ago."

"The temperature here is not abnormal for Vulcan," Spock assured him patiently, "and we have had no nuclear wars nor major nuclear accidents. This is nothing more than a typically volcanic terrain."

"Typical in hell, maybe," David muttered.

Ignoring what was clearly an emotional reference to human religion, Spock scanned the crazed, cinder-covered ground, plotting their next move. As with the rest of the Womb of Fire, nothing grew here but the bright green hallucinogenic lichen and the bright yellow crusts of sulfur, garish against the black rock and gray cinders. Tiny plumes of steam puffed steadily up from the maze of fumaroles, warning of the even greater heat not far below the surface.

Without warning, those plumes wavered and the earth began to shake. A rumbling growl filled the air.

"Volcano!" David yelped, and fumbled the ration bar, which went flying.

"Geyser!" Spock snapped. "Get down!"

Not ten meters from them, an immense geyser spurted out of the blasted land, spraying them with hot, salty water. Spock dropped instantly, covering his hands and face. His desert gear should protect the rest of him from the live steam.

Nothing, however, could protect the ration bar, which sailed right into a shallow, steaming pool. David, peeking out from behind interlaced hands, muttered something in a language that Spock was certain was not Terran standard.

"There goes dinner, such as it was. Spock, if I poisoned your well, I'm sorry."

The geyser slowly subsided. Spock uncurled and peered warily over the edge of the pool. "It is not too deep. We can still retrieve the bar."

"And save the local ecology. Do you still have that collapsing rod?"

Spock passed it over. David extended the rod, then bound it to a pair of pincers also salvaged from the wrecked shuttle's emergency gear and dunked his makeshift device into the water, fishing about till he had hooked the ration bar and pulled it out.

"Would you look at this? The thing hasn't even started to dissolve!" David snorted. "Not that I'm surprised. I wonder if parboiling improves the taste." He waved the bar about to

cool it, then saluted Spock with it. "What I do for science."
Biting into the bar, he grimaced.

"Does that taste 'just like chicken,' too?" Spock asked
without any inflection at all.

"Ha. And ha again. And they say Vulcans have no sense of
humor. And no, to satisfy your curiosity, nothing helps this
stuff."

David resolutely gnawed his way through the rest of his
unpalatable meal. "I don't have to remind you this is almost
the last of our rations. Either we add food to the growing
checklist of things to steal from Sered, or we'll both be
considerably hungrier before long. If we survive."

Spock knew that this was not merely human hyperbole.
The Womb, contrary to its name, was so infertile a region
that only the lichen could thrive. "We must continue. It will
not grow more pleasant for the delay."

David and he edged past a roiling pool that reeked of
sulfur and past a vent that belched fumes so vile it doubled
David over gagging and Spock came close to coughing
himself hoarse. The boys staggered away until they could
sink down, hidden by a cluster of rocks like rotted fangs
covered by a colorful white and yellow coating of dried salts.

"'In the land of Mordor,'" David muttered. "If they
could make it, so can I."

Spock raised an eyebrow, but did not question further.
This was clearly yet another in David's never-ending string
of literary or motion-picture quotes, and if obscure references helped the human, then obscure references were
welcome. He lay flat, glad for the rest, grateful that the fitful
play of fire and steam would camouflage their bodies' heat
from any infrared sensors. Ahead, he could see the top of
Sered's fortress, the small, partially collapsed caldera,
roofed over with its own crumbled rock. A fortress—and yet
Spock remembered from his escape how riddled it was with
vents and lava tubes. Not an adequate fortress at all—more

proof, if any were needed, of Sered's madness. Climbers skilled and foolhardy enough could slip into it and retreat without being noticed.

"Perhaps the hostages are not in quite as great discomfort as we anticipated," he said. "There are enough openings to provide adequate air circulation."

"*This* air's hardly worth circulating," David said. "Stinks of sulfur and who knows what else."

"Yes . . . but air shafts can carry information as well."

"Hey, right! All we have to do is find the way we got out, or some other way in."

"I strongly doubt it will be quite that simple. If we separate," Spock began, "we can cover twice as much ground and double our chances of finding a vantage point. However—"

"What if you fall and break a leg?" David asked.

Spock started to remind the human just who it was had fallen, had to have a thorn cut out, and soaked his rations in scalding water—no. Instead, he contented himself with a more controlled, "That is precisely the point I was about to make. The land is too perilous. Particularly," he couldn't resist adding, "for an outsider. We must stay together. Besides, I will welcome your expertise with a sling."

What David called "all night later" but Spock knew was actually 6.235 hours Terran standard, the two boys had slid, clambered, or climbed over what felt, even to Spock, like half of the Womb of Fire. They had found plenty of openings down into the fortress, but none that led to any area they remembered or weren't outright dead ends.

Slumping on the rocks, the boys drank sparingly from their half-empty water bottles. One could fast a great deal longer than one could remain thirsty.

"We can wait no longer," Spock said at last.

"No, I guess not."

David got wearily to his feet, swaying a little. Spock

reached out to steady him, but the human suddenly tensed. "Do you hear that?"

Spock tilted his head. His hearing was more sensitive than David's, yet the human clearly was listening to something that he had heard and Spock had not.

Fascinating.

"That's my mother," David whispered, his eyes glowing. "I'd know her voice anywhere!" Eagerly, he started forward.

This was going beyond fascinating to astonishing. Humans were not supposed to possess the talents of the Adepts of Gol. Was David hallucinating?

Or . . . am I? Spock glanced down at the rocks and their coating of lichen. Crushing the lichen—and possibly merely stepping on it might constitute crushing—could produce nausea, even vertigo in a Vulcan. He had not told David all: Ingesting it or breathing the fumes caused by its burning not only created hallucinations, it sometimes deranged the victim.

Permanently.

David! The human had nearly reached a vent in the rocks, and Spock hurried forward to block his path. "Careful! The rocks are coated with that lichen of yours"

David grimaced. His hands were covered with not yet healed cuts and scrapes, an ideal situation for infection. "I don't think I've touched any. If I have, it doesn't seem to work on humans. Besides," he added hotly, "right now I don't care. I have to hear what's going on down there."

"If you can hear them, they can hear you."

"I *want* Mother to hear me, let her know I'm alive and well. I have to see, Spock. I just have to." David's voice was rising alarmingly. "What if it were your mother?"

"Let me go first," Spock said in surrender. "I move more quietly. And my hands are less scratched than yours."

David's mouth opened on a protest, then shut again. Was this Starfleet discipline? If it could force the irrepressible human to control himself, it had much to recommend it. "Go on," David whispered.

Careful not to touch any lichen, Spock crawled forward into what turned out to be a rock tunnel wide enough for even an adult. It dropped off precariously, and he whispered back over his shoulder, "Secure me."

David clasped his ankles. Did the human have sufficient strength to hold him if he slipped? Illogical, Spock told himself, to worry about what could not be helped. As he stretched himself down carefully, heat washed his face, growing ever stronger. Ahead, a flaring, uncertain reddish light was reflected in the slick stone surface. A fire? Spock strained out over the lip of the rock to see—then recoiled in shock, nearly banging his head against the side of the tunnel, and scrambled back up with David's help.

"Fortunate," Spock panted. "Fortunate you did not slide down that chute. You would have landed right in a very active pool of lava."

"Great," David groaned. "Did you see my mother anywhere nearby?"

"It is difficult to see or hear when lava is bubbling below you," Spock pointed out. "We must try another spot."

He rose, trying not to look as tired and stiff as he felt. Pain was only pain. He could, Spock told himself, master it. They moved perhaps ten meters, David pausing to listen at every promising crack or crater.

Spock hissed a sudden warning. "I hear them." Ignoring David's small sigh of relief, he investigated the new lava tube. "Less steep," he whispered up to David, "less slippery, and wide enough for both of us."

David wriggled down next to him. "That's my mother," the human whispered anxiously. "She sounds so hoarse! And she's coughing—Spock, we have to do something *now.*"

The two boys crept down the tube as far as they could, then lay flat, staring out and down. The lava pool was to the left, seething and bubbling restlessly, the air above it wavering with heat. By the pool stood a circular, rough-hewn stone altar, half-coated by hardened splashes of lava that didn't quite hide the worn carvings, sigils that made Spock gasp at their antiquity: they must date from centuries before the time of Surak. Crystals set into the stone gleamed a sullen red, reflecting the lava pool. On the altar, adding incense to the injury of burning sulfur, stood ancient bronze braziers with flanged handles, incised with glyphs too worn to be deciphered.

Then a figure stepped to the altar, and the ancient altar and even the seething, steaming lava pool faded from importance. This was Sered: a much-changed Sered. No longer was he the quiet scholar or the daring warrior. Now his robe shone crimson and bronze, embossed with metallic sigils. About his waist hung a heavy, jewel-encrusted belt supporting an energy weapon with a gem-bright hilt and an ancient steel knife, its curved blade marked with the ripples of water, folded and refolded a million times. In the ancient, terrible days of Vulcan history, such blades were neither drawn nor sheathed without a sacrifice.

Is there blood on this blade? Sered's blood? Or human?

As Sered moved, gems gleamed on a massive pectoral, and the sigils on his robe reflected the lava's uneasy fire. Spock struggled to read them. "Mastership of a Great House": that was easy enough to translate, but that other, with the infix that signified sacral mode?

Priest and king. A little shiver raced up Spock's spine as he realized what he saw. Save for the headdress, which presumably he would don later, Sered had dressed himself as befitted one of the ancient rulers of the te-Vikram caves.

Why? They were one of the most warlike and unstable of Vulcan cultures! If we had not turned to Surak's teachings, they would have done their best to destroy Vulcan.

David whispered, "Who's his tailor? And what's all that fancy stuff mean?"

The human's voice was almost cracking with the effort to remain light, flippant, even. His glance kept darting back to his mother, who now knelt beside the children lying against the wall. One coughed feebly. Two more simply lay there, their chests heaving as they fought for breath in the thin, noisome air.

Spock said softly, "He wears the robe of an ancient priest-king of a particularly warlike culture. I think you would call their spiritual leaders ecstatics. They drugged themselves, then went out and performed . . . certain crimes, claiming that they had been . . . guided."

"Hashashiyun," David whispered. "Our very own Vulcan-style Old Man of the Mountain. We couldn't have gotten into worse trouble if we'd planned it."

"Look at the altar."

"What? Chinesey-looking braziers, and . . . ha, that looks like a Mark Eight tricorder. Communicators. And someone's torn-up medical kit—hey, that's tri-ox compound!"

"Evidently this is part of the offworld 'pollution' Sered wants removed from Vulcan."

"Damn him," David hissed. "All that tri-ox compound just lying there doing no one any good. Doesn't he know this air could kill someone? Can't he hear those coughs? Even if Sered thinks this is war, there are still conventions governing prisoners! Doesn't he know that?"

Spock hesitated, trying to find the way to say what he must. "If he truly believes himself a te-Vikram priest-king, he may not think them prisoners, but . . . sacrifices."

David drew his breath in sharply. "No," he said softly to Sered, his voice cold and hard. "Oh no, you don't."

He started blindly down the tube. Spock caught him just in time, holding the human with all his Vulcan strength. "David, wait. Listen."

"That madman has nothing I wish to hear."

"Are our lives worth nothing? Are the captain's words worth nothing? Listen!"

"Your captives are ill," Captain Nechama Rabin was saying to Sered, as if continuing a conversation that had been interrupted only moments ago. "You have not taken proper care of us. Some of us are sick."

"Those are weaklings," Sered returned, "unfit for rebirth from the Womb of Fire. None but the strong, the masters, must survive."

David *growled*. Spock saw Captain Rabin's face go rigid. "That has been said before," she told Sered with cold precision, "by people who thought themselves a Master Race. People who nevertheless fell and whose memory is still accursed."

"It is nonetheless true."

"Is it? Is it true, no, is it *right* that the strong do what they will, while the weak suffer what they must? Have you discarded Surak's morality along with his logic?"

Sered never moved. "It is the way of the Womb of Fire. One must value what is. All else is illusion."

"Then let us treat this . . . illusion as valid," the captain countered. "Let us say your way is truth. That you are the thing whose guise you wear. You seek the expulsion of offworlders and our ways from your world. How? Do you need a hostage to exchange?"

"I have many prisoners, and it may be that I shall not choose to exchange them."

"What, then? Are you going all the way back to the Bad Old Days? Ah, that's just what you're thinking, isn't it? Well, then, if you seek a sacrifice, who will serve you best? Those"—Captain Rabin gestured at the sickly hostages—"or one who is strong and gives herself of her own free will?"

"No," David gasped. "God, no!"

"David, quiet!" Spock whispered fiercely.

Fortunately, Sered, lost in his own world, did not seem to hear either of them. "What logic do you see in suicide?"

Captain Rabin studied him with cool contempt. "Is it not truly said that the needs of the many outweigh the needs of the few? Or of the one?"

"And you offer that as a reason for me to release so many weaklings?"

"Not an offer. A demand."

A fit of coughing cut into her words, racking her body, and Sered . . . laughed, a cold, eerie sound. "How do you presume to demand anything? There is no logic in negotiating from a point of weakness."

Captain Rabin straightened slowly, face drawn but eyes blazing. "I trained to serve and to endure. It is my purpose to make that demand. It is my right. I do not bargain from weakness, but from my sense of purpose—and therefore from my greatest strength."

"Mother . . . no," David whispered, only Spock's grip keeping him from rushing down to her.

Sered studied the woman for a silent moment. "I must concede that you are a warrior born and trained," he observed at last. "But as a warrior, you must understand that it would be imprudent for me to release hostages able to reveal the location of the fortress from which . . ." Sered broke off.

"From which?" Captain Rabin prompted. Her voice was breathy; clearly she was having trouble putting enough air behind it. "The fortress from which you will betray your own people? From which you will lay waste a planet that has known nothing but peace for thousands of years? And you regard sick *children* as security risks?"

Sered lowered his hand to the blade at his belt. "That peace," he said the word bitterly, "has weakened Vulcan. It is time and past time to restore our heritage of battle, the beauty of blades quenched in blood, the blaze of energy that consumes a rival power, the oath of kinship renewed with those from whom this world has too long held itself aloof— too long held itself aloof from victory!"

David gestured at his temple. Spock understood easily enough. The human was right: Sered had deteriorated into total, hopeless madness.

Incongruously, David's stomach took this moment to rumble. Could Sered hear *that?* The human glanced wildly at Spock, biting his lip against laughter that could all too easily burst free and kill them both.

Hastily, both boys scrambled back up out of the tube. David collapsed in a fit of giggles, frantically trying to stop. "I wish I *could* eat that lichen!" he gasped. "Get *something* in my stomach, stop its complaining. The thought of being betrayed by my own stupid innards!" He sat up. "Maybe the lichens wouldn't hit me as hard because I'm human. What do you think? Worth a chance?"

Spock stared at him. "What do I think, David? I think you may have just saved your mother's life and those of the others. Quick, help me scrape up as much of the lichen as we can. Be careful not to crush it! And do not let any touch any open cuts."

It was a delicate, dangerous job, made worse because they both were trying to hurry. "Now what?" David asked.

Spock gestured. "That vent. The one over the lava pool. No, wait, this one is more level. It still will overlook the pool without threatening to pitch us in."

They hurried down the vent. David's mother, caught in a fit of coughing, straightened just in time to glance up and spot them. Her eyes widened, but she continued hastily, covering for the boys, "You others—the ones this renegade calls 'cousins'—you seem to be warriors as well, bred to arms and to honor. Does that honor demand warfare against sick children?"

"When they are hostages for their rulers' word," one of the strangers said uneasily. Another shook his head.

"You seem to have some doubts . . ." Coughs exploded from her, and she bent double.

"Mother could keep this up for hours," David whispered, "if she could only breathe!"

"We should have tri-ox for her in the next few moments." *Either that,* Spock thought, *or we shall be in worse trouble than we are already.* "Drop the lichen!"

"Releasing photon torpedoes," David muttered.

They hurled the lichen down the rocky tube—right into the lava pit. A cloud of incinerated dust swirled up, a wild, sickly green haze, caught in the draughts of hot air, dizzying, dangerous.

And in that moment, Spock, feeling the edge of the hallucinogenic peril, knew with an eerie, not quite drugged certainty that all reality was about to be destroyed.

SIXTEEN

Obsidian, Deep Desert
Day 4, First Week, Month of the Shining *Chara*,
Year 2296

It was cool in the rock shelter, a touch too cool for Vulcan tastes, though Spock refused to acknowledge anything as petty as mild discomfort. Outside, the nomads were quickly and efficiently setting up camp. Their tents were ingenious, he thought, both quickly assembled and lightweight for easy transport: over a framework of springy poles of precious wood went coverings of woven *chuchaki* hair, dyed the exact brownish tan of the desert floor. A flap of hide formed a door, another flap in the arched hide roof could be pulled aside to form a smoke hole, and the coverings could be raised during the day's heat to let air circulate or lowered during the night's chill to hold in warmth.

Quite ingenious, indeed.

The tents were laid out with what seemed a casual lack of organization but, judging from the way no one got in anyone else's way, was probably a planned arrangement of family groupings. The entire encampment, uniform desert-color as all the tents were, would be virtually invisible to outsiders.

Or, Spock suspected, seeing hands never straying too far from weapons, to rival clans.

It would be interesting to investigate the camp, he decided, to see what further adaptations these people had made to their environment. But until the nomads actually offered an invitation, logic insisted that he and Rabin stay where they had been directed. Logical, too, for the nomads to put them here; not only was the cool shelter a compliment to the two unexpected "guests," its solid walls were also a casual way of insuring that those "guests" could not wander away.

Fair enough. Ignoring Rabin, who was pacing about uneasily, Spock turned to study the pictographs painted on the rock shelter's walls: they were of some natural red pigment, ocher, perhaps, outlined with charcoal. The repeated designs were almost certainly sun spirals, the same symbols used by many sentient desert peoples; with each spiral were lines that looked very much like warding-off signs. He had been correct, then. This deep, thick-walled cave was one of the emergency shelters used by the nomads to protect themselves from minor solar flares. They must have some deeper shelters for the more perilous flares.

"Low-tech," after all, does not necessarily mean low intelligence.

The faintest of whispers alerted him. He turned to find himself confronted by a solemn, wide-eyed line of nomad children, boys and girls together. They were, he guessed from their gawkiness and lack of adult proportionings, still somewhere in preadolescence, dark-haired and olive-skinned like their parents. All were a little too thin, perhaps, for youngsters their age—these were, after all, the children of desert hardship—but they showed no signs of illnesses and were scruffy not from neglect but in the way of healthy, active youngsters everywhere.

They were also . . . *Neoteny,* Spock told himself, *is merely a species' logical way of insuring its continuance.* But his mind added in McCoy's voice, *Go ahead, Spock, admit it: They're cute.*

He was obviously meant to say something. "Greetings," Spock began tentatively.

No answer. The children continued to watch him in solemn wonder.

Of course I intrigue them. The young of all sentient species are curious. And I can hardly resemble anyone these young ones have ever seen.

Since he had no idea what else was expected of him, Spock nodded to his audience with equal solemnity and raised his hand in the split-fingered Vulcan salute.

Aha, this seemed to be the right course of action. The children tried to imitate him, bursting into giggles when their small hands wouldn't hold the proper finger positions. Spock kept his face properly impassive, but the smallest spark of enjoyment flicked within him at their cheerfulness. The children kept glancing from their hands to him, grinning openly at him by now, some of them, like human or Vulcan children, showing gaps where milk teeth had fallen away and adult teeth not yet grown.

"No doubt about it," Rabin murmured in amusement from behind him, "you're a hit."

Spock bit back a reflexive *but I have not struck anyone,* recognizing the idiom just in time. And it did seem to be accurate. The children had clearly accepted him as a friend, a fact that he found rather pleasant. Not an illogical reaction, he told himself, not at all. On the contrary, it was quite logical to be pleased that a younger generation of rational beings should be in such good mental and physical shape despite their harsh surroundings.

"It is also a good sign that the nomads trust their children near us. And that they *have* children with them."

"You got it. Not a raiding party, then, with warriors with quick trigger fingers, just a clan hunting fresh pasture or whatever it is nomads like this need."

The children were growing impatient. They didn't want these amusing strangers to ignore them! One boy daringly darted forward to tug at Spock's robe, chattering something about "Again, do it again."

Without warning, Spock's communicator beeped. The boy yelped in alarm, and he and the other children scattered like so many frightened wild things. Even Captain Rabin started, stammering, "What—who—"

But Spock was already thumbing the communicator open. He and Rabin exchanged quick glances, the human with hope beaming on his face, Spock refusing to allow himself more than a raised eyebrow. They heard a faint whisper: McCoy!

"Spock . . . are you there?"

"Dr. McCoy, yes. It is Spock."

"Well, thank God for that! You okay?"

"Quite. What of you, Doctor? Your signal is faint. Are you injured?"

"Only in my pride. And in this blasted communicator, which is losing power rapidly." A pause, and then, voice not quite steady, "We've got a lot of injured people here."

"Do you know where 'here' is, Doctor?"

The faintest of sighs. "Good question. Can't give you any definite coordinates, but I'm in some blasted big cavern with the most incredible metal doors, huge things, barring it from the outside." A pause, as though McCoy was trying to boost the communicator's power. "The cavern's linked by what looks like a network of shiny black lava tubes, so it's got to be somewhere in the mountains. They got me here without using any transporter, and it's been . . . mmm . . . I *think* only a couple of days, so whatever mountains they are can't be too far from where we crashed."

"The Taragi-shar. They are the nearest igneous range."

"Maybe. I haven't exactly had a chance to do any sight-seeing."

There was a sudden long silence. McCoy, Spock thought, must be hiding his transmission from some passerby, probably a guard, and waited patiently for the doctor to continue.

At last McCoy said, very softly, "Can't talk much longer. Too many eavesdroppers. And the damn communicator's almost dead. Listen, Spock, I'm stuck in the middle of some fanatical group that calls itself the Faithful. They're locals. But the big boys, the guys with the guns, are definitely Romulans."

"Romulans," Spock echoed thoughtfully. There had been the mystery of the spy calling him the Fiery One . . . yes. Romulan Intelligence would certainly have placed him on the planet.

"Yeah, I know," McCoy continued, *not* good. But there's worse. Their leader . . . well, brace yourself, Spock. The leader is a Vulcan."

"A Vulcan!" That was Rabin, listening over Spock's shoulder. "You're sure?"

"That has got to be Captain Rabin's voice." Sarcasm dripped from McCoy's own. "Think I can't recognize a Vulcan after all these years of serving with one, Captain? Mind you, this guy, whoever he is, isn't young, but he's straight-backed and haughty as they come. Crazy as they come, too, in flowing white robes like something out of ancient Vulcan history. Coldest eyes I've ever seen on anyone, Vulcan or human. Calls himself only the Master."

"Spock," Rabin said in alarm, "do you know who that sounds like? Our old friend Sered!"

Spock glanced over his shoulder at the human, not quite

frowning. "The odds are greatly against that. In fact, I would estimate them at—"

"I haven't got time for a lecture on statistics!" McCoy snapped. "Listen, I can't prove it, I never saw the man before, but I'd take a good guess that he—damn! Company's coming. Have to sign off. Ignore any other word from me; never know if they might force me to talk. If they can get this cursed thing to work."

"Be careful, Bones," Spock heard himself say, rather to his suprise, in Kirk's tone of voice.

"Now he tells me!" McCoy retorted, and broke off communications.

Rabin straightened, then scrambled to his feet. "Uh-oh. Here comes a committee. Looks like I'm wanted out there. The Master or whoever he is will have to wait."

Spock followed, still mulling over the question of the mysterious Vulcan. But as Rabin said, that matter would have to wait. He watched, curious, as the human, surrounded by the nomads, debated with them.

Or at least Spock assumed this was merely a debate. If so, it was one that sounded only a shade less excited than an argument and that seemed to require a great deal of gesturing on all sides and exchanges so rapid that Spock's translator could barely keep pace.

David told me once that when his people grow excited while debating, their words and gestures accelerate. It would seem true of the nomads as well.

One of the nomads was drawing back, deliberately breaking off the rapid-fire debate, and saying with casual contempt, "You would compare us to *them?* The people of the city, the Tamed Ones trapped behind their own walls? *Tchah,* they lack the sense to come in out of the sun!"

"Worse," another nomad added, "they have isolated themselves from the true desert, the desert which brings wisdom."

"As my people have not," Rabin retorted, and suddenly his mobile face was quite serious. "On both our worlds we have kept the desert; on both our worlds we know that it brings revelations."

That struck home. The nomads drew back in what could only be surprised respect, and Spock heard one murmur, "Perhaps he is not a Kindly Fool, not a Fool, at that."

Rabin glanced at Spock, saying clearly without words: *Help me out here; I'm out of my league.* Spock moved quietly to the human's side, adding, "On my world, as well, we keep the desert. And we, too, respect it and know of similar revelations. But it would seem," he continued with Vulcan calm, "that there are some within your land who have chosen to follow a most unusual path to enlightenment."

"The Faithful!" someone muttered, and the others stirred uneasily.

"The Faithful," Spock agreed. "So we have heard them named. It is of those people we would speak."

But suddenly the nomads were murmuring among themselves, all out of proportion to what he'd said. They stepped reverentially aside to let a small, slender, hooded figure pass.

So-o. I was wondering when we would meet their leader.

The figure's robes were solid tan, totally without adornment, but Spock heard the faintest jingling of ornaments. Judging from the obvious respect the others were showing, these were probably amulets or religious objects.

The nomad stopped before Spock and Rabin, and an aged hand pushed back its hood slightly. Spock felt a sharp, irrational pang stab through him at the face revealed, and a quick, equally irrational thought of *T'Pau.*

No. Illogical. Control. Of course this wasn't the long-deceased Vulcan elder. But the sudden shock of memory was understandable, since this small woman bore a good deal of the same quiet pride, the same calm authority and dignity. Wisdom and a hint of cynical wit shone in her ancient face and dark eyes.

A leader, indeed. But T'Pau had turned down a seat on the Federation Council after the massacre on Mount Seleya: *"We keep ourselves to ourselves,"* as McCoy had voiced it. *Will this leader, too, turn from the Federation—but take her people with her?*

Spock bowed in respect and felt the woman's hand, light as a leaf, touch his head in brief blessing. He straightened, aware of Rabin glancing sharply from him to her and back again. The human, no fool, bowed and was blessed in turn. Then the woman said, her voice not old at all, "I am the Elder of the White Stone Clan of the Benak Haran. You," her gesture took in Rabin, "are the outlander known to us as the Kindly Fool."

"So I've learned," he said wryly. "My . . . uh . . . clan name is Rabin, Elder, and my . . . uh . . . use name is David."

"So. And you, O outlander who is quite clearly from far distant realms?"

Spock straightened. "I am Spock of Vulcan, son of Sarek and Amanda, and now Captain Spock of Federation Starfleet. I regret that I have no clan name to offer you; such subdivisions are no longer my people's custom."

How much of that was translated correctly, with the proper nuances, was uncertain. The Elder's lined face revealed nothing, but her eyes widened ever so slightly. "Yet you know the proper ways of respect."

"Wisdom is always to be respected."

"So," the Elder said again. "This is a good thing." She turned in a swirl of robes. "Come, you of no clan and you of Clan Rabin. We must, I think, talk together."

She led them straight into the center of the encampment, a cleared circle ringed by tents. At her wordless gesture, nomads hurried to erect a *chuckaki*-hair canopy, unroll a carpet under it, place cushions upon the carpet. The Elder sat with careful dignity, robes gracefully arranged about her, then gestured for Spock and Rabin to sit as well. Beyond, squatting with casual ease, was a ring of nomads.

A nervous girl brought water. Once more, the intricate water ritual was carried out. No one spoke until the girl had scurried off into one of the tents. And then the Elder said calmly, "Why are you here?"

It was directed at Rabin. He hesitated a thoughtful moment, then told her, "Why we have come into the deep desert is a matter resting on the backs of other matters. Why we have come to the desert at all . . ."

"Why?" she insisted, face as tranquil as that of a Vulcan.

"Elder, we have come to help. My people, the Federation, that is, we are a union of many peoples. As you can guess, that has not been an easy achievement."

"Impossible," a man muttered, then fell silent at the Elder's autocratic wave.

"Not impossible," Rabin countered. "Yes, we've had our problems, yes, we always will. All sentient beings do. But one thing we learned over the years is that there's no reason to hate someone else just because that someone else doesn't look like you or follow your customs. When that someone is in trouble, the only right thing to do is help."

"Yes," the Elder said. "I know that you have been doing all you can." The faintest hint of amusement tinged the calm voice, as though she were speaking to a child trying to be an adult. "But you," she added, glancing at Spock, "why are *you* here? You, too, are of this same 'Federation,' yes?"

"Indeed, Elder. Elder, I shall not speak of what has already been attempted. I suspect you know perfectly well of those attempts and failures that have befallen the Federation mission this far."

"The affairs of the Tamed Ones behind their city walls do

not concern us. The Kindly Fool means well, but his efforts have not been enough. My people have been speaking with . . . other friends."

"Indeed? Might I ask which?"

"They look like you!" someone blurted.

Both Vulcan and human eyebrows shot up. These "friends" could hardly be Vulcans; other than the rare exceptions such as Sered and this unknown Master, Vulcans did not behave in such illogical, militaristic fashion.

"Romulans," Rabin whispered. "Has to be. McCoy was right."

And what of the Master? Spock seized upon the scanty data, quickly analyzed it.

Fact: McCoy was experienced enough to tell the two races apart. And his description had been quite distinct.

Fact, therefore: The Master could only be a Vulcan. His identity could not yet be proven: insufficient data.

Fact: The Romulans would not have all disavowed loyalty to their homeworld to follow a Vulcan leader. They were here, therefore, on orders. And from that followed, logically, that the Master, whether he realized it or not, could only be one thing: a Romulan puppet.

They would seem to have decided they want this world.

But Spock could not hope to explain that offworld peril to nomads who knew only the desert and referred to anyone else as either Tamed Ones or outlanders. Instead, with a warning glance at Rabin, he asked calmly, "What promises have your friends made to you?"

His totally unemotional approach seemed to impress the nomads more than any hyperbole. The Elder sat back on her cushions, face impassive, signaling them to speak freely, watching as they answered the expected:

"Sweet water."

"Strong children."

"Abundant food."

"I find this fascinating," Spock noted, and meant it. "Have you not already received such things from the Federation? Have you not learned to create them for yourselves?"

There were some stirrings, some uneasy mutterings, and Spock continued, relentlessly calm, "Have the men and women of the Federation not shown you how to build better shelters?" He quickly altered the next logical step, that of planting sturdier crops; nomads who frowned on cities as traps would hardly be interested in agriculture. "How to grow sturdier *chuchaki* and find better pasture for them? Have they not shown you the ways of healing your children from the sun's evil?"

"They've begun . . ." a woman said hesitantly.

It was what Spock had been waiting to hear. With the air of a true scientist, he countered, "Then is it wise to tamper with something so well begun?"

"Clever," the Elder murmured, but said no more.

"When the Romulans make promises," Spock asked the by-now-sizable crowd, "how do they make you feel? Are you hopeful or afraid? Do you feel they can be truly trusted?"

Now the mutterings were definitely doubtful. *Excellent,* Spock thought, and pressed the advantage. "Is there honesty behind their bargaining? Or is there, perhaps, a threat?" The mutterings grew to a roar. Spock held up both hands, the smooth, elegant movement after his calm stillness deliberately calculated. The crowd fell silent, and he continued into the sudden quiet, a scientist merely stating facts: "The Romulans. The Federation. Promises. Threats. Which? I invite you to investigate the possibilities."

Enough. He sat back to let the nomads decide, watching them arguing with each other, very well aware that his words had sparked the storm.

So this was the sense of mastery that his father felt in negotiations. Fascinating. Decidedly fascinating.

But "fascinating," Spock reminded himself, was not the same as "successful," while pride was a most insidious, most perilous emotion, one that even humans listed as a "deadly sin." And at any rate, there was still the Elder and *her* decision to be considered.

I have done what I can, Spock told himself. *Now all there is to do is: simply wait.*

SEVENTEEN

**Vulcan, The Womb of Fire
Day 6, Eighth Week of Tasmeen,
Year 2247**

Spock drew the last breaths he feared he might ever draw as a rational entity.

Fear, Spock? Where is your control?

Quiet, Father. He had longed to say that all his life.

The fumes released by the burning lichen rasped down his throat and seeped into his lungs. He imagined he could see fire roiling in the fumes. They were fire. His eyes were fire. If he opened his mouth to shout, his words would be fire.

Control, Spock. He choked off his memory of his father's usual rebuke, reminding himself as best he could, *You are Amanda's son, not just Sarek's. Trust your human heritage.*

Sudden wild coughing and shouts erupted from below; the fumes were working!

"Everybody down! Cover your noses and mouths!"

That was—David's mother's—Captain Rabin's hoarse shout. Spock could not see her or Sered or anything but the

200

roiling fumes from the hallucinogenic lichen. The humans should survive this. Perhaps the most severely affected would black out; unconscious, one's oxygen consumption decreased, did it not? He could not quite seem to remember . . ..

"Come on, Spock!" David rasped, eyes fierce above his improvised filter of cloth doused in some of their precious water. "Come *on!*"

Yes . . . David would have to be his guide, the control in this . . . this experiment in applied pharmacology. That very logical thought almost made him giggle.

Giggle?

Odd. As the fumes thickened, he found himself actually *afraid,* not just of the action, but of the hallucinogenic fumes. Fear and laughter were human things. Maybe his human side really would protect his reason.

"To me, my brothers!" That was surely Sered's voice, screaming in Old High Vulcan. (A Vulcan, screaming? The lichen really must be working.) "We will seize their wells and hold them against all the nations!"

"To the fires!" his followers roared. "The sword, the forge!"

This savage response brought a hoarse, approving shout from Sered, which in turn brought more shouts from the warriors.

"Sounds like their goose is cooked," David muttered. "When do we eat?"

Spock blinked, blinked again, trying to clear his vision. "We cannot simply rush down there into that war party and grab a communicator."

He fought a growing urge to shout with the warriors, to cry out battle cries of his own—no! Control! But the fumes were eating into his lungs. Their poisons were leaching into his blood, into his brain. They would eat his reason.

They would eat his soul.

"Eat my soul! Yes!"

David stared at him. "Boy, you really *are* on a weird trip."

"No, no, you do not understand! The Eater of Souls— remember? It is an archetype so powerful it makes even my people flinch!" Fighting the fumes, forcing his thoughts to order, Spock continued, "What would its effects be on Sered?"

"Who is already nuts," David added. "Yes, as well as on those vicious 'cousins' of his!"

"One can only see what happens—"

"Especially if that's all the plan one has!"

"Can you make an eerie noise?" Spock asked. "No, not now; when I signal."

"Heh. Trust me."

The two boys edged down into the cavern. Spock gestured David to follow him down into the cavern—into chaos! The warriors were chanting, dancing, a wild, primal group. Some of them were fighting each other, hand to hand. A knife flashed; someone staggered and fell, nearly landing in the seething lava. The human hostages huddled against the walls, some of them alarmingly limp. At least, Spock thought, they were out of the line of danger.

"Now!" he whispered to David. "Wail. And keep wailing!" David set both hands over his throat as if he planned to choke himself, and produced a high-pitched, barbaric shriek that wavered between two notes and echoed most satisfactorily throughout the cavern. Sered cried out in alarm, waving wildly at this eerie wail that seemed to be coming from all sides. The warriors whirled, whirled again. Spock drew a deep breath, ignoring his burning lungs, burning eyes, ignoring the madness eating out his brain, seeking out the choicest morsel. His essence. His soul.

I know this is not true. They *do not.*

"The Eater of Souls!" he screamed with all the will within

him, leaping down to the cavern floor. "The Eater of Souls is here!"

His shout rose above the turmoil, silencing everything for an instant. Then, as David's weird ululations started up again, the warriors erupted anew into wild panic, shooting at each other, screaming war cries, fighting enemies only they could see.

And Sered—Sered stood before the altar, arms outspread, shouting, "Come to me, Eater of Souls, come if you dare! I embrace you, demon, I welcome your strength! Come to me!"

The raw emotion thrilled through Spock (no, no, emotion, control!), its power horrifying him (no, another emotion). *Am I, too, going mad?* The terrifying power was building, building . . . in another instant, he too would scream—

"To me, my brothers!" Sered's voice rang out in new fury. "I have the strength of the Eater of Souls within me! This is the dawn of our victory or our death!" Drawing his ritual knife, the patterned blade blazing red, he charged blindly forward. "May they die, screaming in *plak-tow!* May their issue wither!"

But the hostages weren't totally helpless. Spock heard a tangle of voices, mostly human, shouting:

"The children! Protect the children!"

"Get him! That murdering—"

"They've gone mad! Now's our chance!"

The hostages fought with whatever came to hand: rocks, even pebbles and handfuls of cinders. But Sered's allies were too maddened to know who attacked. One warrior fired wildly at a man in a torn red Starfleet tunic, who disappeared in a blaze of red. The warrior turned with a savage laugh to where an Andorian woman shielded three human children with her body.

"No!" Spock shouted, and threw a rock at the warrior with all his strength. The warrior easily dodged—and then he actually *giggled,* hurled his weapon away from him, and flung himself down, beating his head against the stone until he lay limp.

David raced for the altar and the communicators. Spock ran toward the hostages, fighting his dizzy senses, trying to make himself clear. "Back . . . niches, shadows . . . hide!" Many were too weak to move quickly. Some could barely move at all.

Suddenly Captain Rabin was there, rushing toward the altar and her son. Spock saw David's teeth flash in a grin. The captain's face was grimy, weary, but in that moment it shone more brightly than Vulcan's sun.

I shall bring my mother spoils worthy of a High King, Spock found himself thinking, confused at himself, *spoils so even T'Pau will envy her . . .* "Spider silk and gems as green as heart's blood shall I heap at her feet . . ."

No, those weren't his thoughts, that was a quote from . . . from some ancient play, he could not remember which.

Where is your control? No, that wasn't right . . . *Where is your humanity?* Yes, that was better. Humanity. His human mother did not want green gems. *But if I offered her a Terran evergreen, perhaps then she would smile at me as Captain Rabin smiles at David.*

No, no, and no again, this was as David had said, a "weird trip." It was said that humans deliberately took hallucinogens, that they *enjoyed* this madness. It *must* be madness. There was no other explanation for his seeing, for a moment, the captain wave not a weapon but a harp. And was that really David, wearing not the battered desert gear but a plain hide tunic, brandishing his sling?

Illusion. Atavism. Memories of things David has said of his people's past.

Spock blinked, rubbed his eyes. Reality returned. David had dashed from the altar, clutching a communicator. Captain Rabin had a laser pistol.

"Get moving, people!" she shouted. "Follow Spock!"

Me? Where can I lead them? Ah, there, there, the entrance!
Sered screamed in rage and charged.

Illogical, Spock thought with the distorted clarity of his
still-drugged mind. *If he had attacked silently, he might have
had a chance. But discretion was never the te-Vikram way.*

Captain Rabin whirled and kicked in one smooth motion,
sending Sered's blade flying into the seething lava.

"No!" Sered shrieked in white-hot fury. "The holy knife!
No!"

He lunged at the captain, hands outstretched: the proper
positioning for *tal-shaya.* Maddened, Sered was, but he
could still snap a human's neck. Captain Rabin dropped,
rolled, started to rise—but a glancing blow, struck faster
than human reflexes, grazed her head. She fell back to her
knees, losing her grip on the pistol, which Sered snatched up
with a sharp laugh.

"Mother!" David yelped, and blindly raced to defend
her—only to be straight-armed by Sered with a force that
sent him staggering toward the lava. Captain Rabin
screamed in sudden despair, "David!"

But the boy, twisting frantically about, somehow managed
to land on solid rock, hastily rolling away from the heat,
struggling to free his sling at the same time.

Slingshot . . . Spock thought vaguely, *five smooth
stones . . . courage against all odds . . . yes.*

He stepped into Sered's path, suddenly seeing only this
one foe, the rest of the chaotic scene fading from his
awareness. As Sered stopped short just before trampling
him, Spock challenged somberly in Old High Vulcan, "Is it
only humans that you dare to fight?" The archaic language
held no word for "traitor." Or "madman." *"Lunikkh ta-
Vik!"* he added. "Thou Poisoner of Wells!"

Sered stared, straightened, seemed to . . .

. . . rear up five times his size, his outstretched hands

turned to talons, his mouth open to suck the life and soul from Spock.

The Eater of Souls! It has Taken him—

Impossible. Illogical. David would say . . . would say . . . what? Something boldly mocking. Maybe, "Would you look at that thing?" Yes, and then he would joke about . . . about "dancing theorems." Illusion, that's all this was. Sered was no more than mortal.

No less dangerous! "Half-breed," Sered jeered, raising the pistol.

"I can tell truth from illusion," Spock countered. "Can you?"

"Bah, *child.*" Sered's hands shot up: the position of deadly *tal-shaya.* "Your spine will snap as easily as a human's neck."

I cannot take a grown, trained foe, not hand-to-hand. A weapon—

Yes! A shard of rock like a basalt *lirpa!* He snatched it up, heedless of its weight—

And the battle engulfed him. Suddenly Sered was gone in the crush and a mad-eyed warrior, screaming something about "My life for yours, my chief!" was charging Spock, knife aimed at him in the quick, deadly underhand thrust that was all but impossible to stop. The will to live took over, and Spock blindly swung his improvised *lirpa* with all his might. It cracked into the maddened warrior's head, and hot green blood splattered Spock's weapon, hands, face. The warrior crumpled, twitched once, then lay still, skull crushed.

The shielding haze of hallucination vanished. Standing over the body, Spock could think only, *I never knew how easy it is to kill.* He had refused to slay a *le-matya.* Now, in an instant, he had brought death to an intelligent being.

Suddenly his legs gave way. He collapsed to his knees, retching dryly, wishing himself a thousand miles away, not caring that the very concept of wishing was illogical. Why had it been so easy? He had brought death without thought. And it had been *easy*.

Energy whined right by his ear, one bolt, followed by others. Spock scrambled to one side, suddenly reminded that he was still in the middle of a battle. Sered! Where was Sered?

But with the speed of madness, Sered hurled one of his warriors directly into the line of fire, and fled, glancing wildly about as though hunting a hostage. Somewhere in the struggle, Captain Rabin had regained her laser pistol. Steadying the weapon with both hands, she fired over his head.

"Surrender, Sered! You're outmatched!"

True or not, Sered seemed to believe it. Instead of turning to fight, he raced off into the folds of stone. Spock started after him. He had killed once; why not again, this time in full knowledge of what he did. Sered was a madman; Sered was a criminal; Sered had cost him . . .

"Spock, get back here!" the captain commanded sharply. Involuntarily, Spock obeyed.

"Rabin to Shikahr, come in, come in!" David was babbling into the communicator. "No, I don't know the coordinates. We're on the Forge, the Womb of Fire, Spock says you call it. Can you lock on to my position? Yes? Then *hurry!*"

"I'll take over now, son," said Captain Rabin, only to be hit by a sudden attack of coughing that nearly toppled her to her knees. Pulling away from David's panicky grip with a quick, reassuring grin, she spoke into the communicator, "Rabin to *Farragut*. Yes, I'm alive, never mind that. Lock on to my bioreading. We've got the hostages. We have injured. Beam down medical and security. And as my son said, *hurry!* There's a bunch of very confused hostiles who aren't going to stay confused much longer!"

Within only a few moments, the air shimmered, stirred

wildly as Federation Security beamed in. But there was only the briefest of struggles. The hallucinogenic fumes were all but gone now, leaving some very dazed warriors who would hardly have been an even match for the children, let alone the furious adult hostages who were quite willing to kill all of their former captors. The Federation troops quickly overwhelmed those warriors who maintained enough strength to struggle, doing their best to pacify the former hostages at the same time. Spock overheard bits of "Whoa, enough," and "Yes, I know you want revenge, but hey, we're civilized!"

More quickly than he would have thought possible—or maybe, Spock mused, his time sense was still distorted—the newcomers had removed the madmen and the dead. Shouts echoed down the tunnels and pipes as men and women with the intent gaze of hunters searched for Sered.

"No one," someone said in disgust. "Not even a footprint or heat trace."

"He's gone to ground," Spock heard Captain Rabin say. "Do the best you can. But I think we're going to have to turn the problem, with our recommendations, over to the Vulcans. They've lost a lot of face; you can bet they won't let up."

T'Pau, Spock thought, never forgot and never forgave. There was some bleak reassurance in that.

Within the cavern, the Federation personnel were busy stringing up lights, measuring distances, taking reports in the intervals when outraged physicians and, within a short while, cool Vulcan healers were not driving them away. From time to time, a party beamed in with supplies or out with injured who had been stabilized and could now be transported back to better medical facilities on board Captain Rabin's ship. The communicators beeped and crackled with news bulletins from Shikahr, from the *Farragut,* and the shuttles on their way from the city.

And all the while, Spock did what he could to help, watching his hands deliver medications or assist a healer, yet throughout felt . . . nothing.

David was handling the emotional aftershock in exactly the opposite fashion. "We got here in time, didn't we?" he asked over and over, his voice rising. "Spock said those lichen released hallucinogenic vapor, so we gathered a bunch and dumped them into the lava. He knew what to say to stampede people, and now look at him! I'm ready to pass out, and he's off helping people. He saved my life, Mother. I told him about Starfleet, and how the Academy's looking for Vulcan cadets. I think he's interested, he has to be, he'd be so great—"

"Take it easy, David. We'll talk about this later, I promise."

She paused, catching Spock's gaze. Looking T'Pau—or his father—in the eye might have been easier right then, but he could hardly be rude enough to turn away.

"Are you all right?" the woman asked gently, on her face the look that he'd seen on his mother's face when he had fallen ill or injured himself as a child.

After a moment, Spock shook his head. "I am quite unharmed, Captain Rabin."

"That's not what I asked, Spock."

"There . . . are children still needing help," he said evasively, and hurried off to where a healer trying to inject a terrified little boy with tri-ox gladly let him help hold the child still. The way the boy's color returned almost instantly and his breath steadied eased the ache in Spock's heart to some degree.

He knew the rest would never heal. Not wholly.

EIGHTEEN

Intrepid II, Obsidian Orbit
Year 2296

The amber lights signaling yellow alert had been sweeping the bridge—on and off, on and off—for hours, with the warning alarm, that cursedly calm computerized voice, a constant, monotonous wail in the background. Uhura straightened ever so slightly in the command chair, trying to get more comfortable, refusing to squirm.

A beep from the chair's console nearly made her start. No, nothing alarming. Merely Medical's update. She acknowledged this most recent quarter-hourly report—hull radiation about what could be expected; interior radiation nominal.

"Lieutenant Duchamps," Uhura asked, just as she had every quarter of an hour, "any luck raising the captain?"

The stiffness of Duchamps' shoulders was answer enough, but he reported, "We've still got major static from the flare, Commander."

"Tighten your beam."

"I've been trying . . ."

"Trying is not good enough, mister. Do it!"

Uhura—none better—knew all of the techniques a comm officer might employ to separate static from signal. She itched to leap from the central chair she had taken such pride in occupying, shove poor Duchamps from *my duty station,* and pull a communications rabbit out of the hat just as she'd always done for Jim Kirk.

Spock, I'm failing you.

Worse yet, she was failing the ship.

No. She mustn't think like that; believe you were defeated, and you were halfway there. Uhura made herself sit rigidly still, almost at attention, pretending to review the *Intrepid*'s weapons specs, which she had called up hours ago, when it had finally sunk in that she, Uhura of the United States of Africa, a communications officer, not a fighting captain at all, might actually have to fight. Well, the weapons officer would actually do the firing, but she had to know more about ship-to-ship action than "lock on phasers," "shields up," and "release photon torpedoes." Yes, and (God, she didn't want to hear this one) "Damage control, report!"

Dammit, *Intrepid II* was a science vessel—good legs, she'd heard a captain of her acquaintance once describe the class, but with no real "guns" to speak of. Her captain had been a connoisseur of both elegant ships and armaments. When Jim Kirk had sat in the center chair and had taken his ship into combat, Uhura had watched him out of the corner of her eye, knowing she was seeing a true professional at work. And, as she had told him once when she thought they were both going to die, she'd never been really afraid, because he was in command.

She was afraid now.

Well, at least I've got Duchamps to hound. Right, and medical officers to dodge.

By now, McCoy would have stalked onto the bridge with a tray of sandwiches, insistences that watch relieve watch *including* the commanding officer, thank you, ma'am, and, likely as not, some joke that would have put everyone more at ease, or an observation that would have helped the captain make up his mind. Her mind. Damn.

Yellow alert continued to flash over the bridge. The warning continued to sound. Uhura stared at the viewscreen, its filters partially occluding her view of Obsidian's disk and Loki's deadly light. She listened to the undercurrent of whispers from helm to weapons, weapons to science, science to weapons, where Lieutenant Richards, bless him for trying to defuse things, added a calm briefing on how to divert impulse power into the phasers, boosting their pathetic armament. Too many murmurings. The crew, especially the new ones, untried in battle, were edgy, and everyone was getting pretty tired of "hurry up and wait."

The truth was, it had been far too long without word from Spock or the rest of his people. Too long having to cower on Obsidian's far side, keeping it between themselves and the damnedly unstable Loki.

Too long, too, without a clear fix on the double-damned Romulan ship she knew was out there.

Damn, this chair is uncomfortable. In every sense. Ironic to recall how she had beamed when she'd first sat down in it and heard Spock tell her he had every confidence in her. *Ah well, that good old quote: You knew the job was dangerous when you took it.*

"Mr. Richards!"

"Commander?"

"Romulan Warbirds register on our sensors the instant they drop cloaking. Any sign?"

"I've checked the normal spectrographic bands, ma'am."

"Then check some *abnormal* ones!"

"Aye-aye, ma'am."

You don't have to snap, Uhura warned herself, and added more gently, "I have every confidence in you, Lieutenant."

If not in the safety of the planetary team. But there's nothing I can do about that, so, as Spock would put it, "It is illogical to worry about what cannot be changed."

And maybe *sehlat*s or whatever they had instead of pigs on Vulcan could fly.

Wonder if Vulcans worry, deep down under that unemotional front. Maybe they've all got ulcers. Bet they do. Sure they do. Wonder if Spock is worrying right now—stop that!

"Helm," she ordered suddenly. "Shift course. Two-zero-five mark three. On my order."

"Course laid in, Commander."

"Proceed."

Maybe altering orbit just a trifle would lure the Romulans into thinking *Intrepid* was retreating. Prod those boys into doing something, too. Of course, if the Warbird emerged, they would probably have to fight it, but at least the crew did seem to brighten at the thought of any action at all.

Except that there wasn't any. Nothing happened, save that the whispering started up again. *Just what I wanted,* Uhura thought, *a morale problem.*

All right, go on the offensive. Stop the murmurings before they undermined her authority. Undermined it any worse.

"Lieutenant Duchamps!"

Uhura's voice was as sharp as the crack of a whip, and Duchamps almost shot straight up out of his chair. "Commander. Ma'am. I, uh, I—"

"Lieutenant, you've been doing a fair amount of communicating that has nothing to do with the planet or our people down there. Let's get what you were saying out in the open. Spit it out, mister." *And thank you, Ms. Yemada, Public School Twenty-Nine, Nairobi.*

What had worked for Ms. Yemada worked for Uhura too. Reddening like a boy (quite a weird effect under the sallow lighting of yellow alert, Uhura noted absently), Duchamps muttered, "Begging the commander's pardon. It's just . . . well . . . we're getting a bit edgy waiting and not doing anything. Captain Spock . . ."

"Would tell you your worry is illogical. He can take care of himself, mister."

"Uh, no one's saying he can't, ma'am. It's just—"

"Lieutenant." Uhura stressed the man's title. "What, exactly, would you have me do? Move the *Intrepid* into danger? Would you *like* to find out what solar flares like that could do to this ship and, more to the point, to its crew?"

"No, ma'am."

"Excellent. Now, try to raise that base again. This time, why not switch circuit couplings AF and DX, then . . ." The jargon that tumbled from her mouth turned Duchamps wide-eyed, as she intended.

"As for the rest of you," she raised her voice again, "you hate this delay, and I can't blame you. But I can keep you busy. While the lieutenant here tries to raise Captain Spock or Captain Rabin, the rest of you are going to stop staring at me and start hunting for that Romulan ship. And I won't take 'nothing out there, ma'am' for an answer!"

A ragged chorus of "aye-aye"s trailed off as the bridge crew bent over their consoles. A beep erupted from her own console, and Uhura just managed not to jump.

"Commander," came Lieutenant Commander Atherton's crisp voice, "I must protest."

Wouldn't you just? "Did we throw off your training program again, Commander?" Uhura asked sweetly. "You should have had time by now to do a hundred dilithium remounts."

"It's not the remounts, Commander," Atherton fretted. "It's the radiation."

"Medical says that radiation levels in-ship are nominal."

"Yes, Commander, of course. But I am worried about the weapons systems."

She definitely did *not* need to hear that! "So are we, mister. What suggestions do you have?"

"Withdraw beyond system limits. Let systems cool. Suit up and investigate."

"You mean let that Warbird think it can swoop down on the planet—and our people down there? Get back to me with a workable—" The quick, contemptuous emphasis on "workable" would make Atherton's stiff neck flush, wouldn't it? "—plan. Until then, bridge out."

"Commander Uhura!" It was Ensign Chang, for once too excited to remember to be shy. "I've found it again, or . . ." He added uncertainly, "I did, just for a moment. Their captain must have been trying to watch the planet while keeping clear of Loki. He took the direct impact of one of those flares, and his cloaking device glitched. I got a fix on his position." Chang turned and actually grinned at her. "He got careless. Edged over into the Neutral Zone. Cloaking device is back up, but I'm getting some feedback from it."

Damnation. Entry into the Romulan Neutral Zone by Federation or Romulan ships constituted an act of war. "No Romulan ever 'gets careless,' Mr. Chang," Uhura said. "Lieutenant Duchamps."

"No luck raising the base, Commander."

"Belay that. Send a message to Starfleet Command. Use cipher level D."

"Level D's been cracked for six months, Commander!"

Duchamps, Uhura thought wryly, sounded as if he thought *she* were cracked too. She grinned at him. "The Romulans know that. But they may not know that *we* know it. A little trick I learned from Captain Kirk." This was communications, Uhura thought. This was what she understood. This was pure heaven.

Even if, in the next moment, she might have to fight from a research ship with "great legs and no guns."

"Make it sound a little frantic," she added. "By the time Starfleet gets it, things will be resolved. Always easier to get forgiveness than permission."

Light dawned on Duchamps' face. He grinned back at her. "Aye-*aye,* ma'am!"

Medical signaled. Uhura hit the override. She had more important things to worry about than hull radiation. She'd probably have an angry physician on her bridge in two minutes flat, too. Just like old times.

"Message ready for you to review, ma'am," Duchamps said, all spit and polish now.

"I'm not done yet, Lieutenant. Now, encrypt a message into that one. Pick cipher level F; it's still so secure they won't know it's piggybacking our distress call. Tell them:

"'Uhura, Commander and Acting Captain of the *U.S.S. Intrepid II,* orbiting around Obsidian in the Loki system, to Starfleet. We have just witnessed a clear and deliberate violation of the Neutral Zone by a Romulan Warbird.'"

She broke off to add, "Mr. Chang, transfer your coordinates over to Lieutenant Duchamps for inclusion."

"Aye-aye, ma'am."

"And tell them," Uhura continued to Lieutenant Duchamps, "'This substantiates our prior sighting. Judging from sabotage reports and the evidence of our planetary search team, I have reason to believe that this may be the start of Romulan aggressive action against Obsidian. In accordance with treaty provisions, a state of war now exists between the Federation and the Romulan Empire. We will, nevertheless, endeavor to resolve this situation without hostilities.'"

The message hit her station seconds later. She took a deep breath. "Now," Uhura said, "go to broadband." *Open a*

216

hailing frequency. Yes! "I want the name of every *Constitution*-class starship included in your hail—"

"There aren't any . . ."

"Make sure you include the *Excelsior* as well. The Romulans know another *Enterprise* veteran commands it." Good old Sulu. *Captain* Sulu. "Add the following ships: *Chaka Zulu, Patrick O'Brian, John Paul Jones,* and *Exodus,* cruising in convoy out in . . . oh . . . thataway," Uhura added in tribute to Kirk's preferred choice of destination. "Request their immediate assistance."

"Commander . . ." Duchamps' voice was very small. "There *are* no such ships."

"Very good, Lieutenant. We know that—but can the Romulans be sure of it? Message away!"

She took a deep breath and stood. There were some things for which you wanted to be on your feet. Like the first time you opened your mouth and said:

"Go to red alert."

NINETEEN

Vulcan, The Womb of Fire
Day 6, Eighth Week of Tasmeen,
Year 2247

The last of the hostages had been removed. There was nothing left now for Spock to do but to think. And remember. And neither was anything he really wanted to do just now. The young Vulcan stood frozen, seeing nothing but that sudden flow of green blood and that crumpled, lifeless form at his feet, unable to force himself to move.

David came up behind him, then paused awkwardly. "You've got to cry it out," he said at last. "You're half human, you can do it, I know you can."

After another hesitation, he closed a reassuring hand on Spock's shoulder, and Spock had all he could do not to instinctively slam that hand away. He would not let his instincts betray him again! The last time he had given them free play, he had killed without thought or hesitation. Knowing that David could not see his face, Spock closed his eyes, longing for the serenity of logic the way he had

218

longed for cool water in the desert. *I have poisoned my well.*

David, of course, could not read his thoughts. "I know what happened back there; I saw you have to kill that guy. Hey, don't worry! You'd be as crazy as Sered if you didn't feel bad about it! Remember how I cried at the wrecked shuttle," the boy added, "when I thought Mother might have died there . . ." David's voice cracked. "You've got to let it out, Spock. You won't heal unless you do."

"David, you know we don't touch Vulcans," Captain Rabin said in the rasp seemed to be all the voice she had left by now. She managed somehow to keep track of what was going on in the entire cavern without losing sight of her son. And if her tone seemed aimed at a much younger boy, that was strangely comforting, too.

Spock nodded his gratitude. Gently, as he would put a child aside, he freed himself from David's grasp. "I *am* a Vulcan," he reminded the human boy just as gently. "We do not cry. I will recover. But I must be free to heal in my own way."

Such as it is.

When no one seemed to have any further need of him, he settled himself on a rock, his head in his hands, trying to meditate. He tried for hours. But there was no peace, no balance, in him.

Spock looked up from his fruitless meditations, confused for the briefest instant as to how long a time had passed. The lights that the Starfleet Security officers had strung up were the painful yellow most familiar to human eyes, but his inner senses told him it was night.

Fewer people were about, most of them still pointing tricorders and asking questions. Captain Rabin had finally listened to her medical officer, accepted medication, and consented to sit down. Nearby, David slept, totally ex- hausted, covered by a silvery thermal blanket. His part of the battle over, he seemed, at least in sleep, to have returned to a younger boy's innocence.

Captain Rabin tilted her head at Spock: *Come here.*

He warily obeyed, seating himself at a polite distance, waiting in proper silence for an adult's words.

"Have you heard from your parents yet?" the captain asked after an awkward pause.

He had to fight the impulse—*Aftereffects from the lichen, no doubt*—to flinch and look away. Instead, one eyebrow raised, the only reaction he dared allow himself, Spock answered carefully with what was logical and true: "My father and T'Pau will be occupied with contacting all of the embassies. He would not permit my mother to come here unescorted."

That brought Captain Rabin's eyebrow up. Now Spock did look aside. There had been times when he had dared think his father was not right. Clearly, the captain shared this view. But he could not allow her to think poorly of his mother or, for that matter, his people.

"My mother is not Starfleet," he said in an attempt to explain. And then, because the woman who was both captain and his friend's mother was owed more courtesy than that, he added, "Ma'am."

Not "lady," Spock, as you would speak to one of your Vulcan friends' mothers?

I have no Vulcan friends, honesty compelled him to admit. *Not in the sense that this human has become my friend. And now he will leave, to go to this Academy of his.*

I will miss him.

That was a statement his father must never hear.

"Rabin to Spock," the captain said gently, pretending to open her communicator. "Come in, Spock."

He nearly started. "I ask forgiveness. Lady."

Her smile widened into a grin very like that of David when he thought he'd proved a point. "My son tells me he has spoken to you about Starfleet. He considers you an outstanding candidate, and he says you may be interested."

She watched him carefully. When he just as carefully kept his face blank of expression and said nothing, the captain added, "Enthusiasm often makes David exaggerate, as you must have noticed by now, but you must also know that he is truthful to the extent of his knowledge. Is he right about this, Spock?"

Spock looked down at his hands. "My life's pattern is set. I am to be a scientist, a servant of peace, as my father is. But . . ." Before he could stop himself, Spock heard himself add, "I killed."

"I saw," Captain Rabin murmured. "I wish you had been spared that, a boy your age. But . . . we can't always have what we wish."

"I killed without thought," Spock protested, struggling to keep his voice properly calm. "It was . . . easy, too easy."

"No."

"But—"

"Oh, the physical part's far too easy. But the whole act of killing—it never does get easy, Spock. At least, I pray it never does."

"But I failed in control. Just as my father has admonished me."

"Ah." There was a world of understanding in the one syllable. Captain Rabin started to put out a hand to soothe him as she had her son, then let it fall. *David, you know one does not touch Vulcans.* Frustration. He had seen that expression often enough on his mother's face. He would see it again when Sarek gave permission for Spock's return home. At the most, the Lady Amanda would have the chance to say she was "gratified" to see her son before they packed him off for medical observation. One could not be too careful with a human/Vulcan half-breed, after all. No doubt repairs were expensive.

"Spock?" the captain asked again after another long pause.

"Captain, there are weapons on board your ship, are there not? At your Academy, will David learn to use them?"

"When he must. Only when he must. Spock, there is a quote from my people's writings: 'They shall beat their swords into plowshares and their spears into pruninghooks. Nations shall not lift up sword against nation, neither shall they learn war any more.'"

Spock straightened. "That sounds like Surak."

"Those words are about as old as his teachings. And as true."

"Then . . ." he began, feeling his way along, "there is no conflict between them, the human way and the Vulcan?"

Captain Rabin smiled faintly. "Not in terms of a desire for peace. I know this is all overwhelming for a boy your age—and don't give me that cool Vulcan stare. You are, like it or not, more or less my son's age, and I am definitely old enough to be your mother."

That almost shocked a laugh out of him. Hastily forcing his face back to the proper calm, he bowed his head in respect, hearing the captain's chuckle.

"As a mother as well as an officer, I'm going to ask again: Is David right about your interest in Starfleet? If it helps you decide, I'll say frankly that you're as likely a candidate as I've seen, and I would be proud to nominate you."

The captain's interest, even her unexpected maternal impulses, were far preferable to the discomfort of his thoughts. Cautiously, Spock asked, "Should the recommendation not come from a dignitary of one's homeworld?"

Captain Rabin grinned at him, her face lighting up despite its weariness. "Your mother is of Earth, Spock. And it is a custom among *my* people that parentage follows the mother. By that logic, you are as much of Earth as you are of Vulcan. Don't be afraid of your Earth heritage. It has saved your life—and that of my son."

Spock stared at her but could find nothing to say. The captain's grin softened to a gentle smile. "I'm here for you, Spock. If you need me. If you want to talk. But I will tell you frankly, my offer comes with conditions. I will not go behind Ambassador Sarek's and Lady Amanda's backs. Think about it. If you want to accept my offer, talk to them first and tell me."

"I killed." Spock returned to the almost unbearable truth. "I was not in full control. I did not understand. I am shamed. That is an emotion, yet it is one I believe I fully merit. I . . . need more time to think."

"As do we all. But not now. You, young man, have undergone more than any boy should. You should sleep."

"I do not need—"

"Yes, you do. I know that Vulcans can go for longer than we humans without rest, but you are not fully grown yet. And," she added with a glance that really did remind him of her son, "sleep will help you gain some perspective." She thrust a thermal blanket into his arms. "I promise, I will wake you when the ambassador calls. He will find you awake and about your duties."

Was it continuing weakness from the lichen's fumes or his exhaustion that allowed him to accept her reassurances? Or . . . could it be a childish need for maternal warmth?

He was too weary to find an answer. Spock stretched out near David as he had done every night since their escape from this very cavern. There was comfort in that familiarity, and he should not have felt that either. He had killed.

223

Perhaps Starfleet could teach him how to deal with that, with all his inner conflicts. The idea eased the sickness in his soul.

So, the Eater of Souls had not devoured it after all.

Spock suspected that David would have called it a close call.

TWENTY

Obsidian, Deep Desert
Day 4, First Week, Month of the Shining *Chara*,
Year 2296

Ensign Faisal ibn Saud ibn Turki—Ensign Prince—bit back
a shout of pure frustration. Bad enough that they were stuck
in this cave in the middle of nowhere. Bad enough that they
had such finite supplies that Captains Rabin and Spock had
gone off into the desert on what they said was an attempt to
find aid but could just as easily turn into a joint suicide. But
to put their only real hope for survival in the hands of a
muscle-bound idiot of a Farsi—

"Try it again," Faisal said, and tried not to make it a
snarl.

Unsuccessfully. It earned him a glare from Rustam Kavousi, who was huddled uncomfortably over the makeshift
transmitter. "What," he muttered in Farsi, "do you *think*
I'm doing, you overbearing son of a desert thief?"

Faisal understood Farsi well enough to get the point. For a
moment, pure atavistic hatred flashed between the two men

as they were suddenly back in the ancient days of Arab against Iranian.

Right, Faisal snapped at himself. *And Captain Rabin is Israeli. You going to hate him, too?*

The moment passed. They were both Starfleet, and archaic stuff like racial hatred just didn't belong to the modern age. Besides, Faisal reminded himself, Captain Rabin had left him in charge. Up to him to see that everyone survived.

I'm a pilot. It was a plaintive thought. *A damned good one, too. I never asked for this.*

Who would? Fruitless to argue with what was written. Faisal sighed, patting the other ensign on a burly shoulder. "Sorry. I know you're doing everything you can."

"And I didn't mean to snarl. I *almost* had them. I . . . wait . . . something's coming in."

". . . Federation base . . ."

The signal faded. Swearing under his breath, Kavousi boosted the power again.

". . . calling Captain Rabin . . . shuttlecraft . . . come in, Captain Rabin."

"That's Ensign Chase's voice, back at the base!" someone whispered, and was hastily shushed by someone else before they could drown out the fragile signal.

"Go ahead," Faisal urged. "Answer her."

"This is Ensign Kavousi. Do you read?"

Static.

"I said, do you read?"

". . . Kavousi . . ."

"Yes! Yes! Do you read?"

The static cut off abruptly. Kavousi looked up, stricken. "It's dead. Power's drained."

They were too well schooled to groan, but Faisal could feel everyone's sudden despair and thought, *I don't need this. I really don't.* "What if we tried readjusting the power cells?"

he asked warily. "They should be able to store energy in any form, shouldn't they?"

"Not that I've heard."

"Well, not the ordinary configuration, no. But we've got a real hybrid here," Faisal continued, warming to his argument. "And maybe we can't use all the cells, but at least that one," pointing over Kavousi's shoulder, "looks like a Thomas Adjustable Power Cell. Sure it is," he added, taking a closer look, "good old Series Four One Two Four, maybe A or A Prime."

At Kavousi's startled glance, Faisal shrugged. "I use them in my Beech Four Thousand—that's my plane—back on Earth: don't need anything fancier for an old-style turboprop. The Series Four One Two Four adjusts from standard system powering to solar power with more or less the flick of a switch."

Kavousi snorted. "Solar power, eh? We sure have enough of that."

Lieutenant Diver joined them. "At least we know the home base is looking for us. I vote we give it a try."

Kavousi shrugged. "Can't hurt anything. If we can get any one of the cells working again, we might just have enough power to let them know our coordinates."

"Go to it," Faisal said. "In the meantime," he said to the geologist, "how's your search going?"

"Nothing yet. But there's definitely porous limestone down there, and those stains in the folds of the cliff do look like water."

Faisal rather doubted it. Vulcans, he knew, had keener senses than humans, and if Captain Spock hadn't commented on nearby water, it either wasn't there in any real amount or wasn't really drinkable. Still . . . anything that kept morale high was a good thing. And hell, even Vulcans could be wrong.

"If I can just get down to it . . ." the lieutenant continued.

"Ozmani," Faisal cut in, "you're a rock climber in your free time, right?"

"I am, yes."

"All right, then you're elected to help her. Be careful! Having you two fall off the cliff would be a hell of a way to save on rations."

There was a ragged laugh at that, and Faisal gave them all his most encouraging grin. *Want me to be a leader, Captain Rabin? All right, I'm leading.* "You think this is rough?" he asked. "No way! This is a joke! Remember all those double-time exercise drills back in Starfleet Academy. Remember all those thrice-cursed drill sergeants breathing down your necks! Yes, and remember the cardboard masquerading as food they served us after the drill sergeants had finished with us? Nothing this desert can throw at us could be worse than those bouncing gray meatballs!"

That earned him a genuine laugh, and Faisal's grin widened. Morale booster was never going to replace flying in his list of favorite occupations, but: *Well, what do you know? Look at me: I am a leader.*

For now, a dour part of his mind answered him. *For now. Till the water runs out, or the food, or whatever got McCoy gets us, too.*

Oh, shut up, he snapped.

The nomads, Spock realized, were similar to other desert peoples in that they must, before deciding anything short of dealing with a immediate emergency, debate each and every aspect of a situation. There was no way to hasten such a process, so he merely sat and waited, sipping every so often (one did not waste a chance to drink in the desert, whether one thirsted or not) from the water cup he had been given.

Rabin, much to Spock's surprise, seemed to be showing

almost as much patience. Catching Spock's speculative expression, he grinned and shrugged. "Reminds me of the folks back home." But then the human leaned forward to whisper in Spock's ear, "The only thing that's bothering me is: What's happening to McCoy while we're waiting?"

"One does not harm a valuable hostage. And he is, after all, a Starfleet officer."

"Meaning that he'll be doing his best to escape." Rabin stopped short. "Sounds awfully familiar, doesn't it?"

"It does. However, the doctor would not need the distraction of a tremor. Dr. McCoy is very much a distraction in himself."

The nomads' murmurings were growing louder, more fervent. All at once their voices joined in outright cheering.

"I believe," Spock said mildly, "that they have come to a decision."

There was the softest of chuckles from the Elder, who had been in the midst of the debate. "We have," she said. "We have decided that the men who look like our honored visitor, Spock, son of Sarek, but are *not* his people are enemies and must be driven from our lands."

That, of course, sparked another series of excited shouts. Rabin raised his cup in salute to Spock. Under cover of the crowd's noise, he whispered, "Lawrence of Arabia!"

Catching the reference precisely, Spock retorted, "It is wrong to kill a tribe for the wrongs of one man."

"Heh. Good quote."

"It seemed only logical. Come, my friend. I suspect that we have quite an interesting job ahead."

Ruanek, centurion of the Romulan Empire, member of House Minor Strevon, stood hidden behind a boulder, unsure and full of doubts for one of the few times in his young life. When first he had been given this assignment, he'd been proud of the chance to serve his race and at the same time possibly win glory for himself and his House. It had seemed so simple then: Pretend to obey the Vulcan traitor—who was, after all, merely Vulcan—and all the while obey your own commander. Ignore the slights, the insanities.

Ignore the wrongs done to the savages.

I am a warrior, not some fool of a sage. I should have no doubts.

And yet, and yet, it was not easy to see even savage children suffer, savage children die.

It was different in war. There, death was clean and quick. Honest. Here . . .

Ruanek spat. This ridiculous self-doubt was Makkhoi's doing. Sly, ah sly, that one! Easy to believe the tales about him, with his clever wit: Ruanek had to admit he'd actually come to enjoy their word duels—which was probably all part of Makkhoi's scheme.

It was time for his report. Ruanek opened his communicator with a brusque snap, impatiently adjusting the gain to deal with the cursed, ever-present static. . . .

Ah. The line was finally open. Ruanek whispered the latest series of code words, implanted as had been the first code, which had already faded from his mind (as would this in turn). He waited, refusing to show the anxiety he felt. What if, this time, there was no response? That would mean Avrak somehow knew of his self-doubts, and *that* would mean the end of his career and probably his life.

But then: "Report."

Fighting to keep his relief from his voice, Ruanek said, "We continue to hold the hostage, Makkhoi. The traitor Vulcan continues to preen and pose and suspect nothing."

"Excellent."

"Sir . . . one question, if it is permitted."

A long, unnerving pause: What was Avrak thinking? Would he praise or condemn curiosity?

Why do I do this? Why risk everything?

"One question," flatly.

"Sir, if Makkhoi is so redoubtable a warrior, why was he snared so easily? He did seem confused by the storm, as we, protected by the proper gear, were not. But . . . could he have *wished* to be captured? Sir, I do not presume to great wisdom, but: Can this all be part of some devious Federation plot?"

Another unnervingly long pause. Then: "You are not here to deal with the Federation, Centurion. Obey orders. No more than that."

With that, the link was broken and the communicator went dead. Ruanek stood swearing silently. Why had he been such a fool? How could he have dared question his own patron?

It could have been worse. I could have been stupid enough to mention the dying children.

He had been standing here far too long. Someone was certain to stumble on him and ask awkward questions— someone such as ambitious Kharik, Ruanek's age and distant cousin yet half Ruanek's rank. Oh, Kharik would love to find him dithering here like one of the Federation do-gooders. And if Kharik should manage to worm his way into Avrak's good graces . . .

Ruanek marched on, pretending to be going somewhere. As, he was beginning to suspect, he was not.

It was just about time, McCoy thought, for his latest interview with the Leader of the Faithful. Sure enough, here came his armed escort.

"So nice to see you folks again. Lead on."

He gave them his full-force Southern Gentleman smile,

smooth and charming as they came, and grinned to himself to see their eyes narrow warily. That magnolia-dripping smile always seemed to take the Romulans aback, clearly making them wonder what he knew that they didn't.

Wonder away, boys, wonder away. Wish I did have a scheme.

At least he knew Spock was alive and well and on his trail. That counted for a lot. Nothing like a Vulcan—a *sane* Vulcan—for good old logical tenacity. Better than a bloodhound.

Ah look. There was the Mahdi Wannabe himself, in those ridiculously theatrical white robes.

And those cold, cold eyes. McCoy dropped every wisecrack he'd been considering, recognizing hair-trigger psychosis when he saw it. The Master was definitely *not* having a good day.

Don't want to do anything to set off someone on the edge of violence. Particularly not someone with Vulcan strength. I like my neck unbroken, thank you!

The Master fixed him with that alien stare, flat as the gaze of a lizard. "I have waited with patience," he said with cold, unemotional menace. "I have granted you mercy, time in which to consider the folly of silence. But the time of waiting is over. Now I must insist that you talk."

Oh joy. "I certainly will," McCoy said in as businesslike a manner as he could manage. "Let's see now, where to begin. Ah, I know: with a bargain. Tell you what. You let me treat the ill, no restrictions, and I'll say anything you want to hear."

"No bargain." The Vulcan said the word as though he found it distasteful. "I do not bargain, certainly not with inferiors. You will talk. Now."

Thought we'd get around to the ultimatum sooner or later. Well, I'm ready for you, son. Don't say you didn't bring this on yourself. But then, I bet you've never even heard of a good old-fashioned Southern filibuster. And . . . we're off and running.

Off and running. That prompted McCoy to begin, "First, let me say something about the grand old Southern state of Kentucky, the home of fine bourbon, pretty women, and fast horses. Yes, fast as the wind, those horses."

Now that he was warmed up, McCoy spoke as quickly and smoothly as possible, trying not to interrupt the flow of words with anything as unimportant as breath. "I've seen those horses run, and *man,* you would not believe the sight. The beauty, the speed, the sheer stunning power of them all. Folks hold something called the Kentucky Derby to honor those horses, and it's now . . . what . . . in maybe the Four Hundred and Someteenth running. Then there's the Preakness, the Belmont—horse that wins all three, why he's claimed the Triple Crown for himself! The names of those mighty horses of power have gone down in our history: father of them all, Eclipse, so great they said of him 'Eclipse first, the rest nowhere.'"

The Romulans, to his surprise, were gathering round as though intrigued, Ruanek in their midst. "Are these war beasts of which you speak?" the centurion asked, almost respectfully.

"Why, you could call them that, son. Yes, you could, indeed. In fact, one of the greatest of the Thoroughbreds, those wondrous beasts, was even named Man o' War, only beaten once in all his life, and his son was War Admiral, winner of the Triple Crown he was. Yes, and there were other grand war steeds . . ."

Thank whoever watched over Kentucky horseflesh for giving him the inspiration. McCoy couldn't exactly remember every equine pedigree, but that hardly mattered since no one here was going to be able to contradict him. He could make it up as he pleased. And the Romulans, bless their vicious little hearts, were hanging on every word.

Hell, they already think I'm a mighty warrior. Probably believe all this malarkey is some sacred military epic. Give 'em power in battle.

The Master was another matter. McCoy, keeping a wary eye on him, saw the Vulcan's cold eyes begin to smolder.

Oh, wonderful. What do I do if he erupts?

Nothing *to* do but keep going with his running monologue of horses. "Then there was Seabiscuit, named for the stuff sailors eat—sea warriors, those are. And he was a true warrior horse, ran like the—"

"What nonsense is this?" the Master roared.

But to McCoy's relief, Ruanek, a warrior not impressed by noise, said, "Your pardon, Master, but this is the Captive's Right of Statement. Of honor, he may complete it. Of honor, we cannot interrupt him."

For a heart-stopping moment, McCoy was sure that the Master was going to tear a rifle from someone's hands and shoot him. But the Vulcan wasn't so far gone into madness that he couldn't see the need for his Romulan allies. He subsided, fuming, and McCoy continued, heart racing, "And then there was Citation, like a citation for war heroics, and a heroic horse he was . . ."

And I'll place a bet in his honor on whatever it is they bet on here, if only I get out of this alive and in one piece. Spock, I don't know where you are, but hurry, you green-blooded bloodhound, hurry!

The nomads shouted and shrieked, working themselves up into a joyous, fierce frenzy.

"We will charge the invaders!" they yelled.

"We will hurl them from our lands!"

"They will be destroyed!"

This was not, Spock thought, exactly what he had intended. *Perhaps I was too convincing a speaker? Or perhaps they merely welcomed any excuse for a fight.*

Trapped in the middle of this wild extravagance, his keen hearing assaulted by noise that was rapidly reaching the threshold of pain, he only just managed to keep his face impassive. Fortunate that he was already familiar with explosive human emotions. Otherwise, the experience would be totally overwhelming.

But hysterical crowds too easily turned into mobs. Spock held up a deliberately dramatic hand for silence. Curious, the nomads subsided.

"While your enthusiasm is quite . . . thorough," he told them, picking his words with care, "you must understand that we cannot simply march against the Romulans as though they were no more than another clan. They are . . ." He quickly censored the perilous words *better armed,* since it would hardly be desirable for these nomads to suddenly gain weaponry superior to anything held by their neighbors. "They do not follow any rules with which you are familiar."

That sounded implausibly vague to him, but it served to confuse the nomads for a few precious moments, long enough for Spock to catch Rabin's attention, then ask the Elder, "May we three talk together in private?"

"I think it wise, yes."

They strolled away from the camp in seeming calm, one small, slight, powerful woman between two outlanders. As soon as they were safely out of earshot of the others, the Elder eyed Spock and Rabin slyly and said, "There is more to this than the desire to aid us. I must ask myself what it is you seek, you personally."

Rabin let out his breath in a gusty sigh. "Elder, we won't lie to you. The Romulans are holding a hostage, a physician named McCoy, a colleague of ours. And," he added with a glance at Spock, "a friend."

The faintest of frowns creased the woman's brow. "And yet I know you do not act from selfishness alone. You do genuinely wish to aid us. No, Kindly Fool," she added with the smallest of smiles, "I am not being either foolish or mystical. Your deeds, successful or not, have always been well meant. And they speak in your behalf."

"Elder," Spock said, "I did not intend to rouse an army. Please know that there will be danger for your people. Many may well die."

Her shoulders rose and fell in a slight, almost humanly fatalistic shrug. "So it is, so it will be. At least our land will be freed."

"Yes, but—"

"No. We are not children; we have chosen as named adults what we shall do. Do you know where the enemy has their lair?"

"Dr. McCoy was unable to give us exact coordinates. He did, however, indicate that he is being held in a cavern blocked by two large metal doors."

The Elder stiffened. "A cavern from which runs a network of black tunnels formed from the hardened blood of the world? Aie-ah, is it so? This can only be one place."

"Which is that?"

"I know the location well," the Elder said evasively. "It is not more than a day's riding from this camp."

"Why will you not name it?" Spock asked. "Is this, perhaps, a sacred site?" When she would not answer, he continued, "Please understand that we would not willingly go against your customs or cause insult. But first we must know of those customs."

"There is no insult given by you or intended by me," she answered. "This is simply not the place to speak of such things."

It was said with finality. Satisfied that she had made her point, the Elder turned away to watch her people. The nomads, with the air of people with nothing more constructive to do, were working themselves back up to a frenzy of excited shouting. Someone pulled out a drum, starting up an intricate beat. Someone else began tootling away on a bone flute with more enthusiasm than talent, and an impromptu war dance quickly sprang into being.

"We shall all go," the Elder said. "All the warriors. Indeed," she added, eyeing her wildly dancing people wryly, "I do not think that I could stop them. We shall all go, and your friend shall be rescued. We shall all go, and the outlanders will be forever banished from our lands."

Spock glanced at Rabin, who shrugged helplessly. "Aqaba," the human murmured in Anglic, "by land."

Spock recognized yet another quote from *Lawrence of Arabia*. He thought with not quite properly unemotional calm of the nomads with their foolish bravery and hopelessly antiquated weapons. The nomads he and Rabin were leading into peril against those who were better armed, higher-tech. "Let us only hope," he countered, one eyebrow raised, "that all their guns are pointed at the sea."

The quote raised both of Rabin's eyebrows. "Fascinating," he said.

TWENTY-ONE

It did not seem possible, Spock thought, that so short a time had passed since he had last stood here on Mount Seleya with his agemates. Less than a month . . . 15.6 days, no more than that, since David and he had struggled across the Womb of Fire, facing what had then seemed impossible odds.

And yet, and yet, at the same time how could so little have changed? Surely the rocks, the altar itself, must show marks of the maddened battle that had taken place here! Surely there must be some sign that cousins and sundered cousins had fought and, yes, died here!

Yet the faint mist of early morning continued to rise over Mount Seleya as it had every morning. A *shavokh* rode the first thermals of dawn, the rising sun briefly touching the tip of a wing with gold as the *shavokh* banked, just as it had done before. Of course the altar, the entire site, had been purified, Spock knew that. It was not, in the strictest sense of the word, the same as it had been.

And he—how could he still be the same after he had come so far and done so much?

And . . . killed?

No. He was not the same. Captain Rabin had ruefully mentioned something about "lost innocence," but that was needlessly emotional.

And yet . . .

What was, Spock thought resolutely, was. It was illogical to wish to change the past. Not even his parents knew everything about . . . what had happened. Nor, he had already decided, would they ever know.

When he had returned home . . . no, again. Spock drew a veil over the memory of his mother, control utterly shattered for the first time since he could remember, rushing from the room lest she cause an awkwardness for her husband and son by her unseemly burst of emotion. (But surely, a treasonous little voice whispered in Captain Rabin's voice, there was no shame here? Surely a human mother was allowed to react to the shock of finding her son not dead as she must have feared but alive and unharmed?)

Sarek . . . had said little to him, other than a brief remark that he was pleased to see his son returned unharmed and with renewed proof of his ability to survive ordeals.

Survive ordeals. Is that all he considers Sered's madness and what followed? An ordeal? A—test of my worthiness?

No and no again. This was not the time or place for unseemly behavior. Or dangerously emotional concepts.

At least, Spock thought, allowing himself the smallest touch of satisfaction, though he kept his face properly impassive, one thing *had* changed: His agemates no longer watched him as though waiting—hoping?—to see him fail. Instead, there was almost a wariness to them, especially to Stonn, as though they knew he had already passed beyond boyhood without having needed any ceremony to confirm his status. Or rather, that this ceremony merely reinforced what he had already gained.

There will never be friendship between us now, Spock thought. *But then again,* he added honestly, *there never has been.*

Movement caught his eye, and with it a little jolt of realization: He did have a friend, yes. David was there, standing with Captain Rabin and the other Federation guests. Not unusual that they had all returned here; to do otherwise would have been a subtle snub to their Vulcan hosts, a subtle loss of status for both sides.

Captain Rabin stood with the dignity of a true Starfleet officer, her uniform's insignia gleaming, although Spock thought that he sensed the faintest edge of uneasiness to her, as though she missed the security of a laser pistol at her side; the same not-quite nervousness was shared by many of the guests.

Sered will not attack again, he assured them silently. *Even if we do not yet know where he is.* Some postulated that, alone and insane, Sered must have already perished in the desert. *Even if Sered lives, he is powerless. He has lost his allies, our—our cousins. And even he is not insane enough to try a lone attack.*

I . . . trust he is not that insane.

No. Concentrate on something else.

David? Yes. David was once more dressed as befitted a Starfleet Academy cadet, his uniform spotless. He still showed signs of his desert ordeal, his face a touch too thin, his eyes a touch weary even now. But, being David, he wasn't going to let anything stop him from giving Spock a quick, mischievous, strangely reassuring wink.

The Academy . . . Spock thought, glancing almost guiltily at his father. *I still do not know what . . .*

But then the sound of shaken bells brought him sharply back to the present.

The ceremony had begun. Anew.

"And so it is," T'Pau's calm voice continued, filling the reverent silence, "that we come together once more for the cyclical ceremony, the same as ever—yet with one change."

T'Lar continued, "Change is a logical progression and not to be abhorred. There would be no life without change. Yet ceremony is essential and always will be; it serves the same function in all times and places, here and beyond this world. Ceremony is a force to bind a culture and those within that culture together.

"And so it is only just that we use ceremony to honor those lost to us through change. Through madness. Through," she said the word unflinchingly, "violence."

There was the faintest stirring of murmuring, barely audible from the Vulcans, more evident from the Federation guests, but no one was so ill-mannered as to interrupt.

"There were other than Vulcans among the fallen," the Eldest continued, "and we make no claim to following their families' ways, but understand that we honor them all."

She began a quiet prayer, carefully worded and diplomatically neutral, wishing peace or afterlife or rebirth as was each culture's belief. When she had finished, there was a long silence, broken only by a human voice's murmured "Amen."

"Now," T'Lar continued, and for all her totally unshaken calm Spock could have sworn she was relieved, "we may proceed to the celebration of more predictable and welcome change. As the seasons turn, so youth grows to maturity. We bring forth ancient ritual to honor those who represent the ever-changing, never-changed continuance from past to present, from present to future."

She fell silent, and T'Pau picked up her words. "We honor those so newly come to adult status."

She and T'Lar bowed formally to the young Vulcans. The smallest shock almost of alarm shot through Spock as he remembered that as Eldest of his agemates, he would be the one to lead them to the platform and these two formidable figures. He would be the first to accept formal adulthood and the ritual sword. Numbly he watched and listened as T'Lar, elegant white and silver sleeves flowing like wings (*as they did the first time*) began her formal chant:

"As it was in the beginning, so shall it always be . . ."

This time let her complete it, Spock thought, *this time let there be no interruption, no madman, no violence.*

There was none. Like one in a dream, Spock led his agemates forward. He heard his name spoken: "Spock, son of Sarek and Amanda," saw himself step to the edge of the platform, heard himself proclaimed this day an adult capable of adult reasoning and logic, felt the weight of the ceremonial sword in his arms. Still dazed, he bowed, began to turn away to make room for the next of his agemates—

"Spock." T'Pau's voice was quiet but firm. As he turned back to her, puzzled and fighting down an illogical spark of alarm, she asked, "Why hast thee been gifted with a sword?"

Spock hesitated. There was surely a ritual response, but if there was, he could not remember it. "In memory of our past?" he hazarded.

"That is but part of the whole." Her wise old eyes were cool as a sheltered pool, studying him as though aware of his every thought without needing even a finger's touch to his head. "It is to remind thee not to deny the past, yes. But it is also to remind thee how narrow and sharp is the edge between chaos and civilization. And it is to remind thee, Spock, son of two worlds, that it is only a small, small step back to the days when the sword's edge was the only law. Thee must choose a path with care."

Spock bowed again, struggling with himself for proper composure. "I will not forget."

It was a whisper.

The custom on Vulcan, Spock knew, was for each family to celebrate their newly fledged adult's status privately—but he also realized that there could be no true privacy for the family of Sarek, who was, after all, Ambassador to the Federation. Even so, Spock thought, the list of guests was reassuringly small; he had never believed that a mere ceremony could have been so wearing.

Almost as wearing as being out in the desert again!

By nightfall, he could gladly have curled up and slept like a child. Instead, Spock managed to slip away to the relative quiet of the terrace of his father's estate, wrapping his arms about himself against the chill, craning his head back to stare at the star-crowded sky. Why had T'Pau singled him out? His mixed blood? Or had she seen something in him? What?

A tactful cough made him realize he wasn't alone out here after all. "Captain Rabin. Lady. Forgive me. I did not mean to intrude."

"You aren't intruding." The captain looked very different in her simple blue gown and shawl, but she was still very much David's mother, judging from the amused way she was looking at Spock. "'Today I am a man,'" she murmured.

"I . . . beg your pardon?"

"That's what the boys of my people say when they complete their manhood ritual. 'I am a man,' meaning, 'I accept that I'm responsible for my own actions.'"

"I see. Similar, indeed, to the Vulcan way. But . . . I am not yet responsible for my own life."

"Aren't you?" Her smile was rueful. "Nobody ever said that being an adult was easy. Just when you think you've got it all figured out, life has a way of dumping you on your head."

"David?" he asked in a sudden burst of intuition.

"And Starfleet. I never intended to be a single parent, but . . . well . . . life happens. Don't misunderstand: I love my son. But if it wasn't for Starfleet Academy, I don't know what I would have done with him. A starship is hardly the place to raise a child—yet I'm not ready to be tied down to a planetside job, either."

"But David is going into the Academy, and of his own free will." The faint glow of starlight reflected in eyes that were suddenly suspiciously bright. In a soft voice, blinking fiercely, Captain Rabin added, "I'll miss him fiercely, but at least I know he'll be happy. And that sets my mind at least a little bit at ease."

"I am glad." If that statement held emotion, so be it.

"And what of you?" she added suddenly.

"I . . ." Spock stopped, not sure what he was going to say. "I would like . . . I believe that I would like . . . to . . . apply to Starfleet Academy."

"Ah." Was there the faintest note of triumph in her voice? "As I told you before, I will gladly sponsor you for an appointment in the Academy. But . . ."

"My father."

"Exactly. He *is* a rather important Federation ally, you know; the Federation can hardly up and steal his son away."

"Then you won't—"

"Then I will. I'll be happy to sponsor you—but first you must tell your parents what you're doing. Where you will be going."

"I will." Spock bowed, trying to hide his sudden trembling. "I will."

It would be difficult. He knew that. But Spock thought back to all the hardships he and David had faced—and survived.

If the Womb of Fire could not destroy me, he decided, *I can certainly withstand my father's will!*

I will prevail. One way or another, I will prevail.

TWENTY-TWO

**Obsidian, Federation Outpost and Deep Desert
Day 5, First Week, Month of the Shining *Chara*,
Year 2296**

Lieutenant Shara Albright nibbled worriedly at her lower lip, caught herself at it, stopped, then absently started up again.

Where *were* they? That the shuttlecraft had gone down somewhere out there . . . that was a given. But *where?* All that empty, terrible wilderness . . . she fought down a shudder, thinking about the nice, orderly, and above all *green* parks of New Hampton, her homeworld. No deserts were permitted on New Hampton, no barren waste, and the sun was a pleasant golden thing, not this horrible, horrible monster of a Loki; there, nature knew its proper place.

Yes, and so did the people. Albright had been brought up by nice, proper parents to be a nice, proper lady, and where she had ever found the odd spark to enter Starfleet Academy, yes, and to graduate with honors, even if her parents still hadn't quite forgiven her—

No. That wasn't important, not now. There had been nothing in all her training to cover something like this, nothing in the textbooks to deal with the aching sense that she was far too young for her rank, far too inexperienced—

Stop that! she scolded herself. *You are Starfleet! You are an officer! Act like one!*

"Ensign Chase," she snapped. "Anything?"

The young man, bent over the console, staring at the unchanging equations, shook his head without looking up. "Nothing, Lieutenant." His voice shook slightly with weariness. "I *almost* caught something that might have been a transmission, but that was over three hours ago, and it didn't last long enough for me to get a fix on it. Since then . . . not even a squawk."

"Keep on it. They're out there somewhere, and I want you to find them."

Now he did turn slightly in his chair to look up at her. "Uh, Lieutenant, it *has* been over a planetary day now, and we've had no sign—"

"That was an order, mister!"

"Aye-aye, ma'am."

Had there been a touch of pity in his voice? Almost as though he was adding silently to himself, *Doesn't she realize the truth? Doesn't she realize that they're all dead?*

Nonsense. She would not believe that. Captain Rabin, with all his irreverent humor and cheerful disregard for proper Starfleet behavior—no. Someone that—that utterly infuriating, that full of life, could not be dead. She would not, could not, believe that. He would stay alive out of—out of sheer perversity!

All at once, mortified, Albright realized she was on the verge of tears.

Belay that! she scolded herself. *Regulation 256.15: Officers shall show professional behavior at all times.*

But for once, the orderly world of the regulations handbook could give no comfort.

A *chuchaki*, Spock noted, sitting his mount with as much grace as he could manage, was a natural pacer, which meant each stride involved moving first both left legs then both right legs. As a result, the animal had a most distressingly rough gait, rocking its rider briskly from side to side.

The *chuchaki* also smelled very much like . . . he analyzed the aroma, compared it to the memory of an unfortunate encounter on Terra . . . an ancient, unwashed dog. (There, the dog had decided it was his dearest friend and had shed fur all over him; here, the *chuchaki* all seemed delighted to sniff at his fascinatingly different scent and try to nuzzle him. Equally odorous either way.)

However, he could not deny that the *chuchaki,* the entire herd of them, crossed the desert with incredible speed and efficiency.

Rabin, predictably, was having a wonderful time even with danger ahead of them, leaning forward in the saddle, robes flying, looking like something out of one of his beloved adventure movies. Lawrence of Arabia, indeed.

The land was changing as they rode, no longer as level, rising in slow degrees as the Taragi-shar Range loomed up on the horizon. Fingers of ancient black rock, the weathered remains of old eruptions, reached out over the gravel, and the *chuchaki* slowed their bone-jarring pace, picking their way with care, their cleft hoofs clicking against stone but handling the rougher terrain with ease.

Beside Spock rode the Elder on her own gleaming white *chuchaki,* sitting her saddle with the ease of years of experience and showing no sign at all of stress or weariness. At Spock's glance, she nodded.

"We are almost there. Just beyond the ridge that lies before us."

Behind them, the group of nomad warriors (they were hardly disciplined enough to be called a troop), who had been joking and singing as they rode, fell sharply silent, save for the occasional command to or curse at a *chuchaki*.

The *chuchaki*, beasts of the desert plain that they were, were not as silent. They grumbled and complained to themselves at being made to climb, but after some prodding from their riders, they scrambled up and up the broken lava rocks without too much difficulty, their hoofs mastering the steep slope almost as easily as though it were flat.

With a final surge, they crested the ridge and paused.

"There," the Elder said.

Her sweep of an arm took in a barren plain, absolutely flat, absolutely without vegetation. Beneath Loki's hostile glare, it burned a dull, sullen gold. Beyond loomed the mountains, a jagged black wall, like so many great stone knives towering to the sky.

"What is *that?*" Rabin breathed.

"The Taragi-shar Range," Spock replied.

"I know that, but what is that—that great golden basin down there?"

The Elder said nothing, only prodded her *chuchaki* forward. With much groaning and grunting, the other animals followed. None of the other nomads said a word, either, as they rode out across the flat golden plain: sand, against which the *chuchaki*'s hoofs made no sound. Nor was there any other sound, not even the faintest stirring of wind. The air was very hot, very heavy.

"Eerie," Rabin said, his voice a wary whisper.

To agree would be a needless concession to emotionalism. But Spock could not be unaware of the silence, which did seem more than normal. The air prickled uncomfortably along his skin, and he wondered if there was to be a sudden storm. He twisted about in the saddle, seeing the dark mass of the Taragi-shar before them, the equally dark ridge behind them. On either side, arms of old lava, black basalt with glints of obsidian, fanned out from the mountains to the ridge, forming, as Rabin had said, a great bowl. Not a good place to be caught by natural forces or, for that matter, Romulans.

Rabin glanced at Spock with the air of someone who cannot stand another moment of suspense. "Where are we?" the human whispered.

"This," the Elder said softly, "is the *Te-wisat-karak*, the Golden Hell."

"Oh, good name!"

It was nearly a shout in all that silence. The Elder glanced at him in mild disapproval. "It is an ancient site of sacrifice to one whose attention you do not wish to attract: Khar Hakai, the Eater of Souls."

Spock started in spite of himself, feeling an atavistic little chill prickle its way up his spine. *Control,* he told himself firmly. He had learned enough over the years to prove to himself that similar mythoi, similar archetypes, turned up among even unrelated peoples. It was not extraordinary to find that this culture, too, had a demonic being who devoured sentient essences.

Yet something deep within him, some primitive instinct from the days of Vulcan's ancient past, whispered, *Omen.*

"Omens," Spock murmured, "are pure superstition."

Rabin overheard. "Superstitions or no," he whispered, "let's hope that these omens you don't believe in are as good for us as they were the first time around!"

"One does not," the Elder said in stern disapproval, "make light of the powers of Khar Hakai."

No sooner had she mentioned the Eater of Souls than Loki erupted into a spectacular solar flare, a bright, blinding aurora and sudden sharp ionization of air that made nomads and *chuchaki* alike cry out their alarm as the desert sands crackled and sang about them.

Rabin, fighting his curvetting, frightened *chuchaki,* gasped out, "The radiation in this place is really going to climb, and personally, I'd still like to have kids someday."

Spock, quickly checking his tricorder, corrected, "It has already risen. And I am certain you would wish those children to have the normal human genome."

"You bet I would, but let's not stay out here on this open target discussing it!"

The nomads, meanwhile, were shouting out prayers in atavistic horror. The Elder cut through their noise with a sharp, "It is time to invoke the Sunstorm Truce."

Rabin stared. "What's that?"

Her glance said plainly, *Kindly Fool.* With great restraint, the Elder said, "You have not been a part of our world long enough to know it, not you who have always lived behind city walls like a Tamed One."

"We are behind no city walls now," Spock cut in. "And time cannot be wasted in niceties."

The Elder gave him a slight nod of respect, then flung up an arm in signal and urged her *chuchaki* into a dead run for the wall of mountains. The others followed, no one making a sound now save for the pounding of galloping hoofs against sand, while all around them the air flared and burned. At last the nomads swirled to a stop in the partial shade of an overhanging ledge, and the Elder told Spock quickly:

"The Sunstorm Truce is the oldest law of the desert. Even warring clans will put aside their hatreds when the sun rages, and shelter together against our common enemy. No one may refuse a stranger shelter, not even," she added in distaste, "the Faithful. Come, follow."

She slipped as lightly to the ground as a much younger woman, and Spock and Rabin followed her to a deep cleft in the rock wall. Spock, glancing up, noted a petroglyph carved deep into the rock over it: another sun spiral, inlaid with some garish, blood-red stone, with an equally garish yellow warding-off sign below it. This spot was clearly meant to be easily found.

In the fissure below the petroglyph, protected from the elements, hung a great stone bell. *Clever,* Spock thought in sudden comprehension. This was evidently part of the safety system set up by the nomads to gain them admittance to shelters across the desert; there must be similar bells hidden all across the clan territories. And presumably the placement of all the bells took advantage of acoustics so that they could be easily heard by those already in the shelters.

At the Elder's glance, Spock took up the bronze mallet by the bell's side and struck the stone bell. It rang out with a deep, hollow boom, echoing across the rocks with exactly the extraordinary strength he had expected.

The Elder nodded approval. "Well struck. Continue, if you would. Yes, good. There can be no mistaking the sound. Now we need only wait for the door to open."

McCoy swayed on his feet, almost falling, then caught himself, somehow managing to keep his balance. Couldn't fall, couldn't stop talking. How long had he been spouting this gibberish? Seemed like forever. Couldn't be more than a day. Could it?

God, right now he would kill for a nice, cool drink. He'd even settle for a less than nice hard stone floor on which he could lie down and stretch out and—no, mustn't think of rest or, heaven help him, sleep. Mustn't let his mind wander. If the good ole boys back in the good ole U.S. of A. could keep a filibuster going for days, well then, so could he, and . . . and . . . only trouble was, he was running out of horses or ideas for horses. Got to keep going, though. Make 'em up as he went along. Romulans or that madman in white—none of 'em would know the difference anyhow.

"And . . . and his great-grandfather was Equipoise." *God, now I'm quoting Broadway,* Guys and Dolls *or whatever.*

Gotta keep going, though, even though my throat's starting to hurt and I'm getting . . . oh Lord, a pun . . . I'm getting a little hoarse. "And I say unto you, oh my brethren, that Equipoise, he begat him a whole string of mighty horses, and they went on to fame and glory, and of them folks said such wonderstruck things as—what the hell was that?"

A great hollow booming sounded and resounded throughout the cavern, followed by shouts of alarm from all the Faithful. "What is it?" McCoy asked, daringly snatching at Ruanek's arm as the Romulan hurried by. Ruanek only pulled his arm free with a snarl, rushing off without a word. Left forgotten where he stood, McCoy asked plaintively, "Will someone *please* tell me what's going on?"

But no one answered him.

Ruanek let out his breath in a hiss. That had been a near thing, an almost-disaster. When Makkhoi had seized him, the centurion had very nearly reacted with a warrior's reflexes, weapon in hand. Only by the sternest self-control had he kept from drawing and firing. He would not have wanted to be the cause of that brave man's death.

Besides, Ruanek wasn't so certain himself why the Faithful were suddenly swarming about like some hysterical swarm of *tatri* with an overturned nest. What was this they were shouting, this "Sunstorm Truce"?

Suddenly the Master was among them, white robes swirling, the Faithful recoiling from his furious presence. "What are you doing?" he raged at them. "Do not open those doors!"

"We must!" Their voices were frantic. "It is the Sunstorm Truce! Someone outside has invoked it, and we must, *we must* respond!"

Whatever that truce was—something, clearly, to be invoked due to the wild solar activity he'd been told was going on outside—it was obviously of the greatest religious importance to the savages. Surely, their pleading faces were insisting, their Master, their leader, their messiah, surely *he* would understand this most basic and vital of truces.

This isn't the time to argue with them, you Vulcan madman! No matter who's out there, it can't be that large a troop. We can deal with them. But if you don't yield here and now, we're going to have a riot on our hands!

The Master would not heed. With a brusque wave of his hand, he ordered the Romulans forward, Ruanek among them, to bar the way. The Faithful recoiled in shock at the line of cold-faced warriors confronting them.

As though, Ruanek thought with bitter humor, *they can hardly believe that we, their "heavenly messengers," could ever be so cruel.*

For a moment, he dared believe that the shock would be enough, that the Faithful would sink back into submissiveness.

No. As another hollow boom resounded through the cavern, they surged forward again, and every Romulan hastily drew a weapon.

But the Faithful stopped just short of attack, pleading, *"You* must understand, you who come from higher realms. Stand aside, we beg you, stand aside!"

"Hold your fire," Ruanek commanded his warriors. To the Faithful he said, almost gently, "I am not your Master. I, like you, must obey his will. Have you not served him well? Are you not still loyal to him? Is your faith, then, so weak?" Ha, some of them were wavering. "Go back," Ruanek urged. "We will not harm you."

It might have worked. But at just that crucial point, that Vulcan maniac shouted, "There is no such thing as Sunstorm Truce! I so declare it!"

And with terrible timing, that cursed hollow boom sounded again. "There *is* Sunstorm Truce!" the Faithful cried. "The doors *must* be opened, shelter *must* be granted! *This is our oldest law!"*

Someone snorted in contempt: Kharik, a sideways glance told Ruanek. Kharik looked at him fully, saying without words, scorn in his eyes, *Well? Give the command! Open fire!*

But there were children in the mob, women with babies in their arms, and not a weapon among them.

I am a warrior, not a butcher! There is no honor in cutting down children!

"Laws change," Kharik snapped, as much at Ruanek as at the mob, and fired. A child fell, screaming.

And the mob charged.

"Why will they not let us in?" the Elder said as though speaking about stubborn children. "They can't have failed to hear the summons. And they can *not* have strayed that far from the truth."

Her tone said, *I will not permit it!*

"They cannot," Spock agreed, listening intently. "I hear sounds of fighting from within." He exchanged quick glances with Rabin: *Not the Federation.*

Who, then? The Romulans? Or were the Faithful suddenly and unpredictably breaking faith?

"What," Rabin asked succinctly, "has McCoy done?"

"I doubt that even the doctor—"

But Spock broke off sharply as one great door creaked open ever so slightly, metal groaning as though those trying to open it were fighting with those trying to keep it shut. He caught a quick glimpse of chaos within, of Romulans backed into a corner firing at wave after wave of the Faithful, and heard quick, fiery shouts of "Sunstorm Truce" and "Betrayal!"

Perilous to enter just now. But at the same time, they could hardly stay out here during the solar flare. Besides, there could hardly be any better distraction than a rebellion! Given the circumstances, it was illogical to hesitate.

There was a plan, Spock realized, risky but possible. Rabin would try it, and Rabin would get himself killed, so Spock slipped inside before the human could move. Taking a deep breath, he let his voice ring out with all his strength, cold, logical, precise:

"Are *these* your gods?"

Everyone froze, whirling to him in astonishment. Spock took a sure, deliberate step forward in the sudden tense silence, another, following up his momentary advantage with, "What gods would betray their own sacred laws?"

The Faithful drew back as he approached, letting him pass, staring at him in open awe. The Romulans followed him with hands on guns, but made no move to fire, either waiting for orders or simply curious to see what he would do next.

Beyond the mass of people, a tall, white-robed figure stood waiting, head shrouded by the hood of his cloak.

The one who names himself the Master, Spock thought. *Logically, it can only be he. And who else but someone with so melodramatic a title would stand with such melodrama in such flamboyantly impractical garb?*

Leaving the last of the crowd behind, Spock stepped out into the open, pushing back the hood of his desert robes. He saw the Master tense.

"No," the figure breathed. "Ah, no. The past, not the here-and-now. No."

With a sweep of a long-fingered hand, the figure brusquely bared his own head.

Spock stiffened, staring. He should not have been astonished; there was no logical reason for this reaction; they never had found clear proof of that one's death. And yet, illogical or not, he could do nothing just yet but stare at the sight of this aristocratic face. Older, yes, thinner, per-

256

haps, fierce with an aesthetic fervor that was clearly madness, and yet undeniably:

"Sered!"

Sered, too, was staring in wide-eyed incredulity, as though seeing the boy Spock had been, seeing the adult he now was, trying desperately to reconcile the two. "You are Spock!"

It was almost, Spock thought, an accusation. "Yes," he said. "I am."

TWENTY-THREE

**Vulcan, Sarek's Estate
Day 21, Tenth Week of Tasmeen,
Year 2247**

The sealed door of Lady Amanda's wet-planet conservatory clicked open as she stood pruning her peace roses. Miniature pastel sunsets of rose and yellow brushed her hands as she straightened. Only Spock ventured to interrupt her here, because only Spock believed her when she told him his presence was never an interruption. She had been expecting it. And, since he couldn't yet see her face, Amanda allowed herself a smile of pure joy: Her son was alive. Her son was unhurt.

Her son was changed.

How could he not be changed, poor boy?

After his airlift from the Womb of Fire, a debriefing that would have been arduous for an adult, and his release from the Healers' care, Spock's control had been painstaking. His ordeal in the desert seemed to have honed him to a new edge of power and resolve.

Sarek was pleased at Spock's increased self-mastery. That has to count for something.

But she was Spock's mother: if anyone could perceive in that rigidly still face that he had come to some sort of important conclusion, it was she. "Out with it, Spock."

At least he did her the credit of not asking, *How did you know?* "Mother, I have come to a decision." A human youth might have stammered or blurted out the rest; Spock's words were measured. "I have spoken with Captain Rabin. Her son, David, with whom I traveled, will be entering Starfleet Academy. She thinks that I would be a suitable candidate for entrance."

Very carefully, Amanda laid aside her pruning shears and looked away from the inappropriate loveliness of her peace roses.

What hasn't he told us? What did happen out there?

Whatever, it had clearly been so traumatic that it was going to change Spock's whole future.

"I take it you concur with Captain Rabin."

A nod.

Amanda hastily began adjusting her jacket, an excuse to turn her head away so that her son wouldn't see any unseemly emotion. Sarek would be desolate, and she would miss her son—oh God, would she miss him! But Spock—Spock would be going home! He would see the town in which she had grown up, the cities in which she had studied, the seas and mountains at which she had marveled and that, loving Sarek, she had forsaken to follow him to this forge of a desert planet where the word "love" might be felt, but never, never spoken.

And Spock? What was he thinking? Surely he had never been more thoroughly Vulcan than now, when he was turning his back on all that Vulcan stood for.

All that Vulcan *said* it stood for. There was a difference.

"You could simply have left," she ventured, trying to

break through the shield of control he was raising against her.

Spock raised an eyebrow. "Captain Rabin told me her nomination was contingent on my telling you. And my father."

Not securing their consent nor even their acknowledgment. Just, simply, their awareness that their son has made his choice.

"Captain Rabin's ship leaves Vulcan in seven days," Spock continued. "I wish to . . ."

He hesitated, and Amanda finished silently for him, *Tie everything up in one neat package? Oh Spock.* Her heart sank. *All Sarek's hopes . . .*

But then Amanda reminded herself sharply that Sarek might hope all he wished—even though her husband would reject the concepts of "hope" and "wish"—but she had a son to protect.

"You mean to tell your father tonight?"

Spock nodded. "I plan to notify the Science Academy tonight that I must decline their offer of admission. It is proper for my father to know before I do so."

Besides, Amanda thought, the Academy would probably call Sarek the minute Spock finished his notification. *"Sarek, do you know what that son of yours has done?"* As if he were unfit to decide for himself. *A pity I can't be a fly on the wall at that conversation. Even if, as everyone's told me over and over, Vulcan doesn't have flies on walls!*

"I am glad that you are telling us, not just . . ." She dashed a grimy hand across her eyes, angry that tears had suddenly welled up. "Not just running off to join the army."

He blinked. "That is an idiom with which I am unfamiliar."

"Then learn it quickly, because you're going to hear lots of unfamiliar idioms at the Academy. 'Running off to join the army' used to happen on Earth. Boys who were wild or who . . ." What? Didn't get enough approval? Love? Their father's respect? ". . . who weren't content with their lot would run away and join the military. But my own son, brought up to nonviolence, learning weapons . . ."

Something flickered deep within Spock's eyes. "Mastery of violence is mastery of one's self. Surak teaches us that."

"Oh Spock," Amanda sighed, "you know I can't trade chapter and verse about Surak with you. Just tell me: What brought this on?"

"David Rabin told me how Starfleet prizes the individual—"

"And just because David—"

No. Spock had led his agemates before T'Pau and T'Lar. It was not merely illogical to accuse him of following, conforming; it was inaccurate. Her son was a born leader.

Was that satisfaction in her son's eyes that she'd broken off? Relief? "All my life," he said softly, "I have been under observation. Some have waited for me to fail, and some have wanted it. Others have stood by, ready to excuse me, while still others have just . . . observed. I look no different from the males of my age set. But whenever my control faltered, I was punished more stringently. This is not resentment, Mother," he added quickly, "it is observation. What is more . . ." His voice grew rough, but only for an instant. "I punished myself."

"Spock."

"Look at Sered. If people had watched him as carefully, perhaps, as I have always been observed . . . no. Let that go. Mother . . . do you think I can succeed?"

Oh my son, you are still a boy after all! "I think there is nothing that you cannot do. Except escape the dictates of your own conscience. What does it tell you?"

"You yourself told me that I am a bridge between two worlds. It is logical that I experience both, not attempt to deny half my heritage. Starfleet allows me to do so, not as an ambassador's unworthy son, but as myself."

He bowed and left. Amanda seized her pruning shears and attacked her roses through a blur of tears.

Tonight, Amanda thought, as the family sat together after dinner, her translations seemed lamentably flat. At least working on them spared her having to meet her husband's eyes. Through their bond, she sensed what passed for contentment in a Vulcan: a satisfactory dinner; the company of his family; a wife intent on work that had won her respect on her adopted world; a son who had survived an ordeal with courage and honor; the prospects of an evening's work and an interval of meditation before he retired.

Spock laid aside his holographic sketchcube.

"I must speak," he said.

Sarek raised his head, looking at his son with a surprisingly benign gaze. Amanda felt her heart contract.

"Acting unilaterally is disrespectful," Spock continued, "and I mean no disrespect. But . . . I am about to transmit my resignation to the appointment granted me by the Vulcan Science Academy."

"Indeed?" Sarek's eyes narrowed ever so slightly. "I presume you have alternative plans. Is it too much to ask you to share them?"

Spock swallowed. "Captain Rabin said she would appoint me to Starfleet, but that I must first tell my parents."

Sarek flicked Amanda a *you-knew-this!* glance. A hint of his surprise and pain echoed through the bond they shared. "The Federation knows my opinions of its military. I appear to have valued Captain Rabin's judgment too highly. You will, of course, tell the captain that I do not give my consent."

Spock never flinched. "In all respect, sir, I do not require your consent. I was told that I must, however, acquaint you with my plans before I enter this next phase of my life." He paused, for the first time showing a trace of uncertainty, then added, "I would welcome your acknowledgment and approval."

Look at him, Amanda thought in anguish. *Standing there like a soldier at military attention, waiting for the world to end.*

It ended in ice.

"Never that," Sarek said. "The idea of my son, handling weapons, learning the madness of the ways of violence, is totally unacceptable. You are ill-prepared to deal with such things."

"I confronted violence *and* madness," Spock countered, "in the person of Sered, your colleague. And I prevailed."

Sarek's frown deepened. "We must oppose violence, not embrace it. Your control frequently slips even here on Vulcan where every incentive is provided you for mastering your emotions. If your control fails among offworlders, you do not simply fail, you fail all Vulcan."

"T'Pau gave us weapons on Mount Seleya as a sign that we were adults. Why would she give us swords if we were to shun weapons? Why are the martial arts taught in Vulcan's schools?"

"For discipline." Sarek bit off the words.

"Quite so," Spock retorted. "I require a specific type of discipline that the Science Academy does not provide, but that Starfleet does."

Sarek rose, only slightly taller than his son, but much more solid. "For thousands of years, Vulcan has stood for passion's mastery. In turning aside from our Way, you set yourself in judgment over Surak. If your logic were not impaired, you would not need to be reminded that Surak died by violence."

"Surak followed his own choices, my father," Spock replied. "As must I. Or, the ritual on Mount Seleya notwithstanding, I am no more than a boy to be rebuked, and the ceremony and all I learned in the Womb of Fire are lies."

"The adepts do not lie—" Sarek began, but Spock cut through his father's words.

"On Mount Seleya, I swore to be an autonomous adult, not an extension of you, my father. Or of anyone else."

"You are no part of me," Sarek told him. "Observe what you have done to your mother, to one of those humans among whom you will go. Your very presence will damage them."

"My father, do you consider that your years as ambassador have damaged Earth? In that case, it seems illogical of you to persist."

Sarek cast a glance at Amanda. "I require an interval of meditation. I shall speak to your son only when his reason has returned."

He strode from the room. Even the echoes of his footsteps seemed to ache.

Spock stood frozen, staring after the father who had just repudiated him. "What else could I have done?" he asked, and behind the rigid self-control, Amanda read a hint of plaintive confusion.

"You were very harsh," she told him. "I know that you acted as you logically believed you must, but I wish things had been otherwise."

"Why must it be *my* will that you wish 'had been otherwise'?" Spock demanded. "What of my father's will?"

"That," said Amanda, "is what I am going to find out."

Drawing the soft silk folds of her skirts about her, she withdrew. As she passed through the door, she glanced back at Spock.

She had left him holding his ground in the spacious, silent living room, but now that proud posture had sagged as if he had been defeated, the image of confusion, of anguish.

You are still young, my poor dear, deny it though you will!
As she watched, she saw Spock straighten and take the three breaths with which, she knew, control was invoked. Unaware that his mother was still watching, he turned to the communications console in the corner, clearly meaning to use it, not the computer in his room, to announce his decision and his rights in public, as befitted an adult.

Amanda retreated down the corridor, fighting for self-control. A human needed all the control she could get when Vulcans, even Vulcans loved out of all logic, fought. Was she truly reduced to eavesdropping upon her son and her husband? An irresistible force had met an immovable object. *Careful, Amanda, or the impact will crush you.*

Or break your heart.

For a moment, Spock stood looking about the room his mother had so carefully arranged to mix both Vulcan and human tastes. Right now, its warmth, careful lighting, and meticulous choice of furnishings seemed as much an illusion as his mother's hope that one of them—Spock *or* Sarek—would see reason, or at least the other's point of view.

I cannot live the life my father has planned for me. I am myself, a separate adult.

The thought was not quite as convincing as it should be. He kept picturing his father's face, feeling his father's utter rejection. Quickly, Spock pressed a button, another, opening a specific communications channel.

"Spock!" David Rabin's voice pierced the stillness. "That you? How're you doing?"

The human's voice was warm and friendly, almost overwhelmingly emotional after the so very controlled confrontation with Sarek. But then, David had shown how he could turn emotion, particularly humor, into a survival instinct.

Such techniques cannot apply to me. And yet, how much

has he—and his humor—influenced my decision? Has it been contamination? Or . . . an improvement on the whole?

Not certain, Spock resorted to a formal "I am restored to my customary level of function. And you? Have you recovered from dehydration?"

"Oh, I'm fine. Takes more than a little desert trek to stop a Rabin! But, you know, Spock, about that *plomik* soup you like? They fed me a fair amount of it. Seems it has some valuable stuff in it for recovering humans. But as for taste, well—"

"Am I to assume that it does not 'taste just like chicken'?"

"Hey, he *remembers!* We'll have you punning yet."

"No. I . . . David, I . . ."

"Oh. You told them, didn't you?"

"It was not pleasant, but it is done."

"Spock, I'm—I'm—" Another, longer pause. "I'll get my mother."

"Thank you." Alone in the silence, Spock stood rigidly still.

It was done. He had taken another irrevocable step toward a new future.

And away, a small voice in his mind whispered, *from his father.*

Hesitantly, Amanda laid her fingertips on the closed door of Sarek's study, waiting for her presence to resonate through the bond to her husband.

"Enter, my wife," Sarek called, his voice leached of the subtle expressions that deep love, infinite patience, and twenty years of marriage had taught her to discern.

The small room was serene, almost austere, the walls hung with a few weavings chosen for their soothing patterns, so amenable to meditation. In the corner of the room, a firepot in the shape of a *haran,* a legendary fire-beast, glowed. An incense that Amanda recognized from her marriage, when Sarek's mind and hers touched each other for the first time, filled the air. It was an aid to concentration. One that Sarek rarely needed.

She made herself look at her husband. For once, his meditations had not refreshed him. The furrows in his cheeks were deeply marked, and his eyes were hollow. He looked as if he had fought and was still fighting for mastery.

Of Spock?

Her answer came immediately through the bond.

Not of Spock. Of himself.

He held out two fingers to reaffirm their bond. *Parted from me and never parted. Never and always touching and touched.* It was second nature for her to glide forward and touch his hand. And to respond.

His fingers were hot and dry. The anguish that came through the bond and the ferocity with which he suppressed it made her recoil. Before she could stop them, she felt tears roll down her face.

"Amanda, this is not logical."

His voice was gentle. Amanda forced herself not to flinch as Sarek rose and his fingers touched the tearstains on her face. Illogic lay not in weeping on a desert world, but in flinching away from her husband. He was offering her support, yet his touch told her that he was the one who needed comfort. And she had rebuffed him.

She must. Sarek had no comfort for Spock, and she, therefore, had none for him.

Because dissembling was futile through the bond, she said only their son's name. "Spock."

Sarek drew back. "I should have insisted that an Adept of Gol probe Spock's mind while he was under the Healers' observation."

She knew he sensed her flare of anger, but she managed to

keep her voice even. "Your inference is unfair, my husband. Unworthy. T'Pau would not have honored our son had he been deranged."

"It violates all logic that a son of mine would turn his back on my instruction."

There was a limit to human self-control. "Sarek," Amanda snapped, "if you don't remember the nightmare of those days when we didn't know if we could have a son, I do! Does it matter, does it truly matter, *what* lifepath Spock chooses, provided it is honorable—and that he is alive to pursue it?"

"Spock has rejected thousands of years of peace to choose Starfleet and its ethic of war, its glorification of violence. How long can anyone survive that way?"

"Vulcan survived its wars," Amanda retorted, "long enough for there to be a Surak. And Earth survived, long enough to make First Contact."

"My wife, you use logic as a weapon. That is a human trait."

"Oh no, we are not alone in that trait, my husband. But we *will* be alone, you and I, unless you reconsider your treatment of our son."

"I shall have no son," said Sarek. "Again."

"Is that what it is?" Amanda demanded, while inwardly she winced. Of course she and Sarek sometimes quarreled; it would have been beyond even Vulcan will for twenty years of marriage to have passed completely smoothly. But surely there had never been so much at stake. "You're afraid of being hurt again? Is all this disdain for Starfleet just simple fear? Let me tell you, my husband, I am afraid too. But human women have been sending their boys off to war—"

"In that case, my wife, why do you weep?"

"Because I hate it! And because my child is now old enough to make a man's decision. Chickens can't go back into eggs—and I don't need you to tell me I'm speaking in outworn metaphors! Spock is old enough and certainly intelligent enough to choose his own path. You did not even ask his reasons."

Sarek merely raised a disdainful eyebrow.

"Yes. I know. His choice is so alien to you that you reject it as illogical by definition. But Sarek . . ." She tried to draw breath around the lump in her throat. "When we married, humans and Vulcans both told us how illogical our decision was. Do you recall how many people told us it was a mistake?"

"Seven hundred and fifty-five, at last count," Sarek said, and there might have been the slightest trace of ironic humor in the words. The humor vanished. "Do you now consider our union a mistake?"

Her awareness of him had rarely been stronger. And her fury at him had never been greater.

"I have never felt so, not for a moment. But I tell you, I will not let you destroy our son, or yourself. Or," her voice broke, "me."

Suddenly the small study felt unbearable alien and oppressive. Amanda rushed from it out into her gardens. She walked for hours as the night grew chill, staring out at the Forge on which her son had been hammered into something new.

What would become of him?

And what, O my husband, my love whom I could cheerfully strangle right now, will become of us?

Subtle filters tempered the ruddy violence of 40 Eridani A's light into a glow more like that of Earth's sun. In the discreet restaurant near Shikahr's Terran enclave, Amanda folded back her sunveils and waited for her guest.

Ah. Captain Rabin was punctual and most tactfully wearing civilian clothing much like her own: robes of elegant, flowing fabric that was sturdier than it seemed. After all, she came from a culture that prided itself on its desert heritage; she had proper respect for Vulcan's sun. But then, Amanda had seen the captain under medical care, wrapped in a thermal blanket and sprouting tubes, and had observed at the time that this was the kind of officer whose true uniform was her own dignity.

Whispers rose from the few patrons fortunate enough to secure reservations nearby. *Meet the ladies who lunch,* Amanda thought ironically: the Vulcan ambassador's human wife and one of the first women ever to command a starship. More whispers presented various inaccurate implications and hypotheses. Amanda flashed her best smile, then attempted to ignore the onlookers out of existence.

"Lady Amanda?"

"Captain Rabin."

"Are you often one of the ladies who lunch, Lady Amanda?"

Apparently, Captain Rabin possessed her son's gift for using humor to ease her way. "Right now, Captain, I don't feel particularly ladylike. Please, call me Amanda."

"I'm Nechama. After all, our sons are friends. What can I do for you?"

"Well, for a start, you can sit down and order lunch."

Nechama Rabin looked at the choices. "Vegetables, vegetables, and more vegetables. Ever want a steak?"

"After twenty years, not very often." Amanda could not help smiling at the other woman. The woman who had stolen her son.

"Frankly," said Nechama, after a moment, "right now, I feel as if I am going into battle. I almost think I'd prefer Klingons."

She picked up a glass and drank. Holding her gaze, Amanda raised her glass, murmured, and drank too.

"Water ritual?" asked the Starfleet officer. "Why?"

"You helped save my son's life. I can never thank you enough." *I, not necessarily my husband. She is intelligent enough to understand what I do not say.*

"Please. Spock helped save *my* son's life and, for that matter, mine."

"Let me make this perfectly clear. I do not believe that you meant to steal my son."

"If we're being clear, Amanda, I don't know if I would have told Spock anything about Starfleet. Granted, he's a fine boy, but the Federation is full of fine boys. And girls. But, when David told me that Spock might be interested . . . well, for all David's youth and his habit of turning everything into a joke, his people skills are astonishing." Rabin grimaced. "It would have been worse than illogical not to offer Spock the chance. It would have been wasteful."

She eyed Amanda as shrewdly as her son must have sized up Spock. "So, is that the explanation you wanted from me?"

Amanda looked down at the assorted greenery on her plate.

"I see," Rabin murmured. "The ambassador's taking it badly, isn't he?"

To reply would violate Vulcan privacy. But just then, Amanda realized, faced with an understanding, accomplished, and above all *human* woman, she did not care. "Very badly. Vulcans, for all their obsession with logic, are not passionless." She could feel herself flushing. "But they master their emotions by a discipline so harsh it makes Starfleet look like shore leave."

"I . . . don't envy you."

"Please, don't misunderstand! My husband and I have a good marriage, a very good marriage." *Usually. Just not*

271

now. "But Sarek takes Spock's decision as a betrayal. He refuses to speak to him. Spock pretends not to care and spends his time preparing to leave home." To Amanda's horror, she heard her voice break. She mastered it with every discipline she had learned on Vulcan. "My Vulcan son. One kind word from Sarek would have won his obedience. He adores his father, and he's tried so hard to win his approval!"

Nechama Rabin reached out a hand, then made a small gesture of futility with it.

"It's all right," Amanda said dryly. "I'm Vulcan only by marriage. You can touch me. And I can't really blame Spock for finally deciding that he can't please his father and finding something of his own. Even if it's Starfleet."

Captain Rabin straightened. "'Even'? You share the ambassador's dislike of 'Federation militarism'?"

"I'm not from a Starfleet family. And my family has no tradition of fighting men, much less fighting women. For generations, we haven't needed one."

"I see. The political situation could deteriorate if the ambassador supports Vulcan secession."

"In revenge for Spock's joining Starfleet? No. Revenge is illogical. And Sarek would consider reprisals beneath his dignity."

So he will turn his pain inward instead. After a time, he will believe he truly does not care.

"Amanda, what are you trying to tell me?"

"That I can't fight what must be. Look after my son, Nechama. I know your duties take you away from Earth, but Starfleet is your world. You can help ease a lonely boy into it."

"Don't go imagining Spock as some stranger in a strange land. No, it won't be easy for him at first; it isn't easy for any of the cadets. But as you say, I know Starfleet. And that's why I can promise you that Spock is going to make friends who will last him his entire life."

Amanda dropped her gaze to her plate. For the first time in days, she felt as if she could eat. She raised her glass, a gesture Nechama Rabin copied.

"L'chaim," the captain. "Here's to life."

"To life," Amanda echoed, and almost managed a smile.

TWENTY-FOUR

Intrepid II, Obsidian Orbit
Year 2296

The sirens of red alert whooped in rhythm with the red lights that flashed across the bridge.

"Shields on!" Uhura ordered. "Have you still got a fix on that Warbird?"

"Aye-aye, ma'am."

"Lock on phasers," Uhura ordered Weapons.

"Phasers locked on, ma'am."

"Good," she said. "Now, keep your hands away from the firing button. Sit on them, tie them behind you if you have to. If a Klingon like Azetbur managed to wage peace, so can we."

That drew appreciative smiles from the bridge crew. Well, what did you know? She hadn't thought they had it in them.

Maybe I've underestimated them. Maybe all they needed was action. Our own little private Kobayashi Maru.

"Ma'am?" Lieutenant Richards began. "They don't *seem*

aware that a flaw in the cloaking device is concentrating radiation from the solar flares."

Skeptical, Lieutenant? Shows you have sense.

"Won't that radiation subside when the flares do?" Uhura asked. "Yes? Keep tracking that Warbird. Plot its course on screen."

"Aye-aye."

Warbirds have to drop cloaking before they fire. At least they used to. There'd been some mutterings about the events that had led up to Camp Khitomer, but they'd been slapped with "nosebleed" classification status. There had been a lot of "I could tell you, but then I'd have to kill you" tied up with that conference.

All right. Go with the facts that were, not those that might be. "Let's think this one out," Uhura said. "What Mr. . . . I mean, Captain Spock calls a thought-experiment. We know that Warbirds have to emerge from cloaking to fire." *Or we used to know that.* "So far, so good."

"Aye-aye, ma'am." That was general agreement, albeit mystified. They didn't know where she was going with this.

"But wait a minute," she continued. "We can track the Romulan by the flaw in its cloaking device. But they're no fools, never were. And since they're no fools, I am assuming they mean for us to track them. They're counting on it. So, as far as I'm concerned, they've already chalked us up as a casualty."

Uhura hit the communications panel on her chair's arm. "Uhura to Engineering. Mr. Atherton, how're you coming with that diversion of impulse power?"

"We can boost phaser fire about fifty percent for maybe two broadsides, Commander," Atherton said, as if he was making a vast concession.

"'Maybe' two broadsides?" Uhura asked. "Not enough for a whole battle? See what else you can do by . . . eight hundred hours. And while you're at it, have you got the specs for a cloaking device?"

Long, long ago, Captain Kirk himself had stolen those specs. Even now, tense and frightened as she was, Uhura had to stifle a grin at her memory of Kirk in the command chair wearing tilted eyebrows and pointed ears—and Spock's insistence that on Kirk, they were not aesthetically appealing.

"Aye, Captain," said Atherton. He sounded really apprehensive now.

Getting to know me, are you, Atherton? Good. "Excellent," Uhura said. "How long do you think it'll take for you to build one up from scratch?"

Grinning, she prudently turned down the volume right before an anguished Oxonian howl from Atherton would have split her eardrums.

"Good. Cut that time in half, mister, and get back to me. Bridge out.

"We may want to pull our own disappearing act," Uhura explained to the bridge crew. "Can't hurt."

Well, it couldn't hurt anyone but Atherton and his crew. And maybe a Romulan or two.

The crew dropped into wait-and-see mode. Uhura negotiated appeals from Engineering. From time to time, she reduced Duchamps to apologetic admissions that he'd received no transmissions from any of the ships he had hailed. *Some of those ships are imaginary, mister, remember?* Still, one message from *Excelsior*, say . . .

Uhura stared out into space, as if willing the Warbird to become visible, to finally break the suspense.

Why not wish for a knight in shining armor while you're at it, lady? Jim Kirk's dead, Spock's missing, and you're going to fight this with every weapon you can.

"Commander . . . something's coming in," Duchamps

cut into Uhura's thoughts. "Warbird, Commander. It's dropping its cloaking device."

"Shields on full," Uhura snapped. "Battle stations, alert! Mr. Atherton, how about those phasers?"

"The message is coming from the Romulan vessel." If Duchamps sounded any more surprised, his jaw would probably have thumped onto his workstation.

"Well," Uhura drawled, "will wonders never cease? Put her captain on screen, mister."

She drew herself up into what she privately called her Queen of Sheba pose. Romulans responded to magnificence, and she knew that Romulan women often held high positions on board their starships and in government. Respect for women was built into their culture. She had that working for her—and the fact that she was a veteran of the *Enterprise*. One of Jim Kirk's own.

The figure who appeared on-screen wore no helm. His uniform was finer than most Romulan uniforms she had seen, and she'd seen fewer stars in some nebulae than glittered on his tunic. Dark hair, meticulously cut, pale skin, high cheekbones, a commanding arch of nose, and eyebrows almost ridiculously well arched made this Romulan look more patrician than most. *Hmmm, must be seeing one of the real aristocrats,* Uhura thought. He was definitely worth looking at, *and I'll just bet he knows it, too.*

Keeping her hands out of sight, she brought up Intelligence files, ready to search on whatever name her adversary supplied.

"You are Lieutenant Commander Uhura of the *Intrepid?*" the Romulan commander asked.

"Commander Uhura of the science vessel *Intrepid II,"* Uhura corrected sweetly. "Captain Spock, of Vulcan, is our commander of record."

The Romulan officer nodded. No name? Either he was very rude or very confident. Or he was playing a game.

Uhura wasn't Communications for nothing. She was good at games. "You have the advantage of me, sir," she said, arching her own eyebrows and putting a great lady's disdain into her voice.

"That I have, Commander."

"I was not speaking of firepower, sir, but of courtesy," Uhura countered. "You are an intruder in this space. You use our names, but have not supplied your own."

What the Romulans used for registration numbers appeared on her workstation, and *remind me to log a commendation for Duchamps,* Uhura thought. She ran a fast search.

"Avrak," she said, and saw the slightest tightening of his mouth. "Commander Avrak of the *Adamant.* And what," she added with a second quick glance at the display, "is Senator Pardek's own sister-son doing in this quadrant of the galaxy? A trifle indiscreet of you, isn't it, Commander?"

She had been right. Pardek had been one of the most prominent figures at Camp Khitomer after Nanclus of Romulus had been arrested, and Avrak was his nephew and heir.

"Your intelligence is good, Commander," Avrak said smoothly. Did he seem somewhat peeved at having to share a title with a signals officer jumped up to command? All the better if he did. "But so is ours. I know what your weapons specifications are on the science vessels. Spy vessels, I should say. You are in violation of Romulan space, a clear declaration of war. I call upon you to surrender."

Uhura smiled thinly as her crew whispered objections. "Commander," she said in her best imitation of James Kirk, "I'm surprised at you. Don't you know that we have already transmitted our position back to Starfleet, and in cipher? You're the one who's violated the Neutral Zone, as you know perfectly well. Your cloaking device has been leaking radiation thanks to the solar flares in this system. I'd have that checked, if I were you," she added with false solicitousness. "And put your engineering officer on report while you're at it."

Avrak smiled ever so slightly. "Now you are the one who is overconfident, Commander. Does your crew know that you're planning to fly them straight into the mouth of Erebus?"

Oh, he was a cultivated one, wasn't he, with his references to ancient Romulan battle epics?

"We await reinforcements," Uhura purred. "You may believe you have us outgunned: I would not trouble to dispel your illusions. Nevertheless, when our convoy arrives, you might as well be commanding . . ." Inspiration hit her; Romulans *hated* ridicule. "A rubber ducky."

Did he get the reference? Possibly; at least he knew from her tone of voice that he'd just been insulted.

Atherton, you'd damn well better have those phasers online by now. And a cloaking device of our very own would be really useful.

"Commander," came Atherton's voice, right on cue, "I've got the firepower you want, but please, for the ship's sake, don't go fighting any fleet actions."

Hadn't planned to, mister. She tapped out assent on her console, continuing to keep her hand below Commander Avrak's line of vision.

"Come, come, Commander," Avrak said in the most urbane of tones. "We do not have to charge you with spying. Call it . . . engine failure. A most convenient fiction. You were forced to divert course, and we chanced to find you."

"When someone dies, his heart stops," Uhura retorted. "That doesn't mean that a man shot by phasers dies of a heart attack. Or that a Romulan who's overextended himself can't bluff."

"As can a Starfleet officer who knows she is outgunned."

"Oh no, my dear Commander Avrak, *you're* the one who's bluffing." Uhura kept her face carefully blank. *"Excelsior's* on her way. Commanded by Hikaru Sulu. Do you know him? One of James Kirk's best."

"Ah, what a pity. We broke your cipher, Commander. We know that *Excelsior* has not yet responded to your distress signal."

"You broke *one* of our ciphers, sir," Uhura riposted, "as you were meant to do. We have others. Do you really want to wait around to see if *Excelsior* shows up? Captain Sulu takes a dim view of trespass. As you know. Right about now, he's really not very happy with treacherous Warbirds."

Uhura took a deep breath, thankful that her bridge crew knew to confine their reactions to glances and whispers. It was one thing to bluff with hardware and starships. Now for the real bluff, which was, of course, political.

"Commander." She leaned forward in her best "let's talk equal-to-equal" pose. "It seems to me that you are of no use to your senator and patron dead. Unless, of course, you are of an age and standing sufficient to create an . . . inconvenience. Enough of an inconvenience that he might see an advantage in favoring your heir over yourself."

She flashed a smile that men in several quadrants of the galaxy had assured her was dazzling. Avrak's face flushed darkly, but not as dark as hers, which gave away nothing at all, thank you very much.

"Perhaps," Uhura added, "you came to investigate a few spies whom you might have downworld, hmm? May I remind the commander that Obsidian is a Federation protectorate, secured by a Starfleet outpost? Unless your people are planning to bob their ears and bleed red for a change, it's going to be easy enough to spot them, you know. Or," she asked with sweet malevolence, "have you beamed a plastic surgeon downworld, too?"

No answer.

"Do you know," Uhura went on, "I cannot believe that a senior Romulan officer, a patrician of your Empire, would create an act of war merely because you were too indiscreet to not threaten or bluff. It seems most . . . illogical, especially for a race of Vulcan stock. Perhaps your kinsman is right to focus on your heir, not on yourself."

Leave him some *dignity,* she warned herself. *After all, he's a Romulan. If he loses too much face, he'll fight to the death to regain it.*

"Lady," Avrak forced out between clenched teeth, "you forget yourself."

"Commander," Uhura gave him back as good as she got, "I cannot believe you would declare war—beyond the fact of your illegal presence here—because you were worsted in an argument with a lady. I would suggest you withdraw. Now. I grow weary of this debate."

That tactic had worked for Captain Kirk. Would it work for Uhura? She crossed her fingers, well out of line of sight, and prayed silently.

Avrak allowed himself to laugh. "Commander . . . Lady, how I wish we had met somewhere, almost anywhere other than upon the bridges of enemy ships." That, Uhura thought, was probably the only truthful thing he'd said so far. "I am minded to indulge your bluff for some hours longer," Avrak continued. "And then . . ." His smile broadened in a way that made Uhura want to slap him; he was too confident by half. "We shall see what we shall see." He paused. If they had been in the same room, Uhura suspected, he would have looked her up and down. "Until then, *Adamant* will . . . hold fast."

Intrepid's screen blanked as Avrak ended transmission. An instant later, the Warbird disappeared as its cloaking device engaged.

"Well," Uhura said brightly. "That was interesting, wasn't it? Or, as Captain Spock would say, fascinating.

"Duchamps, are you still picking up those radiation anomalies from the Warbird?"

"Yes, ma'am."

"Good. Well, at least we've got a few new weapons for ourselves." Two, anyhow: the augmented phasers and the cloaking device, assuming Atherton got it online (and she'd bet a month's pay on his success). And maybe, just maybe, they'd get Captain Spock back.

"Commander?" Lieutenant Richards asked warily. "I . . . uh . . ."

"Spit it out, mister."

"Begging the commander's pardon, but it sounded as if that Avrak were . . . uh . . . attracted to you and letting you know it. And during red alert, too." He sounded shocked.

"Did it, Lieutenant?" Uhura gave him another of her dazzling smiles and saw him actually flinch from the impact. *Did you think I didn't know it, mister?* "Now that, too, is fascinating. Reminds me of a little something Captain Kirk taught me long ago. Remember? I've said it before: Anything can be a weapon. Anything at all."

Red alert continued to sweep across the bridge, concealing her science officer's blush.

And, darker skin or no, her own.

TWENTY-FIVE

I am Faisal ibn Saud ibn Turki, Ensign Prince repeated
defiantly to himself. *I am a prince of the ancient ruling
house. I will* not *die in such an ignoble fashion!*

The archaic words weren't much comfort. Faisal looked at
the rest of the group, huddled into the deepest recess of the
cave against the fury of the solar flare outside. (Dramatic,
that flare; too bad that they couldn't exactly enjoy the view.)
Not one of the troop looked happy, or bold, or anything
other than . . . resigned.

*Yes, yes, I know, if it is written we shall die, then we shall
die—but no one can know in advance what is written, so
damned if I'm just going to curl up and—and wait. "Trust in
Allah but tie your camel," and all that.*

But neither Islamic theology nor Arabic proverbs were
going to comfort these people. Instead, Faisal said as briskly

283

as he could, "If I am not mistaken, solar flares of this intensity don't last too long."

"They don't have to," Ozmani muttered. "We'll be out of food soon enough."

"What nonsense is this? We still have plenty of supplies, enough of these . . ." But even Faisal couldn't bring himself to call ration bars food. "These nutrients," he finished resolutely, "to see us through three days. Four, if we're careful."

"Water."

Faisal just barely kept from snapping something hot in Arabic. "We have enough water, too," he contented himself with saying, "as long as we don't get too energetic." No, that was only reinforcing the "curl up and die" idea. *I'm a pilot, curse it all, not a—a psychiatrist! What am I supposed to say?*

Ha, yes, he had it. Faisal continued as brightly as he could, "We did get off that one burst of a message before the flare. The base personnel couldn't have missed it, and brief though it was, they're good enough back there to have gotten a fix on us. Hey, you know those folks! By now they'll be searching for us. As soon as the flare dies down, they'll be coming to get us."

No response from any of them, save a wan smile from Lieutenant Diver. Humoring him, Faisal thought. These were a group of well-trained specialists suddenly stuck in the middle of danger with nothing constructive to do, that was at the heart of it. Of course they were all used to the good old military "hurry up and wait" that hadn't changed since the days when his great-great-however-many-great-grandfathers were out fighting the Turks. But usually the "hurry up and wait" happened when one was amid familiar surroundings. It was asking a lot of these people to combine passive waiting with the hardships of desert survival.

"All right," Faisal said suddenly. "Enough brooding. When my ancestors were stuck in the middle of the Rub al-Khali, the Empty Quarter of our homeland, with nothing around them but . . . well . . . nothing, they could very easily have let all that desert emptiness get to them. Instead, they kept up morale by telling each other stories."

Kavousi sighed, just a touch too loudly. Faisal glared at him, in no mood for sarcasm. "Captain Rabin left me in charge, mister. And if I say we're going to start a storytelling circle, then by Allah, that's exactly what we're going to do. Besides," he added with a quick grin, "haven't any of you ever heard of Scheherazade?"

A few wry chuckles answered him, and Faisal continued, cheerleading, "We're Starfleet, aren't we? If one woman alone could hold off Death for a thousand and one nights, we can damn well hold it off for three or four little days!"

A moment ago, Centurion Ruanek had been surrounded by natives shoving against him, trying to overwhelm him even as he fired and fired again. A moment ago, he had been struggling to keep his footing against the combined weight of their wiry, half-starved bodies, realizing that if he fell, he'd be crushed, realizing that he was actually in danger, he and his warriors both—

And now the battle had stopped so suddenly it was as though he'd been plunged into some fantastic old tale in which living folk were turned to stone. He gaped along with the others, Romulans and natives both, at this sudden bold intruder. The robed figure was actually daring to move right through the lot of them, proud and straight-backed as though knowing no one would attack him. And Ruanek gasped along with the others as the stranger tossed back the hood of his cloak. Another Vulcan—

More than that! Ruanek realized suddenly. *Light and*

Darkness, this is none other than the famous Spock himself. The half-human Starfleet legend—yes, and he is clearly acquainted with our noisy madman.

No, no, more than "acquainted." These two were definitely foes, as rigid with hatred as those emotion-blocked Vulcans could get.

Amazing, Ruanek thought, and again, *amazing,* which didn't begin to relieve his feelings. *And how can I use this?* He glanced sideways at cousin Kharik, thinking, *Maybe all isn't lost after all, maybe we can get out of this mess without killing more children or ourselves,* and raised his hand to his warriors in the Romulan signal that meant "hold your fire."

No danger of disobedience; the others, Romulans and natives both, were all still as intrigued as he.

There will be a battle. Ruanek hardly needed to wonder at that; the icy tension between Spock and Sered was almost a tangible thing. *But this time it will be a battle of one-to-one, Vulcan against Vulcan.*

Akhh, and let this be the end of it! If Sered fell, surely Avrak would accept that as a sign that this mission was doomed to fail. There could be no other possible course of action but to leave, not unless those over Avrak really did want outright war with the Federation.

Unlikely. Yet it might not be a bad thing; there can at least be glory won in warfare. But there can be none at all in serving a madman!

Yes, yes, let him and his warriors at last be free of the madman and let them leave this cursed planet not as servants but as true Romulans! Let them escape while something of honor was still left to them!

I never thought to say this, not of a Vulcan, not of Spock, no less, but: Win! Slay the madman and free us all!

Spock and Sered stood staring at each other, both too stunned to move, each waiting for the other to take the initiative. A familiar, albeit hoarse, voice cut suddenly through the tense silence:

McCoy!

"I hate to break up what's obviously a touching reunion," the doctor drawled, "but can't we just sit down and talk this over like reasonable folks?"

Spock, never taking his attention from Sered, said coolly, his voice deliberately pitched so all could hear him, "These are not 'reasonable folks.' These are those who would break Sunstorm Truce."

The assembled Faithful growled at that, stirring uneasily. But before they could decide on any drastic move, the great metal doors flew open with a thundering crash. Into the hall burst the nomad warriors, shouting gleeful war cries as they rushed into shelter and battle.

The Romulans whirled to this sudden new threat like one well-oiled machine, weapons raised—but the disillusioned Faithful took advantage of the moment for a renewed charge. The Romulans were suddenly caught between two waves of low-tech but highly determined people, the desert nomads and the Faithful for once acting as one. Spock saw the quick bright flash of phasers here, there, and some attackers fell, but there were always more to take their places, too many to be stopped. The Romulans, Spock thought sharply, might have the better weapons, but the tribespeople had something stronger on their side: pure righteous fury.

And better numbers.

It was no contest. The Romulans were swarmed, overwhelmed, weapons torn from their hands.

And in the next moment, the Faithful will become a mob, as only those so suddenly stripped of belief can become, mindless, violent, deadly.

Spock quickly extrapolated the possible results: slain Romulans equaled Romulan retaliation, resulting in potential genocide and certain Federation-Romulan warfare. And he shouted with all his might, "Do not kill them! Do not harm the outlanders! Do not kill them!"

Somewhere behind him, Spock heard McCoy's dry whisper to Rabin, "Was he this nonviolent as a boy?"

Rabin retorted, "No. He killed. He must never have forgotten."

Nor have I. But what I recall or do not recall is hardly the issue.

No time to say as much to McCoy. And Sered—ah, Sered was clearly seeing his holy mission failing yet again, and—oh, most infuriating fact—due to the same blasphemer as before. Eyes blazing with madness, he snapped out, "Enough! Heed me, fools! *Enough!*"

It was a shriek savage enough to cut through any mere mortal noise. At that dramatic sound, the fighting broke sharply off, nomads, Faithful, and Romulans all startled into immobility. Sered strode quickly forward into the sudden silence, spotless robes swirling theatrically, and came to a dead stop directly in front of Spock.

"I thee challenge." The language Sered employed was such an archaic form of Old High Vulcan that Spock could barely decipher it: the true language of the priest-kings of the te-Vikram caves.

"What challenge," he began haltingly in the same dialect, but Sered cut him off.

"Let this be a battle of Righteousness. I thee issue the Holy Challenge of Combat, one to one, hand-to-hand in proper ritual. There shall be no weapon save our strength, no quarter, no mercy."

I am not going to match wits with him in a dialect that handicaps me. "Such archaic terms are not logical," Spock countered coolly in current Vulcan. "There no longer exists such a thing as the Holy Challenge."

"Logic!" Sered spat out the word in disgust. "What has your petty, useless *logic* to do with this? This is a matter of Light, not *logic!* Too long have we been walking separate ways. Too long has our enmity gone unresolved. And Evil has flourished! No longer! At last we are together—at last one of us shall die!"

Not merely madness but melodrama as well. "There is no need—"

"There is!" His eyes fierce as Loki's flames, his whole stance rigid with religious fervor, Sered proclaimed to all the world, "Here it is! Here is the final battle! *Here is the final judgment of Good against Evil!"*

Rabin could hardly have understood the words, but he could hardly have missed the gist of them. He hissed at Spock, "You're not really going to—"

Spock nodded curtly. "I see no other logical way to end this. He must be stopped before more harm is done, but a phaser blast will spark a deadly riot."

Sered was tearing off his spotless finery, till he stood in nothing more than his white breeches, his chest lean and sleek with unexpected muscle. He might be Sarek's age, Spock thought, but Sered had kept himself as wiry-strong as a young warrior from the ancient days.

Still, he cannot have matching stamina. At least I trust that such is the truth.

No other way than this, as he had told Rabin. Spock, too, stripped off his desert robes; he had not fought hand-to-hand in earnest for . . . exactly 6.45 Federation-standard years, and he wanted no encumbrances.

What was that sudden murmuring? Romulan . . . yes. The Romulans—were *wagering,* Spock realized, boldly wagering on the outcome of the duel.

I wonder who they prefer.

Illogical to even consider it, though judging from the

fiercely approving glance of that young Romulan—a centurion, by his garb—he was the favorite.

Shutting this irreverent trivia from his attention, Spock bowed to Sered in the ancient, elaborate Vulcan manner. Sered returned the bow with the same archaic courtesy—

Then they closed with each other.

And the final battle began.

TWENTY-SIX

Spock and Sered circled each other warily, slowly stalking, each seeking an opening, a weakness in the other, each finding none.

His breathing is regular, Spock analyzed coolly, *no fear or hesitation shown. His movements are smooth and agile: no hidden injuries. His eyes . . . are the eyes of madness, which may give him strength or weaken him with anger.* A possibility, not a fact. Useless to speculate on what had yet to be proven. *I must first see the shape of his attack before shaping my own.* Quick extrapolation: *His attack will not be anything as swift-ending or merciful as* tal-shaya. *And it will surely be something far older even than* tal-shaya. *Dating from the time of the priest-kings. Whatever system he uses, I must not kill. For all the evil he has done, his is an illness of the mind, not a rational working of harm. I must not kill.*

There was no emotion to Spock's thoughts; there was no place here for the human side of his nature.

Without the slightest warning of tensing muscles, Sered burst into motion, lunging forward, stiffened hand thrusting like the blade of a sword. Spock quickly parried with a forearm block, ignoring the shock of impact, and Sered just as swiftly sprang back, revealing nothing at all of his thoughts. But the style of his movements, the precise angles of arms and body and legs in this smooth, swift dance, told Spock what he needed to know:

This is ke-tarya.

Logical. It was a style of fighting ancient enough to please Sered though still current—fortunately—as an exercise regime among modern Vulcans; Spock had studied it as a boy, and occasionally still practiced it as an adult.

He feigned a kick that should make Sered dodge to the left—yes. Spock struck, hand aiming at a pressure point intended to send Sered slumping into unconsciousness and end this fight quickly. But Sered moved just as swiftly, blocking with bent arm, unfolding it with enough force to send Spock staggering back a step.

Was this *ke-tarya?*

Sered lunged, hand curved in a claw tearing viciously for the throat. Spock moved smoothly aside, twisting to throw Sered forward with the momentum of the attack— but Sered moved with him, lunging yet again, so quickly that Spock had to block him once more, despite his control aware of the slash of pain as Sered's nails tore his skin.

Skin only. That move was meant to tear out my throat. What is he using? Ke-tarya *has no moves like this!*

Yes, his mind quickly reminded him, it did. This was the most ancient form of *ke-tarya, ke-tar-yatar,* never studied by modern Vulcans save historians; *ke-tar-yatar* was no mere exercise but a style designed for one purpose only: death.

And Spock knew no way to counter it.

God, McCoy thought, *look at those two move, almost faster than the human eye can follow.* Of course he'd always known that Vulcan reflexes were swift, but this—

Too bad it's not just some exhibition match. That would be downright fun to watch, two evenly matched opponents like this, all that speed and grace and no harm meant.

But no, it would *have to be to the death. And in the middle of all these enemies, too, just waiting for a spark to set them off. Like playing with old-fashioned whaddayacallems . . . matches in the middle of dry tinder.*

Never taking his glance from the Vulcans involved in their quick, deadly dance, McCoy muttered hoarsely to Rabin, "Helluva time for a duel."

"When," Rabin shot back, *"is* a good time?"

"Good point." McCoy swallowed dryly, trying in vain to soothe his aching throat. Damn, what he'd give for a cold drink! For any drink. "At least Spock's kept himself in good shape. Desert doesn't seem to have weakened him."

A snort from Rabin. "It hasn't."

"Unfortunately," McCoy added with a physician's appraisal, "it looks like the madman's kept himself in pretty good shape, too. Never mind that he's more than twice Spock's age, and Spock's no kid—age doesn't matter to Vulcans the way it does to us mere humans. Like Faerie Folk, you know? Pointed ears and all."

That earned him a quick, startled glance from Rabin. *Never mind,* McCoy told him silently. *I haven't gone round the bend. Just tired, that's all. And worried.*

God, yes. And not just because they were in such peril.

I already watched you die once, Spock, and once was more

than enough. Dammit, Spock, don't do this to me! We've already lost Jim. I don't want to lose you, too.

Ruanek watched with face impassive and heart racing. Captain Spock moved with the ease and power of a true warrior—but he seemed to lack the true warrior's drive to kill. There! He could have crushed Sered's throat with that blow—yet he turned aside from its full force. And there! There! If he'd continued that lunge, he could have broken ribs, stopped Sered's lungs. Yet he was pulling back!

What is he doing? This is no place to show mercy!

And Sered—akhh, who would have expected the madman to have such strength? And such stamina? The power of the mad, indeed! Not for him to show caution or pity or whatever misguided logic it was that was handicapping Captain Spock. Ruanek let his breath out in a slow hiss of frustration. Sered must not win, and yet honor forbade any interference.

And I still have some honor left.

"A new wager!" he cried out defiantly, glaring at cousin Kharik. "I raise the stakes! Double the score on Captain Spock!"

Had Spock heard? Understood?

It is the only encouragement I can offer you, Ruanek told him. *Let it be enough.*

That it was also open defiance of his patron, of Avrak and his commands—akhh, well, Avrak's plans were already in disarray and sometimes one must risk all upon a single throw of the sticks.

A massed hiss from the Romulans brought Ruanek's attention sharply back to the fight. Spock was staggering back, nearly falling, clearly stunned.

"You," Kharik said with great relish, "are about to lose your wager."

The emphasis on the last word told Ruanek that his

cousin meant far more than a monetary trifle. "We speak of one who nearly held our Empire at bay," Ruanek snapped back. "He is not as weak as you think!"

Let it be true. For both our sakes.

Sered's last blow had come very close to breaking bones. Spock dodged, dodged again, aware despite his stern self-control that his reaction time was 2.55 instants slower than it had been, aware that his body was 6.26 percent weaker than it had been. There was pain, bruising, torn muscles, possibly even a cracked rib, though he would not allow such things to hinder him. But he could do nothing about lungs that were laboring for air. Still, no serious damage had yet been done, and Spock refused to hear the small, human voice whispering at the edge of his mind that *there will be,* that *you must kill or be killed*—no. Humanity had no place here.

Did it not? The hint of an idea slid into his thoughts.

Possible.

Sered? His sleek chest was slick with sweat, and blossoming bruises here and there told of blows that had gotten past his defenses.

I must look very much the same. Hardly the Starfleet officer. Wry honesty forced him to add, *The somewhat winded Starfleet officer.*

Yet Sered seemed not at all distressed, not at all out of breath, and the wild madness in his eyes burned as brightly as ever.

The strength of madness, indeed. He will go on and on until he dies. Or kills me.

Only one chance: not Vulcan but human logic, Jim Kirk's reasoning, insisting *feed that madness.* There was no logic of any kind left to Sered, no self-control, nothing but raw, primal emotion.

As though he'd read Spock's thoughts, Sered lunged again,

hand a claw. Spock countered with a forearm block, and this time all the will in him could not quite shut out the ache in overstrained muscles. He stepped deliberately back, saying as steadily as heaving lungs would allow:

"Do you really think that you can win?"

"Of course!" It was a harsh roar.

"A shame to see such a fallacy."

"What—"

"A shame to see such a once-brilliant mind so over-turned."

"What do you—"

"Look at yourself, Sered. Look. Where is your splendor, Sered? See the truth. No splendor here, no great messiah. Logic, Sered." *Human logic, so that nothing I say does more than shade the Vulcan truth.* "You are nothing but one aging outcast. Nothing but a madman lost in his own delusions. No, more than that:

"Sered, you are nothing but what the humans you despise call 'a crazy old useless fool.'"

With a wordless shriek, Sered charged him.

Wait . . . wait . . . now.

Spock, timing his action precisely, met that maddened charge with a neat, professional, and quite logical punch to Sered's solar plexus, followed by an equally neat uppercut.

Sered collapsed as though strings holding him upright had just been cut. There was a whoop, quickly suppressed, from the young Romulan centurion, then stunned, total silence.

Silence which Spock, standing over his unconscious foe, green blood on his knuckles, broke by saying simply:

"Let us assume that Good has won the day."

That started a sudden storm of shouting, Faithful, no-mads, Romulans all trying to be heard. *And so I have not brought peace but sparked a new riot—no! I did not go this far to see more deaths in this place!*

"Silence!"

Ahh, he certainly did have a cracked rib or at least severe bruising: his body did *not* want him shouting like that. And it would be quite pleasant to sit somewhere and regain his breath. There were, though others might deny it, limits to Vulcan strength.

Control, he told himself sternly. *Control. There is no time for weakness yet.*

McCoy, being McCoy, hurried to Spock's side, heedless of danger, all set to examine him. At Spock's fraction of a "not now, Doctor" frown, the human contented himself with draping the discarded desert robes back about Spock, "so you don't get a chill on top of everything else," and knelt at the fallen Sered's side, diagnostic tools in hand, his face a study in conflicting emotions.

Rabin, being Rabin, had just as quickly moved to guard Spock's back, whispering something about "Turned a kung-fu movie into a John Wayne movie, didn't you?"

It was the only logical move. Or movie.

But he kept that rather feeble pun to himself. "You," Spock said sternly to the Romulan centurion. "Here."

The Romulan wisely obeyed without an instant's hesitation, signaling to his uneasy warriors to follow. The centurion was shorter than Spock by a small margin (1.2 centimeters, Spock's brain told him), and young enough to actually allow himself a quick grin of relief before fixing his face in more properly solemn lines. He gave Spock a crisp military salute.

"I am Ruanek, Centurion of the Empire. Of House Minor Strevon. I formally request honorable protection for my warriors and myself."

Good. The youngster was quick-witted. But then, he never would have risen to the rank of centurion at such an early age if he had been anything but clever.

"Granted," Spock said. He added with more force for all the others to hear, ignoring the strain it put on aching muscles, "I have placed these people under my protection. They were but tools of the foe, not the foe himself. They are not to be harmed."

Were the murmuring Faithful accepting that? Probably not; those deprived of their illusions usually wished to destroy the illusion-maker and, failing that, the illusion-maker's allies.

But the Elder stepped smoothly forward, her easy grace yet again belying her age. "There will be no war," she said, and it was not a request.

At her calm gesture, the nomads moved to encircle Spock, Sered, McCoy, Rabin, and even the startled Romulans. At a stern glare from the Elder, the nomads lowered their weapons and merely . . . stood, a solid, implacable ring.

"There will be no war," the Elder repeated, and nodded solemnly to Spock.

"Peace," he agreed with an equally solemn bow.

"Peace," the centurion repeated, again proving his quick-wittedness, adding in a wry whisper to Spock, "Besides, you've just made me a nice bit of money."

Before Spock could find a suitably logical retort to that, there was a great roar from outside, a familiar rush of noise—shuttles setting down? Federation equipment? Yes, surely that. McCoy and Rabin said simultaneously, "Here comes the cavalry over the hill!"

They paused, stared at each other in astonishment, then burst into laughter, gasping something about "You, too?" "Old Westerns?" "Love 'em!"

Which makes as much sense, Spock thought, trying not to rub muscles that were nagging him about their soreness even through his control, *as anything else that has happened this day.*

The cavalry, as it were, had indeed arrived.

TWENTY-SEVEN

Spock restrained himself from flexing his fingers diagnostically again. He had ascertained that no bones were broken and that the most superficial of the grazes on his hand from delivering what humans referred to as an "uppercut" were already healing. A human would permit himself to slump, to admit that at least one rib was probably cracked, possibly broken, and that he felt as bruised as if he had been trampled by a stampeding *chuchaki.* Dr. McCoy would no doubt make ironic comments Spock had no desire to hear.

Fortunately, however, McCoy was preoccupied with Sered. Conscious once more but at least as battered as Spock, the madman had permitted his robe, trampled and soiled with blood though it was, to be thrown over his shoulders, protecting him from Loki's light but not, in his current state, from the pain of his injuries. His sides and chest were as bruised as Spock's, and his jaw had swollen to twice its size.

We each wear the other's blood. The thought was one from which he would be glad to escape.

Sered's eyes were glazed, the veils flickering aimlessly back and forth across them as his mind retreated almost into catatonia. He was standing, which was the best that could be said of him.

He must be returned to Vulcan, where his madness could be treated and he could be interrogated—by someone other than Spock.

Touching Sered's dementia would be worse than that ugly, ancient crime of rape—and not necessarily just for Sered.

The late T'Pau had known all along, Spock realized. Any investigation would have to include what she, no doubt, had preserved in meticulous personal records. It might even be deemed important enough for someone of T'Lar's stature to commune with T'Pau's *katra.*

"All Vulcan in one package," Jim had once called her. She had refused a seat on the Federation Council rather than reveal who the intruders at Mount Seleya had actually been. Had that been a betrayal?

No, T'Pau had protected her own.

Spock protected his own, too, even when he wanted no more than to indulge in the luxury of a Vulcan healing trance. Many of Spock's "own," the nomad warriors who had followed him so joyously into battle, now stood on the sands of *Te-wisat-karak,* watching his every move. Even some of the former Faithful had dared to follow him, stretching out their hands, pleading with him to remain and be their new Master.

"You need no Master," Spock told them patiently. "You have the Law. You will have wise leaders of your own once more. This Revered Elder will aid you in choosing them.

And you have the friendship of this good man." He gestured toward Captain Rabin.

"Let's move out a ways from the rocks," Rabin said. "The *chuchaki* put up with the first shuttle landing, but there's a limit to what they'll tolerate. You folks don't want to *hike* all the way home, do you?"

That made the nomads actually chuckle, and Rabin grinned.

"A wise precaution," Spock said, referring to both the shuttles and Rabin's winning friends with a jest.

Someone wasn't laughing. Spock glanced over at the Romulans, now under his protection. All but one: young Kharik, a cousin to the centurion Ruanek, whom two of the Romulans were holding under close guard. Spock admitted to himself that seeing the anger on the subcenturion's face, with its Vulcan features, was . . . disconcerting.

Ruanek, as Spock had commanded, stood close to McCoy in case Sered's madness turned violent again.

"Don't worry about me," Spock heard McCoy tell Ruanek. "Worry about how you're going to smuggle horses across the Romulan Neutral Zone."

Horses?

"Assuming, of course," McCoy continued, "that you won enough money to set yourself up as a breeder."

A breeder? Of horses? Perhaps exposing Ruanek to McCoy's notions of humor constituted abuse of a prisoner!

But Ruanek actually laughed, a breach of control for Vulcans but not, apparently, for Romulans. Typically, McCoy had won the young Romulan's liking.

For all I know, that had something to do with the centurion's support of me, with the support of most of the Romulans here, during my duel.

Although none of those who had exiled themselves from Vulcan knew the deep discipline of Gol, the Vulcan gifts lay latent in them. Spock had felt their strength, their will, reach out to support him as he fought Sered.

My victory is yours, he thought at them, wondering if they would hear. If he could sense their will, their support, it might be possible, one day, one year, for Romulans to learn the ways not just of Surak but of Gol.

The next time Romulans stand on Mount Seleya, let it be as pilgrims and peacemakers.

Spock believed that McCoy would say he had his work cut out for him.

"I give you my word," Captain Rabin said to the Elder, "on my mother's soul. I shall return with help, and if not I, then my children." He began the ritual three bows of respect, but the Elder forestalled him, drawing him into the formal embrace of equals.

After a polite moment, the captain drew away. Gently, he disengaged the small hands of two children who had attached themselves to his legs and strode toward Spock. At the last, he turned to wave to the nomads, then snapped down his protective visor with a dramatic gesture.

What movie hero is he imitating now? Spock wondered with the barest hint of amusement. *No matter; it is effective.*

Rabin gestured. Spock turned and saw Loki's violent light flash from the incoming shuttles. The human snapped shut McCoy's communicator with a satisfied grin. Spock's hand flexed again, waiting to take the communicator from him, try again to raise his ship.

Impatience? he asked himself. *Illogical.*

The solar flare had subsided, although it was still too risky to attempt using the transporters. Uhura must have a good reason for continuing the communcations blackout. The more powerful communications equipment at Rabin's headquarters would help him find it out.

"They evacuated our people first," Rabin said. "Ensign

Prince and all. Wanted to airlift the lot of them back to Kalara, but they insisted they weren't going back until we were safe. I've got a mind to put them all on report for insubordination."

"No doubt," Spock remarked blandly, "your sickbay will suffice as a brig."

Rabin chuckled, then gestured again at the landing shuttles. "Faisal's not piloting. That's probably punishment enough for him."

Guards swarmed out, faces hidden by protective helms and visors, their bodies stiffening at the sight of the Romulans. Spock and Rabin stepped forward just as a very bedraggled knot of familiar officers tumbled out of the shuttles behind them. One of the latter gestured passionately, critically, over his shoulder at the hatchway, pushing up his visor so there could be no mistaking his disapproval.

"What was that supposed to be? Touchdown at twenty-nine point five, twenty-nine point six, twenty-nine point seven, take your pick? A sloppy landing like that makes us all lose face before our captain!"

"Faisal!" Rabin exclaimed, pushing up his own visor. "You, all of you, you're a sight for sore eyes!"

He blinked hastily, not just from the sun, Spock realized, but from a wave of emotion so powerful that even his human friend sought to control it. "Now, put your visor down," Rabin snapped, voice not quite steady. "You want to go blind?"

Ensign Prince was actually quivering with the effort not to dash forward and hug his captain—and possibly Spock and everyone else, as well—but managed to stay put, more or less at attention, particularly after Rabin said something in Arabic that made him raise his head with pride. Spock watched as his friend somehow managed to greet everyone by name, pat everyone on the back, and still preserve some semblance of military bearing all at once.

He, too, looks after his own.

"Welcome back to civilization, Lieutenant Diver," Rabin was continuing. "I hope my people gave you every consideration."

"They kept us alive, sir," the young lieutenant said.

"And the lieutenant's got to finish the Tale of the Three Princes of Serendip," Ensign Prince cut in, grinning. "We were rescued just when they'd found the princess."

At Rabin's blank stare, Lieutenant Diver added, blushing slightly, "You . . . ah . . . just had to be there, sir."

"I see. Well. All the same, it's a pretty sorry welcome to Obsidian, Lieutenant. You'll just have to come back, perhaps when the ozone layer's had a chance to start healing. We can all stroll around, you, too, Spock, sample the local food, give you, Lieutenant, your first ride on a *chuchaki.*"

Lieutenant Diver studied the Taragi-shar with a geologist's longing. "With rock formations like that, sir, just try to keep me away!"

The guards started forward to take the Romulans into custody.

"They are under my protection," Spock said.

"But—Romulans!" one of the guards protested. "Just the fact that they're here, in Federation space—that's an act of war!"

Spock raised a bruised hand for silence. "If one were genetically accurate, one could say that they are, in fact, family members, distant cousins to myself. That would logically eliminate the need to think of them as Romulans."

The guards warily backed down, not wanting to argue with a Starfleet officer—and a Vulcan. Rabin surreptitiously gave Spock the thumbs-up gesture.

That means approval, I know. I suspect Jim would rather have approved as well.

After all, Jim had always tried to avoid fighting with the

Romulans and had never been above a certain . . . creative interpretation of the facts.

"Well," asked Rabin, "now that that's settled, hadn't we better go mind the store?"

Spock flinched—

"Only me," McCoy said laconically. "Didn't mean to startle you." His tricorder whirred busily as he scanned Spock's rib and kidney areas—"not that your innards are anywhere a sane man would have them, mind you."

Spock acquiesced. It was better to let the doctor believe he had been startled than to ask pardon for his loss of control at hearing *"hadn't we better go mind the store,"* words his dead friend had often used, in the mouth of a friend who still lived.

"Nothing too serious," McCoy muttered.

Spock raised a brow. "Are you disappointed, Doctor?"

"Naw. A cracked rib, lots of bruises—not bad for a prizefighter, amateur division."

Spock permitted McCoy to ease him into the shuttle. It was simpler than arguing. And by now he had to admit that sitting, as the nomadic saying went, would be far better than standing.

"You're going to rest on the flight back," McCoy warned, "or so help me, I'll sedate you."

The doctor darted back outside before Spock could reply, returning with the nearly catatonic Sered, whom he strapped in before returning to Spock's side with a wry grin.

"The Invalid Express is under way."

Spock suppressed a sigh.

David Rabin just barely kept pace with Spock as he strode past the painted letters on the outpost's walls and into CommCen. "If you please, Ensign, connect me with *Intrepid II.*"

Impossible to believe that the ship was no longer there,

Spock thought. If not to the degree that Jim had bonded with the *Enterprise,* he was at least partially bonded to it; he would have sensed if it had been destroyed, as he had years ago when the original *Intrepid* had died.

Behind him, the outpost's staff was clustering around their leader. "Yes, Captain Rabin," Lieutenant Albright was saying. "I took my medicine. In more ways than one. And I am—we are all very glad that you're back."

Her voice almost managed not to falter.

"I'm trying, Captain Spock." The ensign looked up at him with concern.

Spock could see his own reflection in the brightly polished console. He could agree with the doctor and, apparently, with this young man—did all of David Rabin's people worry so?—that he belonged in a sickbay rather than on the bridge of a ship. Nevertheless, he raised an eyebrow, a silent order to the ensign to try again.

"Not to worry," he could hear Rabin telling Lieutenant Albright. "When you've got a little more experience in the field, you'll have more perspective on these things. Meanwhile, if you could send a yeoman with something to eat, some water, maybe . . ."

"Yes, sir!" The precision was back in Albright's voice.

The signals ensign sighed with relief, and Spock came fully alert. "I've got contact, sir."

Spock heard the familiar crackle of sublight communications. His aches receded. "Spock here, Commander Uhura," he said crisply.

"Captain Spock!" That was definitely Uhura. "Good to hear your voice!"

Static crackled between the base and the *Intrepid.* As well as if Spock already faced Uhura, he knew she reproached herself for giving way to emotion. He must make her know he reproached no one for acting in accordance with his nature. Or hers.

Communications went live once again. "Ship's status is operational, Captain." Uhura had disciplined her voice into dispassionate briefing mode. "We pulled into Obsidian's shadow. Radiation levels were well within hull tolerances, no overdoses were reported, and hull levels are returning to baseline norms."

"Summon a security team to the transporter room, Commander. The ground team will beam up, plus seven others."

"Negative, Captain, negative." Uhura's voice cut across his. As she boosted the volume, Spock raised his eyebrows at the *whoop/whoop/whoop* of red alert. "We've got this Warbird in the vicinity. It's cloaked, so we're in no immediate danger, but I'm keeping shields up until reinforcements arrive. I've opened negotiations with the Warbird's commander, Avrak. Sister's son to Senator Pardek."

So, now. Fascinating. "Most understandable, Commander. You seem to have prepared for any eventuality. My compliments."

"Thank you, sir." The ring of pleasure in Uhura's voice eased some ache in Spock that he had not known he possessed.

"Spock?" David Rabin stood at his shoulder. "Since you're not going anywhere just yet, I'd like to discuss something with you."

"Indeed." Spock followed Rabin into a conference room where food, water, and a savory hot drink had been set out. "I see you have already planned for this event."

"Sit down," Rabin commanded. "At the risk of sounding like a stereotype: Eat something. On the flight back, I was making plans that I want to run by you. Now that we've got the nomads working with us *and* no more Romulan interference, I want to set some priorities."

"Wise."

"The first thing is to tell the whole story. No more myths. No more secrecy. No more fear. Then, we start to rebuild

307

the ozone layer. I know we've only got outpost status here, but with the cooperation of Obsidian's people—all of its people," he added with immense satisfaction, "we can ask for a change in planetary status so that Federation technology can be brought in."

"The Prime Directive?" Spock asked with an eyebrow lift.

"This is a devolved culture," Rabin reminded Spock. "I'd wager paleoarcheologists and archivists could pinpoint precisely at what cultural level they regressed."

Spock nodded. "Proceed."

"Ozone layer is going to be our long-term project," Rabin said. "Where we're really going to make our short-term gains is in the area of medicine. If we could borrow the services of a really first-rate oncology center . . ." He shook his head. "When I die, what I'd really like as my epitaph is that I helped see that the only thing that made kids get sick around here was the local equivalent of a cold. We can cure a lot of those cancers and stabilize the ones we can't against the next breakthrough. Are you with me, Spock?"

"Not literally. I will be returning to Vulcan so that Sered can be treated. But I find your priorities flawlessly logical. I suspect," he added with the smallest upward crook of a corner of his mouth, "that you have heard the last of the title 'Kindly Fool.' I have one more suggestion."

"What's that?" Rabin poured hot tea for Spock and glared at him until he drank.

"More diplomatic missions to work with the deep-desert nomads. The Elder we met is a powerful ally. No doubt she is connected with tribes halfway across the planet."

Rabin shook his head. "Spock, all I can say is that I wish you were going to be here to take charge of that. Seems you're a born diplomat."

Spock set his teacup down almost too quickly. Rabin might even attribute any shakiness to the fact that Spock had used his damaged hand to lift it. A diplomat. Like his father. His father who had tried to force him into a pattern designed before Surak's birth.

But I broke free to create my own pattern. Now . . . where is that pattern leading me?

He looked past Rabin and out a floor-to-ceiling window of polarized steelsheen into a dry-planet garden, remembering the conversation he had had so many years ago with his mother in her wet-planet conservatory. The stars of Romulan space shone up there, far beyond the poison of wounded Loki. Perhaps Sered had had the right idea after all, even if his means were as desperately flawed as his mind. If more Romulans and Vulcans of goodwill could only speak together honestly and openly . . . Perhaps it must wait until a younger generation grew up without the old, illogical fears that kept the cousin races sundered. Ruanek, after all, had even wagered on him.

Spock's hearing picked up a beep in CommCen, and he rose, his abused muscles protesting.

"Commander Uhura from the *Intrepid*," said the ensign. "Commander's compliments and she'll be happy to beam Captain Spock on board now. Just the captain, she adds, sir."

Interesting.

Spock started toward the transporter booths. "David, kindly look after my people for a while longer, please."

Rabin grinned and waved the transporter chief away from the controls. "Next time, don't forget to write. Shalom, Spock."

He saluted Spock in the Vulcan fashion, which he had once told Spock had religious significance for his own people. Spock returned the gesture.

"Live long and prosper, David Rabin. And . . ." How would someone of Rabin's people word it? Ah, yes. "Do not be a stranger!"

Transporter effect took him before Rabin could retort.

TWENTY-EIGHT

**Intrepid II
Year 2296**

Spock had an instant to wish, illogically, that he could have materialized on his ship minus his injuries before a young officer greeted him.

"Lieutenant Duchamps, sir. Commander sent me to brief you en route to the bridge."

"Commendably efficient," Spock approved as he headed toward the nearest turbolift. Uhura had even chosen someone able to keep up with his long-legged stride, not expecting to see him return somewhat the worse for wear.

"Bridge," Spock ordered.

The turbolift hummed, then lurched. The ship screamed red alert again, and lights went dark as power flickered. Spock lunged for emergency controls, ignoring strained muscles. The lights struggled back on, and the lift returned to operations, although somewhat more slowly.

"Powersave," Duchamps explained superfluously. "Captain—I mean Commander Uhura said to channel power to the shields to compensate for being outgunned."

Captain Uhura. He had always valued and respected the communications officer, but he had had no idea that she could so quickly weld his bridge staff into a fighting crew.

The turbolift's hum faded, the door slid open, and Spock strode out as fast as his battered body would allow.

"Captain!" The gladness in Uhura's voice was replaced by concern at the sight of him. Spock hoped that the alternation of red light and shadow that marked red alert would hide the brief frown that crossed his face.

"There is no serious damage," he assured her, and moved forward. Uhura fairly leapt out of the command chair so he could seat himself, standing beside him as he quickly scanned her records of the past few days. "Creative adaptation to maximize weapons," he noted.

"A science vessel just isn't up to exchanging broadsides with a Warbird, so I was trying to bluff. I thought I had Avrak convinced!"

If diplomacy worked with Klingons, how much more effective should it be with Romulan kinsfolk? "We shall provide him with another demonstration of the validity of your logic, Commander," Spock told Uhura, and saw some of the tension leave her body.

He glanced at the crew, seeing an almost imperceptible difference in them. Commander Uhura had welded them into the same sort of cohesive unit that David Rabin had created on Obsidian. (And was that the merest twinge of a very human jealousy he felt, that she should succeed where he had not? Impossible.) The crew looked back at him. Their spines straightened. One or two of them even smiled.

Spock nodded. "Open a hailing frequency."

Duchamps turned, exchanging a grin with Uhura. "With pleasure, *sir!* I mean, aye-aye, sir."

Spock awarded the lieutenant an ironic eyebrow and received a grin in exchange.

The screen blanked, then filled with the image of a Warbird's cramped bridge with Avrak, sister-son to Pardek, seated in the command chair.

Civil wars are always the worst, McCoy often said. Still, if Romulans and Vulcans both wished it, they might at some point in the future again be one people. A quick flash of thought: Was this why T'Pau had refused to allow the subject to be discussed, why she had kept herself aloof from the tremendous contribution she might have made all these years on the Federation Council—so that the family might have a chance to heal itself?

Avrak's eyes widened at the sight of Spock.

"Commander Avrak," Spock greeted him bluntly. "Let us admit that it would be glorious to measure our ships' strengths and our crews' courage. Glorious, but illogical. Your attempt to sabotage the Federation's efforts on Obsidian have failed, and your plot to exploit a renegade has been exposed."

He turned to Duchamps. "Lieutenant, raise the outpost on Obsidian. Captain Spock's compliments to Captain Rabin, and would he kindly patch in transmissions from his sickbay and brig?"

A second screen came live, the image forming of Sered, lying slumped on a diagnostic bed, eyes blank, clearly not living in reality.

"You relied too greatly on a weak reed, Commander," Spock told Avrak. "Commander Uhura has already summoned reinforcements, but she faced certain . . . limitations of knowledge."

"Your lady the officer is a fierce one, Captain." There was more than a touch of admiration behind the words, possibly even a hint of something unexpectedly warmer. Beside

Spock, Uhura stiffened, and he felt her hand tighten ever so slightly on the back of his command chair.

Interesting, Spock thought, and stored the data away. "I value my officer appropriately, Commander. She very properly called for reinforcements. But she did not have access to certain information."

Spock gestured as imperiously as Sered ever had, and an image of Centurion Ruanek, his cousin Kharik (still under guard), and the other, surviving Romulans, formed on-screen.

"You have not just suborned a Vulcan in broken health—and who must be returned to Vulcan for medical intervention," Spock began, coolly listing facts, "you have illegally landed an armed force on a world protected by the Federation. You have crossed the Neutral Zone and fired on a Starfleet vessel. At least two of these actions are acts of war, while the first is what my crew might call inhuman. Do you truly wish the entire Federation—and your Praetor—to know that it was all your doing? Or shall we simply be polite and call the matter a slight . . . miscalculation or misunderstanding? I leave the choice of word to you."

After one quick glance at Sered, Avrak had ignored him. But he was unable to look away from the Romulans in the brig on Obsidian. "My warriors," he said.

Spock arched an eyebrow. "All but one of them gave me their parole. I took them under my protection to save their lives. They deserve nobler purposes than these."

"They deserve better than a Federation prison!"

"So they do, Commander," Spock agreed. "And we have no desire to be their jailers. Accordingly, I am returning them to you."

"On what terms?"

"Why, Commander Avrak, what logical terms are there in this situation but those of honor? Captain Rabin, respond please."

Rabin would have been within range the instant that Spock hailed his outpost. "Captain Spock." His voice was properly formal.

"This is Commander Avrak of the *Adamant*. He has a slight problem with missing personnel. Do you think you can assist him?"

"With the greatest of ease, sir." Spock heard Rabin activate a communicator. "Transporter room? Six to beam to . . . ?"

"Commander?" Spock asked. "Will you transmit coordinates to Obsidian?"

Avrak looked as if he would rather order Spock's slow execution. He gestured curtly. A centurion saluted. From the planet, Rabin nodded.

"Coordinates coming through. Prepare to beam six up."

Lights swirled about the Romulans, forming into columns. Their bodies flickered, and the lights faded. Avrak turned his head as if listening to the Romulan equivalent of a transporter chief report that six warriors had come on board.

As David would say, good luck attend you, Ruanek. I think you shall need every bit of your cleverness.

"I have my warriors back," Avrak snapped. "Those who still live. I shall disavow knowledge of the misadventure in which the others died. Now, what of the Vulcan renegade?"

"I shall return him to Vulcan for therapy and interrogation. Any knowledge that remains in his damaged mind is valuable to us."

"I do not envy you the shipmate, sir."

"Envy is an emotion, sir. This is a matter of duty, not . . . enjoyment." And he shaded the word with the faintest disdain.

Avrak smiled. "Game well played, Captain Spock. I shall anticipate our next contest. And . . ." He let his eyes stray from Spock to Uhura. "My compliments to your officer."

His glance was openly admiring. A flurry of amusement went around Spock's bridge crew. Uhura shrugged.

"There would be no games," Spock said quietly, "if we could, perhaps, deal together as friends. Or perhaps one day as kinsmen, once again."

Avrak's gaze snapped back to Spock. He raised a thoughtful eyebrow. "Stranger things have happened," Avrak admitted after a moment.

The screen blanked. Instants later, the Warbird's cloaking device engaged.

"Check to see that it's still emitting radiation," Uhura ordered, turning toward Lieutenant Richards's scanners. "Begging your pardon, sir," she added to Spock. "But I'd bet that Commander Avrak will keep that glitch so we can track him out of Federation space."

"It is illogical to bet on sure things, Commander."

Spock turned to Lieutenant Duchamps. "Mr. Duchamps, will you please contact Obsidian and ask when Dr. McCoy will have his patient stabilized for transport on board?"

"Aye-aye, sir."

Spock allowed his spine to touch the back of the command chair. Even this more relaxed posture was uncomfortable. The chair simply was not a proper fit, neither literally nor figuratively.

Logic required an accurate assessment of his own skills. He could command satisfactorily and more than that; but command was a task in which "satisfactory" was insufficient. He was also, he knew, an outstanding science officer, and Jim used to call him "the best first officer in the Fleet." Those roles were in his past. What was his future?

You're a born diplomat, David Rabin had told him. Decades ago, as a boy, he had been right about Spock and Starfleet. Was Rabin right now, too? Despite his humor and the passion for the frontier that made him avoid promotion as assiduously as Jim Kirk, Rabin's mind had always been adept in making the intuitive leaps that Spock only now had begun to realize might represent a form of logic entirely new to him.

He would need, Spock thought, to give serious consideration to the issues he had raised with Avrak.

Was I, too, impelled by an intuitive logic? One that parallels David's own?

Reconciliation of the Sundering would truly be a worthwhile goal—the crowning scientific expedition of his life.

McCoy's call from Obsidian found Spock in his quarters, where he had turned up the climate control to a luxurious approximation of Vulcan's restoring heat.

"You should be in sickbay," McCoy accused him, face frowning from the viewscreen.

"Not just yet, Doctor."

David Rabin's image was right beside that of McCoy. Gratifying, Spock thought, to see peace between the two.

"They're gone, Spock," Rabin assured him, "though you probably know that already. Centurion Ruanek withdrew his parole so that . . . let me see if I can remember his exact words . . ." Rabin's mobile face took on a faraway expression. "'I withdraw my parole that I may be free as befits a warrior, a vassal to Avrak sister-son of Pardek, and a son of House Minor Strevon.'"

Spock inclined his head a fraction. "The centurion speaks with propriety."

"Property too," McCoy added. "You may not have made him a wealthy man, but when his bets on you paid off, he at least had the sense to be grateful. Knows how to cover his . . . ah . . . tail, too."

Good. Such a youngster should not be wasted. "What is your patient's status?" Spock asked.

McCoy hesitated. "If he were a human, I'd say he was in shock. Denial, but not quite to the point of true catatonia.

And I'd put a human on suicide watch. But given what I've learned of Vulcan physiology and psychology—" He eyed Spock ironically. "—I'd say he's as tough as the rest of you, despite his craziness."

"Is that a technical term?" Spock asked mildly.

"As technical as I'm going to get! I would think that any neurological damage should be reparable once we get him to Vulcan. We *are* headed to Vulcan, I take it."

"You are finally learning logic, Doctor."

"I think I'll ignore that comment from a patient-to-be," McCoy remarked: his form of revenge. As Rabin leaned back, grinning widely, the doctor continued, "As I was saying, I think that the Science Academy can probably regenerate any damage. However, the consequences if, as, and when Sered returns to sane awareness—can you imagine a Vulcan with a guilt complex?"

"I'm not sure I want to," Rabin said.

And he met the doctor's eyes with complete, if ironic, understanding.

"Captain Rabin, thanks for your hospitality and all your help."

"Is Sered ready to beam up to the *Intrepid?*" Spock asked.

"Spock, I'll meet you in sickbay," McCoy responded.

"Negative, Doctor. I will receive you in the transporter room myself. With guards. I will not risk you again."

McCoy rose hastily. "I'm on my way."

"Take care of him, Doctor," Rabin said.

McCoy raised his eyebrow in a Vulcan-like gesture that made the captain smile. "Take care of *him?* He'd tell you it's the other way around."

"So?" Rabin asked. "What else are friends for? Shalom, Spock."

"I will think about what we discussed. Live long and prosper. Spock out."

No doubt McCoy would press Rabin for an explanation. After all, as *Intrepid*'s chief medical officer, McCoy had a duty to participate in any major decisions.

Spock signaled Security, ordering, "Armed party to the transporter room." He rose slowly, allowing himself to wince since he was alone. A day or so in sickbay might be worthwhile, even if he had to listen to McCoy's ranting.

He adjusted climate control back downward. There was absolutely no logic in giving McCoy the satisfaction of knowing he had succumbed to the lure of physical comfort.

Then, with the slightest tightening of his lips, Spock adjusted the control back up. There was also no logic in giving the doctor the chance to nag him about removing himself from a healing environment.

Either way, I must admit that the doctor's presence will be quite welcome.

TWENTY-NINE

Intrepid II and Vulcan
Day 21, Tenth Week of Tasmeen,
Year 2298

"Captain's log, Stardate 9835.7." Spock paused for a moment, organizing his thoughts, then continued:

"I have reviewed the performance of the bridge crew of Intrepid II, *and hereby confirm the commendations made by Commander and Acting Captain Uhura to Lieutenants Duchamps and Richards, as well as to Lieutenant Commander Atherton of Engineering.*

"I should like to log additional commendations: to Chief Medical Officer Leonard McCoy for his courage and humanitarian assistance on Obsidian, and to Commander Uhura as well. I would like to recommend that, at her next fitness evaluation, she be offered a ship of her own. Perhaps even this one."

Her reaction to that should prove most interesting.

"Helm reports that we shall soon enter orbit around

Vulcan, where Sered will be transferred to the care of Vulcan Science Academy Healers."

Someone was at the door to his chambers. *"Spock out,"* Spock ended, and closed the log. "Come," he called, and the door opened, revealing McCoy.

"Ah, Dr. McCoy. I have been expecting you."

He raised an eyebrow at McCoy's finery. The doctor wore a new, hot-weather uniform, acquired against a trip down-world into Vulcan's heat.

"If I'm going to be a consulting physician to the Vulcan Science Academy," McCoy explained, "I can't look like something the *sehlat* dragged in."

"What a *sehlat* drags in, Doctor, would undoubtedly be of more interest to pathology than psychiatry."

McCoy grumbled, conceding the point, and set a bottle of Romulan ale down on Spock's table.

Spock awarded his friend another eyebrow.

"Well, I'm all out of Saurian brandy, and I've never been able to civilize you into liking mint juleps, so we'll just have to make do."

"I thought," Spock said, "that the ale might be part of your . . . I believe the appropriate term is 'syndicate' . . . with Centurion Ruanek."

"Nice youngster, isn't he? Deserves better than . . ."

Breaking off, the doctor extracted glasses from a shelf, and poured. "Spock, are you by some chance planning to help them out the way you did the Klingons?"

"You have a genius for intrusion, Doctor."

"Hell, Spock, what else are friends for?"

Spock raised his glass to McCoy as if in the ritual of water welcome. "Absent friends," he said, and this time meant living as well as deceased.

They both drank to the toast. Then Spock continued, "I have begun to think that friends are for keeping one honest, a gift you and David share. In fact, Doctor, I would probably have been consulting you soon enough. I have been thinking of making some changes—"

"Dammit!" McCoy exploded. "Out of the frying pan— which is a pretty good metaphor for Loki, if you ask me— into a Learning Experience. Uhura told me you've asked her if she wants a ship of her own, and she's considering it. Now what?"

"Captain Rabin suggested that I had the skills suitable for diplomacy. Because he was the one who first suggested I might successfully enter Starfleet, logic compels me to consider his suggestion."

McCoy set his glass down, propped both elbows on Spock's table, and leaned forward. "Doctor to patient, if you don't mind. It's true you don't have the same flair for command that Jim did or the style that has Duchamps sitting up and saying 'arf' every time Uhura smiles at him. But you do have people skills: we saw that with the Elder on Obsidian—hell, we saw that with the children down there. If you want the honest-to-God truth, I'd say that your skills actually parallel those of your father, down to the last drop of charisma. Probably explains why the two of you fought like—like *sehlat*s and *le-matya*s for so many years. Oh all right, *sehlat*s and *le-matya*s who'd studied logic at Surak's feet. You know perfectly well what I mean."

Spock inclined his head.

"Spock, you've already made up your mind, haven't you? And if you have, what's the point of calling in your friendly neighborhood doctor?"

"Doctor, it was you who called yourself in. The 'point,' as you call it, however, is what I believe humans used to call a 'reality check.'"

McCoy took a careful sip of ale. "Dealing with Sered sort of makes you want to make sure your mind's in the right place, doesn't it?"

Spock awarded him a level glance. "Logic posits change.

Even you will change, Doctor. For all I know, you might return to Obsidian one day. My assumption is that between my hail to the base and your return message, David was trying to draft you."

"Wouldn't be the first time Starfleet pulled that stunt on me. Dammit, Spock, I'm a Starfleet surgeon, not a—a pediatric oncologist."

"Before you are either, Bones"—it was a deliberate use of the old, familiar nickname—"you are a healer. You will go where you are most needed. As must I."

"We're not talking about me, Spock."

"Nor about me," Spock replied. "But about logic and change."

As McCoy assumed his most exasperated "give me strength" look, Duchamps signaled from the bridge.

"Captain, I have located Ambassador Sarek."

Spock's hand tightened ever so slightly on his glass. Logic and change, indeed. "Patch the ambassador's call through to my cabin, please."

"You don't want me here. No, don't argue. Just give your father my greetings," McCoy said, with an odd, sympathetic little smile, and slipped out, tactful and acerbic to the last.

Spock had beamed down alone in what was sunset at Shikahr, at a point he had chosen for its view of what had once been his home.

From the low hilltop on which he stood, he could admire the brilliance of the red light that struck the Forge, hammering out individuals, a civilization, millennia of history with the ruthlessness of an artist. A *shavokh* veered, rising on a wingtip before it mounted a thermal to soar out toward the Forge. Spock followed its flight for a moment. Beyond the

Forge was the Womb of Fire, where he had been reborn as a Starfleet officer in the reek of sulfur and fear. The evening air was fragrant, enticing with the desert's lure.

The Veil slid down over his eyes as he stared into the splendid light, peering through it to focus upon the subtle curved walls and courtyards, set among his mother's gardens, of his family home. The air and sight of home were . . . highly satisfactory. McCoy might call that hyperbolic language if he chose.

House and gardens both were still meticulously maintained. Neglect was, of course, illogical, as was regret. It did seem, however, that while Spock's mother lived, the gardens had possessed a studied disorder in the raking of the gravel and pebbles of the paths, the arrangement of just one blossoming shrub, placed with slight, satisfying asymmetry to the others, even the casual untidiness of one fallen spray of leaves upon a hollowed rock, that they now lacked.

Although Spock had known the door codes since he had been old enough to venture out-of-doors alone, he signaled his arrival. Sarek greeted him formally at the door, ushering him ceremoniously inside.

Always sealed against Vulcan's heat, dust, and dryness, the house now felt instead hermetically closed off from the rest of the world. Sounds echoed in the austerely furnished rooms. These days, Spock thought, Sarek traveled as light as Spock himself.

"May I offer thee water after thy journey?" Sarek asked formally.

"I am honored by thy welcome," Spock replied, just as formally. "I give thanks."

He bowed deeply, son to father, guest to host, as he accepted the water that Sarek brought from a bubbling courtyard well in cups even older than the house, each carved from agate that gleamed in the sunset.

Father and son saluted each other and drank. Sarek

gestured Spock to a chair. At least, Spock thought, it was not the one reserved for honored guests.

They sat admiring the sunset until it faded. Subtle light radiated from the walls of the house, glittered in the gardens.

"I have received a report from the Science Academy on its most recent patient," Sarek began after a long, almost meditative interval. "I am struck by the symmetry of your and Sered's interactions."

"Dr. McCoy would say, 'What goes around, comes around,' or perhaps, 'The wheel has come full circle.'"

For a tense moment, he was certain that his father would reject the metaphor.

"Yes," Sarek said. "Events do possess a symmetry that is aesthetically appealing as well as logical." He paused. "Although that is a redundancy."

"Captain Rabin and I proved to be the agents, finally, of Sered's return to Vulcan, just as we helped to exile him."

"Sered chose his own exile," Sarek corrected. "At some point, surely, before the madness took him, he had awareness, volition enough to have sought counseling. Instead . . ."

This measured, logical conversation was perfectly proper—between acquaintances, not family. "T'Pau knew him for what he was," Spock said, and to his chagrin—another emotion—heard criticism in his voice.

Sarek drew himself up in the way that had proved so daunting to Spock as a boy. "Thee has no right to judge where thee chose not to belong," he said in Old High Vulcan. "Thee made thy choice."

But Spock was no longer a boy to accept a reproof he did not deserve. "My father, we both know why I chose Starfleet. It is illogical to argue the past."

Sarek bowed his head ever so slightly but said nothing,

knowing as Spock knew that their last quarrel had set eighteen years of silence between them. Without Amanda's conciliatory influence, any quarrel they had now might prove irrevocable. Drawing a deep breath, Spock began again, this time more cautiously, "Yet, my father, it is of my former choice that I wish to speak."

His choice of the word "former" brought Sarek's head up with more haste than was seemly, a strange light glistening in his eyes. "Walk with me, my son," Sarek said. And rose somewhat quickly.

Spock followed his father out into Amanda's gardens. Her memory was very vivid here, too, almost as if some human essence akin to a *katra* remained in what she had loved and tended for so many years.

"My father," Spock began, "I have formed a working hypothesis regarding a solution to a long-standing problem. It is logical for me to conclude that I have arrived at this solution because of the very choice that I made as a boy to go out among the stars and serve with beings of many races." Trying to ignore Sarek's ever so slight tensing, he continued, "I have been doing so, however, in a way that I suspect that Dr. McCoy would term 'making it up as I went along.'"

The faint tension relaxed. "As always, the doctor speaks in metaphors."

"As always, the doctor speaks emotionally," Spock agreed. "But, as we both have found, logic almost always underlies his words. I . . . have thought to change my life's course somewhat. Because you are the most experienced xenodiplomat on Vulcan and perhaps in the entire Federation, logic demands that I consult you. As does . . ." He hunted for a word that was not too emotionally charged, settled on "loyalty."

"Speak, my son."

Was Sarek finding breathing difficult? Spock glanced quickly at him but perceived no indications of cardiac distress. Best to say quickly and concisely what there could be no turning back from.

"I require advice on how best to apply to the Vulcan Science Academy for advanced study in diplomacy and alien cultures."

"You would resign your commission?" Sarek's voice rang out over the Forge.

The words, illogically, hurt. *Service,* Spock reminded himself, *is service, no matter the variation. And it is only logical to serve in the most efficient possible way.*

"The position of ambassador," Sarek continued, voice sternly controlled, "is a civilian position, and an important one. It must not be abused."

"Sir, I would not abuse the position I seek—one that you have always fulfilled with such honor—by attempting to hold both it and my current rank. As soon as Starfleet confirms my choice of replacement, I shall resign."

There. It was done.

Sarek stood watching him, his eyes hooded.

Spock hesitated. "Your recommendation would be of the utmost assistance."

"If I refuse, no doubt you will apply on your own."

"No doubt. Nevertheless, I would value your approval. Because I . . . consider it worth the having." Spock felt his chest tighten, as though, illogically, he were a human in need of tri-ox. "I always have."

Sarek's hand, outstretched to straighten a branch laden with fragrant white flowers, faltered. He started to reach out to Spock instead, but then let his hand drop and glanced quickly away.

"I ask pardon for my loss of control," Sarek murmured.

"I see no need to ask pardon, sir."

Dammit, Spock, McCoy's voice yelped in his mind, *sometimes there's such a thing as too much logic!*

So be it. Spock closed a hand on his father's shoulder, letting the touch say what he could not.

And now he will brush me away. Refuse me. Again.

Yet Sarek did not rebuke him. They stood motionless, father and son, and then Sarek said, very softly, "I give thanks."

Spock released him, and, moved by unspoken agreement, they began to walk again.

"My father," Spock said, "you and I have both studied human culture. Over the past few years, I have become . . . reacquainted, I should say, with human writings that are as old as Surak's epigrams. For example: 'To everything there is a season, and a time to every purpose under the heaven; a time to be born, and a time to die; a time to plant, and a time to pluck up that which is planted . . .'"

"'A time to love,'" Sarek's deep voice blended with the night wind, "'and a time to hate; a time of war, and a time of peace . . .'" He paused. "I am acquainted with the text."

Of course. Doubtless, if Spock searched, if he could bear to search his mother's effects, he would find the large, battered volume that she had brought with her from Earth and from which she sometimes had read aloud when Spock was young or when she, like her husband, required a period of meditation and reflection. And he had always thought her life had been so serene.

"Your explanation is highly unorthodox, my son. Nevertheless, your logic is most . . . eloquent. If I may be permitted another quotation, I shall quote your mother, who derived great satisfaction from telling all we met, 'We are very proud of Spock.'"

"You honor me, sir."

"There is no honor in expressing the truth."

"On the contrary, my father, there is no honor higher."

Father and son stood together as the wind wreathed them and died away. Chimes rang, then subsided, leaving a stillness too precious to shatter.

At length, Sarek sighed and spoke. "With your mother gone, the house seems to possess echoes that are not harmonious. Accordingly, I often dine in the common room of the Science Academy. Would you care to accompany me? It would be an ideal beginning."

He is lonely, Spock thought with a shock of realization. *My father is lonely.* "An excellent idea, my father."

Together, they walked toward the Science Academy; starlight glittered on their upturned faces. Their accord, at least for the moment, possessed all the harmony of music resolving into a tonic chord, Spock thought, aesthetically as well as logically pleasing, although, as Sarek said, the two concepts were one.

A veteran of Starfleet, an accomplished scientist, Spock could enter the Vulcan Science Academy as a peer now, rather than on the sufferance that would have been granted Sarek's half-blood child. He had come home by choice, and by choice would go back out into the stars again.

He glanced toward the stars that marked the boundaries of the Romulan Empire, seeing not merely their light but the faces of memory, as well as the faces he had yet to meet.

I am coming, he told them silently.

They would wait for him.

Ambassador Spock's Story Will Continue in

Star Trek®
VULCAN'S HEART

by
Josepha Sherman and Susan Shwartz

Coming Fall 1998 from Pocket Books

Science Fiction, Fantasy, and Me:
To Boldly Go Where No Book Has Gone Before

JOSEPHA SHERMAN

The first book I remember reading on my own was *First to Ride,* a story about a Stone Age boy and his horse. Nothing fantastic there; in fact, the establishing of that age-old bond between human and equine is a theme that runs through the lives of a good many fantasy and science fiction writers!

The second book was something else again. Though I have forgotten the exact title and author, it was a science fiction adventure, possibly called *The Angry Red Planet,* involving a group of Earthlings making First Contact with Martians who had evolved from a plant origin. (Intelligent plants? Perhaps the author of that book was remembering John Campbell's "Who Goes There?") It was this reader's first introduction to that good old "senzawunda" we all crave from science fiction, that hint of the exotic, of—yes— strange new worlds and new civilizations. And from then on, I was hooked.

Fast-forward to the 1960s. Not much in the way of science fiction had been on television, with only a few exceptions. I opened the *TV Guide* edition featuring new shows—and came face-to-face with the color photo and listing for STAR TREK. One look at Mr. Spock, exotic features, pointed ears, and all, and the "senzawunda" kicked in. This was going to be one good show!

So, of course, it proved.

Life being the unpredictable thing it is, I went on to get a degree in archaeology (learning from hands-on experience that buckets of earth are *heavy* and that ancient cesspools retain their aroma for several millennia—ah, the romance of archaeology), then became a fantasy writer and folklorist.

I remained a fan of STAR TREK in all its varied incarnations, and attended science fiction convention panels such as the one on which Dorothy (D. C.) Fontana, story editor for The Original Series, revealed, deadpan, that the "T" in "James T. Kirk" stood for "Tiberius." (A wonderful moment, that: several hundred people as one echoing in disbelief, *"Tiberius?"*) I even wrote my one and only filksong about STAR TREK—about tribbles, to be precise. (A definition of "filk" for the Fannishly Challenged: it was originally a typo for "folk" that caught on in fannish society and came to mean original words, usually related to science fiction or fantasy, set to older melodies.)

But never did I guess that I would ever have a part in the STAR TREK phenomenon. In fact, I first came into closer than fan contact with STAR TREK through one of my folklore books, *Once Upon a Galaxy* (published by August House), which deals with the ancient folklore behind the modern icons. An entire section features STAR TREK! The original *Enterprise* on its five-year mission "to seek out new worlds and new civilizations" has its cousin in the ancient Greek *Argo,* and quick-witted, clever James T. Kirk is certainly cousin to the *Argo*'s captain, Jason.

But then came John Ordover, editor of STAR TREK for Pocket Books, who asked, "Want to write a STAR TREK novel?"

Good question. I told him I'd get back to him, but then was too busy finishing fantasy novels or folklore books for a time. Meanwhile, John had asked the same question of Susan Shwartz.

And suddenly inspiration hit me. I called up Susan and asked, "Want to do a STAR TREK novel together?"

Not long after, we were both guest speakers at Mount Holyoke College, in South Hadley, Massachusetts—in January. Susan tells the rest of this story in her section, so I'll only add that out of that speaking engagement, a novel was born!

Here's to you, Susan, my fellow collaborator! Here's to you, John, STAR TREK Editor Extraordinaire! It's been a fun voyage. And here's to the *Enterprise*s, one and all! May their STAR TREKs never end!

Thirty Years After First Contact—
Join Starfleet and See the Worlds

SUSAN SHWARTZ

The year I turned sixteen, my father gave me the sun, the moon, and the stars—at least the stars of Federation, Klingon, and Romulan space. (The Organians might have something to say about Dad's land grab, but so far, they've kept discreetly silent.)

"Susan," Dad shouted. "I want you to come in here and watch this show with me." I was quite happily ensconced with a James Bond novel I'd swiped from my mother, but Dad had cheered when I started reading Heinlein, Norton, and Asimov, protecting me from "she's so smart, why does she have to read That Stuff?" So, if he said something was good—apart from the ongoing battle about "practical" shoes I couldn't possibly let him win—I knew he wouldn't let me down.

He didn't. Neither did the STAR TREK episode I started with: "Charlie X." "What *is* this?" I asked, fascinated.

"It's called *Star Trek,*" Dad told me. "It's like the stuff I used to read in *Planet Stories.*" Now, what's odd is that I had remembered hearing the program's name and thinking it sounded interesting before I had to run off to marching band practice. Dad had remembered, though. He always did. As I said, he wouldn't let me down.

Over the three years of Classic *Trek*'s run, marching band, homework, and other hassles often prevented me from watching the episodes as they came out. And in the intervening years of college and graduate school, as often as not, the revolting species Pretentious Aggressive News Watchers usually swarmed into the TV room at *Trek*-time, claiming a majority at the last moment and preempting my dormitory's lone TV. Nevertheless, I managed to catch up, then to stay current. I was a Trekker, and a Trekker I've remained.

Certain episodes come to mind as favorites: "The City on the Edge of Forever"; "The Trouble with Tribbles"; "Shore Leave"; "Amok Time"; "Journey to Babel"; "The Conscience of the King." Over the next thirty years, as Susan-as-graduate-student became a lapsed academic and Susan-as-fan began, slowly and painstakingly, to transform herself into a professional writer, I was to establish First Contacts with writers, artists, and what I can only call Closet Trekkers. (I think you had really better let me explain that . . . please!)

I've had the chance to meet Harlan Ellison and to be on panels with him. David Gerrold, the father of all tribbles, is a colleague. I once stayed up till 4:00 A.M. listening to the late, great Theodore Sturgeon, author of "Shore Leave." Twice, I got to meet the late Mark Lenard at conferences where I, too, was a guest, and, as I write these lines, I have just returned from his memorial service, where, with the courtesy and generosity Mr. Lenard's characters always showed (well, maybe not the Klingon, but the Romulan commander and Sarek, definitely), his family welcomed relatives, friends, and those of us from the STAR TREK community who were able to come—or to mail in via the Internet—to pay their last respects.

Just last week, at Thanksgiving dinner on New York's Upper West Side, a distinguished guest (distinguished at that moment by a toddler crawling on each shoulder) told me his father had been in "some STAR TREK episode or other as a Shakespearean actor with a troupe." "Good grief!" I said. "Your father's Anton Karidian."

I think it was very polite of me not to say "Your dad's Kodos the Executioner!"—don't you?

Over the past thirty years—twenty years of it as a friend of Trek writers like Ann Crispin or an almost-wedding-guest of Diane Duane and Peter Morwood at Boskone (hey, it's not my fault I got waylaid by a Latvian intellectual, and I did manage to get to the reception)—I've found STAR TREK in the most unlikely places. Here, in no particular order:

A first-year student at the Harvard Business School has forgotten his assignments, and the prof is in a mood to nail him. The student pulls out his wallet, flips it open, and orders, "Beam me up fast, Scotty."

A person in terminal chipmunk mode—me, recovering from surgery on impacted wisdom teeth—lies in the hospital, hurting. "I think Bones would have done better," I mumble to the nurse. "Well," she tells me, "this isn't the *Enterprise*, but we'll do our best."

James Tiptree's poignant short story "Beam Us Home."

It is the late 1970s in upstate New York (think Darkover, and you've got an idea of the weather), and some Ithaca College students are lining up to watch *Star Trek: the Motion Picture*. They see their Medieval English prof—me again. Not only has she beat them into line; she's got Starfleet insignia on her ski jacket.

I walk into the office of a vice-president at the financial organization that employs me. Someone's got a tribble on her desk, courtesy of the handouts promoting "Trials and Tribble-lations." (My own tribble, named Charmin for obvious reasons, remains at home.)

And, of course, the wonderful moment as I watched the first Space Shuttle being pulled out of its hangar and the Alexander Courage theme from STAR TREK started playing. Just as Clark Gable absolutely had to play Rhett Butler in *Gone with the Wind,* the first Shuttle *had* to be named *Enterprise.* I am convinced that when some future-day Chuck Yeager or Zephram Cochrane or Sally Ride or Shannon Lucid breaks the light barrier, he—or she—will do so in a ship that they're going to have to call *Enterprise.*

It is, of course, the only . . . logical . . . name.

Sometimes, of course, people look askance at my interests. You probably know from your own experience that Some People look askance at any enthusiasm at all. More often than not, however, I've found that my enthusiasm kindles matching fire—a Webmaster who wants to go to conventions; a financial analyst's father, now retired from a professorship of plant pathology, telling me "you need xerophytes" (he was right); the way the phosphors on the Internet sparkle when I mention what I write.

So, what took me so long to put my name to a STAR TREK title when at times it seemed as if I were the only member of Science Fiction and Fantasy Writers of America on the block not to have one? I haven't the faintest idea. Maybe, just maybe, I was a little shy of presuming to ask to be on a team I'd admired so long. That didn't stop John Ordover from asking me in Round Table Conferences on Genie (yes, the SF outpost there is holding out!) if I'd ever thought of writing a STAR TREK novel. And had I thought of this, and had I thought of that . . . and meanwhile, Josepha Sherman was getting the same line of questions.

Jo and I talked about it online, on Broadway, and at Saturday movies, but nothing really coalesced until January

1996, when we trekked out to South Hadley, Massachusetts, to speak to the undergraduates at Mount Holyoke College, from which I graduated far too many years ago and which realizes that science fiction and fantasy now form part of its undergrad gene pool.

By Friday night:

The students were gone.

The bar was closed.

And there we were, snowed in in South Hadley on a Friday night. As I remember from four years of college, there is nothing to *do* in South Hadley on Friday night unless you're a glutton for reserve reading.

Well, almost nothing. Jo and I hiked up from the alumnae center (looks like a ski lodge) in the center of the campus to a restaurant in the town center (looks like an even bigger ski lodge). Over salad, shrimp, and wine, we started plotting. And laughing. And gesturing. Some impeccable parents spotted, and flinched from, my gesture with an—imaginary, I promise you—obsidian dagger.

"Star Trek?" they asked each other, bemused. They were, of course, much too decorous to ask us. Besides, we would have told them. In detail.

We came back from college with an outline. A few months and several revisions later, we had a contract. A few months after that, we had *Vulcan's Forge*—which I hope you like. And that's why this book is dedicated to Bellatrix, Mount Holyoke's science fiction club.

I wonder what the people at my twenty-fifth reunion are going to say.

Well, as we say on the Net: <G>.

A very big grin indeed. I have never been so happy to be on any team in my life.

About the Authors

JOSEPHA SHERMAN

Josepha Sherman is a fantasy writer and folklorist who has written books and short stories for adults and children. Her fantasy novels include *The Shining Falcon* (Avon, 1989)—winner of the Compton Crook Award—*Child of Faerie, Child of Earth* (Walker & Company, 1992, an ALA Best Book and a NY Public Library Book for the Teen Age), the bestseller *Castle of Deception* (with Mercedes Lackey, Baen Books, 1992), *A Strange and Ancient Name* (Baen Books, 1993, Science Fiction Book Club edition, 1993, a NY Public Library Book for the Teen Age), *Windleaf* (Walker & Company, 1993, an ABA Pick of the List, a Junior Library Guild Selection, and a NY Public Library Book for the Teen Age), the bestseller *A Cast of Corbies* (with Mercedes Lackey, 1994), *Gleaming Bright* (Walker & Company, 1994, a Junior Library Guild Selection), the bestseller *The Chaos Gate* (Baen Books, 1994), *King's Son, Magic's Son* (Baen Books, 1994, a NY Public Library Book for the Teen Age), *The*

Shattered Oath (Baen Books, 1995, nominated for the Nebula Award and a NY Public Library Book for the Teen Age), and *Forging the Runes,* sequel to *The Shattered Oath* (Baen Books, 1996). She is also the author of the picture-book *Vassilisa the Wise* (HBJ, hardcover, Houghton Mifflin, paperback, 1988), and over one hundred short stories, plus a script for the late, lamented television series *Adventures of the Galaxy Rangers.* And, of course, she is co-author, with Susan Shwartz, of *Vulcan's Forge!*

Sherman's folklore titles, all from August House, include *A Sampler of Jewish-American Folklore* (1992), *Rachel the Clever and Other Jewish Folktales* (1993), *Once Upon a Galaxy* (1994), and *Greasy Grimy Gopher Guts: The Subversive Folklore of Children* (with T.K.F. Weisskopf, August House, 1995), *Trickster Tales* (1996) and *Merlin's Kin: World Tales of Hero-Magicians* (1997).

Josepha Sherman is an active member of the Authors Guild, SFWA, and the American Folklore Society. She has lectured on fantasy and folklore to writers' groups around the country and told stories to groups of all ages. Personal interests include (in no particular order) aviation, computers, horses, and travel. She is a diehard fan of the hapless Mets (wait till next year!) and a founding member of EHA, the Editorial Horseplayers Association, a motley group of writers and editors who hold their board meetings at the finish line at Belmont Racetrack!

SUSAN SHWARTZ

For the past fourteen years, Susan Shwartz has been a financial writer and editor at various long-suffering Wall Street firms. For the past twenty years, she has written, edited, and reviewed fantasy and science fiction. Her most recent books are *Shards of Empire* (Tor), set in eleventh-century Byzantium, with *Cross and Crescent* (Tor), a novel of the First Crusade, to follow in 1997. Her other books include *The Grail of Hearts,* and, with Andre Norton, *Imperial Lady* and *Empire of the Eagle* (all from Tor). Her anthologies include the two volumes of *Sisters in Fantasy* (ROC) and two volumes of *Arabesques* (Avon). She has published more than sixty pieces of short fiction and has been nominated for the Nebula five times, the Hugo twice, and the World Fantasy Award and the Edgar once each. She has written reviews for various SF publications and *The New York Times, Vogue,* and a variety of other places. A lapsed academic, she has a Ph.D. in English from Harvard University, enjoys writing polemical letters to major newspapers, and spends entirely too much time on the Net that she could use going to the opera, shopping, or even—heaven forbid—having a life. She lives in Forest Hills, New York, with two computers, a lot of books, and a notorious shoe collection.